RUNNING
THE RISK

LEA GRIFFITH

sourcebooks
casablanca

Published by Sourcebooks Casablanca, an imprint of Sourcebooks, Inc.
P.O. Box 4410, Naperville, Illinois 60567-4410
(630) 961-3900
Fax: (630) 961-2168
sourcebooks.com

Printed and bound in Canada.
MBP 10 9 8 7 6 5 4 3 2 1

checkups and stayed clean as whistles. Jude acknowledged that the thought of her being pregnant with his
child didn't make his heart seize in fear. It did the exact
opposite. He shook his head as he lowered her legs and
came down beside her. Being inside her was as close to
heaven as Jude would ever fly.

She rolled over, and he curved around her. It was
still hot, still humid, but he needed her against him. He
no longer questioned that need. Like his lungs required
breath, his body called for hers.

"You're wheels up tomorrow?" she asked.

The sound of her voice made his heart beat heavier.
Every single thing about Ella Banning made Jude want
to be a better man. Made him want to rise above the
things he'd seen and done and just be—*better*.

"Yeah, baby. Zero dark thirty," he said and then
pressed a kiss on her shoulder.

"I'm logistics point on this mission, Jude. That means
I'll be at base. I won't be *there* to watch your six."

He snorted and ran a hand down her side, over her
hip, and back up again to cup her breast. "You're my
light in the darkness, Ella," he said solemnly. "You're
always with me."

Her breath hissed in, and she turned in the circle of
his arms. Her body molded to his, her softness con-
forming to his hardness. It was an ecstasy all its own.
Her fingers traced the planes of his face, across his
eyebrows and over the bump in the bridge of his nose.
It'd been broken at least four times, possibly more.
Ella didn't seem to mind that Jude was an ugly motherfucker. Nope, his woman found beauty in the face of
the worst hells.

Her gaze met his. "You are mine, Jude. You come home to me."

Some nameless emotion swirled in the depths of her blue-gray orbs. "Hey, what's this about?" he asked as he ran the back of a finger down her cheek.

She veiled her eyes, and his heart stuttered. She was worried. Damn. He hated that. "I would move heaven and earth to get back to you, Ella. Stop it," he murmured at her lips.

"You can't control everything," she whispered.

"This is me…who I am. Hell, it's you. We knew what this was when we signed up for it." The reminder had her stiffening.

She pulled away from him and got off the bed, pulling the top sheet with her and wrapping it around her slight frame. She made her way to the sliding glass door and stepped onto the deck.

He'd bought this tiny house on the beach the day after he'd first made love to Ella. Two hours away from Endgame Ops' base of operations in Port Royal, Virginia, Jude had wanted a house they could escape to. They both loved the ocean, so he'd bought this.

She stared out over the waves kissing the lips of the beach not even a hundred yards from them. He stepped behind her and enfolded her in his arms. He couldn't be this close to her and not have her against him. It was even becoming difficult when they pulled missions together. They always maintained professionalism— but yeah, it was getting hard to avoid the small touches that eased him.

King had mentioned his concerns in a meeting a week ago. Jude had reassured his leader that he was a soldier—cast in the mold—and Ella was an absolute professional. King reminded him they were also human and therefore subject to all the frailties inherent to that condition.

Jude wondered now if that was why Ella was pulling logistical support at base while Jude ventured to Beirut with the team.

"He pulled me off the ground op for this one," Ella said softly.

She'd read his mind. Jude sighed and settled his chin on top of her head. She relaxed back into him, and the band around his chest eased somewhat. "Nah, he just knows you're a whiz with tech logistics and this mission's FUBAR potential, while not high, is still there. We'll need your expertise if sugar goes to shit."

"Great sentiment, Jude, and yeah, I know where my skill set is the strongest, but I need to be there at your back," she said.

A chill skated through Jude at the urgency in her tone.

"It's simple: go in, blow shit sky-high, and we're out. I'll be fine. Hell, we'll all be fine. Plus, I have you to come home to," he said and pressed his lips to the soft flesh of her neck. "I'll have you in my ear the whole time. And then I'll have you in my arms when I come home."

"Yeah," she said as she turned and rested her head on his heart. "You will."

He held her for a few more minutes, soaking in the setting sun throwing golden sparks over the writhing blue of the Atlantic. When darkness finally began to creep in, he guided Ella back inside, removed the sheet, and kissed her from the bottom of her feet to the top of her head. He made her back arch and her breath break, and then he started all over.

And when it was time to leave the next morning, he nuzzled her cheek, kissed her lips, breathed her in, and left.

Six hours later

"Hey, Keeper, I heard your mama's in town," Micah Samson called across the room.

Jude let his smile show his teeth. "We ain't talking about my mama, dude." Micah was as good as they came—solid, straight shooter, and strong. He was probably the best friend Jude had, but he loved to jack with Jude about his mama.

Micah laughed. It was a strange sound coming from the big man. Strange enough it made Jude bark out a laugh too, even though the topic of his mama wasn't funny at all.

Brody Madoc grunted. "Not sure if you know this, Keeper, but Micah doesn't want to *talk* about your mama."

Harrison Black—the crazy ex-SAS officer who'd come into Endgame right after he left his country's service—followed up on Brody's comment by making a kissing noise. It was designed to piss Jude off. It did, but not for the reason Black thought.

"That's right, Keeper. I wanna give your mama a little sugar," Micah said with another laugh and a wink. Even though his best friend teased him, something had been off with Micah for a few weeks. A darkness filled his eyes, tension rode his shoulders, and he'd been distant. Jude would take him out for a beer when they got back and ask him what was up.

But he couldn't let the teasing go without a pop of his neck and a glare, giving them all his patented shut-the-hell-up look. Why he bothered, he had no idea. It never worked. "Seriously, man, stop talking about my mama."

Jude didn't even like acknowledging he had a mother, much less having his teammates talk shit about her. She'd once been the light of his meager family, but then she'd abandoned him for a career in, of all things, Mexican soap operas. Becoming famous in her home country had been more important than her son. And yeah, there was a whole story there that Micah knew well and Jude sure as hell didn't want to dwell on, so he turned his mind to this mission's spec ops and tried to drown out the sound of Rook Granger and Jonah Knight joining in on the amusement. Even though this wasn't Jude's favorite subject, the tension in the room eased with the men's laughter.

A shrill whistle sounded in the bunker room, and Jude sought out the source. What met his eyes was Ella striding confidently into the war room like she owned it. And there went the tension—right back through Jude's roof.

"Ella-Bella got called up, huh?" Chase Reynolds's voice was loud in the sudden silence.

She smiled at the man, and Jude's hands clenched. Her smiles were his. Not Reynolds's. Chase was his brother-in-arms, his teammate, but he'd drop the man with a punch to the throat if he didn't stop ogling Ella's ass.

"What are you doing here?" Jude asked and almost winced at the harshness of his voice.

She speared him with her gaze.

"She got the call. Nina can't ride because she's sick, maybe food poisoning," King McNally said from the doorway to his office before Ella could respond.

Jude met his leader's eyes and let his frustration communicate along the path between them. King shrugged, but there was zero apology. Each of the men and women of Endgame had been hand-selected for their various talents. So while Jude may hate the fact that his woman was going to be in harm's way, there wasn't shit he could do about it. This wasn't his kingdom. He was simply a member of the king's court.

So he lowered his eyes and went back to making sure his jump bag was ready. They were taking off in a few minutes for DC. From there, it would take them roughly twelve hours to make it to Israel and then on to Beirut.

"You okay?" Ella's soft voice tickled his ears and made his dick harden behind his cargo pants.

"Yep," he responded in a clipped tone.

She didn't say anything else. Goddamn, he hated when she was near danger.

He felt her staring at him, but he had to shut it down. If he kept her in the forefront of his mind, the chance he could fuck up and put her further in danger increased. It took a will of iron, but he'd been honed in the fires of BUD/S training. They called him Keeper because that's what he did. He kept his calm in the midst of danger and kept his team safe. And Ella was a part of that team— albeit the most important, but she was still team. And he'd not treat her any differently than he would the other men heading out with them.

He'd at least try.

He put his bag over his shoulder and stood straight, staring at her across the bunker until her gaze rose to meet his.

"Safe, Ella," he said with force. They were the only words he'd take her on this mission with. He wouldn't speak to her the same way they did at the house on the beach; it would be spec ops only.

She held up six fingers. "I've got your six," she said in an equally hard voice. Then she smiled and ruined the effect. His Ella was softness incarnate.

He nodded, and the men around them didn't acknowledge the interaction between him and Ella. They knew better. Hell, he'd almost kicked Chase's ass a few weeks ago for daring to bring it up. Jude wouldn't have her embarrassed. If this were a regular branch of the service, they'd have been discharged months ago for fraternization.

"Wheels up, men," King ordered.

They piled into the C-130 transport plane, and as they rose and their view of the ground grew fainter, an eerie feeling swept over Jude. He pushed it down and chalked it up to the fears his woman had voiced last night. He glanced at her and found her staring at him.

As the feeling wound its way through his mind, he let her gaze center him. He'd never give in to the doubts. He couldn't afford to. He was a soldier and, as such, dealt in possibilities and outcomes. He knew there was always the possibility he wouldn't come home, and accepting that brought calm in the midst of every storm. Still the feeling persisted, raising the hair on the back of his neck and not letting him go.

In thoughts of all the potential outcomes, he allowed a single assertion to keep him moving forward. She was his, and he would do his job on this mission to ensure that nothing was allowed to harm her.

Nothing.

He rested his head against the hard metal bowels of the plane, needing some sleep before they hit their target.

When he opened his eyes again, they were landing at an Israeli airfield. Endgame was a private entity, providing security for contractors and military personnel alike on the ground throughout the world. In reality, they were black ops, always working in the undefined gray. They took the missions the United States couldn't—traversed some of the worst hellholes the United States couldn't send their military personnel into.

They were hidden from the public behind the persona of a military contractor, doing the things that needed to be done but couldn't be admitted. Because of their founder, a man known as the Piper because he pulled the strings, they had access to military installations the world over, and they had access to allies of the United States. Hence the C-130 and the Israeli airfield.

Once they disembarked, they checked their weapons, went over mission spec ops once more, and boarded a Black Hawk helicopter. The feeling Jude had had when they'd left the States had dissipated.

Ella was seated beside their team leader. Kingston McNally was a fine soldier and an even better leader. He'd pulled Jude out of a bad situation in Syria last year and had had his loyalty ever since. Not that he hadn't had it before, but there was something about having your ass saved that engendered lifelong fealty to your savior.

And still Jude loved jacking with his team leader. "Oh, Your Hiiiighness…"

King flipped him off and kept his head tilted back against the wall of the bird. Jude let his laugh escape on a rough bark. King was a tough son of a bitch, but he hated helicopters. It was a source of much laughter among his men.

"Seriously, sir, Ella wants to hear about Serbia." Ella's anxiety communicated across the small space between them. It was abhorrent to Jude. He'd do damn near anything to lighten the atmosphere. Messing with his team leader helped him meet his goal.

She hated conflict. How the hell she'd ever migrated to the CIA and military service was beyond Jude.

King opened his eyes and stared hard at Jude. Jude grinned and pointed to Ella, trying to get the other man to understand why he messing with him. King flipped on his communication unit. "Jude, you're a pain in my ass."

"Sir, if it's—" Ella began.

King held up a hand and shot Jude a look. Jude was unperturbed.

Already the brackets of stress around her mouth had disappeared. "It was fifteen men, Your Highness. You were pinned down behind a building in the middle of the country, and you fought with nothing but a—"

"I know the damn story, Jude," King said firmly.

"I'm just saying," Jude began. "It's a damn *good* story."

A beep sounded over their comm devices. "Five minutes until touchdown, boys and girls," Vivi informed them.

Olivia Granger, a.k.a. Vivi, was a CIA analyst who'd joined Endgame when she'd refused to let her man, Rook, leave her. Jude smiled at that. Vivi was a tiny bit of nothing, but she had badass Rook Granger wrapped around her little finger—and he loved it.

Jude understood it. He hadn't when he'd been told Vivi was joining them in Port Royal, their home base. But damn did he understand now.

King's gaze touched on them all, and Jude watched the other man's face transform to warrior. Every person on this bird was a warrior. And just like every other mission they took, this mission—under the cover of darkness in the middle of a desert outside Beirut, Lebanon—could very well become a war.

Jude let his gaze settle on Ella. Her eyes were closed, her nostrils flaring as she drew in deep breaths, preparing. He knew why King had chosen her to go when Nina came up sick. Ella spoke Lebanese.

Hopefully, they'd be in and out so fast nobody would need to use her translating skills.

"Two minutes until insertion," the pilot relayed.

"What the hell is that?" the copilot asked suddenly.

Jude's neck tightened. That didn't sound good.

"Bogeys in the air! Repeat, bogeys in the air!" the pilot yelled over the comm links.

Jude immediately glanced at Ella, warning her with his eyes to brace herself. Fear raced up his spine. It left an acrid taste in his mouth and a burning in his gut. He pulled his helmet on and watched as she did the same.

Antiaircraft fire peppered the fuselage of the bird as it tipped into an evasive maneuver. Jude grabbed his oh-shit handle and saw his teammates do the same. His gaze snagged on Ella.

"Safe," he mouthed.

She nodded and held up six fingers.

"In, out, protect yourselves. Remember the alternate extraction point," King ordered. "Ella, you're behind me at all times, you understand?"

Jude's gaze narrowed on his team leader.

He knew if he looked at Ella, he'd see the terror clouding her bright-gray eyes.

Everything in Jude screamed for him to cover Ella's

body with his own. This insertion had just gone straight into clusterfuck territory. He needed to protect her.

"You got something to say, Jude?" King asked harshly.

Instead of moving toward her, Jude shook his head at King and pulled his visor down as he breathed in deep. King would shield her with his own body, give his own life for any of them. Jude knew that and wouldn't disobey him, even if it went against every instinct he possessed.

"We're hit! We're hit!" the copilot yelled over the comm units.

The bird swayed, dipping sharply to the right and turning in a gut-swirling three-sixty. They were going down hard.

Please let her live, Jude pleaded to the God he rarely acknowledged. *Please, if anyone needs to die, let it be me*.

"We're going down, Your Highness!"

Chase's voice was panicked in Jude's ear mic. There was nothing he could do. He was impotent here—at the mercy of the wind and the same God he'd just lifted up a prayer to. The dying whine of the bird's rotors blew through his mind. This was it.

"Brace for impact!"

The helo fell rapidly. Jude couldn't get his bearings. He needed to see Ella. And then the helo slammed into the ground, and Jude's world snapped to black.

Chapter 1

JUDE ADJUSTED HIS SCOPE'S SIGHT AND SETTLED DOWN in the slight depression between two trees. Pine straw, dying leaves, and branches covered him. He'd made the blind to blend into the landscape seamlessly. The sun was behind him now, its heat nothing more than a fading promise. The wind had picked up an hour ago, and he allowed its bitter cold to seep into his soul. It was soothing to a degree, though Jude doubted anything could ever completely cool his rage. He'd been here for two days, following intel that would hopefully lead him to... *her*. He'd stopped even thinking her name months ago. The sound of it reverberating through his mind caused unbearable pain that spread from his heart through every limb. It was debilitating, that pain. And unending. Instead, he remembered her face, the way her body had once moved beneath him, and the promises she'd made that had inevitably been nothing more than lies.

Movement in the compound below had him tightening his grip on his rifle. He'd been trained to take down targets a mile away, but today was simply reconnaissance. When he'd seen her in Beirut six weeks ago, after a year of believing her dead and gone, his mind had denied what his heart had immediately recognized.

El—*her*.

Then she'd disappeared in the smoke and confusion, and he'd had no choice but to leave her again.

In the hell that was Lebanon.

He tightened his grip on his weapon, tamping down his dangerous emotions. Below him, four white Range Rovers pulled up to the concrete warehouse that had once been a chemical engineering facility. Unsubstantiated rumors had it that the facility's purpose was to conceal Horace Dresden's biochemical weapons stash. Whatever the case, those rumors had hit Jude's ears and his skin had prickled.

For two years, Endgame's mission had been the elimination of Horace Dresden. For Jude, the mission had morphed. Oh, he wanted Dresden, but his motivation resided in the fact that if he could find that murdering son of a bitch, he'd find *her*.

The right-side driver's door of the lead Rover opened, and a dainty foot encased in a nude stiletto heel lowered to the ground. The leg attached to the foot had his gut clenching. He'd tasted the arc of that calf, tongued the indention of that knee, and had his hands all over that thigh.

She stepped out of the Rover completely, and his gut clenched, then relaxed. It was a reaction he'd only had with her. Jude was a warrior, a soldier. He'd spent most of his adult life training, fighting, and killing. He was damn good at what he did. Had never even realized something was missing from his life until she'd stepped into his sphere and taken him over.

The wind caught her overcoat and tossed the ivory folds, allowing him a glimpse of a body that was thinner than he remembered but no less captivating. Through the scope, his gaze trailed upward over her hips and then higher across her breasts and up along the slope of her collarbone. Her skin was the same color as her coat but softer, glowing. The flavor of that skin danced like a phantom over his tongue.

The trees above him bowed to the wind, and in his spot on the ridge above the compound, his nostrils flared, a stallion scenting its mare. He swore he could taste her on the breeze. She moved to shut the door and, in an instant, froze.

She slowly lifted her hand and removed the dark sunglasses that hid the frost of her gaze from him. The scar at her temple mocked him. It was the only mark on the otherwise unblemished face that stalked his dreams. And then she angled her head toward his location.

His heart locked in his chest. No way she had any idea he was here. He hadn't even told King where he was headed—had kept the information about Dresden's supposed compound from the Piper, King, and his team-mates. This was what he'd been reduced to. Spying on a woman who'd betrayed him…betrayed them. Desperate for a glimpse of her. Desperate to make her pay.

The wind settled at that moment, but still she gazed up toward him. The man who'd gotten out of the Rover on the other side must have called her name, because she glanced at him and her lips moved before she began walking toward the building. Jude was too far away to hear her words.

Six men got out of each of the remaining Rovers, each carrying a small metal briefcase. Jude would bet his left nut they were here to obtain some of Dresden's horde of biochemicals.

He trained his gaze on her again, watching as her long legs ate up the distance between the Rover and the building, and for a crazy second, Jude remembered her as she'd been the night before his world had been blown to hell. He saw her walking on their beach in Virginia, the wind whipping her long ebony hair, the waves playing havoc around her delicate ankles. He saw her head turn as a grin broke across her face. He saw the flush of their recent lovemaking on her body.

A hawk screamed in the distance, and Jude was jerked to the present. Instead of seeing his woman through the sight of the scope, he saw *her*. A stranger. A traitor.

Jude's sight remained locked on her, his finger caressing the trigger as he let the anger flow through him. He'd heard the whispers—maybe she was a double agent. Maybe she wasn't the traitor he knew her to be. Maybe she was both and neither.

Maybe he hadn't given everything he was to a ghost.

He needed the truth, and he'd resolved that he'd have to be cold and merciless in finding it. She'd led them on this path. She could damn well walk it with him.

The man entered the building, but before she stepped in behind him, she once again turned her gaze to Jude's location.

She couldn't see him, but for Jude, it didn't matter. She knew he was there. He knew she knew. She raised both hands, holding up six fingers. It was so quick that Jude wondered if his mind was playing tricks on him as his heart threatened to burst from his chest. Had it been supplication or warning? He didn't know—but the sadness that passed like a cloud over the contours of her face in that moment had him swearing.

Then she lowered her hands as the soft curves of her mouth lifted in a travesty of a smile.

Jude cursed again, the wind taking the foul word and

tossing it to and fro. As she moved out of his sight, his gut clenched once more. King had warned Jude that all was not as it seemed, to give him time to figure it out.

Jude hadn't been inclined to give himself that time. Until this moment.

Because there'd been one other emotion on her face just now that ripped a hole right through Jude's shriveled heart. He'd seen it many times over the course of their year together but had despaired he'd ever see it again. It had been the truest of all the emotions she'd ever displayed with him.

It was the one thing that stayed his trigger finger. It was the only thing that could save her.

Love.

—⁓—

Her neck had been itching for weeks, as if a scope's site was embedding itself into the skin there, and she knew why.

Jude.

Her past. She swallowed the agony of that truth. He would always be her past because the simple fact was that Ella didn't believe she had a future.

As soon as she stepped out of the Rover, she'd felt him on her skin, tasted him on her tongue. Of course, that was fanciful. But she knew he was up there, watching. When she saw him at Dresden's place in Beirut, she'd known he would come for her, and she knew that Vivi Granger was too good not to locate her.

Ella winced. All the subterfuge of the last year was a terrible weight she carried every day. Endgame thought she was a traitor, and even though she'd had an opportunity to explain parts of her story to King, it was impossible to recap her hell in a single conversation. And that was all they'd had before Dresden's men had caught up to them.

Did Jude hate her? Want revenge for the perceived betrayal her own team leader had believed? Why was he here now when she was so close to figuring out how to dismantle Dresden's operations?

"Where's your ape?" Segorski asked.

She assumed he was referring to Brody Madoc. Brody had been her constant companion over the last year. She'd managed to plead for his life when Dresden and Savidge had been intent on killing her teammate. All she'd had to do was give up an innocent to see Brody saved.

Ella had done it and not blinked. Team before all else. Did she wish she could have made a different decision? Now that she'd met Allie Redding, yes, she did. But hindsight was always twenty-twenty, and Ella didn't have time for gazing into the past.

Except when it came to Jude.

"Your ape?" Segorski demanded again.

"Obviously, he's not here. I'll be sure to tell him you asked about him," she responded waspishly, cutting her gaze to the small Russian as she removed her overcoat. The factory was kept cold due to the temperature-sensitive nature of what was housed here, but Ella burned on the inside. Fear, rage, and love threatened to choke her. She wished Brody was here, but he was back with Endgame. She'd forced him back to the team and now bemoaned her choice. He'd been a rock for her, a link to her team, safety, when she hadn't deserved it.

Segorski smiled, which brought Ella back to her present. She shuddered, suddenly wishing she hadn't removed her coat. Segorski was all teeth and no soul. The pistol resting in a holster on her thigh soothed her. Segorski had accompanied her here to Dresden's factory on the outskirts of Sarajevo in Bosnia and Herzegovina with the intention of counting his shipment prior to payment. Normally, this was a duty reserved for Ella, as she'd worked herself into a position of trust with Dresden. But Segorski didn't trust Dresden. One of the only men Ella knew who had told Dresden that to his face and lived to tell the tale. Ella wondered if Segorski understood he stayed alive not because Dresden was scared of him, but because Dresden still had use for him.

Segorski moved closer to her and ran a hand down her arm. "Perhaps now we can become better acquainted."

Not a question, a statement.

She turned her head and stared at him, saying nothing.

Segorski was still smiling, but the expression slipped when he realized Ella wasn't. The Russian cleared his throat and then his eyes changed, slitting as his face went red. "I'll have you." He breathed in deeply and smoothed his gray hair back from his face. "Dresden can only protect you for so long."

Ella found his statement humorous, but her face remained blank—as empty as the heart inside her chest. Dresden didn't give a shit about protecting Ella. She was a means to an end.

"The product is through those doors. Count the vials, transfer the money, call your men in, and take possession. I don't have time for small talk, Segorski."

"One day you will," he promised.

As Segorski strutted to the containment room, Ella thought over how she'd manipulated Dresden into his current position of extending her a measure of trust.

Oh, he watched every move she made, but when she'd handed over Allie Redding with no hesitation a year ago, she'd begun a long journey toward becoming integral to Dresden's operations. She still didn't know the structure of his conglomerate—you had to be his right or left hand to have access to that—but she was close to the inner sanctum, and she was willing to do whatever was necessary to gain that information.

She owed Dresden. She owed him a bullet to the temple. But not until she knew how to take down his entire organization. Cutting off the head wouldn't kill the snake in this instance. The bastard had put a system of checks and balances in place that rivaled the U.S. government. There was something behind all that paranoia. Ella was going to find out what that was.

Dresden's operation made Al-Qaeda and ISIS look like poverty-stricken amateurs. The fact that the bastard was one of America's own—born and bred in New York City, no less—was just another reason to take him out.

But for Ella, this was much more personal. Yes, Dresden had killed innocents, two of her Endgame teammates included, and he was responsible for arming most of the terrorists and warmongering monsters on nearly every continent on earth. His biggest mistake? Aiming for Jude Dagan.

And Ella was going to make him pay for it.

Every emotion she'd trapped inside herself for the last year bubbled up. Jude would never know it, but he'd taken every step in the last year with her—in her heart and mind.

And he was right outside now. So damn close she ached with it.

"It's all here. The transfer is made. Confirm it." Segorski's high-pitched voice pulled Ella from her musings.

She pulled her phone from the pocket of her dress and hit a preprogrammed button.

"It's done," the person on the other end answered her unspoken question. The money had been transferred into Dresden's accounts.

She hung up and nodded to Segorski. "Enjoy your death dealing, Segorski."

He smiled that reptilian smile again, only this time Ella smiled too. She knew something Segorski didn't. Ella had contaminated his entire shipment of ricin powder two days ago. She'd raised the temperature of the poison to over a hundred degrees Celsius by placing burners under the metal containers holding the vials. She had cooked it so much that the ricin had been inactivated.

She wouldn't be able to stop the bombs Segorski would likely use in his quest to disperse the powder, but at least the ricin itself wasn't going to kill thousands. He had aims to cement Russia's incursion into the Crimean Peninsula. Ukraine, along with Crimea and all of its precious oil, was ripe for the taking, and Mother Russia was making her move.

Ella's victory was a small one, but it was a victory nonetheless. And maybe when Segorski didn't get the end result he wanted, he'd come after Dresden. Do Ella's dirty work for her.

But not until she'd found out the details of Dresden's

organization. Please, God, not until then, or everything she'd gone through over the last year would be in vain.

"Dresden promised me a bomb maker," Segorski reminded Ella.

She turned and began striding away from the Russian.

"Bomb maker," Segorski called out, snapping his fingers at his men to hurry up and get the product loaded into the briefcases, which contained metal cylinders to house the vials.

She didn't stop. "Not my concern," she said over her shoulder. Then she pushed open the door and stepped back out into the chilly day.

That feeling of being watched was gone now. Ella mourned it but continued to the Rover. She got in, drew in a deep breath, and started the vehicle.

She had to leave Sarajevo. Her heart raced, threatening to beat out of her chest. The heart that had been dead for months.

Jude was onto her now. There was too much risk with Jude involved.

She had to run.

Chapter 2

SILENCE GREETED JUDE AS HE PICKED THE LOCK AND made entry into the loft in the middle of Sarajevo proper. This particular building still held pockmarked evidence of the three-and-a-half-year siege of Sarajevo that had ended in 1996. Bosnian Serbs had surrounded the city and pounded it with tank artillery and small arms fire. The city had burned, and nearly 14,000 people had been killed during the conflict. Sarajevo had managed to recover, but some of the buildings remained sentinels to the war that had nearly decimated it.

The loft Jude had sought was on the third floor, and though the building looked battered on the outside, the loft had been transformed into a posh condominium with hardwood floors and floor-to-ceiling windows along the south side of the space. The interior was filled with all the accoutrements of a well-to-do tenant. A leather sofa, ebony end tables, and a large, heavy oak dining table with twelve chairs for entertaining dominated the two main rooms. Heavy, steel appliances appeared brand new and unused in the spacious kitchen.

Jude made his way through the condo, his gaze cataloging every surface, finding nothing intimate or personal in nature. This was a safe house for her. She'd purchased the property under an assumed identity, Alejna Hurtic. Age twenty-six, daughter of a farm worker, Alejna was known for her escort work and lovely, vivacious nature.

She was considered a dark beauty, much sought after but rarely caught.

And she'd apparently managed to amass a fortune in her scintillatingly dubious profession because her digs represented a lot of money. Logically, Jude knew it was part and parcel of what they did in the world of black ops. Create an identity, assume it with as much or as little engagement as needed, and use every resource at your disposal to garner money for your activities. Off-grid was how black ops worked, and there was no better way to survive the game than to re-create yourself.

She had done well with this one. Had she in fact earned her money in the business Alejna supposedly excelled at? Jude's mind went there, knowing it wasn't true but unable to stop the wave of possessiveness that tightened his scalp and fisted his hands.

Goddamn her for driving him to this madness. Stalking her and now resorting to ambush. But she had yet to show, and he was worried he'd lost her again. He'd left that rise above Dresden's compound knowing that hanging around and blowing the building sky-high wasn't going to accomplish anything. Dresden only used manufacturing facilities and storehouses once before moving on. So Jude had immediately headed here.

A source of his—okay, *Vivi Granger*—had listed this city as having potential as Alejna's, a.k.a. Ella's, location. Vivi was the only one who had never stopped believing in Ella's innocence. She'd reached out to Jude two weeks ago and agreed to feed him as much information as she could get. And she had. Ella had become a master at evasion, but Vivi was wicked with a computer and excelled at possibilities and pattern recognition. She could find anyone, or at least a link to them. She had access to Ella's CIA workup and file, so she knew how Ella moved, how she thought.

Jude didn't know how he felt about Ella's ability to outmaneuver him. The conflict inside him was buried under the need to be in her space, breathing her in. Anger could wait, right? He just needed his hands on her for a moment to make sure she was alive.

But now darkness was falling, and with it, Jude's hopes of catching El—*her*—off guard.

Damn, Dagan, get your shit together. Her name is Ella. You've held her. Loved her. You thought she died, but apparently it was all a lie. Don't let her steal the last part of you by refusing to say her name.

He breathed in deeply, let the oxygen work its magic on his muscles. Slowly, he relaxed. And then a key inserted into the lock of the front door, and Jude froze in the shadows beside the enormous bank of windows.

There wasn't a single sound after the almost silent snick of the door behind whoever had entered. No footfalls echoed over the oak flooring, no small sounds rode the air. There wasn't even the soft shush-shushing noise of cloth over cloth as someone moved. But they were in the condo now. Jude could feel them.

A small trail of light nearly blinded him as a hall lamp flipped on. Then the last person he expected to see entered the living room area, and Jude tensed.

"I knew you'd find her, son," the tall, silver-haired man said as he came fully into view.

Fuck me, Jude thought. "The Piper?" Endgame's creator. Looked like shit was about to get interesting.

The man nodded, a sadness in the gesture that brought

every survival instinct Jude possessed into full alert. The Piper sat down on the large leather couch and leaned back negligently, resting an ankle over his knee and remaining motionless. "You shouldn't have looked for her, Dagan. Why couldn't you just let this go?"

Confusion bombarded him. "Let what go?"

The Piper lifted a hand and gestured to the entire loft. "This."

Jude knew then. Ella might have started out CIA, but she was Endgame all the way. She was working for the Piper. "I'm not following, sir."

Another shake of his head and the Piper smiled, unhappiness again riding the bare twist of his lips. "You follow, son. You always follow. They don't call you the Keeper for nothing, do they? She knew that about you and cursed herself every time she gave in to her emotions for you. She knew you wouldn't let her go, and if anyone ever needed to be let go, it's her." Silence followed his words. Jude didn't dare to breathe. Something big was going on here. He couldn't get a grip on it though. "Dagan, I'm going to have to ask you to leave and go home."

Jude bristled at the proprietary tone in the other man's voice. "And if I don't?"

"Son, I may have phrased it as a request, but it wasn't." The Piper's voice was hard, implacable, and completely at odds with his nonthreatening persona. The man was every bit sixty years old, but his body was well maintained.

Noah Caine was the chairman of the Joint Chiefs of Staff for the United States of America. He was the principal military adviser to the president and the secretary of defense. He'd graduated from Army Ranger School, Marine Corps Amphibious Warfare School, *and* U.S. Army War College on top of having a PhD in government and international relations from Tufts University's Fletcher School of Law and Diplomacy. The man had served at nearly every level in the military. He was a bad motherfucker. He'd also created a private entity to do the things America's regular military couldn't do. Endgame Ops was his brainchild, and it was his funding that kept them operating and doing the things they did to keep America safe.

Jude knew the man. Had eaten barbecue with him and the rest of the team at Port Royal. Had watched him take the heat for failed military incursions even when he'd advised against them. Hell, Jude had watched a damn documentary prior to joining Endgame that had touted the man's military achievements during Operation Iraqi Freedom.

And none of that mattered. Not the respect he held for Caine or his position, nothing. The fact that he was here, where Ella was supposed to be, enraged Jude. He didn't want to kill an old man, but damn if he wouldn't.

Jude palmed his KA-BAR neck knife and waited where he was. He knew this man's background. Knew his training. Jude had the advantage of being younger and stronger, but when equals met, that advantage was always limited. Still, something about the Piper's eerie stillness led Jude to believe he wasn't anyone to screw around with, so he would wait this out.

When Jude continued to remain silent, the Piper drew in a rough breath and stood. The man's body was motionless, his breathing even.

"I came here because you're one of mine. I don't like it when mine are hurt. But she's one of mine too. And no one on this team has sacrificed as much as she has. Go home, Dagan, and if she survives, she'll come home too."

"What is she involved in? What do you have her doing, Piper?" Jude kept his voice even, but inside the fury rolled, a tidal wave that threatened to choke him.

The Piper shifted, and Jude noticed the man's hand slip behind his back. "That's not your mission, Dagan. I believe you need to check in with your team leader. It's never good to go rogue."

"Don't," Jude warned him.

"Yeah, don't," a woman said from behind the Piper. Her smoky voice, though soft and low, reverberated through Jude. She took the weapon the Piper had been reaching for and tossed it to the side.

The tension in the room shot through the stratosphere as Ella Banning stepped in from the kitchen, pressing a gun to the back of the Piper's head. Jude hadn't heard her. Had she been here the entire time? Goddamn, he was losing his edge. She had him so wrapped up in misery that he wasn't even covering his own ass.

The Piper stood as still as stone, but a smile tracked slowly across his face. "There's my girl."

Jude tensed, unable to let his body relax or clear his mind as this went down. Normally he was ice cold. But the circumstances inside this condo at this moment wouldn't allow him that. She wasn't *his* girl. She was Jude's. Or she used to be.

She had yet to look at him, but Jude's gaze tracked over her features—across her high cheekbones, over her straight, slightly upturned nose, and down across her mouth, the mouth that had pleasured him and spoken of love and lies.

"You promised," she whispered in the Piper's ear, though loud enough for Jude to hear.

"I have promised a lot of people a lot of things, Ella. He can't have you. There's still too much to do," the Piper returned, his voice deep and sad.

"I will do whatever needs to be done, but he is, and always will be, off-limits." Her voice had hardened, a bitterness riding the dulcet tones that carried caution. And she still hadn't looked at Jude.

"I'm wondering if I get a say in any of this?" he threw into the conversation.

Neither of them looked his way.

Jude sheathed his knife and pulled his 9mm Smith & Wesson M&P from its resting spot in his back waist-band before thumbing off the safety. His skin tingled, a sure sign something wicked his way came.

"Someone's at the door," the Piper said suddenly.

Between one breath and the next, that same door was kicked in and a small canister bounced into the living room, smoke immediately pouring from it and infiltrating the condo. Jude squatted, finding Ella unerringly.

Finally, she looked at him, her gaze filled with fear and something he'd seen earlier outside Dresden's stash house…love? Or was it hate? "Run," she mouthed as she lowered her gun and allowed the Piper to begin pulling her to the inner recesses of the condo.

No way in hell was anyone getting to her. Not before him. "Get her out of here," Jude shouted as automatic weapons fire began peppering the walls and windows above him.

The Piper said nothing, and Jude was left alone with an unknown number of assailants and an unknown situation. He lowered fully to the floor, trying to stay beneath the smoke.

They were silent, but under the smoke Jude counted four sets of feet, moving in a coordinated way that spoke of a concentrated effort to eliminate a target. He knew their moves. Had moved that way himself for years.

He rolled as one man breached the living room, raising his gun and firing a single shot, hitting the man in the forehead. The man fell like a rock.

More sporadic fire came Jude's way, adrenaline kicking his senses into high gear. He could see them through the smoke now, darker shapes that seemed phantoms in the midst of a nightmare. He took down another one as he plastered himself to the wall and began inching toward the back of the condo. They were trying to locate him, their eyes covered by night-vision goggles that probably also allowed them to track heat signatures, unhampered by the smoke they'd thrown as a distraction.

He wouldn't be able to avoid them much longer. He lined up his shot, but before he could squeeze the trigger, two shots rang out. Jude recognized the report—H&K VP9—Ella's choice of handgun. The remaining two attackers fell, unmoving, clearly dead.

Her hand settled on his arm, and he looked down, the moment surreal and unbelievable. Her touch warmed him at the same time it settled something cold and vicious in his gut. His gaze rose and met hers, and where before there had been fear, now there was nothing. She was closed off to him.

"You never run when you should," she bit out, loading another magazine into her weapon.

"You always run when you shouldn't," Jude responded, the lash of his voice scoring even him.

Her eyes narrowed, the only sign she was angry. "No time for idle chitchat, Dagan. There are more where those came from," she said, gesturing toward the fallen men.

Then she disappeared into the back of the condo. Jude followed, one ear trained to detect any incoming threat, the rest of his attention on Ella. She scurried through a small door in the wall of what looked to be a bedroom, turning as she passed through to watch him.

He stopped for a split second, caught as he always was by her beauty.

"Hurry up, Dagan! For the love of God, hurry the hell up!" She turned away from him again and began hotfooting it through to what looked like a neighboring apartment. All he could think was that she'd never, ever, called him by his last name.

He squeezed his big frame through the tiny opening and took off after her. She was quick, always had been, but she wouldn't elude him this time. He caught up to her as she came to yet another small opening and entered another apartment.

"Set this up pretty well, didn't you?" he asked as he once again squeezed his body through the tiny hole in the wall.

"Gotta do what you gotta do," she threw back at him as she stopped suddenly and turned to stare at him.

"What?" he asked, brushing dust off his face and checking his weapon. Men were following; he could hear them making entry into the other apartment. He didn't know how many, and he had limited ammunition. Hell, he hadn't come here for anything other than her.

"Keeper," she whispered.

He cocked his head at her, wondering where the hell this was going. "Why?" He didn't know if he was asking why she'd left him or why she was calling him Keeper.

She took a single step toward him, raising the hand not holding her weapon to his face. She ran a finger along his bottom lip. "Because I won't ever allow anyone to hurt you. You're the Keeper, but you're mine."

She moved so quickly he couldn't track the action, then a sharp prick pierced his neck. "They're coming. Don't do this, Ella. You're killing me." He never would have made that admission before. He hated himself in that moment for making it now.

She caught him as he fell, and then her soft voice was at his ear. "My love, I'm *saving* you. I'll always have your six."

Then she laid him gently on the floor and stepped over him. The last thing he saw past his drooping eyelids was her raising her weapon and firing.

Chapter 3

WHEN HER MAN SLEPT, HE SLEPT LIKE THE DEAD. Ella smiled ruefully. Not that they'd ever done much sleeping. A sharp pang hit her heart. He wasn't hers anymore, was he? She drew in a deep breath, hoping to find the calm center that had served her so well during the last year. Now wasn't the time to deal with what she'd left behind. She had to keep him safe in the here and now so she could hopefully explain everything to him when the time was right.

She'd taken down the remaining four attackers, and then the Piper had helped her relocate Jude to another safe house on the outskirts of Sarajevo. This one belonged to a longtime Endgame associate, Adam Babic.

Ella had to make sure Jude was okay before she took off. Adam would handle Jude's safety until he woke. The Piper was doing his best to find out who had sent the two teams of killers after her. Ella thought it could be any number of people, though she'd ruled out Segorski fairly quickly. He wanted her alive, and it was clear by the shock-and-awe method of attack that the teams had been there to eliminate their target, not capture.

An insidious thought crept in. Maybe they hadn't come for her at all. Maybe the two teams of assassins had followed the Piper. Ella acknowledged the goose bumps breaking out on her skin. Fear was a fine emotion. It kept you sharp. But Ella hadn't been born to this life like Jude had. She'd been trained, but being a soldier wasn't in the fabric of her bones, and the fear was her friend and foe. She had to work to overcome it.

If they'd followed the Piper, that meant someone was onto him. He had suspected for a while that someone even higher up in the presidential administration than him had been gunning for him. They'd started by trying to take out Endgame. It wasn't common knowledge that Noah Caine, a.k.a. the Piper, had created a private spec ops entity, but it wasn't buried six feet deep either. On paper, they provided logistical support and security for private contractors rebuilding countries like Afghanistan and Iraq. It was unspoken but understood that they delved into the gray whenever they needed to. Whose feet had the Piper stepped on? Or was it just Dresden?

Ella needed to have a little sit-down with the Piper. It really was time he came clean on some things.

She rested her head on the bed beside Jude's arm. She was so damn tired.

"He's got to stop." One of the men who'd cost her damn near everything had entered the room. Ella sighed soundlessly.

"He'll never stop. I told you that, and you said you could handle him, keep him busy on missions that wouldn't get him killed and keep him far from Dresden," she reminded the Piper. She stopped for a moment and really looked at him. "You look really tired, old man."

He snorted before rubbing his eyes. "I am old. Too old for this shit."

Ella shrugged. "You set the board, and now moves are being made. This was what it was all about," she bit out.

The Piper nodded. "I did my best, but the bastard just keeps coming, doesn't he?" There was a rueful note in his voice as he disregarded her comment.

"Yeah," she returned. "He does."

She raised her head and stared at Jude. His eyes remained closed, but she felt his attention. He was awake. Ella stood and moved away from the bed. Jude's eyes opened immediately, the black of his gaze snaring her, refusing to let her leave completely.

Always it was Jude. In every dream, in every breath, it was always Jude.

She watched him, noticing the exact instant he realized he was strapped to the bed. He tugged on each arm once and relaxed. Or at least he appeared to relax. With Jude, that was never reality. He was ready for anything at all times.

"Take them off," he demanded in a deep voice. His gaze never left hers.

She opened her mouth—to say what, she didn't know—but the Piper beat her to it. "No."

Jude continued to stare at Ella. "Take them off, or when I get free I'll make you both pay."

There was so much in his gaze. Questions, pain, rage—the tangle of emotions traveled the air between them. And Ella was in no position to give him the answers or assurances he needed from her. Had needed for over a year now.

"Jude—" she began.

"I don't deal with traitors," he bit out.

Oh, that hurt. Cut bone deep and left her bleeding inside.

"No one has asked you to, son," the Piper said, his

voice now low and carrying a hint of frustration. "Then again, no one here is a traitor."

The skin over Jude's cheekbones went ruddy. Ella had really only seen it do that when he was buried inside her, so it was unique to see it now, and for an entirely different emotion. He was furious. Unfortunately, there was nothing she could do about that.

Jude's gaze finally shifted to the creator of Endgame Ops. "Take off the restraints."

The Piper shook his head and stepped beside the bed. "No. There is work to be done, and while I would love nothing more than to release you, we appear to have different objectives. Ella Banning has a mission to complete, and you, Dagan, have to return to your team. If I let you out of the restraints, you'll take her, and I know what you're apparently blind to. She'll go with you, willingly, if it means you stay safe. And that will destroy any chance we have of finding out who is pulling Horace Dresden's strings."

Jude sat abruptly, reclining one second, upright the next. The chains attached to the leather cuffs on his arms and legs jangled against the metal framework of the bed he was on. The sound was strident, and Ella winced. The Piper shifted to his right. Her back snapped straight, and she reached for the weapon in her side holster, snapping the strap holding it in place.

Jude's head rotated, and once again she was pinned under his night-sky gaze. "You gonna shoot me, Ella-Bella?"

Her breath left her in a rush. He doubted her and it—*hurt*. She would never shoot Jude. But she'd earned his doubt and would have to carry it with her when she left. The Piper's head swiveled in her direction, and his pupils dilated. He lowered the hand that had been reaching for his weapon and took a small step back from Jude.

"I wouldn't shoot him," the Piper said wearily.

"I wouldn't let you," she responded, making sure her voice didn't waver but conveyed her intent.

"I'm going to reach for my pocket, Ella. I've got something to leave Dagan." The Piper waited for her nod and reached in, pulling out a sheet of paper. He set the paper on the small table beside the bed and stepped away again.

"We have a plane to catch," the Piper tossed in her direction as he left the room. "Say what you need to say, and let's go."

Ella closed her eyes and drew on the dwindling core of strength inside her. She could leave him again. She had to.

"Don't do this, Ella." Jude's voice reached inside her, and whether he would ever know it or not, it bolstered that failing strength. "Whatever has happened, let me help you."

Ella allowed her gaze to rove over his big body, up his wide chest and up farther over his face. She appreciated his tanned skin and the black hair that had a tendency to curl when he let it grow past the shorter style he preferred. She prized the bump in the bridge of his nose. She treasured his ebony eyes. She had always enjoyed his big hands and the tensile power of his corded, muscular body. She cherished his pride, his loyalty, and the way he had shown her he was hers. He wasn't a beautiful man; he had been too much of a soldier not to bear the scars of his profession. But he was sexy as hell, and to her, he was everything.

She loved Jude Dagan. She always would.

Ella pushed down every bit of love and loss she felt, burying it under her duty.

"I had hoped you'd never see me again. That I'd never have to see you and remember what I've given up. But we rarely get what we want." She spoke quietly as she walked to the end of the bed. "Sometimes though, you have a chance to apologize."

He laughed, and it was harsh in the silence of the room. "Is that why you're standing there? To apologize?"

Ella allowed a smile to curve her lips before shaking her head. "No. It's not time yet to apologize for the things I've done. You, probably much like King, will think what you want. It's not my job to change your mind or bury myself in recriminations."

He sighed and rattled his bindings again. "Then what the hell is your job, Ella?"

"Why, it's the same job we've had for nearly two years, Jude." She saw him wince and knew instinctively it was because she'd used his first name. Yet another thing she loved about the man before her...his name. "Destroying Horace Dresden."

"Then let me go, and let me help you," he said, more demand than request.

She straightened then, giving him the full force of her gaze. "You need to return to Endgame. Following me will get you nowhere but dead. Go home, Jude, to your teammates."

"It's time, Ella." The Piper's voice rang out from the other room.

She would try one more time. "Don't come after me." She let her gaze slide once more over the man who owned her heart, body, and soul. Then she turned.

She'd made it to the doorway when he spoke.

"I'll come after you. I'll never stop coming after you. You owe me the truth. And I owe you for what you allowed to happen to Micah and Nina. You almost killed us all. Dresden would have loved that, wouldn't he?"

She breathed in deeply through the pain of his words. She hadn't set up what happened that night in the desert surrounding Beirut, but she'd definitely taken advantage of it. Micah Samson had been one of Jude's best friends, and he'd fallen that night. Nina had been one of Ella's, and she'd fallen back in DC, before they ever set foot on the C-130 headed to Beirut. Both of their losses haunted her. She had no choice but to push through it.

She took another step, and again his words stopped her.

"One more thing… When I find you, and I will find you, I will make you pay for this, Ella. I thought my life ended when I saw you *die* in Beirut. But if you make me hunt you down again, what I do when I find you will destroy us both. I'll say it one more time: don't do this. Make me understand, Ella. Let me help you." His voice was sandpaper over gravel by the time he finished.

And she was shredded by it. She glanced over her shoulder at him. His face was ravaged by what he'd gone through over her. Such a strong man, his purpose embedded in the framework of his bones—and she'd nearly broken him. She was scalded by the rage in his eyes, but it was nothing less than she deserved.

He'd move on from her. And even though a tiny part of her, the most jealous part, prayed he never forgot what they had shared together, the bigger part prayed he did indeed move on. Because Ella was living on borrowed time. She had resigned herself to her fate when she'd agreed to work with the Piper. She would probably die ending Dresden. There was nothing for her with Jude, no matter how much both of them wished it could be so.

"I said I wouldn't apologize, but as fickle as fate is, this might be my last chance," she whispered. She lowered her head, unable to look at him and still have the strength to walk away. "I love you, Jude Dagan. I will always love you. I'm sorry."

Then she walked away, hearing him curse her and struggle against his bonds.

Chapter 4

"AH, ELLA! YOU'RE BACK," HORACE DRESDEN CALLED out from his position at the head of the enormous dining table.

Ella walked in, portraying a casualness she did not feel. She walked a tightrope with the monster that was Horace Dresden. She could be neither too strong, nor too weak. Instead, she struggled to place herself right in the middle between those two approaches.

Anton Segorski sat to Dresden's left, and to his right sat Abrafo Nadege. Segorski was a worm. Nadege was a vulture. The African warlord had spent the last two years setting up shop in Burundi, Africa, stealing wealth and mining diamonds. He'd amassed a following of ragtag, disenfranchised mercenary fighters from all over Africa, but his specialty was taking young boys and forcing them into his army.

It was interesting that Segorski was already back with Dresden. Ella figured the Russian would be gloating about his ricin and formulating plans to maim and destroy innocents.

"I'm back," she acknowledged in a neutral tone, hitting the high bar and pouring herself a shot of Jack Daniel's. It had been Jude's whiskey of choice. Ella did whatever she could to hold him close.

She tossed back the shot, letting the burn hit her gut

before she turned and rested against the large, oak high bar. She raised an eyebrow at Dresden, waiting.

"Come," he urged. "Sit and eat with us."

Ella snorted, unladylike and loud in the silence of the giant dining room. "Eat dinner with murderers and terrorists? I'll pass." She turned and poured another shot, placing a single ice cube in the crystal highball glass before adding two fingers of whiskey over the top.

Dresden laughed as she knew he would. He'd once told her he preferred her feisty rather than meek and obsequious. Of course the only reason she'd been obedient had been because he'd allowed Vasily Savidge to break her into tiny pieces.

She tossed back the second shot and waited for it to numb her.

Vasily Savidge couldn't hurt her anymore, ever again. He'd perished under the onslaught of two bullets—one courtesy of King McNally, the other thanks to Loretta Bernstein. Where was that woman, anyway? Ella knew she'd survived the CIA's blitzkrieg of Dresden's Beirut property. She'd left as Endgame hustled Allie Redding out. Loretta had been hurt but not bad enough to prevent her from running and holing up somewhere Ella hadn't been able to locate yet.

And she *would* locate the woman. She had some explaining to do. She also had intel Ella needed.

"*Ella*, come *sit* and *eat* with us." Ahhh, there was the Dresden Ella knew and hated. No more Mr. Nice Guy.

She had to play the game if she wanted to win.

Ella took a seat at the opposite end of the table. Segorski mumbled something, Abrafo Nadege laughed, and Dresden merely watched her, chin in his hand, finger slowly rubbing over his lips.

Horace Dresden. Ella had been labeled a traitor, but the man across from her had defined the word. Born thirty-six years ago and raised in New York City, he'd graduated cum laude from Columbia, then gone on to join the Navy. He'd made his way through BUD/S training and become a decorated soldier.

Then something had happened approximately four years ago that set him on a very different path. Ella was after that something. It was the key to his destruction. When the Piper had first contacted her to work a mission within a mission, she'd been hesitant. Then he'd told her about Dresden's past, and she'd known that somewhere inside that past was the way to destroy the man who'd turned on his brothers and his country. Hell, he'd turned on the entire world.

And his rise in the murky world of arms dealing had been meteoric. Within two years of going AWOL from a joint task-force team on a mission in the Kunar Province, he'd been at the top of the arms-dealer shit pile. He'd raided weapons depots belonging to the United States and Russia and become a billionaire, taking out competition swiftly and efficiently. By the time the world's powers had realized there was a new player on the international arms-dealing stage, it had been too late. Dresden had been too powerful.

All of this was bad enough. But one of the most curious things about Dresden's past was exactly who some of the members of that joint task-force team had been—Kingston McNally, Rook Granger, and Jonah Knight.

Men who had since dedicated themselves to the eradication of Horace Dresden.

"She will bow to me before it's all said and done," Anton Segorski said from his perch beside Dresden.

Dresden lifted a brow to that. "Ella bows to no one. Even Vasily had difficulty breaking her."

Was that pride in his voice? Ella wanted to vomit.

"Are you missing Vasily, Dresden?" Abrafo Nadege queried softly. For such a large, brutish-looking man, he spoke with a refined air, voice hell-deep and cultured. To be expected, considering he'd been schooled in London. "I know he was your right hand."

"Vasily's loss was…unexpected," Dresden admitted. "Right, Ella?"

Ella chuckled, the sound strident in the cavernous room, as she watched a server fill her glass with red wine. "It happened too fast. I would have preferred he suffer a bit before having his head filled with holes." She shrugged, lifted the wine, and mimicked taking a healthy swallow. She'd had two shots. It wouldn't do to dull her senses around these killers.

Dresden threw back his head and guffawed. Finally, he ceased, dabbed his eyes, and lifted his own wine and sipped. "Ella, you never fail to impress me. I've broken you, killed your friends, and still that fire you always try to hide makes an appearance."

"I can break her again," Segorski bit out.

Dresden struck then, standing so swiftly his chair flew out from behind him. He was on Segorski in the blink of an eye, pulling the man's head back so far Ella wondered if his neck would snap. Dresden held a butter knife to the Russian's throat.

"Maybe you haven't been listening to me, friend. Ella will never be yours," Dresden hissed in the man's ear, pressing the butter knife into his throat so hard he began to bleed.

The Russian didn't move, and Dresden didn't either.

Ella sipped at her water casually. She allowed her eyes to drift to Nadege, who stared at her, his cold, hard gaze trying to ferret out her secrets. She lifted her glass to him before running a finger along her throat in a slitting motion, a salute of sorts, as the tableau in front of them played out.

Long moments passed, but finally Dresden released Segorski, who coughed and wheezed as the air rushed back into his body. Other than gasping and trying to right the damage done to his hair, he didn't move, not even mopping up the blood dripping down his neck.

Dresden straightened his suit coat. "Now where were we?" he asked, looking down the table at Ella.

She smiled at him. He smiled back. And so the game continued.

"We were celebrating another successful sale, Ella. I'm so glad you could join us for a time." He turned then and addressed both Nadege and Segorski before his gaze slid to her. "I believe Ella and I have some business to discuss. Shall you finish your dinners in your rooms?" Dresden inquired. Read that as ordered. Again, Ella wondered why Segorski was here with Dresden instead of in his own hole counting containers of ricin.

She would have shuddered but giving Dresden that much of a response would have been a win for him. And that she would not do. It was tough calling back the response because nothing about being alone with Dresden was good.

Instead, she smiled. "It's been a pleasure as always, Segorski. Don't choke on your food, and fellas"—she addressed them both—"watch those butter knives, okay?" They both stood and left the room.

Dresden took his seat again at the table, picked up his silverware, and began slowly eating the rare filet mignon that sat in a bloody pool on his pristine white china. Silence reigned for several minutes while he finished his food. He was at his most obnoxious during these times, when he had someone hanging on the hook waiting for him.

He finished, drained his wine, and wiped his mouth. Though his gestures screamed of refinement, there was a desperation to each movement that belied any belief that the man had been raised wealthy. He seemed more of a rabid predator wearing a thin veneer of civility. Some of that animalistic nature had no doubt been drummed into him by the military.

He steepled his hands and rested his chin on them, staring at her down the length of the table, quiet with a bored look on his handsome face.

"So, Ella, you have once again met my expectations. Tell me, how does it feel to work for the dark side?"

She had to tread carefully here. In the tones of his voice was a warning: *Answer me wrong, and I'll have you gutted. Answer me the right way, and I'll let you live. Maybe.* The game continued.

She shrugged, took a pull on her wine—for real this time—and let it go down slowly. The warmth of the earlier whiskey had faded. She longed for it now. "I do what I'm told, Dresden, and I live."

He chuckled and pushed back his chair, strolling to take the seat beside her. He leaned close, the smell of his aftershave a noxious scent of sandalwood that turned Ella's stomach. He brushed a single strand of hair from her face and cupped her chin. His grip tightened, and he pulled her face to meet his. "Look at me when I talk to you."

She lifted her gaze and met his. The blue of his eyes would have been appealing, were it not the gaze of a sadistic monster. "I'm looking."

His grip on her chin hurt but she didn't let that show, willing herself to keep calm in the center of this new storm.

"Yes, you are. Now." He released her and sat back. "I have something else I need taken care of."

Ella tightened her grip on the stem of her glass. She could break it easily and embed it in his throat before he could blink. But there was still something she had to have from him, and until it was in her hands… "What do you need?"

"There's a meeting in Moscow in two days. I need someone there representing my interests. Someone to report back to me, should Segorski and Yevgeny Markov betray me. It wouldn't do to have the prime minister of Russia benefitting from my hard work before he's paid for it."

She inclined her head. "The oil is yours."

"It is, and I'll make billions off it after the Russians complete the takeover of the Crimean region. Say it again," he demanded, his voice still full of warning.

"Say what?" Push a little, and this would go well for Ella. Push too much, and he'd crush her.

He grabbed her face between his big hands and squeezed. The pressure was also a warning. "Say it."

She stared at him, hoping the loathing she felt for him didn't show in her gaze. "The oil is yours."

He released her so suddenly that her head snapped back.

"And so are you," he informed her. "Say it."

"So am I," she parroted.

He sat back negligently, crossing one leg over the other and watching her. "My sources tell me Jude Dagan is actively searching for you."

Ella said nothing. Perhaps his *sources* had noticed Jude when they'd torn into the flat in Serbia yesterday.

"I have yet to take him out, but I can rectify this with a single call. Someone always follows him, and it would only take a split second to put a hole in his skull with a bullet. Do you know why I haven't?"

Here was the line she couldn't cross. "I don't, Dresden. But you're going to tell me?"

"Because he keeps you in line. Don't they call him that? Keeper?" He didn't laugh as she expected him to, which put her even more on the razor's edge.

"They did. I don't know what they call him now," she answered, making sure her voice remained even and distant.

"You loved him once. Don't tell me you no longer feel that same emotion for the brute," Dresden mocked, tracing the scar along her temple.

Hide the truth behind a lie. She'd become a master. "I feel nothing for anyone, Dresden. You and Savidge made sure of that. What Jude Dagan is called or not called is no longer my concern. I once felt an emotion for him; that's true. My course has changed, and Endgame and Dagan are in my past. I'm curious why you think he keeps me in line."

He grunted. "I think your words are…the right words. Because of that, I'll give you the reason I think Dagan's life keeps you in my pocket. He was your world, and you're a woman."

She allowed a mirthless chuckle to escape. "You noticed."

Dresden sat up straight at that. "I notice a lot of things, Banning. That's why I'm on top. I noticed that your flat in Sarajevo mysteriously blew up after the sale to Segorski went through. I noticed that sixteen men were found dead in or around Sarajevo in a matter of hours after that explosion. I noticed that you entered my home a day later and immediately poured yourself a whiskey neat, which by the way is also Jude Dagan's favorite drink, and I noticed that now your pupils are dilated in fear."

"There's a point to this conversation. Can we get to it?"

He laughed then. It was evil. "You always seek to hide behind whatever persona you feel I need from you. I let you because it amuses me. The point is this: Dagan controls you because he lives. And because I like having a way to control Dagan, I keep you alive and doing my bidding."

Ella should have felt fear. It was true her pupils had dilated, but it wasn't with apprehension. It was with rage. Dresden thought he had her figured out. He thought he *knew*. It took her a few seconds to control herself, to not snap the stem of her glass and shove it in his right eye. Or the left. Either would work. She continued to breathe through her nose, not rushing her breaths, keeping them even and controlled. She had a goal. She could do this. He held her wrist, gauging her pulse no doubt, and she managed to control even that.

She had become ice cold.

She hated herself.

"I would clap for your keen sense of observation, but you're holding my hand. I will grant you instead mental applause for the way you've managed to manipulate every situation to your advantage. Good job, Dresden."

"It is all a game to you, isn't it?" He huffed, sounding like a petulant child. "I broke you, and still you come at me like it's all a goddamn game. Tell me, do you really no longer feel anything for Jude Dagan?"

She had one shot at this. If she said no, he'd eliminate Jude. If she said yes, he'd eliminate Jude. "I don't feel. You removed the ability. I work. I succeed. Dagan is a way for you to control Endgame? Okay. Keep the Keeper on the line. But if you think that either eliminating him or keeping him alive gives you control of me, you're wrong."

"I let Vasily work you too long," he said mournfully. "You've become a puppet."

She glanced at him dismissively. "Is that not what you wanted?"

He stood then, and she held herself still. "It's not your concern what I wanted."

His phone rang, and he answered it. "Speak." His face reddened, and his gaze went flat. "Kill him."

Ella's heart stuttered.

"I don't care if his daughter is in the car. Destroy him." He hung up and threw the phone across the room, shattering it against the marble floor.

Not Jude. Not this time. She hated herself for the relief she felt.

Dresden walked to the entry of the dining room and

turned back to Ella. "I want you in Moscow tomorrow. Crimea is mine until I say otherwise. Make sure Segorski and Markov stay in line. And, Ella? If Dagan doesn't keep his fucking nose out of my business, it won't matter to me if he's a way to control Endgame. Ultimately, Endgame will be mine, just like you, and I don't need Dagan to make that happen."

"I don't control Jude Dagan," she countered. She needed to throw him a bone. "And I'll say again, he is no longer my concern."

"Good. Make sure it stays that way. The jet will be ready for you when you're ready to travel. Meet with Svetlana Markov when you arrive, and she'll fill you in on the specifics. Ella?"

She met his gaze.

"I control Svetlana Markov as I control you."

"And how is that, Dresden?"

"Completely," he dropped into her silence, and then he left her with a small, triumphant laugh.

She drained her wine and motioned to the mute server in the corner to refill it. Then she drained that one too. She was a long way from drunk but wished she were safe enough to engage that state.

She had no idea how much longer she could do this with Dresden. Though every interaction with him brought her closer to the information she needed before she took him down, each meeting with him, each conversation, left her deadened on the inside. Hiding herself from his keen gaze took a measure of skill she'd had no choice but to perfect. But it took its toll on her soul. She was losing herself.

This conversation had given her Svetlana Markov,

wife of Yevgeny Markov and apparently as deep in Dresden's pockets as Ella herself was.

She closed her eyes and let the last drop of wine slip down her throat. Black eyes taunted her. She had it all, and she'd walked away from it because the evil that was Horace Dresden could eat up the world and spit it out irreparably broken. He'd set into motion deals all over the world that would disrupt the economies of every major power. The few would be in control of the many, and the many would suffer because of it.

Her country would be the first to fall—all because of greed. Dresden had been right; she was a puppet. One of many. And he wasn't the only puppet master, because someone was pulling his strings too—and that's who she needed.

Endgame thought Dresden was the top of the pyramid, but though he was really close, there was someone, or a select group of someones, higher than him. Losing Dresden would cripple that entity. And it would save Jude.

That's all Ella wanted or cared about. Yes, her teammates were important. But nobody was as important as Jude.

She needed to find out why the Piper hadn't told Endgame and King McNally the theory of someone being higher than Dresden. Ella knew it all led back to that fuckup in Kunar Province more than four years ago. Endgame had been born out of that failed op. The Piper had secrets Ella was beginning to suspect tied him to Dresden in some way. He also played a dangerous game. Kingston McNally was nobody to mess with. And his team was his number one priority. Well, his team and now Allie Redding.

King wouldn't appreciate being kept in the dark. Though maybe he had secrets she needed to discover as well.

She rubbed her head and stood, heading to her room.

Sleep would probably evade her, but she would try. Tomorrow promised to be trying. More games to be played, more people to maneuver and watch.

Ella removed her heels, skirt, and shirt, showered, and then dressed in jeans and a T-shirt. She never slept in anything else when she stayed here. Dresden was public enemy number one, and Ella wanted to always be prepared to run at a moment's notice.

She flipped off the lamp beside the bed and watched the moon climb through the sky. She wanted to dream of Jude but knew that falling asleep opened her up to nightmares rather than dreams. Instead, she closed her eyes and counted every breath she took, keeping track so that if she was lucky enough to live through this, she could take them all over again with her man.

With Jude.

Chapter 5

"WHAT DO YOU WANT, JUDE?" VIVI GRANGER ASKED for the second time since he'd entered the room.

"The same thing I always want, Vivi," he replied, crossing his arms over his chest and watching her. A big part of him felt remorse that he kept coming to her. There was no way to skirt around the fact that he was asking her to keep information from their team leader.

Yet still he did it. Ella was a piece of him he thought he'd never get back. After being close enough to her to see where the gray of her irises bled to black, after having the regret on her face cut him like a knife, there was no way he could walk away from her—even if that took him through the hottest fires of hell.

Vivi huffed and blew a strand of long, curly brown hair out of her eyes while her gaze roved over the computer directly in front of her. She paused for a second to throw him an exasperated look before she glanced at the computers sitting to the left and right of the main laptop. "I've got things to do, and you're bugging me just standing there staring. Don't make me get Rook."

"I don't know if you know this, but I'm not scared of Rook," he said with a small grunt.

"I don't know where she is exactly, Dagan," Vivi hissed. "And if you keep coming in here asking, eventually my man will find out I'm feeding you information, and then my ass is grass."

"Your man already knows" came from a deep voice behind Jude.

He shifted to the side, and Rook Granger walked into the room, oozing confidence along with no small amount of anger, both directed at Jude. The man moved like a cold wind, silent and lethal. He'd lost a leg in Afghanistan ten years ago, but you couldn't tell unless you looked down and saw the blade he wore. Even then, you doubted what you were seeing because Jude knew some warriors with two fully functioning legs who didn't move the way Granger did.

"And he's pissed," Rook finished.

Jude shrugged. Vivi gasped and removed her glasses, rubbing her eyes wearily. She put her glasses back on and glared at Jude. He shrugged again. He needed to know where Ella was. It had taken him an hour to maneuver that damn bed she'd strapped him to enough to get the key and unlock himself. By then, Adam Babic had walked in and laughed at Jude. The Serbian had a wicked sense of humor, but when Jude was the butt of the joke, it pissed him off.

Ella had been long gone by then, her trail cold. Adam had given him nothing but his well wishes. Jude had spent the flight back to DC angry, determined to talk to Vivi and then the Piper.

Vivi knew things. A lot of things. And what she didn't know, she could find out with an ease that left all of Endgame Ops shaking their heads. Jude had thought no one besides him knew Vivi was helping him locate Ella.

Apparently he was wrong. And he was desperate enough that he didn't give a damn—hell, two damns—about being wrong.

"I need her, Rook," Jude told his friend and teammate.

"She's busier than hell, and you're pressuring her, Dagan. That's not cool," Rook bit out. "Plus, King told you not to continue your little sideline ventures if they relate to Ella Banning."

"I don't mean to burden Vivi, Rook." Jude sighed and ran a hand down his face, recognizing he needed to shave and not really caring. "But I need to find her."

Rook faced him from behind his wife. His wife. He had his woman. Jude didn't.

"If *her* is Ella, then you're screwed. Because Vivi isn't going to give you anything else about *her*," Rook told him, his voice hard and very, very final.

Vivi gasped again and turned in her seat to face her husband. Her husband. She had her man.

"You don't get to do that, Rook Granger," she said as she stood to her diminutive five-foot-nothing height and shoved a finger in Rook's chest.

Rook's face softened. "I earned that right when I went all in, Vivi. And we'll talk about why you felt a need to hide this from me."

Her finger lost its point as she flattened her hand on her husband's chest and stepped closer. "That's not what that meant, Granger."

Jude had had enough. Seeing them together—loving, being with each other when he couldn't be with Ella—hurt. He cleared his throat. "Can you hash this out later?"

They both straightened and glared at him. Vivi huffed. "You're causing me issues, Dagan. I have nothing more to give you, and I'm buried in deciphering this code from the file Jonah and Rook retrieved yesterday."

"I need to find her, Vivi. She's in danger," Jude bit out.

He'd run over every single second he'd been with Ella and the Piper, and nothing added up the way it should.

He could say with spectacular clarity that Ella had been playing a dangerous game while working for Endgame. Double agent indeed. She'd manipulated them all, signed on for the cause, and done the dirty work for the Piper.

The hell of it was, the Piper was Endgame Ops' creator. Why would he instigate an op within an op? What was he hiding? The latter question bothered Jude the most. If they couldn't trust the man who'd created them, who the hell could they trust?

Jude had yet to speak to King about his theories. King had ripped him a new asshole earlier, telling him to leave the issue of Ella Banning where it was…in King's hands. Jude hadn't even tried to lie to his team leader. He'd shrugged and ignored the edict. It had frustrated King, but Jude wouldn't say one thing and do another. It wasn't in his makeup.

"She *is* in danger. But she knew what she was getting into when she signed on. I guess we could all talk to the Piper about the danger she's in, yeah?" Vivi asked around the pencil she now held between her lips.

Rook went on alert, hands on his wife's shoulders, squeezing. "What the hell does that mean, woman?"

"He's been pulling all of our strings for years, Rook. He started with you and Jonah four years ago, then he brought in King to lead you all. He allowed the CIA to put not one, but two analysts on the team, knowing you already had me. He's had that damn file you took from that safety deposit box in Oklahoma City, and he hasn't let me see it again. He's got answers…"

Rook spun her chair around and leaned over her. "You told me you wouldn't dive into that disk, Vivi."

Vivi's hand shook as she brushed a strand of hair away from her face. Jude noticed it all, but even in the midst of that, the woman carried a secret smile on her lips. She loved playing Rook.

Jude rubbed his chest. He missed *her*. "Come on, people. Focus." He really needed them to stop their shit.

Rook glared at him. Vivi continued to look up at her man. "I only peeked, and he took it before I could copy it—"

Her words cut off because her husband's hand covered her mouth. "Stop." Rook glanced at Jude and said, "Not a word to anybody."

Jude raised his right hand. "Swear it. But only if she gives me Ella's location."

"I'm good, Dagan, but she's gone ghost, and not even I can track a ghost," Vivi told him, a mournful quality to her voice that stung him.

Jude cursed and ran a hand over his hair.

"But I do know that Svetlana Markov is headed for Moscow. In fact, she landed earlier today and registered a room at the Four Seasons…ummm, a penthouse suite," Vivi dropped into his silence.

Rook straightened and sighed. "Stop doing this to him, baby. You're tearing him apart."

Vivi grabbed Rook's hand, entwining their fingers, locking them together. "He looked at her the way you look at me, Rook. The way I'm sure I look at you. What they have doesn't die. Besides, I owe him one…or twelve."

"For what?" Rook asked in outrage.

"Ukraine," Jude answered. He'd buried himself in

intelligence gathering when he'd first heard rumors of a woman with a gaze of frost and a bullet scar at her temple making waves for Horace Dresden. During a two-day stint in Ukraine tracking a former Russian FSB agent, Jude had hit a gold mine. He'd managed to get a shit-ton of information from the former agent. Of course, he'd had the man strung up and hooked to battery cables at the time, but the FSB agent had sung a nice tune. Jude had netted information about Dresden hunting Rook's wife.

Dresden had it bad for the former CIA analyst. Whether it was to kill her or have her skill set for himself was anyone's guess. Had Jude not given Rook the intel, Vivi might well be in Dresden's clutches today.

Rook let a really foul word slip out before he looked at Jude. "She's right."

Jude nodded in agreement.

"But this is it. She gives you this, and you don't ask her anymore, Keeper. King would have my ass, and man, this shit just isn't good for you. If she wanted to be here, she would be. She's obviously a lost cause."

Jude was in the other man's face just that quick. He pushed Rook against the opposite wall and got real close. He didn't spare a second to acknowledge that Rook was allowing this to happen. Rook and Jude were evenly matched, but Jude had rage bleeding through him. Rook only had pity.

"Don't say that," Jude pushed out between clenched teeth.

"Somebody needs to," Rook responded.

Vivi reached for Jude, placing a hand on his back. Rook growled, but Vivi just shushed him. "There's more at play here. King's right. We don't know every-thing. You find her and keep her safe, because I have a bad feeling the Piper is using her for something bigger than any of us realize."

Jude snapped his gaze to her. He hadn't breathed a word of what had happened in Sarajevo to anyone. That meant Vivi had her own suspicions. He wanted to talk theories with her, but he needed to get to Ella. His gut told him something huge was about to go down, and every instinct he possessed urged him to find her... protect her.

"The Piper is a good man. But even good men do bad things to get an end result," Vivi said as she stepped back. "Let my husband go, Jude."

Jude pushed away from Rook. "I'm sor—"

Rook threw him a look from narrowed eyes. "Don't apologize. I wouldn't. But I mean it. After this, no more. You leave Vivi out of this shit. Consider Ukraine my debt, you feel me?"

Jude nodded. "Yeah." He turned to Vivi. "Where?"

"Start with Svetlana Markov. I'll send you an encrypted file on her and her husband, both known associates of our good friend, buddy, old pal Horace Dresden. Word on the street, a.k.a. my hack of an FSB database, indicates there is a meet and greet between Yevgeny Markov, Anton Segorski, and the Russian prime minister in two days—and rumors are being tossed around about Crimea and oil. Lots and lots of oil. Oh, and money. Lots and lots of that too. Read the file, Dagan. You'll find it interesting how they all intersect with Dresden."

"You'll have a twelve-hour head start. She's got to

give this information to King," Rook warned. "If we can get Dresden…"

"I know," Jude replied. "I'll set up shop. I'll give King everything I have once I arrive. Chances are that Dresden won't show but his players will." And by players, he meant Ella.

Rook and Vivi both nodded. "I don't know who King will send, but I'll be volunteering," Rook said. "You might want to consider letting your team leader in on this, Jude. Otherwise, he'll bench your ass, maybe even kick you off the team. You do remember you have a team, right, Dagan?"

Jude hung his head. Shame speared him. "I never forget my team." He raised his head and stared at Rook, letting everything he'd felt over the past year infiltrate his gaze. "She was my soul. I have to know. But I won't compromise my team. Ever."

Rook took a step toward Jude and held out his hand. "Brother. I'll see you in Moscow."

Jude grasped Rook's forearm in the way all warriors had, inclined his head, and stepped around his teammate to Vivi. He placed his hand on her cheek and bent his forehead to hers. "Thank you. I'm sorry King's going to rip you a new ass over this."

"Big, bad CIA operative here. I can handle King." She smiled, and Jude knew shame again. "Find her. Bring her home. She's been gone too long, Jude," Vivi whispered.

Jude headed to his room, grabbed a go bag, and walked out of the Civil War–era mansion they'd taken over as their headquarters in Port Royal. And he kept walking—to his car where he got in, gunned the engine, and screeched out of the driveway.

Time was ticking down. He had to get to Moscow and set up shop, do recon, and figure out what the hell was going on.

He had to find Ella. Before she did something neither of them could come back from.

Chapter 6

ELLA STRAPPED THE SLEEK, BLACK MATTE-FINISHED H&K VP9 in the holster at her back and slipped her combat knife into its special scabbard at her side. She put her fawn-colored leather coat over them both, thinking about the meeting she had with Svetlana Markov in around thirty minutes.

She had researched Markov ad nauseam over the last two days, and what she'd discovered could fit in a thimble. The woman had supposedly been born in Moscow, raised in Moscow, and if she moved the wrong way with Ella today, she'd die in Moscow. Other than that, Ella had no idea what to expect.

Dresden had told her nothing other than that Yevgeny Markov's wife was in his pocket and Ella was to meet with the woman.

A brief knock sounded on the door, and Ella reached for her weapon. She was expecting no one.

"*Obsluzhivaniye nomerov*," a disembodied voice called out.

"I don't speak Russian," Ella answered. It was a lie. She knew Russian as well as she knew Lebanese, but today she was a corn-fed, straight-out-of-Nebraska tourist. She wouldn't tip anyone off by speaking fluent Russian.

No one knew this, but Harrison Black had kept her supplied in identities for the last year. She didn't trust Dresden, so she'd reached out to Black through Brody, and he'd reluctantly—okay, had his arm twisted by the Piper—agreed to supply her.

Nobody did fake identities like Harrison Black. The surly former SAS agent knew his stuff, and though he grumbled every time she contacted him, he still called her Ella-Bella. *Team.* King was going to be so pissed off when he discovered Black had helped her. Hopefully, she'd get a chance to run interference for Black before King took his head off in anger.

"Message," came the stilted reply, pulling her from her musing. "For you."

Ella cautiously opened the door, prepared for anything. A slight man dressed in the accoutrements of a bellhop was holding a single sheaf of paper, which he handed to her before turning on his heel and leaving.

Ella took the paper, unfolded it, and read.

Meet me in Saint Basil's.

Ella's mind whirred. She'd love to have Brody around to bounce things off. He'd served as her friend, teammate, and handler for the last year. He'd couriered information for her to the Piper, and he'd been her sounding board when shit got bad.

Right now, she'd love to have him at her back.

Ella had been told to meet the woman in the State Historical Museum. She didn't care for the change in venue, but it wasn't tourist season and there were ongoing renovations at Saint Basil's. Perhaps that's why Svetlana had chosen it—less line of sight, more barriers to hide behind. Still, Ella was prepared for anything at this point, and it was too late to turn around.

How many times would she have to tell herself that?

Instead of continuing to beat herself up, she made her way to Saint Basil's Cathedral. The beautiful, multi-colored onion domes played supplicants to a stunning blue Moscow sky. The air was crisp, and all around her, tourists were snapping shots and laughing, completely unaware that somewhere in the world Horace Dresden was plotting their demise in his bid to line his pockets.

Ignorance could be bliss.

Ella didn't sense anyone watching her, which was a marked difference from Sarajevo a mere three days ago. Her steps didn't falter, but she wanted to fall to her knees at the shot of pain she felt in remembering Jude's face.

Betrayal. Rage.

She'd caused that.

Ella entered the cathedral but didn't pause to admire the colorful murals and mosaic tiles the cathedral was known for. Ivan the Terrible had created an ode to Jerusalem as only a proper Byzantine Christian could, and it had stood the test of time. For Ella, it was nothing more than a place to meet and discuss business that would bring her closer to eliminating Horace Dresden.

To her left, she saw a woman standing in front of a large section of wall currently under renovation. A beige drape was her backdrop. The woman was taller than Ella, maybe five nine or so, with startlingly blond hair pulled into an elegant chignon, and wearing sunglasses.

Ella came closer, willing the woman to take off her glasses, and surprisingly she did, meeting Ella's gaze with no small amount of aggression. The aggression gave Ella pause. This was a simple meet and greet—get some information, and get out. The meeting between

Segorski, Svetlana Markov's husband, and the prime minister wasn't until tomorrow, yet the woman acted as if they were about to plot to overthrow the entire Russian government.

Chills skated down Ella's spine, and the feeling of being watched made an appearance like a hammer to the back of her neck. She smiled at the Markov woman, hoping to ease the tension as she held out her hand.

Svetlana Markov dismissed her hand with a look. "You're late," the woman hissed so softly that Ella wondered if she'd spoken at all. "Do you not know what I risk meeting you?"

"I'm right on time," Ella replied, coming to a standstill about three feet from the other woman. "Shall we?" Ella inquired as she motioned to a small alcove to their left.

"Here's fine," Svetlana said. She cocked her head and stared at Ella from head to toe. Finally, she gave Ella a look that said she found her lacking. Ella almost laughed. The nerve. "For some reason I expected more of a...soldier."

"Your expectations aren't much of a concern to me, Svetlana. Now, why am I here?" Ella inquired politely, her face blank, her mind whirring. The woman had no accent, and she kept both her face and body absolutely still. Only her eyes betrayed her—as if they couldn't contain her wrath at the world around her. She was...disquieting. And very, very trained. Ella hadn't anticipated that.

"He didn't tell you? Perhaps you aren't as important to him as he led me to believe," Svetlana said, running a red-tipped nail over her lips.

"We can play games. I'm okay with that. But if I leave here without the information Dresden has been promised, you will lose. And, Svetlana?" Ella said, leaning closer to the woman so she could whisper and still be heard, getting all up in her personal space. "I've seen what happens to people who lose to Dresden." Ella slowly lifted a finger and traced the scar at her temple.

"Back away," Svetlana responded harshly.

Ella did, giving the woman a moment to collect herself. Though fear wasn't visible on Svetlana's face, it permeated the air.

And still Ella's neck felt the weight of either a scope or someone's gaze. She turned discreetly, seeking the shadows in every corner and seeing no one.

Svetlana Markov had been bred wealthy. It was another thing besides the fear and aggression she reeked of. Her clothes were Dior, her shoes and purse matching. Her hair color was flawless, though definitely from a bottle. She smoothed back the wispy strands of hair that had escaped her updo, and fidgeted, just once, from foot to foot.

Ella made her nervous, and that pissed Svetlana Markov off.

"Why am I here, Svetlana?" Ella was done playing.

"He will want to know what Yevgeny's plans are," Svetlana said, glancing around and finding no one paying any undue attention to them.

"And you're going to tell me?" Ella pushed.

Svetlana stared at her, eyes pinning Ella in place. "He plans to crawl into the prime minister's pocket by offering up Horace's location."

She called him Horace. How cute, Ella thought with disgust. *Was she a lover?* She dismissed that immediately. Svetlana's angst didn't have a jealous lover vibe.

Ella was missing something, and she couldn't put a finger on it. "So he's going to tell the prime minister where Dresden is, and then the prime minister will attack? I don't understand what that nets your husband."

Svetlana waved her hand dismissively. "He'll take Horace's place if he's successful. It's kill or be killed. Power cannot be attained until you reach the inner sanctum, and most of the time, by then you are already dead. Do you not understand the game?"

Confusion numbed Ella. Her body seemed frozen as her mind ran through scenarios. *Endgame, endgame, endgame…* The words whispered through her like a cold wind. It was all a game. And what the hell was the *inner sanctum*?

"You didn't know," Svetlana said, shock threading her tone. "How could he send you here and not give you this information? Do you not know who he is?"

"Who Dresden is?" Ella asked. "Yes, he's a—"

Svetlana threw up a hand. "Not Dresden, the Pi—"

A cough-like sound split the air, and just as suddenly, blood sprayed from Svetlana Markov's chest. Ella caught the woman as she fell, noticing the woman's shock had spread to her face. Her lips were moving as Ella lowered her to the ground, her head swiveling as her gaze sought the shooter.

They were alone in the hallway.

Ella lowered her head to Svetlana's lips. "Get to Kazansky Railway Station, locker 2207, combination 24-17-24. Take the packet inside and run. Get your ass out of here. Tell your boss I tried. He must hide my sister."

The woman was gasping now, pain and loss of blood making her pallid and gray. "I can get you help," Ella urged.

Another coughing sound, suppressed gunfire Ella now knew, and the woman's head split open between her eyes. Blood the color of night poured from the wound, and as Ella watched, the life fled from the Russian woman's eyes. Ella lowered the woman's head to the ground and pivoted on her feet before ducking farther and diving behind the small alcove she'd tried to get Svetlana into earlier.

No more shots rang out, but Ella wasn't stupid enough to believe the shooter was gone. They wouldn't risk Svetlana having given her any information. She was the target now. She was damn lucky they hadn't taken that final shot at Svetlana through *her*.

She took a quick peek around the corner and winced as another coughing shot heralded the bullet that embedded in the wall behind her. She dodged another bullet as it found a home in the rock across from her, spitting chunks of stone onto her face.

She pulled her gun from its holster, chambered a round, and waited. *Five, four, three*—she stepped out from behind the wall of the alcove and began firing in the direction the shots had come from. A man was on his knees, a rifle bearing a suppressor held to his shoulder. She had no idea where he'd come from. He'd appeared as a ghost, and she hoped to make him one for real.

Ella aimed and fired, but the man fell before her bullet could take him, his head rocking sideways from the impact of another bullet. From the hallway to the dead man's left, another man stepped out, his black gaze piercing hers. He walked swiftly to the downed man, kicking away the weapon and checking for any identifying information. He moved like her dreams.

Warrior.

Ella turned and ran.

"Ella!" Jude called out. "Goddamn it, wait!"

Everything in her wanted to freeze. The command in his voice was absolute, but it was the plea buried beneath the order that had her heart demanding she turn around and run to him, not away.

Dresden would kill him. Whoever had ordered Svetlana killed would kill him. So she ran away, dodging tourists and security guards running toward the scene she'd just left. She didn't slow or look back until she made it to the turnstiles at the front entrance. She didn't see him, but that didn't mean he wasn't close.

Jude was a big man, but he had the uncanny ability to blend into any surroundings. It was what made him such an excellent hunter and sniper. You never saw Jude unless he wanted you to, and right now, he was probably content to follow her.

But Ella had learned a few things in the year she'd been gone from him. Hiding was what she did best, and she'd take refuge in that now. She turned to her left as she exited the cathedral, once again dodging tourists. In the distance, sirens wailed, drawing closer. Ella had to ghost quickly.

She took a direct track across the Red Square, heading toward the State Historical Museum. Ella didn't look back. She was fast but realized Jude was faster. It was colder today than it had been yesterday, and the air burned in her throat. She sprinted across the length of the square and dodged into the museum. Once inside, she stopped and searched for a security guard.

There were four lined up along the wall to her right,

and she approached them. "*Yest' chelovek, presleduy-ushchiy menya! Pozhaluysta pomogi*," she pleaded. It was true. There was a man chasing her, and she did need their help.

"Don't do it, Ella," Jude warned from behind her.

Her body warmed even as her heart raced. She couldn't do this much longer. Running from him went against everything inside her. How she found the strength, she didn't know. She did feel bad for a split second that she was throwing the security guards to the wolf, but having to deal with them would slow Jude down, hopefully giving her enough time to get away from him.

"*Kto etot chelovek k vam?*" the most intrepid of the guards inquired.

Who was he to her? Everything. Instead she answered, "*On nikogo net. On pytalsya zastavit' menya pogovorit' s nim, a zatem poluchil grubyy. Pomogi mne.*"

All four men moved around her, meeting Jude some-where behind her.

Once again, Ella ran. And then she ran some more. She could hear punches being landed behind her and winced. Those poor men were going to take a beating. She didn't slow down though. She had to get to the rail-way station Svetlana Markov had mentioned, and then she had to get whatever packet the woman had spoken of somewhere safe.

She'd have to call Dresden. She'd have to contact the Piper.

Ella stopped on the stoop of a souvenir shop and picked up a trinket, glancing behind her surreptitiously in the glass front of the shop. Nothing seemed out of place, but again, Jude could be anywhere.

She had to rely on her senses, and nothing flared out to grab her. Her skin didn't prickle as it always did when he was near. Her neck didn't itch the way it had in Sarajevo and then again earlier today, as if Jude's scope pressed into the skin there, branding her. Ella put down the trinket and began walking at a sedate pace toward the Bolshoi Theater. The railway station Svetlana had urged her to was close to the theater.

It took Ella ten minutes to reach the station, and she once again stopped, glancing over her shoulder casually before she entered. She searched for a map of the station, ignoring a lady's offer to direct her wherever she wanted to go, and when she found the location of the lockers, she made a beeline toward them.

Locker 2207 was innocuous enough looking. At the end of a row, it had a single combination lock that looked like something the KGB had probably invented. It seemed that impenetrable. She stepped up to it, used the 24-17-24 code and, with no small amount of amazement, opened the locker.

Inside was a single packet, close to the back. Ella pulled it out, noticed whatever was inside was about the size of a thumb drive, and stuck it in the pocket of the jeans she wore. Then she walked away. She ducked into a restroom, checked each stall to ensure she was alone, and then pulled her shoulder holster off before putting her gun at the small of her back inside her waistband. She pulled her sweater down over it and trashed the holster before pulling her coat back on.

She exited the bathroom, keeping her gaze forward and searching out of her periphery for any sign someone was following her. All seemed clear. A homeless woman was sitting beside one of the active tracks, and Ella removed her heavier coat and handed it to the woman. The woman smiled and removed her light-weight sweater. With winter bearing down on Moscow, she was probably enjoying the promise of warmth. The slight woman offered up the lightweight sweater she'd been wearing. Ella took it and put it on.

Then she walked out of the station's back entrance. She hopped into the first cab she came to and demanded to be driven around Moscow until she told him to stop. The driver glanced at her in the mirror, shrugged, and set about doing as she'd asked.

And it all happened just in the nick of time because as they pulled away from the curb, Jude walked out of the station, spotted her, and went completely still. He was too far away to catch her, and there were no traffic lights close enough to hold the car still for him to catch them.

Ella's heart jumped to her throat. His lips moved, forming the only word he ever left her with on an op... *safe*. Her sob caught her, ripping from her throat as she did the only thing she could do. She pressed six fingers to the window and watched him until the cab carried her out of sight.

Chapter 7

ONCE AGAIN HE WAS IN THE SHADOWS OF AN APART-
ment. This one was being rented by a Daisy Harper of
Omaha, Nebraska—a.k.a. Ella Banning. The flat was a
total of four rooms. Kitchen and living room were com-
bined into one large area, with a small bedroom down a
short hall and a bathroom at the end of the hall.

The furniture had probably been around for forty or
fifty years and the same with the appliances. It was in
a building right in the middle of Moscow, surrounded
by offices and other flats. The paint was peeling, the
wallpaper had been stripped bare in some places, and all
in all, it was a small hellhole.

So while he was in the same kind of shadows as her
Sarajevo safe house, the digs were definitely different.

She hadn't shown yet, but Jude felt in his gut that it
was only a matter of time. He'd followed her to the train
station and lost her, finding her again as she hopped a
cab and drove away. Always she was running from him,
and he was sick and tired of it.

"Objective in sight," Rook informed across his ear mic.

"Roger that," Jude responded.

"Disable the objective and wait for us." King
McNally growled this time.

Jude didn't respond to that. He estimated he had
approximately five minutes from the time she entered
until King and Rook made their entrance. He wanted

to get one answer out of her before his team leader and teammate arrived.

"She's in the building," Rook said, voice whisper quiet.

"Disable, Jude. Do not engage her in conversation. Do you understand?" King was adamant that Ella wasn't what she seemed.

It was shocking for Jude to realize that wasn't the most important thing to him anymore. He didn't care one way or the other. She was his, and she was in grave danger. She would go willingly or not; King would get angry with him or not, but Jude was going to ask his question, and he was going to do it today.

A soft click heralded her entrance into the flat. Night had long ago fallen, the threadbare curtains covering the windows almost no hindrance to the lights of Moscow. Outside, horns from irate drivers blared, and night traffic noises infiltrated the silence.

Ella stepped in and went completely still. She sensed him, no doubt about it. Jude's body came alive—adrenaline spiking, breath roughening, and dick going brick hard behind the fly of his cargo pants.

It was always like that with her. He grimaced. It always would be.

"I want to know why," he bit out.

Her chin dropped almost to her chest, and then she straightened her shoulders and lifted her face, finding him unerringly in the darkness.

"Goddamn it, Jude," King said across the mic. "Disable. Do not engage."

Ella smiled, sad and haunted. "Things happened, Dagan. I just didn't want us anymore."

"Lie," he growled. The tense line of her body, the

way her pupils contracted in the low light, showed she was lying through her teeth. "That's a lie, and I won't hear another one from you, Ella."

She turned, shaking her right arm and more than likely dislodging the small blade she carried on the inside of her forearm. "Lies are all I know now."

"Tell. Me. Why." He was demanding it of her. She owed him at least that.

The thump of boots echoed through the small flat. Jude was out almost out of time.

"I won't," she whispered, and her agony rebounded through Jude. "I can't."

He nodded. She wasn't going to give him what he needed. So he'd take it.

He moved fast—in his space beside the hallway one second, on her in the next. She lifted her right arm and tried to cut him with her blade; he dodged, knocked her arm to the side, and used the momentum to turn her.

With his front to her back, he took both of her wrists in one of his hands and pulled the syringe King had given him earlier from a side pocket of his pants. She struggled, and he inserted a knee between her legs and spread them far enough apart that she had to concentrate on not falling instead of kicking back at him.

Dodging her head as she threw it back to clock him in the nose, Jude uncapped the syringe with his mouth. "I'm sorry," he whispered in her ear a second before he pressed the syringe to her neck.

She didn't say a word, just went lax in his arms with a soft release of air. The door opened, and both King and Rook entered, looking ready for WWIII.

King's eyes swept over Jude, reprisal in their depths.

"At least you disabled her. She's become quite a handful, hasn't she?"

Ella had done something for King she'd not done for Jude. Answered his questions...hell, given him something. She'd given nothing to Jude.

His heart mocked him. *She gave you six fingers against the cab's glass.*

It wasn't enough. Was it?

"You got her?" Rook asked.

Jude nodded as he shifted her in his arm and lifted her small body high against his chest. King and Rook turned as one and left the building. There was no reason to search the flat; he'd handled that and loaded up anything of use earlier. Jude left behind them, carrying the most precious of his burdens close to his heart.

They walked down the hallway and took the tiny service elevator to the ground floor. Rook exited and took point. King glanced at Jude. "You okay?"

Jude had never been more vulnerable than right that second. Every emotion he'd felt during the last year bombarded him, nearly sending him to his knees. He'd seen her, smelled her, but until that moment, he hadn't held her in nearly four hundred seventy-three days.

"Dagan," King demanded sharply.

"I don't know what 'okay' means." He met King's gaze, took a deep breath, and said, "But I can do this."

King nodded slowly and held open the doors. They exited the back of the building and got into a blacked-out Range Rover they'd appropriated from a used car lot on the outskirts of Moscow.

It took them an hour to reach the abandoned farmhouse in Sergeiv Posad. Known for its monastery, Trinity Lavra, the town was a quiet one and just what they needed to handle business. They weren't going back home to DC. Not quite yet, since King felt it would be better to question Ella before returning.

Rook glanced at Jude in the rearview mirror before looking down at Ella. Jude ignored the warning in his teammate's eyes. He wasn't letting her go until he absolutely had to. Jude returned his gaze to Ella's face, the lights of the roadside lamps highlighting her and then casting her in darkness. Her hair was pulled back into a severe ponytail, braided and then wrapped into a bun near the top of her head. Jude longed to release the shiny tresses, run his hands through them, and hold her still for his mouth.

His hand fisted, and he slowly removed his glove, the temptation to be skin to skin with her damn near overwhelming. Her lashes lay like fans over her cheeks. The wings of her black brows arched over eyes that could skewer a man or make him feel like king of the world.

He loved staring at her while he entered her because everything she felt was mirrored in her gaze. Her face could remain passive, but those eyes? They were truly the windows to her soul, and she'd never been able to hide from Jude.

He lifted his hand and was shocked to note a tremor. He was shaking. He lowered a single finger to her lips, stroking over the lush bottom one.

A touch was all he could stand because as he came into direct contact with her, his skin heated and he knew he was going to lose it.

Never had he loved anyone as much as he'd loved her.

Never had anyone hurt him as much as she had. Not even his mother.

He dropped his hand, used his mouth to tug his glove back on, and then stared at everything but her face.

It was the longest hour of his life.

They let King out of the Rover half a mile from the abandoned farmhouse they'd reconned and set up for tonight's purpose. He would make sure their surroundings remained clear and return to them.

It had taken Jude hardly any time to read what Vivi had sent him, and then he'd called King. Rook's words two days ago had reminded Jude of why he was in Endgame Ops...brothers, family, teammates. He couldn't continue to let down his brothers-in-arms, because the relationships he had with them were now the most important.

He couldn't let Ella, or what he felt for her, interfere with that anymore. He'd resolved that he would use tonight to get his answers, and then he would leave her alone. He wouldn't chase her any longer.

It was clear she didn't want Jude, no matter that she'd held six fingers up to a goddamn window. No matter that he still loved her like hell on fire. She didn't get those pieces of him anymore.

He'd contacted King, given him everything he had, and he'd listened to the man he respected more than any other tell him they'd figure it all out. King was angry, and that was to be expected, but he was a leader, and all leaders knew when to ream you out and when to let it ride.

Jude wouldn't get a free pass, but the fact that King had let him stay on this was proof that his leader had his back.

King returned, waving them forward and walking

beside the Rover as they drove up the dirt path to the farmhouse. Within a minute, they were out of the car. King stepped up, adjusted the strap on his rifle so the weapon rested on his back, and held out his arms.

Jude froze. First steps were a bitch, but if he was going to do this, he had to let her go. He transferred her to King's hold and walked into the house. They had set a tarp on the floor of the living room. There was a huge hole in the ceiling, and once the clouds had cleared from the rain earlier, the moon shone through, giving them enough light so they didn't have to set anything up.

The original structure had been built well over a hundred years ago, and time and Russia's climate had taken over. Weathered walls and floors, furniture moldy and falling apart—the place had an ancient, broken feel. It probably wouldn't last much longer, but it was perfect for their purpose. There were ghosts in this house, and even more now with Ella's presence.

King placed her in a chair in the middle of the tarp. He blindfolded her—Jude thought for effect. She'd have to rely on her other senses, and when a body was stressed, those senses could lie. Ella had been a wonderful CIA analyst, but like Rook's Vivi, she hadn't exactly been a dyed-in-the-wool soldier.

Rook wound long lengths of rope around Ella's torso and each leg, strapping her in place. She could move— Jude was sure Rook hadn't tied her tight enough to cut off circulation—but she couldn't escape. Rook was a master of knots. Jude steeled himself to remain impassive. Those ropes represented so much.

They told of failure and betrayal. Love and lies.

"She'll wake soon. We didn't give her enough to

keep her out for very long," King murmured as he walked to the other side of the room and leaned against a doorjamb, facing Ella.

Rook moved to the opposite side, taking up much the same position. Jude moved to behind her and waited.

The air felt charged moments later, and Jude knew she was awake. He tamped down his body's response to her by force of will alone. His pain at her betrayal helped him.

Silence reigned. She'd obviously decided she'd let this play out. King took a step toward her, and she straightened in her seat.

What was she feeling? Trapped? Did she know the fear Jude had felt when he'd thought her dead? Why did it bother him that she might understand that?

King walked until he was standing beside her. Ella's chin notched in the air.

"Just say something," she demanded roughly. Her voice was strained and gravelly.

Jude found himself wanting to give her a sip from his canteen. He fisted his hands and crossed his arms over his chest, holding himself back.

"What are you doing in Russia, Ella?" King asked in a bored voice.

"Oh, you know, touristy things. I've never spent much time here, and so…" she said with a small, gruff laugh.

King laughed with her. Then his voice lowered as if Satan himself were speaking through him. "What are you doing in Russia, Ella?"

She cleared her throat. "I told you, I wanted to see Russia." She coughed, and Jude lowered his arms, almost walking to her, but her words stopped him. "Let's see,

I know you're here. I'm guessing Dagan and, hmmm, Rook? Yeah, Rook's here too, isn't he?" she questioned in a polite tone. Making everyday conversation, huh?

"I'm here, Ella-Bella," Rook informed her in an easy tone. Rook had a soft spot for women.

"Rook, how's your wife? You know, I meant to talk to you about that in Beirut a few weeks ago. You have got to control her better. She's really nosy, and she's sticking hers in places where it might get lopped off."

Rook straightened at the underlying warning in Ella's voice.

She laughed again, the sound ricocheting off the walls of Jude's heart. "*I* won't hurt her, but Dresden is a real bastard, and he does his best to watch every move she makes." She turned her head so she seemed to peer over her shoulder, and Jude was grateful for the blindfold that kept him from seeing her eyes. "Hey, Dagan, Rook know you're pumping his wife for information on me?"

"He knows," Rook said before Jude could reply. The man threw Jude a look that told him to keep his mouth shut. Jude ground his back teeth together.

"Aww, scared of Rook, Dagan? Since when are you scared of anyone?" She seemed to taunt him.

"He won't bite the bait, Ella," King said. "Now tell me why you're in Russia."

"How about I tell you to kiss my ass, team leader? How about that?" Ella intoned. "If you hadn't left me to Dresden, none of us would be in this!"

Finally a truth from her. Her words, the pain in her tone, scored Jude. It was the one question he'd not allowed himself to dwell on—had they left her to Dresden? Could they have saved her?

King moved then, sweeping the front legs of the chair with his foot and causing her to fall back. He caught the chair inches from the ground. Ella gasped and then laughed, the sound shrill after the pain of her admission. "Take off the blindfold, King. If you want to talk to me, this isn't the way. I seem to remember saving your ass in Spain. Oh, and the ass of your woman... I saved that too. Doesn't that merit at least some civility?"

"The same ass you put in play to begin with." King grunted but lifted the chair, reaching for the blindfold and removing it. Ella blinked a few times, accustoming herself to the low level of light. Jude moved around to the side of the chair and watched her, arms still crossed, fists still clenched.

"Really, all I did was confirm what Loretta Bernstein had already given Dresden." She tilted her head. "Can you guys not just leave well enough alone?"

"Not when it involves Dresden. And not, apparently, when it involves you," Rook said conversationally.

Ella sighed, making sure it was loud and conveyed how put out she felt. "I just want to live my life. Do my own thing. What's a girl gotta do to make that happen?"

"Tell the truth," Jude bit out, his silence a thing of the past.

She hung her head and just as suddenly raised it, spearing him with those eyes of frost. "Ah, Dagan, the great hunter. Keeper. Just haven't gotten the memo yet, huh?"

"What memo is that, Ella?" Rook asked.

"The one where I obviously want nothing to do with Endgame Ops, and that includes your teammate, Dagan." Her words were forceful, but the underlying layer had Jude's ear perking, making a liar out of her once again. Why she persisted with this, he had no idea, but he realized that the truth lay within her lies.

"Just can't get that telling-the-truth thing down, can you, Ella?" He kept his tone light, but she shuddered.

Yeah, she still felt it. As much as she denied it, denied him and their past, she felt him in her bones as much as he felt her.

She looked away from him. "Let me go, King. This is too big for you to step in and jack it up now."

Steel underpinned her words. *What was going on?*

"Tell me," King demanded.

"Talk to the Piper," she responded.

King shook his head. "What does he have to do with this?"

"I can't give you any more than that," she whispered. "Let me go."

Jude stepped up to her now and sank down on his haunches in front of her. She stared over his head, refusing to meet his gaze. He took a gloved finger and ran it slowly down her thigh. The muscle quivered, and Jude fought his reaction. "Tell me why," he urged, watching her face for every nuance she'd give him.

"Don't do this to me," she pleaded.

"You've asked me that a lot lately, but I'm not sure what I'm doing. I mean, you left with Dresden a year ago, watched as he shot Madoc and killed Micah. You stayed with him *willingly* and have spent the last year doing his dirty work. You claim we left you with the bastard, but at every turn you've run from us. All I've asked for is the truth. So what exactly am I doing to you?"

She bit her lower lip. Jude continued to trace down her thigh. "If I ever meant anything to you, you'll let me go."

He barked out a laugh and stood abruptly. "Let you go? I never had you, Ella. So let's cut the bullshit, yeah? Tell us what you're doing here for Dresden, and we'll let you go."

He took a few steps back because the need to rip off those damn ropes and pin her beneath his body was raging. She was lost to him, and his mind couldn't accept it. His heart refused to accept it. Goddamn, he was a soldier to his core, but he was human too.

She drew in a deep breath and looked him in the eye. That look almost took him to his knees. "Dresden has aspirations of selling Crimea and all of its oil to Russia. I'm here to broker the deal."

King hissed in a breath. Rook cursed. Jude shook his head. "How can he sell something that isn't his?" he queried.

"He bartered with Ukraine, vowed protection from Mother Russia if they gave him the rights to the oil in Crimea. They did. Dresden can be persuasive when he has something you want very badly."

"What did he have of Yoraslav Schevchenko's?" King asked.

"Schevchenko's sons, daughters, wife, mother... Dresden had his entire family. The prime minister caved quite easily once he was delivered his youngest daughter's head on a platter." Ella's mouth twisted. "Dresden doesn't care who he kills, only that it nets him something he considers valuable. In this case, Schevchenko's three-year-old daughter netted him the oil rights to the Crimean Peninsula."

"Jesus Christ!" King ran a hand through his hair. "And you work with this bastard?"

She pinned King with a hard, cold glare. "I do what I'm told. As should you and your team. You're wading into waters you haven't been invited into. Talk to the Piper, and stay in your lane, team leader."

Jude cleared his throat and cocked his head. "Is that a threat?"

Ella moved her glare to him. She had developed quite an attitude over the last few months. "I think we both know I can't make good on any threats. I mean, look at me. Bound and trussed like a Thanksgiving turkey."

"She's got you there, Keeper," Rook said while rubbing his chin.

Jude shrugged him off. "Why were you there with Svetlana Markov yesterday?"

"It's none of your concern," she answered crisply.

"What did you pick up at the train station?" he asked, not giving her time to breathe.

"Again, none of your concern," she replied, that waspish tone making another appearance. "You really have no control over him, do you?" She directed the question to King, but it was Jude who answered.

"He does. I mean, you're here, right? Not somewhere locked up at my mercy."

Jude turned his back to her and walked into the kitchen area. He just needed a few minutes to get his shit together, and he'd go back in and have another go at her.

"She's working with the Piper," Jude said as King came up at his back.

"I know," King responded, and it was the last thing Jude expected.

A bitter chuckle escaped. "She pulled an op within an op with us, didn't she?"

King nodded. "Looking more and more like just that."

"What is he doing?"

"He won't tell me. He points and directs, and I lead my team into whatever hellhole he says to." King's tone suggested he was beginning to question doing so.

"She's on Dresden for a reason. We need that reason. She's been close enough to put a bullet through his skull, yet she hasn't. That means the Piper wants him alive. What the hell is going on, King?"

"I don't know, but let's—"

A muffled groan from the living room sounded, interrupting King, and it happened a split second before the noise of an engine cranking invaded the house.

"Motherfucker!" Jude shouted. He took off, sprinting outside the main door only to see the taillights of the Rover disappearing. "Damn it," he raged at the sky.

He hustled back into the house and found King tending to Rook. The man had a goose egg on his forehead. "What the hell, dude?"

Rook glanced up at him, and what Jude saw there had him frozen. "She's not the same Ella. She took me like I was a babe in the manger. Quick, effective, and deadly accurate."

No way that tiny slip of a woman had overcome Rook Granger. "She was tied up, man."

"She had a knife. Nobody checked her," Rook said as he pushed King away. "I'm good."

Still Jude didn't believe it.

"She wanted me to tell you something, Jude," Rook told him.

Jude didn't want to hear it. "What?"

"She said she's let you go. Now it's time for you to do the

same. But then she gave me something else…said you've got a tail, and they're watching every move you make."

King bit out a curse. "She'll head back to Moscow. If Dresden is selling rights to that oil to Russia, there'll be a meeting. Rook, talk to Vivi. Have her tap every resource she has to find out where that meeting is and when. Jude? Get Knight and Black here ASAP."

"On it," Rook and Jude replied at the same time. "What about the tail?"

"I'll handle it." Jude pulled out his satellite phone. "How are we getting back to Moscow?"

King sighed. "Rook, get Vivi to find us transpo too."

Rook grumbled something, and Jude dialed up headquarters. Once he'd talked to Jonah Knight and gotten assurance that he and Harrison Black were headed their way, Jude disconnected and turned to King.

"They're on their way," he told him.

"Do you still have that contact in the FBI… What's her name? Greta? Gerta?" King asked.

Jude rubbed his jaw. "You mean Georgia?"

King waved a hand in the air. "Whatever, but yeah, her."

"I haven't talked to her in a couple of years, but I'm sure she'll answer my call," Jude replied. He'd dated Georgia on and off two years ago. Once he'd seen Ella Banning, he'd never had another thought about Georgia until King had just mentioned her.

"Call her. I need to know everything she can get me on Noah Caine," King ordered. "Oh, and I'm going to contact Chase. Have him be on the lookout for Abrafo Nadege in Burundi. He's in Dresden's pocket, and I want to know why. What does he have or supply Dresden with that makes him valuable?"

"Who is that?" Jude questioned.

"Nadege? He's an African warlord who hit the radar last month. Chase mentioned in his last report that he'd discovered intel while questioning a local mercenary. The merc mentioned a link between Nadege and Dresden. Don't know if Nadege is working for or with Dresden."

"And he just gave up that info out of the goodness of his heart, huh?"

"Chase did mention he had the merc spread-eagle in a wooden chair and a ball-peen hammer in his hand," King shrugged as he answered with a dry tone.

Jude nodded. "Now tell me why we're researching the Piper."

"He's withholding information from us. If he won't give it, we'll take it. I'm not losing her again, Jude. I'm not losing any more of my men because he's playing games with my team."

"Give me more than that, King," Jude requested.

"Like you gave me on Ella?"

Ouch. Point to his team leader. "He's pulling her strings, and it's torturing her."

King's head swiveled to Jude. "Where did you see him?"

"In Sarajevo."

King's brows lowered. "And you're just now telling me this?"

"Ride's here," Rook said, jogging back up to them from the road. His arrival saved Jude from having to answer.

"You'll tell me about Sarajevo, Jude," King ordered.

Jude nodded and watched as a dilapidated truck made its way down the dirt road toward the farmhouse.

"House is clean?" King asked Rook.

"Yep. Let's go."

Jude, Rook, and King all loaded up. The arrival of the truck had saved Jude that time. Before the night was out, he'd told King everything—how his last months before they'd rescued Allie from Savidge in Beirut had been spent doing everything he could to discover the woman with eyes of frost and a bullet scar at her temple.

King nodded a lot, grunted some, and in the end he clapped Jude on the back and said seven words that let Jude know they were okay.

"I would have done the same thing."

Jude lay down on the cot in the apartment they'd rented on the outskirts of Moscow. But he didn't sleep. Ella kept running through his mind. Until they could draw a better picture of what was going on, they were simply going to do recon. Vivi was working on getting them a location of the meeting taking place tomorrow.

During the course of their situation report, Jude had silently come to a conclusion: he loved Ella, but he had to let her go.

Before that happened though, he'd make sure she was safe and out of this game the Piper had embroiled her in. Because Jude might have lost her, but if she wasn't somewhere in the world, alive and well, it would destroy him completely.

He'd lost her once. He wouldn't do it again.

Chapter 8

THERE! MOVEMENT ON THE ROOF OF THE BUILDING across from them. Jude put his night-vision monocular against his right eye and waited. He'd moved to the upper level of the warehouse, picking a window that had been shattered before Endgame ever appropriated the building for this op.

He'd gotten a few hours' rest and risen prepared to eliminate whoever thought they could follow him. He'd become sloppy over the last months, ignoring the prickle of the tiny hairs at the back of his neck. He'd been so focused on Ella that he hadn't taken care of the threat.

He must have done something right in a past life or God was feeling favorable, because the fact that he was still alive was either luck or providence. How long had the tail been on him?

Why had Ella told Rook?

Jude was now fully committed to eliminating the threat.

"Come on, you son of a bitch. Give me something," Jude whispered.

Shadows shifted in the night. Car headlamps offered light and then took it away, making those shadows writhe in the black of the night. Whoever it was, they'd make a mistake, and Jude would put a bullet in their head.

They were Dresden's. That made them the enemy.

What about Ella? his mind taunted.

His heart didn't respond. Jude had managed to lock

it away somehow. His love for her was now buried beneath a layer of purpose. Purpose to protect her and keep his ass moving. She didn't trust him enough to give him her truths. The foundation of any relationship they'd had in the past had crumbled, if it had ever been built on anything but straw.

King, Rook, and Jude had talked about the merits of taking the tail and decided it would be better just to eliminate him. Dresden had low-level assassins at his beck and call. He was a crafty bastard who kept his eye on targets for a reason. The assassin would likely have no idea why he was following Jude. So he was going to become a kill tonight.

Jude wasn't sad. Did he mourn the need to take life? Yes. But life was a constant battle of good and evil. It raged in the hearts of men every minute of every day. If Jude was confident of anything in his life, it was that he was a good guy. Endgame Ops were the good guys.

So anything attempting to destroy Endgame Ops was the enemy and therefore would be eliminated.

As Jude continued to sift through the varying shades of darkness across the street, a separate shadow moved like a wraith over the rooftop, headed toward a point directly across from him.

Through his ocular, he recognized the way the ghost moved—sinuous, feminine—and his heart stuttered. "No, damn it, Ella. Stop," he pleaded silently.

Her target hadn't noticed her yet because he hadn't moved. Suddenly she stilled. And then her target moved, showing himself as he twisted and came up. A passing car's lights hit the assassin's scope glass, giving his location away more than his movements.

Jude stood from his perch, knowing he'd never make it to her in time, fear beating through his body and making his scalp tingle. He held his breath as the target rushed Ella.

She dropped into a crouch right as the moon made an appearance from behind a cloud, highlighting the blade she wielded. With a swift flick of her wrist, she took out the man's left Achilles. He fell and she was on him, caressing her blade across his neck with a very practiced, very professional movement. Then she casually wiped her blade on the man's clothing, stood, and turned to the warehouse Jude was in.

She held up six fingers again, turned, and disappeared off the roof. Nothing but mixed messages. She'd become the queen of them.

Jude took off, sprinting down the metal stairs and out the front entrance. He headed across the street and around the right side of the building. He skirted the corner and came to a standstill.

She'd waited there, facing him in the shadows.

He cocked his head and waited on her.

"He reported to Dresden that you took me," she said softly.

He nodded. "But he had no clue what you told us, if anything."

She shook her head. "Didn't matter. His orders from the moment I reported that I'd escaped became kill orders."

"Me?"

She didn't move, and the air between them became charged with energy. "Yes."

The moon once again played peekaboo from behind a cloud and shone its light down on her face. She was breathtaking under normal circumstances. That she'd just killed to protect him made her the most beautiful thing in Jude's world. "Dresden wants me that bad, huh?"

"You're a tool," she replied.

"For what purpose?" he asked, though he already knew—had known from the moment she held those six fingers against the cab's windows.

"To hone me." She wiped a weary hand down her face and removed the skintight hood of the spandex suit she wore. Her hair fell in soft waves that glinted in the moon's glow.

"For that to be the case, I'd have to be important to you, Ella. Surely Dresden knows I mean nothing to you," he bit out.

She laughed, and it was low and ugly. "You're fishing, and it's not like you, Jude."

He moved into her space. He'd always been fast, but had she wanted, she could have evaded him. She'd become quite the black ops operative in the year she'd been gone. Maybe she'd been one before she ever left him.

"Why, Ella?" She sighed as he lowered his head to hers, his mouth right at her ear. "Tell me why."

He felt her heart give as her body relaxed against his, and he knew a moment of triumph.

"He can't have you," she whispered. "He will *never* have you."

White-hot anger moved through Jude, but he remained still, half afraid she'd bolt. "Don't tell me you did this to protect *me*." In his world, men protected their women, not the other way around. He couldn't wrap his mind around what she'd just told him.

She turned her head just enough that their mouths

were inches away from each other. "All I know are lies, but what I just told you isn't one. All I've had are my memories. Give me something, Jude. Something to keep me warm when the lies ice me over," she pleaded.

That quickly, his anger evaporated. Their breaths mingled. She'd just taken life, and all he wanted to do was give her his.

His lips covered hers, and he drank her sigh. She didn't move as he sank into her. Ella was satin and heat, vanilla and spice. He licked into her mouth, feeling her tongue tangle with his and draw him deeper.

She angled her head and he did the same, pushing as he fell further and further into his woman. A car backfired somewhere in front of the building, and a shudder ran through her. She danced with him once more and pulled away, their heavy, heated breaths frosting the cold Moscow air.

She backed away and he watched her, let her.

"There's a meeting tomorrow at Petrovka House—a mansion at the end of a street by the same name. Big players, including Anton Segorski and Yevgeny Markov. The prime minister will be there."

Jude nodded. "The oil rights?"

"Among other things."

"Why are you giving me the location?" He didn't think their kiss had changed anything. Ella was still going to run. What she didn't know was that Jude had just changed tactics.

"Because there's a particular player of interest to Endgame Ops who will also be there."

Jude's skin prickled. "Who?"

"Loretta Bernstein," she responded with zero hesitation.

"I thought she went boom in Beirut," he said.

Ella smiled at that. Jude almost rubbed his chest at the ache that settled there. "I think we all know Loretta's good at what she does. She's like a cockroach surviving nuclear fallout. She always turns up."

Jude grunted at that.

Ella spun and began to walk away. Jude stayed where he was, something telling him he needed to let her go this time. The meeting tomorrow was huge, and whatever the hell she was doing for the Piper was big enough that she'd betrayed her team for it. There was also the fact that she could obviously take care of herself. Had been doing it for over a year now.

Before she got too far, she pivoted and turned back to him. "I never left you, Jude. Not really. Let me finish this, and I'll do my best to come back to you."

He didn't say anything because she was gone just that fast, her words ringing in the empty air.

Chapter 9

"ELLA, I'M SO GLAD TO SEE YOU," ANTON SEGORSKI chanted as he stood and walked toward her.

Fear settled at the base of her spine and spread through her body. He looked her up and down and then did it again. She'd worn Givenchy, the flaring skirt of her dress giving her ample room for the H&K strapped to her thigh. Her bodice was heavily beaded, and the entire dress was crimson. The same as the blood that would no doubt be spilled here tonight.

She licked her lips coyly and wished she hadn't lost the taste of Jude on them. She allowed the man to air-kiss her but then stepped back and turned to greet the man she'd received orders last night from Dresden to kill—Yevgeny Markov.

Dresden had been furious when he'd found out Svetlana had been slaughtered. Of course, Ella had said nothing about how she'd obviously been a double agent, working for them both but leaving only a little something after death to the Piper. Ella hadn't sent the thumb drive to the Piper, but to Brody Madoc.

Brody had promised to ascertain what was on the drive and get back to her. She was still waiting. It was either encrypted and Brody had to decipher the code before he could open it, or Brody didn't have her back anymore. Ella doubted the latter. The former was more likely. She and Brody had been through hell in Ukraine at the hands of Vasily Savidge. The bond they'd formed would stand the test of time.

She hated to ask anything of the man who'd lost most of his voice to the tender care of Savidge, but he was all she had. Jude was a no-go because he'd take the information straight to King. Their team leader had his loyalty, and after the kiss she and Jude had shared last night, Ella seriously doubted Jude wanted to do anything but protect her.

"You look lovely, Ella," Markov intoned, his nasal voice sending chills down her spine. She'd heard that voice in nightmares. Markov had enjoyed watching Savidge perpetuate his torture. He'd been especially fond of watching Ella scream under Savidge's knife.

She shook it all off and smiled at Markov. "Where's Svetlana?"

Markov went still, and Ella wondered if she'd screwed up. "You know Svetlana?"

Ella smiled. "No, but I know of her. She's your wife, Yevgeny. Dresden would have my head were I not polite."

He nodded as if that made sense. "Sadly, my wife can't be here tonight. Perhaps you'll meet her another time." Then he moved away and sat down beside the prime minister.

Ella wouldn't be meeting Svetlana Markov anywhere ever again. But she couldn't let the woman's husband know she knew that. It was interesting he was hiding her death though.

Ella took the seat assigned her beside Segorski. Two other people entered from a side door—good old Loretta Bernstein and a man Ella had never seen in the flesh—Baron Meadows, a former CIA operative turned traitor to Russia.

Meadows had evaded capture and kill by the United States for twenty years. He'd sold secrets related to some of the United States' top aeronautical plans, and he'd given rise to a league of hackers who did their best to crack into any United States database they could locate. He wasn't quite public enemy number one—that was Horace Dresden—but he was in the top five. He'd been a player on the international stage for years, although it looked as if that was changing.

Loretta glanced at Ella and raised her chin, but her eyes remained blank until she turned her gaze to Baron. Then she became a fawning lover. Baron drank the attention and smiled at Ella, gaze lingering on her cleavage as insinuation flared in his eyes.

"Shall we get to business?" the prime minister inquired in Russian. Ella understood Russian. So did Segorski and Markov. Loretta and Baron glanced at him questioningly.

"Fucking Americans," the prime minister snapped. "Shall we get to business?" he asked again in perfect English.

They both nodded and smiled. Ella really wanted to know what Loretta's game was here and hoped she'd get a chance to ask her.

Everyone's head swiveled to Ella.

She took a drink of wine and a deep breath, smiling even as her gaze sought every corner, searching for exit points. She'd memorized the plans of this house last night after leaving Jude. But it had been remodeled recently, and she'd not had time for recon after offing one of Jude's assassins-in-waiting.

"It's time to talk negotiations, eh?" she asked, her gaze stopping on the prime minister.

The man smiled at her and nodded. Greed echoed in the curving of his lips. Greed and death. He thought to eliminate Dresden, but Dresden had one up on the leader of Russia. He had Ella.

"Prime Minister, what would you have of Dresden?" She opened the foray.

"I want Ukraine," he returned simply.

Ella nodded and contemplated the napkin folded in front of her before once again meeting his gaze. "My employer is aware of what you want. So the question begs, Prime Minister, what are you willing to pay to have what you want?"

The prime minister snapped his fingers, and a very large, very heavily armed security officer stepped forward with an envelope. The prime minister motioned for the man to take the envelope to Ella.

Ella's hand fell to the folds of her skirt, finding the slitted opening in the fabric that allowed her hand to wrap around the butt of her weapon. The officer brought the envelope to her and placed it on her plate before stepping away. Ella relaxed and inclined her head.

Markov sat back in his chair, also relaxed and waiting—for what, Ella didn't know. A secret smile played about his lips. She wondered about that smile, knew it meant bad things.

"Open it, Ms. Banning," Segorski encouraged, dollar signs making his eyes bright. Or maybe that was fear.

Ella glanced at Loretta. The woman's eyes were glued to the envelope, but stress masked her face, lines making her look older than Ella had ever known her to look. Baron Meadows looked infinitely bored.

But they all had a part to play here, didn't they? Ella

really hoped Endgame was close. She was a lamb among lions here, and it was about to go down.

She carefully peeled back the flap on the envelope and pulled out a gold-engraved card. There was a phrase in Russian on the card, simple and succinct.

Kak poseyesh', tak pozhnesh'.

Ella smiled as everything inside her tightened, then expanded. *As a man sows, so shall he reap.* She'd known once Svetlana Markov had gone down under a sniper's bullet that the trip to Russia was leading to this. Dresden wanted Markov dead because the bastard was betraying him. Ella would be forced to put a bullet in the head of a man she found herself ironically wanting to high-five.

Because she hated Dresden as much as Markov apparently did. Or at least as much as he wanted to betray the man.

"Perhaps you've given me the wrong card, Prime Minister?" She infused steel into her voice because this was about to get very, very ugly.

The three security officers in the room all stiffened and palmed their handguns. Loretta and Baron both reached under the table, clearly palming their own weapons. Segorski wiped a bead of sweat falling down his temple.

Markov grinned outright.

The prime minister laughed. "I would have preferred to eat first, but that was never really an option, was it, Ms. Banning?"

Ella cocked her head and ran a finger over her lips, seemingly contemplating the prime minister. What she was really doing was praying her shot was straight and true. "I can't help but feel a certain affront. I came here in representation of my boss, and you gift me with this vague threat as a way of answering my query. Mr. Dresden will be disappointed."

She allowed a sigh to color the air. Infinitesimal movement behind Markov, air moving a heavy curtain, as the red dot of a scope appeared on the green silk above the Russian's head. Endgame was there.

Markov picked that moment to lean forward. "You're a killer, no?" he asked Ella.

"I am whatever I need to be whenever I need to be that particular thing," she answered, pulling her gun out and placing it on the table. No need to hide anything anymore.

"Dresden is a nuisance. There are riches beyond measure if you accept our proposal," he said into the tension.

"You can't ask that of her, Markov," Loretta said in a furious whisper.

Markov glanced at Loretta dismissively and to Baron he said, "Keep your bitch quiet."

Segorski stood then, outrage pouring off him. "You promised I'd have her, Markov!"

Ella got it then, and it was so much worse than Dresden had thought. Both Segorski and Markov were betraying him, the prime minister simply a means to an end, a moneyman. Segorski had aligned himself with his countrymen, and Ella wondered why Dresden hadn't seen that coming.

"Oh, Segorski, I am no one's but my own," Ella said with a laugh.

"So you are not even Dresden's?" the prime minister interjected.

Ella sat back in her seat, hoping to portray calmness she in no way felt. "Your card, Prime Minister, while so very short and eloquent, is probably not the response to Dresden you want to give. I'll allow you a single minute, that's sixty seconds, to contemplate changing who you've allied yourself with. Otherwise, you'll leave here very much an enemy of the one man you never wanted to be an enemy to, if you leave here at all."

The prime minister went red in the face. "You dare!"

Loretta gave her a quick nod. Ella knew what that meant. She moved fast, as she'd trained to move, raising her gun, but before she could fire a shot, another one rang out. A single shot right into the forehead of Yevgeny Markov. The man fell back into his chair with a smile on his face.

Segorski sat down quickly, placing his smoking gun on the table before he wiped his forehead with his napkin. "He promised me" was all Segorski said by way of explanation for the assassination of Markov.

Ella trained her gun on the space between Segorski and the prime minister, prepared for anything.

The prime minister's security team moved to flank his chair. Shit was about to hit the fan.

"You thought to frighten me. You thought to cow me with Markov. But he's a weakling," Ella mused, holding her gun steady. "I would thank Mr. Segorski for eliminating an irritant to us all, but I've made it a rule never to thank the devil for anything. And so, I'll ask you again, Prime Minister, do you really want to give this response to my employer's offer?"

One of the security men leaned down to the prime minister's ear and whispered. The prime minister raised his gaze to Ella. His pupils were dilated, and a bead of sweat tracked down his cheek. "We will deal."

Ella smiled. "I thought so. Now, how do we get out of this with no one else taking a bullet?"

"What do you need?" the prime minister asked hurriedly.

"I need your security men to leave," she stated quietly. They wouldn't. They were about to rain hellfire on Ella's position. She just needed a small diversion first.

And just like that, a smoke canister rolled into the room, and orange smoke began pouring from it. *Thank you, Endgame.*

Ella dropped out of her chair and rolled, coming to a stop beside a set of Wellco combat boots, size twelve if her eyes weren't deceiving her.

Jude stooped, pulled her with one hand to her knees and calmly stepped in front of her, lifting his large sniper rifle, the look in his eyes daring anyone to shoot.

"Shoot them!" the prime minister yelled.

Smoke was a barrier between them, but gunfire began in earnest. Ella dropped to her stomach, felt Jude come down beside her, and they both made their way to the main entrance.

"Two down!" King said from her right.

"I've got one, more coming from the back," Rook echoed.

"I'm going after Bernstein," King bit out.

"No!" Ella called. "She's not the target. Not yet."

She had no idea if King listened to her, because right then Jude picked her up around the waist and pushed her out the door into a waiting SUV.

Doors slammed as Jude followed her in, and Rook and King got into the front. Two seconds later, they were speeding down the quiet residential street, taking a corner on two wheels and heading hell-bent for leather out of Dodge.

"You look real nice, Ella," Rook called out from the front, a smile in his voice.

Ella lifted a hand to her hair and pushed a hank behind her ear. She smiled at the man, because of everything he could have said to her, that was the last thing she expected.

"So do you, Blade Runner. So do you," she returned.

She took a deep breath and glanced at Jude.

"She actually looked at him," Rook said to King in the front. "I'm putting five large on them being in bed together by the time we land back in DC."

Jude smiled, something so inherently sexy in it that Ella's heart fell into her stomach.

"That's a lot of money," she called out to the front.

"It's a sure bet," King answered.

"Did anybody get Segorski?" Ella asked, her gaze still pinned on Jude.

His midnight eyes remained locked on hers, something moving behind them that Ella wanted to sink into.

"No," King replied.

That was not good at all. Ella needed to report to Dresden before Segorski had a chance to do the same. Otherwise, Dresden would know Endgame had shown and that Ella had once again been with them.

"I need to hit my hidey-hole before we go wherever we're going," she demanded.

"Directions?" King queried.

She gave her team leader directions. Wait, was he still her team leader? No, best not to get ahead of herself at this point.

"I'm going in with you," Jude said beside her.

She turned to him as she opened the door to the SUV. "No, I'll go alone."

His face went blank.

"I'll come back."

She exited the vehicle, entered the two-story brick house, gathered her duffel, and walked back out.

"I wish Vivi packed that fast," Rook grumbled.

Ella laughed. "I was already packed."

Silence took over as King maneuvered them to an extraction location. Ella's heart, now back in place, thumped heavy in her chest. She couldn't go home with them. Not this time.

They came to a small farm, again on the outskirts of Moscow, and everyone got out. King stopped and turned to Ella.

"We're team, Banning. You in or out?" he asked, his gaze pinning her in place.

She wanted to scream in frustration. "It's not that easy."

"Team is always easy." Rook threw in his two cents.

Jude said nothing, just stared at her.

She blew out another frustrated breath and reached down to pull her heels off. They were sinking into the snow anyway. "I'm in. Damn it. For now."

"Hooah," she heard Rook mutter.

Jude still said nothing.

"We're here for the night. Nothing to be done for it. We'll head out on a transpo plane at 0600," King told them. "Bed down. Stay quiet. Rook, you've got first watch."

"Who's after me?" Rook asked.

"Me," King replied.

Rook glanced at Jude. "That give you enough time to work *things* out?"

"Screw you, Rook," Jude responded, but there was a smile in the heat of it.

"You are such dudes," Ella bit out and pushed past Rook to enter the small farmhouse.

She entered a musty, dank structure that was falling down around their ears, but it was warmer inside than out. She took the stairs and headed up, entering the first door on the left at the top and finding a sagging bed in a wrought-iron frame.

She threw her duffel down and headed to the window that looked out over the front yard. From her vantage point, she could see Jude speaking with Rook and King. Her gaze roved over him. She started at his Wellcos and worked her way up over long, firm legs encased in black cargoes. She wished he'd turn around so she could see him from behind.

"I'm in so much trouble," she muttered. Still she continued to look.

He was a big man, no two ways about it, but he wasn't too heavy with muscle. He was lean with thick thighs, chest, and arms. His shoulders were broad, and from experience she knew they could carry her entire world.

Jude looked up, as if sensing her perusal, and when their gazes met, Ella had to lock her knees to stop from going to him. He undid her.

His eyes narrowed, but something King said drew his attention again. He'd lost weight, and it showed in his face. He wasn't gaunt by any stretch of the imagination, but he was leaner...meaner. His face would never be classified as beautiful, unless you spoke with Ella.

To her, he was the most beautiful man she'd ever seen. There was a scar bisecting his right eyebrow and one just above his lip from a bottle he'd taken to the face in a bar fight at seventeen. She still didn't know what he'd been doing in a bar that young.

What she did know is that she loved licking that scar because it made Jude's hands clench on her body. And that scar in his eyebrow was proof that he'd fought hard and taken his fair share of licks. Yet here he remained. Strong. Stalwart.

Hers?

Ella shook her head. It was folly to head down that path. She had to get back to Dresden. But first?

She changed clothes, balling up the Givenchy gown and stuffing it into the tiny closet. She put on her own pair of black cargoes and a black thermal, and paired them with an equally black sweatshirt. She sat down on the bed and pulled on thick socks and combat boots. Then she located her sat phone, took a deep breath, and dialed Dresden.

He answered on the first ring. "So Markov is dead?"

"He is."

"And Segorski? Did you take care of him as well?"

"He escaped."

A long pause. Never good with Dresden. "I'm going to have to kill Jude."

Her heart stuttered. "Do what you must."

"Did you really think I wouldn't know what happened in that meeting as it went down?" he asked her softly.

"I know you have eyes everywhere, Dresden. I did what I could. Markov was handled, and your interests were protected as you requested. Your deal with the prime minister will go down exactly as you want."

"If I hadn't had eyes on that meeting, you would already be dead. As it is, I know you used Endgame to escape. You're better alive than dead to me, so I appreciate their help. But he will die, Ella. He's an end that must be tied up."

"Again I'll say, do what you must." She rubbed her chest and wiped the single tear that escaped. She had to get Jude to safety, and that meant returning to Dresden. "I have more news I can't share right now."

"What is it?" Dresden demanded.

"I'm not secure. I'll be home"—she almost choked on the word—"tomorrow evening."

"Yes. Come home, Ella. We need to talk." Then Dresden disconnected.

She threw the phone down and walked back to the window. The three men of Endgame were still there, talking.

Ella would take tonight, talk with her former team, give Jude some truths. But come tomorrow, she'd have to continue the game. She needed a name. Just one. So she would walk once again into the lion's den.

And this time she might not survive.

Chapter 10

DARKNESS HAD FALLEN, AND WITH IT, MORE SNOW. Ella had thrown together a quick meal of rice and beans for herself and the men, and now they all sat around a hastily constructed fire outside the house.

"Dresden is worse than any of you know," she said as she stared off into the darkness.

No one replied. So she continued.

"When the Piper approached me over a year and a half ago, I had no idea what I'd be stepping into. I only knew that everyone I'd ever loved was in danger—hell, my country was in danger—and I potentially had a way of mitigating that danger."

She took a drink from her water pack and leaned her head on the tire she was reclining against. "I was recruited by Gray Broemig for the CIA while I was still in college. When the opportunity to insert me into Endgame showed itself, he jumped on board with both feet. Broemig wanted access to Endgame via one of his own—someone on the inside who was willing to manipulate Endgame Ops to be a tool for him. I wasn't that person. Once I settled in, actually became Endgame, he recognized my allegiance had shifted and he backed off, but the expectation hung over me.

"Instead, he settled for having another one of his analysts on your team, under the guise of sharing information with the Piper, but Broemig's ultimate goal was always to gather as much information as he could from Endgame so he could activate me to go after and eliminate Dresden. It's why he allowed the Piper to put Nina into Endgame as well. He'd doubled down on Broemig's bet that he could turn Endgame and make it his. There's a story there, boys. Something deep, dark, and dirty about why the Piper allowed Broemig—no, *asked* Broemig—if he could have analysts for Endgame. We'll have to tackle that soon. But not today, right?"

She shrugged, took another pull on her water, and continued to stare out into the darkness.

"I knew Dresden was moving the pieces on the game board, and I knew my time evading the Dresden situation was running out. See, what you may or may not have figured out by now, is that the Piper had recruited me for a little side job. Something similar in nature to what Broemig wanted but a bit different. The Piper didn't want to kill Dresden; he wanted to insert me into Dresden's operations. He wanted me to gather as much information as I could so he could begin to dismantle Dresden from the inside out. The Piper had already planned to insinuate me, but it's important you understand that I never had any idea it would be on that Beirut op. I had no idea that was going down."

Silence reigned for long moments. She'd lost her best friend, Nina, another analyst she'd suspected of being a plant for Broemig, the very thing Ella herself had refused to do, but she'd never been able to confirm that. It hadn't mattered. She and Nina had shared Thanksgiving for two years, both having no family to speak of and glomming on to each other like bees to honey. They'd shared hopes, dreams, laughter, and fears—something Ella had never done with another woman. Her loss still stung.

And Endgame had lost Micah Samson. Jude had lost his best friend. Those memories were hard to relive. Hard to think about.

"I knew Nina was sick that day, but I had no idea she'd been poisoned. I don't know to this day if the Piper was responsible, and I haven't asked. All I knew was that I was supposed to be support for that operation, not on-site with you."

She laughed, and it was mirthless. "I was as surprised as you, Dagan, when King called me up for the op. And I was scared."

"You should have been," King finally said.

"When we crashed, I came to and found myself face-down in the sand with Brody and Micah on either side of me. Then I saw Savidge gun them both down, and I knew I was next. I could feel you all out there, watching. When he put the barrel against my temple, I knew that was it."

"But it wasn't, was it?" Jude bit out.

She shook her head and closed her eyes, blocking out the sounds of the gun going off and the red spray blotting her eyes a split second before oblivion took her down. She woke to that sound from her nightmares. She would never forget it.

"No. When I woke up...well, let's just say Dresden doesn't treat his prisoners of war very well. After a few days, I discovered Brody was alive but that they'd buried Micah in a graveyard outside Beirut. It took me another few weeks to h-heal." She stuttered on that word because she had never fully healed. Not from what Savidge had done to her. She swallowed thickly, refusing to give in here. They didn't need her memories of that horror. "Then I realized that I had the perfect way in. Hell, I was *already* in. I just had to make Dresden believe I was his."

"The Piper didn't have to work too hard, did he?" Rook mused out loud.

It was akin to treason, the words he spoke. Endgame was a private entity on paper, but they were all soldiers to their cores. Insinuating that their creator had been the master manipulator in all of this walked the line of treason.

More silence, pregnant with all manner of unspoken questions she couldn't answer and hoped they never voiced. She'd have to tell Jude the truth if she survived. But that was a big *if* and would be an even bigger one eventually. She wondered if being around him, kissing him, had bestowed her with some kind of false hope.

Still, she had to give them something. "He got everything he could have asked for when we went down in the desert."

She felt Jude's gaze on her—the hot, tactile caress of it dulling her pain for a few precious seconds. She lifted her head and met that obsidian gaze.

"I didn't leave you," she whispered. "I *never* left you."

Jude didn't acknowledge her statement, and that was okay. She'd put herself in his place a million times over the last year. She'd have been devastated if he'd done to her what she'd done to him.

"Where can we find Dresden? What's his weakness?" King asked, breaking the rising tension.

"Here's where we part ways," Ella replied mournfully. "I can't give you that. I asked you to talk to the Piper."

If she gave these men Dresden, she'd lose all hope of finding out who was in charge of him. After the last year of pain and sorrow, and for all the future horror Dresden could inflict on the world, she would not do that.

"I told you back in Moscow, you're either in this with us or out. This is your fork in the road, Banning," King told her.

"I can't give you Dresden. Not yet," she responded, skirting the line between giving them something and giving away nothing.

"You're coming back with us?" Rook asked the question, but she addressed her reply to Jude.

"Not yet." *Please, don't give up on me*, she pleaded silently. *Please.*

"Then there's nothing to say, is there?" King asked. "We're done here. You'll go your way; we'll go ours."

She nodded, and it nearly broke her. The Piper had warned her these men and women of Endgame were no joke. They believed in the team over everything, and leaving them meant she might never be able to return.

To keep Jude safe, she'd risk everything.

"Rook, you're first watch. Then me, then Jude," King said.

"What about me?" Ella asked before she could stop the question from escaping.

King simply looked at her and didn't reply.

Ella stood then, grabbing the shredded shards of her heart, and headed inside, up the stairs to the sagging bed. She placed her gun within easy reach beside the bed and lay down. She needed to rest because tomorrow she walked back into hell. For tonight, she took refuge in the fact that she slept in the company of soldiers.

She closed her eyes and prayed for a sleep uninterrupted by nightmares.

Jude opened her door as quietly as the rusted hinges would allow and stepped into the room. She was asleep, the steady rise and fall of her chest obvious in the moon's light. He strode to the bed softly and sank down beside her, the bed sagging in the middle so badly that she slid back into his body.

He wrapped his arms around her as her body conformed to his, sinking into his hard places, her butt into his hips, her head finding purchase on his bicep. He waited for her to wake, but she didn't.

He didn't know if he was relieved or frustrated. Besides two nights before when he'd carried her on the car ride to the other farm, he hadn't held her in well over a year. His body screamed at him to take her, to make her his again.

His heart demanded a different wooing.

Always with Ella, his hardness could find no foothold. She softened him, made him easier. He'd accepted it before that last mission. Now it came perilously close to pissing him off. But even in the midst of that burgeoning anger he held her close, protecting her the only way she'd let him.

He wanted to follow her tomorrow. He would follow her. Because everything she'd left unsaid earlier haunted him. Dresden had to know by now that she was still Endgame. When Jude, King, and Rook had spoken earlier, they'd decided that Dresden most likely had had that entire meeting wired and knew how everything had gone down.

But they hadn't been able to figure out Ella's part in everything. It was frustrating because King had said that the Piper categorically refused to give him anything when it came to Ella's mission.

Before he'd come up here, Jude had spoken with King. He'd told his team leader his plans to follow Ella. King had been against it, but in the end, he'd given in because Ella was still Endgame whether she admitted it or not.

"Jude?" she whispered, her breath feathering his skin.

"I'm here, Ella. I've got you," he whispered in return, pressing a kiss on her neck.

She was his. She always would be.

She settled at that and Jude breathed her in, knowing he was going to let her enter Dresden's on her own, but also knowing he'd be close if she needed him. Jude had an ace in the hole meeting him tomorrow in Ukraine.

Ella could run. But she'd never be able to hide from him again.

Chapter 11

"I AM SO GLAD YOU'RE BACK," DRESDEN SAID FROM HIS perch beside the enormous blazing fireplace.

"Do tell," she responded as she walked into the room and sat down across from him. She was so brittle that she was about to break. She had to shove thoughts of Jude to the back of her mind. It took a force of will that she would have doubted she could achieve.

She'd left the farmhouse separately from Jude, King, and Rook. Alone. She'd left alone.

"You know I'm going to punish you?" the monster asked softly.

She shrugged. She might be scared he'd break her again, but she'd be damned if she'd show him her fear.

"Being with your team has made you bold," he said, his tone unchanged. "That doesn't bode well for you."

"Segorski isn't an ally. He needs to be eliminated," she responded, refusing to engage with Dresden. He liked that, and she didn't want to give him anything he liked.

Dresden rose and walked toward her. "We'll talk about Segorski...*after*."

"After what?" she asked, infusing the appropriate amount of caution into her tone.

"I've got something to show you," Dresden said with a smile.

Ice washed through her veins. This could not be

good. She'd expected something twisted, but normally he crowed about things before showing her.

She followed him down to the cells. She'd spent a fair amount of time there. She remembered the smell, the cold, the fear, and the pain. God, how she remembered the fear and pain. As they descended the metal steps, her trepidation grew. She didn't get the feeling he was going to hurt her—not physically anyway, not yet.

He flipped on a light as they came to the bottom, and all of the space he used for torture was revealed. There were five doors around the edges of the large circular room. The doors were made of heavy wood and impenetrable from the inside.

Ella knew; she'd tried at one time to escape.

A man stepped forward from behind them, holding a ring of keys.

"Open the door," Dresden ordered.

The small man scuttled to do as he was bid. Ella tensed, afraid suddenly of what was about to be revealed.

The man opened the door and stepped back. Dresden stepped forward and entered the room. He exited after only a few seconds, pushing a small, blond woman ahead of him toward the center of the room. The left side of the woman's face had a large bruise, but the rest of her body, dressed in a simple though dirty shift, was untouched. She didn't fight, didn't make any noise at all when Dresden grabbed her arms behind her back and forced her to kneel on the cold stone floor.

Ella winced as the woman's knees bounced against the stones. All of Dresden's moves were to belittle and show his captives that ultimately they had no power. Whoever this woman was, she was in trouble.

"Do you know who this is, Ella?" Dresden asked as he walked to Ella and stroked a finger down her cheek.

"I don't," Ella replied, keeping her gaze on the woman, looking for signs of life besides simply existing. Other than the shallow rise and fall of the woman's chest, there was nothing.

"This is Anna Beth Caine," Dresden said with a small, evil laugh. "She was once my fiancée."

That name… Something about that name niggled at Ella.

"You're probably wondering why she's here, right? Is her name familiar?" Dresden asked as he stepped behind Ella and rested his chin on her shoulder.

Like lovers, she thought. He was treating her like a lover.

"I don't like it when you don't answer me, Ella."

"I'm not wondering why she's here," Ella pushed out of a suddenly dry throat.

"No?" Dresden laughed. "I'll tell you anyway. She's here because Svetlana Markov tried to undermine me by giving your Piper information that she thought would break me. So I decided to break Svetlana first."

Svetlana Markov's whispered dying words floated through Ella's mind. Something about a sister…

"She didn't say anything to me," Ella said, denying what Dresden obviously already knew. Did the bastard know everything?

"We won't talk about your propensity to lie to me right now. I want you to concentrate on the woman kneeling so beautifully on the floor in front of us. Are you watching her, Ella?"

Ella nodded.

"Svetlana Markov's real name wasn't Svetlana. It was Cameron. She and her sister, Anna Beth, are—or in Cameron's case were—daughters of a prominent American military leader who has made it his number one priority to destroy me." A pause, a draw of breath, and then he continued. "Can you imagine trying to destroy me?" He laughed then, sinisterly and softly. "Anyway, I digress. Anna Beth was at one time my beloved fiancée, her father a pawn in my pocket. She loved me unconditionally until she couldn't love me anymore. It's a sad truth that I tend to break my toys."

Caine…the name… The woman couldn't be… "What have you done?" Ella whispered in horror.

"Svetlana—excuse me, *Cameron*—decided to try to hide her sister from me. Cameron and her father did their best, but ultimately, well, I'm me and I know everything. Cameron decided she would try to hide Anna Beth from me. Nobody leaves me. Nobody hides from me." His whispered edicts had every hair on Ella's body standing on end.

She didn't know how to deescalate this situation. Dresden was cold and methodical. This woman's torture was a means to an end for him. Ella didn't doubt his sanity. The bastard simply had no soul. He'd sold it to the devil to attain power. The woman on the floor had once been important to him, and she was Svetlana—um, Cameron—Markov's sister. Now? She was a tool. And today she'd be used to bring Ella back in line. For Dresden, it was just that simple.

The truth circled Ella's mind… Noah Caine's daughter. So was the woman who'd died in Ella's arms in Russia.

Noah Caine. The Piper.

Goddamn it.

"It looks like you've won, Dresden." Ella pointed to the woman. "She's right there at your mercy, just like you like them."

He smoothed his hair back and straightened his jacket. "Yes. Yes she is. How does it feel to know the bastard that created you, created Endgame Ops, has such a deep tie to me? God, you and your team are pathetic. Put her back into her cage, Ella. Do that for me, will you?"

Ella nodded and walked to the woman, stooping to help her up. The woman was smaller than Ella and lighter. She rose with Ella's assistance, though it seemed a painful transition if her gasp was anything to go by.

Ella glanced at the woman and was surprised to find her deep-green gaze locked on her. Inside them was acceptance and, strangely enough, a clarity that spoke volumes about her mental health. She wasn't insane with pain or torture. Not yet. Not by a long shot.

Ella would save this woman. She vowed it right then. But first she had to get her out of Dresden's line of sight.

"Prepare yourself," Ella said so softly that her words went no farther than the woman.

She closed her eyes and did as Ella instructed.

Ella pulled the woman's arms behind her body as gently as she could. She was a pawn. Another piece on the chessboard.

How much longer until an endgame in this seemingly endless game with their lives?

"Put her up," Dresden spat out.

Ella pushed lightly on the woman, who walked to the room. "I'll be back for you," she whispered before she turned and closed the door behind her.

Before the solid oak door latched, Ella heard the woman say, "I'll be ready."

Then Ella locked the door and turned around. Dresden was right there in her face.

She didn't have time to brace herself for his fist. It connected with a snap, and she fell to the floor, shock coating her tongue, the blow to her cheek rendering her insensate for a precious second. Ella rode the wave of pain that threatened to carry her down.

"If you betray me, I will kill you, Ella. But first I'll make you watch as I gut your man. Would you like that?"

He didn't say anything else, just hovered over her until she finally opened her eyes. He wasn't even out of breath from his exertion.

Yet, the sanity remained in his eyes. The calculation absolute and so very real she wondered if she could touch it.

But Ella was hurting now. All she wanted to do was curl into a ball and weep.

"Get up and clean yourself. We'll speak tomorrow," he ordered and then turned and calmly walked away.

"You won't be able to save me. You can't even save yourself," the woman behind the door whispered.

"You have no idea what I'm capable of," Ella said to the woman. She pulled herself up off the floor, wincing at the ringing in her head. She pushed the pain down deep and made her way up the lower stairs, her mind clearing with every step.

Then she made her way slowly up the grand staircase and to her room on the second floor of the huge mansion. Maids and hired help passed her, but none of them looked at her, avoiding any repercussions of helping someone Dresden had gone out of his way to hurt.

Ella ignored them too, instead focusing on what she'd learned tonight. It was information that threw everything the Piper had asked her to do out of perspective.

She concentrated on what she knew. Dresden had taken over this property from a well-to-do Ukrainian businessman who found himself no longer needing a place to sleep since the hole Dresden had dug and placed him in suited him quite nicely in his deceased state.

Dresden had taken refuge in Ukraine. The Russians wanted him. The United States would never stop hunting him, but the Ukrainians? Ah yes, the Ukrainians wanted his power and wealth because it seemed not even the Russians knocking at their door would cross Dresden.

It was all a huge game to Dresden. Because even as he played false with the Ukrainians, he sold biochemical weapons to the Russians. Or at least he sold them to Segorski. A Russian who wanted the Crimean Peninsula and all the oil that lay within it.

Ella slowly made her way to her room and walked to the balcony that overlooked a small, picturesque meadow. A stream cut through the middle of the field, and the moon reflected off the dark water. She took several cleansing breaths and wondered how in the hell she'd managed to survive this long.

"Ma'am?" A tentative voice sounded from the door of her room.

Ella turned and saw a woman standing there, hands folded in front of her, dark auburn hair in a severe bun, the lace apron she wore confirming she was a maid. "Yes?"

"Do you need anything?" the maid asked, and Ella swore she heard another question in the woman's voice.

Where did she start? A broken laugh escaped Ella. "No. I'm good."

The woman nodded and without warning grabbed Ella by the arms.

Ella tried to pivot, but the woman was stronger than she looked. Soldier strong.

Surely they wouldn't...

Oh God, what had Endgame done? Ella could only pray they weren't coming for Dresden. Or worse, herself.

Ella twisted and backed away. "Who sent you?" she asked, her voice nearly silent for fear of rousing other staff or, worse, Dresden.

The maid's head rose swiftly. She was caught and knew it. "Jude," she admitted with a small grimace.

Damn it! Damn Jude and his interference!

"Listen to me," Ella hissed. "Dresden will kill you if he discovers what you're doing here. I can't believe Jude attempted this!"

The woman shrugged as if Ella's words didn't matter a whit. She pulled a square of fabric from a pocket in her maid outfit and shoved the fabric into Ella's face.

Ella's vision swam immediately and she sagged, the bitterness of defeat nearly as heavy as the sweet taste of the drug coating her damaged tongue. For the second time within the span of a few days, she'd been taken. Damn it.

Ella lost her ability to fight, her limbs going numb even as her vision cleared. She wondered who the woman was to Jude even as she cursed the wayward thought in the middle of this clusterfuck of a situation. She had to be here. She had to be accessible to Dresden, or everything she'd sacrificed would be for naught.

And now there was Anna Beth Caine...

She tried to plead with her eyes for the woman to leave and let her be, but the woman was a force.

In less than a minute, Ella was wrapped in the duvet cover and shoved into a laundry cart. She was growing more and more tired, realizing that whatever she'd been given was meant to paralyze and eventually knock out the recipient.

Jude had warned her, and as the maid-slash-operative working for or with Jude dumped the contents of the laundry cart into the chute, Ella wondered where the hell she was headed.

Because none of this was good.

Not at all.

Chapter 12

JUDE WANTED TO RIP HORACE DRESDEN INTO TINY pieces, rebuild him, and do it all over again. The right side of Ella's face was bruised. Once he'd cleaned her up, he realized nothing was broken. He'd checked her over completely, not sure she hadn't been tortured. The rest of her body appeared untouched. She'd taken a punch from a man around Jude's size. Dresden. Jude knew it, and he wanted to kill that motherfucker.

Once the laundry truck Georgia had used to spirit Ella away from Dresden's had arrived at the airfield, Jude had loaded Ella onto the small charter plane they'd then taken to Moldova. From there, he loaded her onto another larger charter, and they'd flown to the States. Each charter had owed Jude a favor, and he'd called them in with zero hesitation. He hadn't wanted anyone to know his plans, so he'd not involved Vivi or his other Endgame teammates.

Had they been there, Jude could have taken his shot at Dresden. Without their involvement, he couldn't risk busting in there like a one-man army. That could result in damage to Ella. So he'd made the decision to sneak her out, knowing she wouldn't go without being disabled. Georgia had signed on with Jude. She'd also owed him a favor or two. When she dropped Ella off, she'd complained about his woman's right hook and even had a shiner to match the one coloring Ella's face.

Georgia had assured him she hadn't harmed Ella too much, that the mark on Ella's face wasn't from her.

He didn't know if Dresden would be able to track them, but he knew once the bastard realized Ella was gone, he'd guess Jude had her and was taking her to the United States.

She'd roused once on the flight from outside Atlanta to the abandoned airstrip in Texas. Jude had knocked her back out, feeling only fleeting remorse when her confused gaze had met his and then gone blank as she fell back into the arms of Morpheus. Then he'd driven eight hours through Texas to the mountains of New Mexico.

He pushed off the doorjamb and entered the massive bedroom, moving to the side of the bed she lay on—the bed he'd had handcrafted when he'd had this cabin built almost two years ago. This had been designed to be his escape. He'd brought her here because no one but his *tia* Rosa knew about this place. They were as safe as he could make them because the only other person who knew about his home away from home was dead.

He'd purchased the land under a shell corporation Micah had helped him set up for them both. Micah had built in Alaska. Jude had built in the Cimarron Range of the Sangre de Cristo Mountains in New Mexico. He'd hunted these woods with his great-uncle as a child. Some of Jude's happiest memories had been created in these mountains.

And now she was here.

It had snowed last night—not the light, fluffy stuff, but the heavy, wet snow of a fall storm—and Jude had had a bitch of a time getting the dilapidated Range Rover up the pass to his home. Once he'd gotten them there safely, he'd taken Ella inside, removed everything but her bra and panties, and placed her in the huge California king-size bed made entirely of the cottonwoods that dominated the landscape outside his windows.

She'd wake soon, and then he'd deal with what he'd done and what had been done to her. But until then…

He allowed his gaze to roam over her features. Even with the black-and-blue marks covering her face, she was hands down the most beautiful woman Jude had ever seen. He knew that under the bruising, her ivory skin was tinted with freckles across the bridge of her aquiline nose. Her almond-shaped eyes were closed, and he missed the cold frost of her gray eyes. Eyes that could turn to molten silver when she was in the throes of passion. Long, black lashes lay like fans on her pale cheeks, and her dark-brown eyebrows were gently curved over her eyes.

His gaze traveled south, over her thinner upper lip and deliciously full lower lip. Those lips could flatten in anger, lift in a soul-destroying smile, or open in ecstasy. He stopped when he came to the dent in her chin and licked his lips. She would always tempt him. Jude wondered if he'd ever be able to purge her. The need that had simmered under his skin from the moment he'd seen her almost two years ago continued to beat at him, heating him from the inside out, making him fist his hands.

Then his gaze traveled over the scar at her temple, and rage lit him. He pulled on a single thread of his control, finding other threads and winding them together until he could breathe without the fury.

Still he stood there and watched her breathe, ironically realizing that's all he'd wanted for over a year— nothing more than to be able to watch her breathe.

Of course, that had been when he'd thought her dead. And she wasn't dead. Not physically anyway.

He pulled his gaze from her, assured she was resting easily, and walked to the chair beside the wide bank of windows facing the southeast ridges of Baldy Mountain. Snow blanketed the top of the mountain, and the trees swayed in the wind of the continuing storm overhead. A pale-gray sky taunted him. It would weep snow again soon.

Could he survive in her presence for as long as he knew it would take to force her to give him information? Could he save her from herself?

He ran a hand down his face and tensed. She shifted on the bed, and everything in Jude went on alert. He heard her rise to a sitting position before she stilled. How would she play it?

Her breathing didn't change from slow and even. But Jude was a hunter by nature, and he recognized the fear she was giving off in waves. He turned and simply watched her. He stood beside the window in the shadows of the intentionally darkened room, and unless she turned her head, she wouldn't see him.

Could she feel him?

He wanted to know, but he waited.

"You have to let me go," she said, her voice rough and low.

Jude didn't respond.

She turned her head, finding him unerringly, her gaze narrowed and dark. "You don't know what you're doing here, Dagan."

Anger rose again. Always, it was the anger now. He stepped from the shadows and turned the chair around, sitting down and crossing one leg over the opposite knee. "Why don't you tell me then, Ella?"

"Let me go," she demanded, her voice rising, the notes of the fear she was obviously feeling ringing strident in her tone.

"I've tried." He answered her demand with the truth. He had. Once he'd found out she was alive, he'd gotten rip-roaring drunk and tried to drown his pain. Then he'd woken up with a bitch of a headache and a resolution. He would find her and force her to make him understand why she'd done what she'd done.

"Try harder," she whispered. "For both of us, try harder."

He rubbed his chest before he could check the action. She was scared. And not of Jude. What did she know? What the hell was she doing for the Piper? "Do you need some water?"

She shook her head, the nearly black strands of her hair falling to curtain her face from his view. "I need you to let me go, Dagan."

"My name," he said in a gruff voice.

"I can't," she returned, voice breaking at the end.

He sat up, both feet on the floor, fisted hands on his knees. "Use. My. Name."

"Please…" If it was possible, her head hung lower.

This was the beginning. If he was going to break her, he'd have to start now. "Please…who?" He kept his voice low, almost a whisper.

She straightened then, giving another half-hearted tug on the soft leather cuffs attached to her wrists. "I won't beg. Never again."

He stood at that. He'd never made her. "Who made you beg, El?"

Jude winced as he automatically switched to the shortened version of her name. It was intimate and something he'd fallen back into far too easily.

She turned away from him, staring at the opposite wall and refusing to answer.

The fury that had been his best friend since the night she'd *died* rose again, swift and supernova hot. "Who made you beg, Ella?"

She took a deep breath and met his gaze. "Let me go."

He shook his head and stood, walking to stand right beside the bed. She shrank from him, and that also enraged him. "When you tell me what's going on, then I'll let you go…maybe."

He turned and walked to the door.

"I can't give you what you want. Not anymore," she said softly.

Bullshit. He didn't turn around when he spoke. "You'll give me everything you've got, intel, spec ops. You'll give it all to me, and then I'll decide what to do with you."

Then he left, hearing her breath break and a strangled sob escape her. He almost, *almost*, turned around and went back to her.

Instead, he put one foot in front of the other, descending the stairs quickly lest he do what his heart demanded.

Ella lay back down gingerly on the bed. She was in so much shit. Once the maid-in-disguise had switched her from the laundry cart to the laundry chute, she'd known Jude was in control of this round. She'd have no choice but to ride it out and see what was going on.

She couldn't have fought anyway. Her head had been muddled from Dresden's blow, and once the woman Jude had sent dumped her in the laundry chute, Ella had passed out for good, not waking until a few minutes ago. She'd dreamed she'd woken on a plane, meeting the gaze of her lover and seeing him smile at her the way he used to. But that's all it had been…a dream.

Because the resolution that had masked his face moments ago told her just how deep in the shit she was. Jude Dagan wasn't a man to play with, and she knew that's what he thought she'd been doing.

Ella stared at the gorgeous cedar wood that comprised the ceiling and closed her eyes against the pain of her circumstance. He wanted the truth, and that she couldn't give him. Not yet. It had nothing to do with trust and everything to do with her mission. The Piper had made it very clear she was to tell no one her mission objective because, he'd said, all of Endgame Ops would try to stop her. King and his men wanted to kill Dresden. The Piper wanted Dresden so he could interrogate and dismantle him.

And the Piper had another huge reason for wanting Ella's mission kept quiet…his daughter, Anna Beth. The thought of the other woman sent fear tripping through Ella. No one knew better what it was like to be at the horrible tender mercy of Horace Dresden. Ella needed to contact Brody as soon as possible. The woman needed extraction the moment they could discern that Dresden was away from his mansion.

She sat back up and glanced around for a clock. The one on the bedside table said it was five in the afternoon. Darkness was falling outside, and the clouds above them were beginning to drop their load of snow. She had no idea where they were, but if she had to venture a guess, she'd say New Mexico. The Cimarron subrange of the Sangre de Cristo Mountains, to be specific.

Jude had told her stories about him and his great-uncle hunting these mountains and their passes. He'd always spoken of New Mexico as home, even though his mother had left the state when he was a baby. Jude hadn't returned until he was a young teenager. His mother, sadly, had not returned with him. Too eager to become Mexico's next soap opera star, she'd let Jude return to his father's people in New Mexico and never looked back.

He hadn't told Ella much else, but his mother's desertion had hurt him. Hell, she'd hurt him so much that he denied her existence to most people. Ella had heard their teammates ribbing him about his beautiful mother. Jude tried to ignore it, shrug it off, but sometimes it got to him.

The sound of his footfalls coming back up the stairs tightened her muscles. She didn't know how to breathe with him so close to her. All she wanted was to sink inside him and never come back out. Would he let her?

The answer rang through her mind unequivocally… No, he wouldn't. Not until he had the truth. And that she couldn't give him. Hell, she didn't even know it now.

"I brought you some soup," he said as he walked in and placed a heavy-looking ceramic bowl on the bed-side table.

"I'm not hungry," she responded, a part of her just wanting to be contrary. She was frustrated at getting caught. But how could she have anticipated that Jude would come for her inside Dresden's house?

"Yeah, you are." He laughed, and the sound rolled through her tummy. "I can hear your stomach growling."

"That's anger you're hearing," she sniped back.

He laughed again and sat down in the chair he'd taken earlier. "Eat, Ella. It looks like you haven't been doing much of that lately."

The smell of potato soup wafted through the air, and her stomach growled loudly, again. She sighed and reached for the bowl, coming close to grabbing it before Jude grunted and beat her to it.

"It's hot," he warned her, placing the oven mitt that lay beside the bowl in her hand.

She put the mitt on and grabbed the bowl. He towered over her, and her gaze rose, roving over his strong features until she met his look head-on. Something flared in the depths of his ebony orbs, warming Ella in a way the soup in her hands never could. Then he veiled his eyes, long, dark lashes falling as he made sure to brush her fingers before releasing the bowl into her hands.

Electricity arced between them. She wanted to touch him, to feel that lightning zing between them and settle between her legs before spreading throughout her body. It had been this way between them from the first moment she'd seen him. He'd had his back to her when King had introduced her to the team. Gray Broemig had warned her that King didn't play well with the CIA but that he'd be fair. Broemig had just wanted someone inside Endgame who could report to him. Vivi had defected and wasn't forthcoming with intel on Endgame anymore. He'd needed a new patsy. What he hadn't anticipated was that Ella would *become* Endgame in her bones. Broemig had lost Ella the moment Jude Dagan had turned around and looked her up and down, his gaze finally centering on her own. Ella had never experienced that type of connection before—had never even known she wanted it.

He had owned her in that moment, and the men he called brothers had become hers as well. She took a delicate bite of the soup and nearly moaned. She'd forgotten how well Jude cooked. His great-aunt had taught him everything she knew, and he'd kept practicing long after he'd grown up.

He said cooking kept him close to his roots. Right now, Ella and her stomach were glad for it.

It took her less than five minutes to empty the bowl. The heat initially stung her bruised tongue, but nothing could stop her from shoveling in the food. The whole time she ate, Jude's perusal was a tactile caress. When she finished, she turned and found him holding a glass of water and three small white pills in his hand. Aspirin. He wouldn't drug her again. He'd get no information out of her that way.

She took the glass and the pills, drinking them down before she handed the glass back.

He took it and placed it on the nightstand. Then he sat back down and waited.

She realized then that she was nearly naked under the covers. She tucked them tighter around her body, using her arms to hold them close.

Ella heard him chuckle, and then he said, "I've seen everything you've got, Ella."

But he hadn't. Her body was nothing like he'd known it. She'd been marked irrevocably by Vasily Savidge— had the scars on her back and thighs to prove it. Jude had obviously stripped her, leaving her some coverage with her bra and panties. Had he seen her scars?

She guessed not. His first question upon her waking would have been about them, if he'd seen them.

Instead of responding, she lay back on the pillows she'd stacked behind her. Fatigue was threatening to pull her under, much like the drugs had. How long had it been since she'd slept deeply? Safely?

Since the last night she'd spent with Jude at the beach—and even that had been short because she'd preferred to spend the time loving him.

"You're going to have to talk to me, El," she heard him murmur. Her heart stuttered.

His voice when he called her *El* made her want to weep. He could destroy her…weaken her resolve to finish this thing with Dresden, make her want to just stay holed up here with him and forget the world.

But she didn't have that luxury. She had Anna Beth Caine to save and a name to glean from Dresden. Didn't look like rest was coming anytime soon.

"Sleep now, baby. We've got all the time in the world," Jude said as he tucked the plaid duvet around her. His smell—cedar and nothing but man—sank into her pores. She licked her lips, wishing she was licking his.

She heard his declaration and allowed herself the pain of hope for a few precious seconds. Warmth stole over her, combining with her exhaustion to pull her under. She wanted to believe his words but knew the truth.

Ella's clock had been ticking down for two years. She had hardly any time left. But Jude? Jude was a different story.

She'd make sure he had plenty left. Or she'd die trying.

Chapter 13

"I'VE GOT HER," JUDE TOLD KING VIA A SECURED SAT phone connection.

"When you know anything, I need the specifics. She's got information on Dresden's locations and hideouts—hell, his whole operation—that we need to take him down," King reminded him.

Jude didn't need the reminder. He'd given King Dresden's location. Rook, Knight, and Black were all over that location now. Only Brody Madoc and Vivi remained at Endgame's base in Port Royal, Virginia. Chase had been sent to Burundi, Africa, two weeks ago and was gathering intel on Abrafo Nadege.

"Chase reported in?" Jude asked.

"He's got eyes on Nadege. Says the bastard is a sadist who enjoys two things: killing and diamonds. We don't know the nature of the connection to Dresden yet, only that it's there," King responded.

Jude heard the weariness in his team leader's voice. "How's Allie?"

"Lobbying in DC. She's determined to get to the root of what's going on. Woman swears it comes from higher up than we realize and is working every angle like it's going to straighten at any moment. She'll be the death of me," King said, a laugh in his voice. And love.

Had Jude sounded that way before Beirut a year ago? Probably.

"When I know, you'll know, King," he said.

King sighed. "Be safe. We'll be back stateside tomorrow morning. We know he's probably there, in that big mansion in Ukraine, but he's not moving, and he's added more men to his security force. The prime minister of Russia has gone to ground, and Segorski is nowhere to be found. Oh, we did find out something that might be of interest to you."

Jude went on alert. "Yeah?"

"Lo-Lo Bernstein was sighted in DC yesterday. Apparently, she enjoys visits to Gray Broemig's residence where she sits outside on the hood of her car and stares at the CIA director's house."

"What the hell?" Jude asked, confusion spearing him.

"Yeah, weird right? When one of Broemig's men made contact, she left. Didn't say a word, just got in her car and drove away each time."

"Allie safe?"

"I've got Madoc on her."

"Wise choice," Jude affirmed.

King grunted. "It bothers me that Lo-Lo was with Baron Meadows in Russia. There's an angle there that Brody is working on. Oh, and Brody has requested to speak with Ella. Give that some thought, yeah?"

"Sure," Jude replied. *When hell froze over.* Brody had known how much Ella meant to Jude. Hell they'd all known—the entire team. And he hadn't even given Jude a hint that she was alive. He would have to answer to Jude for that eventually. Maybe there was logic in there somewhere that Jude simply couldn't see because of all the emotion clouding things.

But right now, he'd be damned if he'd let Brody talk

to her without him having access to the entire conversation. She wasn't hiding anything else from him. Not until this was over and he could walk away.

If he could walk away. Which he doubted, but he was giving himself some consolation that the choice was his.

"I'm out," King said. "Check in with me, Dagan. Don't keep me in the dark on this."

"I'll check in," Jude promised. He'd kept King in the dark for too long.

But he was unwilling to do anything right now except relearn Ella Banning.

He leaned back in his chair and glanced out the window. Snow was falling in earnest, coating the ground in an even heavier blanket than last night. These mountains were beautiful. The only other place he'd felt the peace he felt here was inside Ella.

And he hadn't had that in over a year.

Already, he could smell her in his house. Maybe he was just being fanciful. She had a scent he'd imprinted on the first time he'd gotten close enough to smell her. Her skin held a combination of berries, sugar, and sun-kissed rain. He could taste her now—tactile memory.

His heart skipped a beat. He'd never be able to scrub her from his mind.

She'd never been to the cabin. It'd just been completed the year he'd met her, and they'd been balls to the wall the two years since. He'd only been here once himself. His great-aunt kept it up for him.

He smiled when he thought of his *tia* Rosa. She and his uncle Herman had been Jude's rock through his teen years. His mother hadn't had time for a husband, much less a fourteen-year-old son. She hadn't had time to cook, clean, work. What she had had time for was fame.

Sophia—formerly Dagan, now Ortiz—had only had time for the Mexican soap opera on which she'd been cast by pure chance. She'd been a beautiful woman with a heart colder than a witch's tit in a brass bra, his dad had always said. Of course, that had been when he was falling-down drunk or close to passing out in the shed. Eventually, his father, Carron Dagan, had killed himself, driving straight off the side of one of the mountains outside Jude's window.

Jude had been left solely with his father's uncle and aunt. They'd been old when Jude was a teen, but Uncle Herman and Tia Rosa had taken care of him. Uncle Herm had taught Jude how to hunt, fish, and live off the land. Tia Rosa had taught Jude what little he knew about love and loyalty. Oh, and how to cook. She'd taught him that too.

At the thought of food, Jude grimaced. He needed to go back up and check on Ella. He rubbed his chest. She gave him those gray eyes, and it slayed him every time. She was a land mine for Jude, and in the midst of gaining her secrets, he'd have to step carefully.

He walked up the stairs cautiously. She'd escaped rope ties in Russia. He'd taken her clothes and weapons when he'd undressed her, but the woman had proven she was more than capable of handling herself. She hadn't quite had time to fashion a knife's edge out of the spoon she'd used to eat her soup, but she was an unknown to him now and he had to be careful.

He came to his room—yeah, he'd given her his room. There were only two bedrooms in the whole house, and it felt right for Jude to have her in his. Her eyes were closed, but he felt her awareness.

"Do you need anything?" he asked, his voice neutral, nonthreatening.

"I've got to pee," she said softly.

Of course, Jude thought. Of course that's the first thing she'd say to him. He made his way over to the bed, gauging her reaction. She kept her gaze trained on him the entire time, her body tense and ready.

What had happened to her that conditioned her wariness around him? He'd never hurt her. Never would. When he'd told her in Serbia that he'd destroy them both if she made him chase her, he'd only been partially lying. But he'd never hurt her physically. No, Jude was worried about the lengths he'd force their hearts to before one of them broke.

"Bathroom is through that door," he said, pointing to the other side of the room.

She sat up, rubbing her neck, wincing. He waited for her to move, his gaze focused on her motions. When she didn't try to get up, he raised his eyes and found her staring at him, some indefinable emotion playing over her bruised features.

The mark on her cheek was growing into a deeper, darker purple and blue. Dresden would pay.

"What is it?" he asked roughly.

"Will you leave and let me handle my business?" she questioned, her tone sharp.

He shook his head.

Her brows lowered, and her gaze went flat. "Seriously, Dagan?"

He was sick of her calling him by his last name. It was

time to initiate Project Bring Ella Home. Jude almost laughed. Hell, he'd not even known he was making her a project. She was here physically, sure, but emotionally she was too far from him. It was anathema to his soul that she was so far away from him. "Don't ever call me Dagan again, Ella. We clear?"

He didn't move into her space, barely moved anything more than his lips, but his voice conveyed how precarious her situation was at the moment. He was tired of the distance between them. A year. Hell, over a year. Four hundred seventy-three days he could have been loving her, touching her, and she'd *left* him. *Lied* to him. Forced him to believe she was *dead*.

Get a grip, Jude, he told himself.

She didn't respond. She didn't do anything more than look away from him, but a flush rose up her chest. She was angry.

And Jude didn't care. Not at the moment. He had to gain her confidence somehow so she'd spill her secrets, and somewhere in there, he had to earn enough of her heart so that she didn't leave him when all this came to a head.

Is that what you want? his mind asked.

Hell yes, his heart answered unequivocally.

Jude needed to be truthful with himself. As she sat there, breathing, very much alive, he had no choice but to recognize his heart's truth. He wasn't leaving her. And she damn sure wasn't ever leaving him again.

Period.

End of discussion.

I hear you, his mind screamed at his heart.

Damn right, his heart responded.

He sighed. First steps were indeed a bitch. He turned away from her, giving her the illusion of privacy while in reality he could see every move she made in the mirror on the opposite wall. She eased to the edge of his massive bed and glanced over her shoulder. He barely restrained his smile. Trying to make sure he wasn't looking, no doubt.

When she felt assured he wasn't looking at her, she pushed the covers down and stood.

Jude's breath hissed in when he saw her back.

Scars. Everywhere. From the line of her panties to the base of her neck. His woman was scarred. Most were thin and looked to have been made with a very sharp, small blade. The thinness of the marks indicated the cuts weren't that deep, but the presence of keloid scarring on some of them told Jude something had been done to make them scar in such a way.

Salt? Acid?

He was around the bed in a heartbeat. "Who?"

Her head fell, her chin touching her chest. There was so much sorrow in that gesture that Jude's breath locked in his throat. The top of her head came to his breastbone and rested there. He reached for her, but she said, "Don't."

A shuddering breath, and then she whispered, "Don't touch me. I might break if you touch me right now."

He froze, hands partway up, and then he felt the scalding heat of a single tear fall on his skin, and he lost it. He scooped her up, turned, and sat down on the bed, holding her close. Her head tucked beneath his chin and she shook, deep, racking sobs that rocked her body in the cradle of his. Her tears scored him. Her sobs shattered him.

He held her tight, arms crossed over her. "Shhhh, El. I've got you."

Still she cried, as if his touch had indeed broken the dam on her sorrow and she had nothing to hold it back any longer.

He waited for her to calm, and when her sobs eased, his hold loosened and his hands began roaming over her cold skin.

"Tell me," he demanded. "Get it out, Ella."

She shook her head, denying him.

"Woman, you're killing me," he whispered against her hair. Something told him he couldn't push her on this right now. She was too fragile. And while Jude had a hard time reconciling the woman in his arms with the one who'd taken out an assassin on a rooftop in Russia to protect him, she was the same woman, and he couldn't hurt her any more than she'd already been hurt.

He felt her withdraw and let her get up from his lap. She stood in front of him, quivering, hands twisting, quiet.

"Go use the bathroom. Take a shower, clean up. I left a bag in there with some underwear and clothes for you," he said softly, making an effort to keep the rage out of his voice.

Someone had hurt her. Badly. Jude knew one man, in league with Dresden, who enjoyed his knives.

He drew in a deep breath. "I wish King had let him live."

Her head rose sharply, the question in her eyes clear.

"So I could kill Savidge again and again for what he's done," he promised her. "I'd do it for you, Ella. Over and over."

Something akin to relief lit on her face for a few seconds, and then she straightened her shoulders and turned, walking to the bathroom and closing the door behind her.

What had happened to her in Dresden's clutches? Her story was vague, but her scars, her wariness, didn't lie. She'd been devastated over the last year.

Jude rubbed a hand over his face, finding his cheeks wet.

Where did this leave him? How was he going to earn her trust when she was so splintered?

He'd have to love her harder.

So that's what Jude set out to do.

———

Ella pressed her forehead to the heavy wood of the bathroom door. Pain ripped through her, rending and biting, taking chunks out of her soul—chunks she couldn't afford to lose. His face when he'd looked at her?

Devastated.

He was hurt by her scars.

This man. The one she'd given everything to before Beirut. The one she'd given up everything for so he'd be safe. He was going to finish taking her apart, and Ella didn't know if there would be anything left when he was finished.

She knew Jude. He was planning and plotting a way to earn her trust so she'd give up her secrets. But there were too many, and she didn't know where to start— hell, if she *could* start. She was so locked inside herself, and she'd buried the key inside him.

He'd have to find it because she didn't dare.

He'd held her, and she'd cried. There was more where those tears had come from. A tidal wave of pain that could eventually bury them both. He'd been her reason for carrying on with her mission, and now he was the reason she wanted to curl up with him and leave the mission far behind.

She made her way through the large bathroom, bypassing the sink and mirror and handling her business on the toilet before running nothing but hot water in the enormous sunken tub.

She turned off the hot water and put on the cold for a minute before she turned it off too. Then she removed her bra and panties, still avoiding any look into the mirror. Her face felt numb. She probably looked like hamburger meat.

Everything was a blur. How long had she been out? How long was he planning on keeping her? How long could Anna Beth Caine survive in Dresden's hold?

She needed to contact the Piper. She needed answers.

Who was she kidding? She needed Jude.

And he was the one person she refused to pull any deeper into this than he already was.

Ella was off her game. Emotions she'd buried for a year were pressing against the back of her eyelids, threatening to pour forth from her throat and eyes.

She sank beneath the water gingerly, allowing the heat to soothe her knotted muscles. She bathed slowly, inhaling the scent of Jude in the soap he'd placed on the side of the tub. Mint and cedar, both scents she'd always associated with her man.

Ella sank beneath the water, washing her hair before she rose and dried off. The water gurgled out of the tub as she dressed slowly. The underwear was service-able, nothing girlie, just plain cotton. He'd left her with sweats, a T-shirt, and a sweatshirt that had *New Mexico*

State emblazoned across the front. There were thick socks, but no shoes.

In spite of her situation, she smiled at that. Jude wasn't going to make her escape easy.

She searched for a hair dryer and found one under the sink. Turning her back to the mirror, she dried her hair and pulled it up into a ponytail. She hadn't cut it in over a year. It reached her mid-back and was a serious detriment in a fight, but she didn't have the energy right now to put it up any other way.

Bathed, dried, and dressed, Ella reached for the toothbrush on top of the vanity, tearing off the wrapping and putting a liberal amount of toothpaste on it. Jude used to make fun of her for how much toothpaste she used. "Damn, how big is your mouth anyway?" he'd once teased her.

A smile creased her lips, causing her cheek to hurt, and her gaze instinctively rose to the mirror.

As she wiped the condensation off the mirror, her gaze roved over the planes of her face. Her cheek was a mess. Green, blue, and purple covered the left side of her face. The scar at her temple taunted her. She stuck out her tongue and eyeballed the damage. It wasn't split but looked like it'd been chewed on. It was healing though, so she wouldn't complain. Dresden's physical strength was formidable. Or maybe his rage lent him such power. She looked like she'd barely survived a prizefight.

That didn't bother her. Not the bruising. Not the pain. The only thing that bothered her was that Jude had seen her this way. That he hurt because of her.

She finished brushing her teeth and gingerly wiped her mouth. She couldn't waste any more time in this bathroom.

Ella reached deep for her strength, felt it flicker to life, and opened the bathroom door. Jude was nowhere to be seen.

She quickly searched the room for anything that would tell her where she was or that she could use as a weapon. If her time with Dresden had taught her anything, it was that weapons could be as small as a thumbtack or as soft as a pillow. Pick your poison, and you could temper it to the perfect degree of deadliness.

She searched for a few minutes until her mind reminded her just who had her right now. And it wasn't Dresden.

Jude Dagan must have been born a soldier. His every move was calculated to win whatever campaign he was currently engaging in. Ella was the current war he was fighting. He'd made sure there was nothing in the room that could be used against him.

Points to Jude, she thought.

Ella glanced out the window and noticed the wind blowing snow all over the place, so hard and thick she could barely make out the mountains in the distance. Damn. She wasn't going anywhere anytime soon.

She walked to the door of the room and listened. The sounds of pans banging together below assured her that's where she'd find him. Her stomach rumbled.

Her heart ached.

She took the steps and came to the lower level. The cabin was huge, and the more she saw, the more she had the uncanny feeling it belonged to Jude.

He'd never told her about another property. She'd only known about the beach property they'd bought so they could steal away between missions.

She swallowed thickly and pushed those memories

down. They had no place here. Ella needed to get her bearings, remember why she was here, how she'd come to be here, and where she was headed.

His smell haunted her though, pleading with her soul to come out and let Jude ease her. There was a time, before Savidge had hurt her, that she would have sheltered in Jude and allowed him to fix everything for her.

She'd been confident in her strength then. Confident enough to let her man carry the load. Now? She was nothing more than cracked glass, waiting for the hammer that was Horace Dresden to complete the break Savidge had begun. There was no way she'd allow Jude to carry her load now. It was way too heavy.

"Dinner's ready," he called out from the kitchen.

Ella walked to the huge living room opposite the kitchen. She was delaying the inevitable, but somehow she needed to pull the tattered pieces of herself together before she saw him again.

Then he was there in front of her. His broad shoulders blocking her vision, his eyes taunting her to give him everything.

She loved him. She loved Jude Dagan.

And she wouldn't allow him to be harmed by her decisions.

"Did you hear me?" he asked, but her gaze snagged on his full lips. Strong lips that had suckled at her skin and given her more pleasure in a single kiss than she'd ever known before him.

His head cocked, and a small grin curved those lips. Her knees weakened.

His mother was Hispanic, from the Jalisco state of

Mexico. He'd inherited her coloring—from his sienna-toned skin to his black hair and eyes. His father had been American, a "big, blond motherfucker" Jude had called him. Jude had gotten his size from his dad. The only other thing she knew about his father was that he'd been a mean drunk who'd given up on Jude the moment his mother had left them both.

Jude rarely spoke about his mother, but Ella knew the woman had hurt him deeply. So much, in fact, that when he said her name, it was usually with a sneer. He never talked about his father. Anything Ella knew, she'd learned from his *tia* Rosa. His great-aunt was the only family member Jude had left.

He'd been alone most of his life, and then Ella had left him too.

"Ella? Are you hungry?" he asked, pulling her from her musings.

"Yeah," she said, her voice rusty from her earlier tears and the restraint she was pulling on to keep from jumping into his arms and begging him to save her.

He smiled at that. "Then come eat."

He turned and led her into the kitchen—another big space dominated by large, stainless-steel appliances and heavy wooden furniture. He'd set the table that resided in front of a bay window. Two place settings, no candles.

It's not a romantic dinner, Ella, she admonished herself.

She took a seat with her back to the wall. He took the opposite seat, spearing her with a look. Before Beirut, she would never have made sure to keep her back away from the door. He'd noticed.

He loaded her plate with stewed beef, potatoes, and carrots, liberally pouring gravy over everything before setting a basket of bread between them. "Eat," he said and then dug in himself.

The food smelled amazing, and her stomach reminded her she needed to build up her strength. The drugs she'd been pumped full of over the last few days were still making her sluggish, and she'd barely eaten.

She picked up her—she laughed out loud—her *spoon*, and she dug in. She saw the smile that lit his features a second before the taste of the meal hit her taste buds.

Ella groaned. "That's delicious."

"I know," he said with not a hint of humility. "Tia Rosa left me stocked the last time she was here."

Ella took another bite, watching her food instead of Jude. "You didn't cook it?"

"No time," he said around a bite.

She didn't ask him why he had no time. She knew. He'd been hunting her hard the last six months. Brody had warned her and done everything he could to keep proof Ella was alive from Endgame, but in the end, the world of spec ops was only so big. Word got around. Once she'd save King in Spain, she'd known her gig was up.

She hadn't anticipated the scenario playing out quite like this though.

"This place yours?" she asked. She needed information on him. Had to have it. Like the Jude junkie she was.

"Well now, Ella, I don't think that's any of your business," he answered in a hard voice.

She winced.

"Unless you're willing to trade information?" Jude asked with a milder tone.

She couldn't not look at him anymore. She raised her gaze and found him staring at her, his face blank, his eyes hot. "Don't ask that of me, Jude."

She couldn't call him Dagan anymore. He was Jude. She could give herself that much at least.

He barked out a laugh that was anything but humorous. "I'm going to ask that and more, Ella."

She kept her gaze on him, and he returned it, refusing to look away. "If you'd just give me some time—"

He cut her off. "There's no more time. We're out of it. Dresden is making moves that will decimate world order. We need to know everything you've got, and we need it yesterday."

"That's not my mission, Jude," she protested.

He took a bite of his beef and then a drink of tea Ella knew she'd find unbearably sweet. He wiped his mouth, never looking away from her. "Fuck your mission, Ella."

She snorted. "You have fucked me. Royally." She wondered where her anger was. He'd taken her off grid somewhere, was making it plain as day he was going to do everything in his power to get information from her, and she was as far from angry as she'd ever been.

"Not yet, lady," he said with a wink before picking his fork back up. "But that's coming too."

Her breath caught, and an errant piece of meat lodged in her throat. She coughed, choking even as she laughed at his overwhelming gall. He started to get up, but she held up a hand, managing to dislodge the meat before she took a drink of his tea.

"Damn that's sweet," she complained.

"Only way to drink tea," he responded.

He was lulling her, and damn him, it was working.

She was falling back into her pattern with him, and the comfort of it was a draw she could barely resist.

She couldn't allow this. She was going to hurt him when she left again. Because she would leave again. She had to take Dresden down, and the only way to do that was from inside his organization.

He was probably wondering where the hell she was and mobilizing to either find her or destroy Jude. And beyond all that, Ella's skin continued to crawl with worry for Anna Beth Caine.

Fear prickled her skin. "Where are we?" she asked suddenly, her fear communicating in the waver of her voice.

He held up six fingers.

Her eyes watered. *Damn tears!*

"You're sure?"

He peered at her, intense and a bit put out, if the look on his face was anything to go by. *Yes,* she thought, *how dare I question the ultimate warrior, Jude Dagan.*

"I need to hear the words, Jude," she admitted.

"We're safe, Ella. I won't let anything hurt you ever again."

"Not a promise you can make," she countered.

"You don't think I can keep you safe?" Oh, the affront in his voice!

"I don't think you have to. I've done enough to stay alive the last year, Jude. All you're doing by keeping me here is making things exponentially more impossible for me."

He grunted. "They were impossible before you left with Dresden in Beirut. I'm trying to keep you alive."

"And mine my secrets in the process? Come on, Jude, let's be honest. The only reason you've got me here is because I've become your mission. King wants answers. Endgame wants Dresden's head. What none of you seem to realize is that there is more in play here!" Ella slammed her hand down on the table and stood up, leaning over the table to get in his face. "I can keep myself alive. It's *you* I'm worried about!"

He stared up at her, his gaze moving over her face, his expression giving her nothing. She had never yelled at Jude. Ever.

But she wasn't the same Ella anymore.

"Sit down and finish eating," he said softly. He picked up his fork and did the same, ignoring her outburst as if it'd never happened.

She plopped back into her chair, picked up her spoon, and ate. Silence reigned through the rest of the meal. When Ella finished, she picked up her bowl and carried it to the sink, washing it and her spoon before putting them in the drying rack. She attacked the rest of the dishes and finished them off. As she was drying her hands, Jude came up behind her.

His hands settled on the granite countertop at her sides, his front pressing against her back. His heat wrapped around her as his scent toyed with her emotions. "Let's establish the rules right now," he said at her ear, his voice gruff and hitting her right between the legs. "I don't need you to keep me safe. I don't need your protection. I need your cooperation. I need your secrets. Because, Ella? You're mine. You have been since the moment I saw you, and you always will be. It is my right, my goddamn *privilege*, to take care of you. And if I have to fight you to do that, then by God, I will. I've been waging wars for a long time, lady, and when I fight, I win. You're too important for me to walk away from."

Her head fell back against his shoulder, and he took advantage, breathing his fire across her neck. She swore she felt the tip of his tongue on her skin. She went molten. "Don't do this to me, Jude. I begged you in Russia, and I'm begging you here."

"It's too late to beg. The game is in play, has been since you began working Dresden. The difference is that I know I'm a major player now."

"You don't know what you're asking me for," she whispered desperately.

"I'm asking you…for you, Ella. Your lies, your truths, and everything in between."

Her heart climbed out of her chest and sank to his feet. "The rules?"

"Nothing but truth from now on. If you don't want to answer me, tell me, but always give me the truth," he answered, biting the tendon that ran from her neck to the shoulder.

Ella hissed in a breath as lust speared her midsection.

"What else?" she questioned him breathlessly.

"Truth in everything, Ella. That's the only rule," he said against her skin.

"Is sex on the game board?" She had to know what was in his mind and, for the life of her, was too afraid to ask him.

"Fucking is always on the board between us, beautiful lady."

Well, then. Fucking was the same as making love to Jude. He'd gone to great lengths one night to prove that to him, when he was with Ella, there was zero difference.

God, the pleasure she'd had in his arms. It had sustained her these long months without him.

"If I give you the truth, you have to do the same."

He smiled, and she felt the curve against her ear. "I'm not the one who's lied here, Ella."

She pushed a hand to her chest. His truths were already painful. "I'm fooling myself...allowing myself to be placated with my desires." Who was she talking to?

"I appreciate that truth, Ella. To know that you desire me is a relief, considering how far you've gone to show me otherwise. But I don't want the waters muddied too much. As you stated, there's too much at stake here. Fucking you has always been my greatest joy. Loving you my greatest reward. I'll do what I can to keep my hands off you, but I can't promise. My body needs yours, but my soul needs your secrets just as much."

Then he stepped away from her and walked out of the kitchen.

Ella blew out a rough breath, gathered her wits, and finished cleaning up the kitchen. Fatigue pulled at her. With her belly full and the warmth of the cabin tugging at her, she made her way back upstairs to the room she'd woken in.

Chapter 14

ELLA STARED OUT THE WINDOW FROM THE BIG recliner, watching the fat flakes fall from an ebony sky and contemplating her next moves. She'd gone back and forth with herself for hours about whether she should just unload the truth on Jude and let the chips fall where they may. Her gut said to do it.

Her training, her word to the Piper, said don't.

Where did training end and loving Jude begin? Was it that easy?

He was her teammate, and there was every possibility the Piper was playing games with them all, reaching for a conclusion he wanted for reasons that weren't quite as virtuous as he'd portrayed to Ella in the beginning.

She was tired but not sleepy. She hadn't seen Jude since he'd left the kitchen earlier. She had no idea where he was or what he was doing.

Jude had taught her how to love. How to trust. The Piper had taught her how to survive.

She was missing something in the puzzle though. She traced back over what she did know, ticking off every fact she'd amassed over the last year. Horace Dresden was a monster who needed to be eliminated. Endgame had been brought on two years ago to effect that outcome for the Piper. The Piper was the chairman of the

Joint Chiefs of Staff. He'd served as the highest-ranking
official in the military world for a long time and had the
ear of the Secretary of Defense and the President of the
United States. He had so many contacts in the world
of intelligence that he was probably more powerful
than any CIA or FBI director. And he had a hard-on for
Horace Dresden, the reasons beginning to seem entirely
too personal for Ella's liking.

And why did she think that? Well, there was the matter
of his daughters, Cameron Markov and Anna Beth Caine,
former fiancée to Horace Dresden.

Ella needed her laptop. Hell, what she really needed
to do was pick Vivi Granger's brain and resources.
Nobody infiltrated information like Vivi. Ella was good,
but not Vivi good.

The Piper had originally wanted to put her into
Dresden's organization so he could watch Dresden from
the inside. He'd seen a way to do that when Endgame
Ops team's mission in Beirut went bad. He'd been lucky
they'd survived the rocket-propelled grenade that had
taken down the helicopter. He'd hit the jackpot when
Dresden hadn't allowed Savidge to kill Ella.

There were so many things the Piper hadn't been able
to control on that mission—so many potential outcomes,
most of them really bad—that his willingness to go
ahead and give up Endgame stank of desperation. There
was also the possibility he hadn't given up Endgame;
he'd just gone with the flow.

And now Ella understood why. His daughters were
on the playing field too. What was the Piper's endgame? She'd only be able to figure it out if she knew
his motivation.

Ella bit a nail as she ruminated. She really needed her laptop and a sat phone.

"Stop biting your nails," Jude said from the doorway.

Ella allowed her smile to show as she turned her head to look at him. His arms were raised, his hands holding on to the doorjamb as he leaned casually with one leg bent at the knee. He'd showered and now wore jeans and a long-sleeved dark-green T-shirt. A sliver of tanned, muscled abdomen peeked out at her. There was something so innately sexy about that space between his jeans and the bottom of his shirt that she had no choice.

She licked her lips.

His gaze zeroed in on her movement, and he licked his own.

She almost groaned.

"I need to borrow a satellite phone," she told him.

Jude started to shake his head, but she cleared her throat. His gaze snagged on hers, and he stopped.

"Seriously. I need one now. There's a woman in trouble, and somehow, some way, I need to get word to someone to help her."

"Who?" he asked succinctly.

"Brody would be nice," Ella responded, mentally crossing her fingers that Jude would let her contact the man who'd helped her survive Dresden.

It took him a long moment of staring her down, but eventually he left and returned with a satellite phone.

"Do not tell him where you are. Make it quick," Jude demanded.

"You're bossier than His Highness," Ella muttered.

"Brody is speed dial number 4."

Ella hit 4 and waited.

"Yo, Keeper. What's up?" Brody's broken voice was music to Ella's ears.

"It's me, Brody," Ella said around threatening tears.

What they had been through together…sometimes it promised to rise up and choke Ella.

"Goddamn it, Ella-Bella! You haven't contacted me in a week! A week! Where the hell are you?"

Ella smiled. Brody took that whole handler moniker pretty seriously. When the Piper discovered Brody had survived as well, he'd immediately recruited her big teammate to become her handler. Once he'd agreed, Brody couriered information between the Piper and Ella when they were unable to meet in person. He'd also stepped up into the role of bodyguard. Hence the anger she was getting from him now.

"Stop yelling at me, Madoc. Big girl here. I've got this," she told him firmly.

"Then what do you need? Word on the street is that you've left Dresden, and he's got the hard-on of all hard-ons looking for you. Where are you, Ella?"

"Safe," she whispered, sneaking a glance at Jude.

He made a wrap-it-up motion with his hand.

"Look, Dresden has a woman in the cellars. She needs evac immediately, Brody. He's going to end up killing her if we don't get to her soon," Ella pushed out.

"I need more than that, Ella. Who is this woman? Why is she important?" Brody asked.

"Hurry up, El," Jude growled, now standing in front of her.

"I don't have time for that now. Do what you do, Brody. I'm going to send you some information when I disconnect, and I'll touch base with you in a few hours and give you more. Right now, I need you either prepping a resource or getting your ass to Ukraine to help her yourself."

"Damn it," Brody said on a heavy sigh. "You're a pain in my ass, Banning."

"One more thing, Madoc." Ella breathed out. "Tell the Piper that Dresden has Anna. He'll know who you're talking about. Hell, he may even give you the details I haven't amassed yet because that's the woman Dresden has in the cellar. Ring this phone once you've landed in Ukraine, okay?"

"You owe me, dropping this in my lap and hanging up," Brody said darkly. Then, "It's good to hear your voice. I worry."

"No need, Madoc. We've survived worse."

Ella disconnected and let out a long breath.

"I need a laptop," she said baldly.

"No." Simple answer.

It pissed her off, his continuous resistance to letting her have the tools she needed to do her job. "I need a laptop, Jude," she reiterated.

"No," he answered again.

"Damn it, Jude!" she said, coming to her feet in a rush.

He walked into the room and stopped in front of her. "Give me a truth, Ella."

She huffed. "I need a laptop. There's a truth for you," she bit out in frustration.

He laughed at her and then reached for her, tracing her lower lip with his forefinger. Then he stepped closer to her, bringing them chest to chest. "Why do you need a laptop? And what's going on with this mystery woman Brody needs to save?"

"I need to search, and I'll tell you everything once I

have it all together," she replied automatically, the need to find the truth damn near making her shudder. Or was that the proximity to Jude? Both maybe?

Yes.

"For what?" he asked, continuing to trace her lip.

"Huh?"

"What do you need to search for?" he asked again.

She stomped her foot. "You're like a dog with a bone!"

"Only if the bone is five four and curvy as hell, with eyes that melt like frost in the sun," he responded calmly.

"Do you have any chocolate?" she asked suddenly.

He threw back his head and laughed. "Yes."

"I need it and the laptop. Meet me in the living room," she demanded before she headed to the bathroom.

He caught her hand as she tried to pass, and before she could blink, his lips were on hers.

"Open up to me," he pleaded.

She did.

He moved so gently, his lips covering her in a whisper, his tongue tracing, licking. It was nothing like the kiss they'd shared in Moscow. That had been heat and need and anger. Desperation.

This one was soft, pleading, holding too much emotion for words. He sipped at her, careful of her bruised face, loving her lips even as his tongue requested permission to enter her mouth completely.

She gave it, sucking on him, tasting him. She heard herself moan, felt his body harden, and knew she was going to lose herself to him.

Wait, he demanded only truth, and that had to begin with herself. She had to acknowledge this truth—that she was already lost.

He pulled away slowly and made his way out of the room with a husky chuckle. Ella went into the bathroom, ran some cold water, and splashed her face. She needed to cool down, get her mind right. Eventually, she took the same path Jude had, still in the fog of the heat he built in her so effortlessly as she slowly descended the stairs.

She stopped on a step and watched him. He sat on one of the leather couches, and on the low coffee table in front of him sat a laptop and a Hershey bar. His big body leaned back against the leather as if he hadn't a care in the world, and the vixen in her responded. Yes, she had responsibilities—Anna Beth Caine, finding out who was controlling Dresden, figuring out what the Piper was doing—and they weighed on her. But she needed this with Jude. She needed what she found inside his arms to cement her to the present and make everything real.

His chest rose and fell as his fingers drummed on the back of the couch. His eyes were closed, the black depths of them hidden to her. She could lose herself in him for a little while—remember her reason for setting out on her journey a year ago. It was all about Jude.

Need thrummed through her, poignant and heartbreaking. She knew what she had to do. Slowly, she reached up and pulled her hair down from its ponytail. Ella wasn't as weak as he thought her to be.

And she was about to put something on him he'd never forget.

It was late. She should be asleep, resting to refuel her body and heal. Instead she was up, thinking, plotting. Jude could practically smell it on her. She only bit her nails when she had a puzzle to solve—it was the analyst in her. She hated conundrums and had to solve them, determine every last piece and its place, before her brain would give her rest.

She'd demanded a satellite phone. He'd given it to her when everything in him said not to. He didn't want a soul knowing anything about her or her whereabouts. He'd given in because his Ella was fierce when she demanded something. Then she wanted a laptop.

He sighed and rubbed his eyes. He'd give her his, but only after he knew what she was searching for. Give and take. That's what they were now. Until he could trust her anyway. Or until she trusted him.

And now she walked toward him like every wet dream he'd ever had. Dressed in sweats and one of his ratty New Mexico State sweatshirts, with beautiful dark-chestnut hair down around her shoulders, she was a vision. He didn't even see the bruises on her face, because all he knew was Ella.

His cock hardened behind his fly. Instead of acting on it, he nodded to the laptop. She looked conflicted for a few seconds but eventually grabbed the computer and sat across from him. Within two minutes, she'd handled whatever business she'd needed to—and he'd be asking her about that shortly—before closing the laptop.

She stood once again, teeth worrying her lower lip, tongue sliding along the curve of it. Heat flowed into his extremities, and he sat forward. But she didn't hesitate, coming directly to him and pushing his shoulders until he reclined once again, before she climbed up onto his lap.

Goddamn.

She sank against him, aligning her core with his

jean-covered hardness and rotating her hips just once. She played the move off as if she was simply settling, but he knew her. Knew her wants. Knew how she moved.

She tugged on his T-shirt until he lifted it over his head, and then her hands were all over him, stroking down his pecs, nails scraping his nipples. He groaned and she laughed, the sound a spear to his midsection because it was so damn sexy. His fingers flexed on her thighs, and she bit her lip. Then she settled her hands on his shoulders, fingers digging in, yet another indication of her need.

Ella lowered her head to his, her mouth hovering over his, sweet breath fanning his face. "Let me give you a truth, Jude."

He moved his hands to her hips, and he nearly gave in to the temptation to move her over him, back and forth, until they both yelled in release. "I'm here," he said in lieu of acting on his baser urge.

"You were the last thing I saw before Savidge shot me. I watched your face, saw your horror, and knew I was about to die. You were my last thought before my new existence began."

He hissed in a breath, pain knifing his gut, rendering him incapacitated in the face of her words. "What was it?"

She cocked her head, still hovering right at his lips, so close he could taste her. "What was what?"

"Your last thought."

Another infinitesimal centimeter eliminated as she lowered even more, hips fully cradling him now, fingers still digging in deep. "I love you."

God, he'd never experienced pain like what she'd just

given him. It was horrible. It was beautiful. Her truth was redemption. He lifted, taking her mouth firmly, swiftly moving to her neck, licking, tasting any inch of her skin she'd allow.

His hands took over, moving her over his hardness, seeking to meld it into her skin. She moaned, and he answered her with a harsh groan. He pushed her sweatshirt up, then her bra, then he just looked at her.

He'd uncovered smooth, creamy skin. His. All his. "Mine," he growled. He watched her eyes as he lowered his mouth to her breast. Then she closed those gray orbs with irises like shattered glass, and he took her nipple in his mouth. She cried out as if her need were a violent thing seeking escape. Her hands settled in his hair, tugging, pulling, pushing.

He smiled against her, and then he let himself do nothing but feel—the softness of her skin, the pebble of her nipple, the ripest, sweetest of berries. He kissed the area over her heart before he began laving attention on each mound, unable to pull away, her cries in his ears, her taste and smell dominating his senses.

Her hips writhed over his even as he pushed up, trying to alleviate the bittersweet pain in his cock.

He reached for the drawstring of the sweatpants and lifted her slightly as he pushed the pants and her panties down one leg, baring her to his gaze. Her downy brownish-black curls taunted him. He gazed at her there, splayed over his lap, legs on either side of his, pussy open and hot. He could feel her heat through his jeans and wanted nothing more than to release his cock and impale her on it, move her over him until they both released.

Reverence slid through him, peaceful and calming.

His need didn't abate, but for this moment, he would please her and show her everything he felt for her with his mouth and hands.

"Please," she whispered brokenly.

He'd heard that word from her too much. She'd never beg him for anything else ever again.

Slowly, half afraid it was all a dream, he moved his hand to her opening, sliding a single finger through her folds until the center of her heat was *right there*. He touched her, her wetness coating his finger, easing his way inside her body. Her hips moved, allowing him greater access.

She opened like a flower above him. So much heat. He wanted to taste her there, but with her head thrown back, her chest flushed, and his need hammering at him, he needed her to finish before he blew his top.

One finger surrounded by her warmth. Her body milked him, and he added a finger. Her breath blew out roughly, and she keened softly. Her head bowed, hair hiding her face from him as her chin came to rest on her bunched-up sweatshirt. With his other hand, he pushed her back until he could wrap his hand gently around her neck, holding her head up so he could watch her eyes as she exploded. Her hair was silk against his skin.

Had he ever wanted this badly?

With one hand between her legs and one around her neck, Jude worked Ella. She was so damn tight, clenching and releasing around his fingers. He sank deep, hitting the spot he'd longed for, and her eyes closed.

"Open them," he demanded.

Her mouth opened first, on a gasp saturated with sex and desire. Her eyes followed, locking on his, and in them was every emotion he'd missed from her during the last year—need, love, joy, pain, frustration, followed quickly by need again. She was spiraling tighter, her body moving faster on his hand, her chest rising and falling, her nipples hard and begging for his mouth.

His tortured cock cursed him. Through it all, he watched her. Ella. His lady. The absolute love of his life.

"Give me another truth, Ella," he ordered, his tone soft but uncompromising. "I need your truths, baby."

"There are too many," she pushed out around a moan.

"Give me the most important one," he pleaded.

Her body rippled, their fire burning her up from the inside out. He scissored his fingers once and then swirled her wetness around her clit. One more entrance into her body, one caress of his index finger against her chin, and Ella gave in, crying out in her pleasure, her body undulating as it sought the last vestiges of pleasure from his hand.

She never looked away from him, their gazes locked, and in that moment he was both proud of her strength and humbled that she'd given herself over to him. She was magnificent in her release.

Slowly, because this was part of his reward for not taking more than she was ready to give him, he brought his hand to his mouth and licked his fingers. "Beautiful," he said when finished.

"You'll take it all, won't you?" she asked.

He nodded. "But don't worry, Ella. I'll give it back tenfold."

It was a vow from his heart.

She collapsed against his chest and snuggled, legs still spread over his, her core against him once again.

She fit so perfectly in his arms. God, he'd missed this. More than being inside her, just holding her, being wrapped up in her.

He shook his head and wiped his eyes.

"Another truth, hmm?" she asked and sounded as if she was moments away from sleep.

"Yeah, I'm ready," he told her. "Give it to me, El."

"I dream of you, even when I'm awake. I never let you go, Jude."

Her voice was so low that he wondered if she'd said what he thought she had.

A shuddering breath left her limp against him, and he knew she'd gone to sleep.

With her words, she put a piece of him back in place. It was a piece he'd been missing since she'd "died." He somehow managed to get her pants completely off, and then he started to work on her shirt. Once he'd removed those and her bra, he settled her against him and then lay down with her.

Jude pulled the throw over them both and finally relaxed. A sigh escaped him at the skin-to-skin contact. Outside, the wind howled and the sky wept snow. Inside, Jude held his woman in his arms. For now, his world was right.

Chapter 15

HIS HANDS WERE EMPTY. THAT WAS HIS FIRST THOUGHT upon waking. As empty as they'd been during the last year, and that was unacceptable. He came up in a rush, hands fisting, gaze cataloging the entire room. Empty.

Where was Ella?

He glanced out the window, noticed dawn was just breaking over the mountains and that it was still snowing. A sneeze sounded from somewhere in the direction of the kitchen. Jude followed the sound and found the reason why his hands were empty.

Ella, head buried in his pantry, gorgeous ass in the air, hummed softly. "You know what, kitty, I don't see any food for you," she said as she stood up and backed out of the pantry. "I guess—" She stopped when she spotted him, a wry smile curving her split lips.

She was so lovely. She'd obviously showered and was dressed in a fresh pair of his sweats, another New Mexico State sweatshirt covering her torso. Jude wanted to rip it off her.

"When did you get a cat?" she asked him, a saucy note in her voice.

"I didn't," he said, glancing at the tortoiseshell-colored feline.

"She was at the door when I opened—"

He crossed his arms over his chest. "Why were you opening the door?"

She didn't respond.

"Ella? Give me the truth," he demanded.

"Perimeter check, okay? I did a perimeter check," she told him, raising her chin a notch.

Shock ran through him, followed closely by anger. "You went out into that weather dressed like that?"

Her gaze narrowed, sparks flying from her winter-gray eyes. "I put on shoes."

"She put on shoes," he muttered. "It's ten below out there, Ella. We're in the mountains, and it's snowing. You need more than just shoes!" Why was he yelling?

"Stop yelling at me. Someone had to do a perimeter check. Your ass was out stone-cold on the couch," she reminded him.

"We're safe," he said firmly. "I wouldn't have you anywhere you weren't completely safe."

She moved to the cat that wasn't his and began absently petting the animal. The cat preened underneath her hands. Jude wanted those hands on him.

"You and I both know that nowhere is completely safe, Jude," she said patiently. "And if this cat isn't yours, where'd it come from?"

"No clue. Put it out," Jude snapped.

She eyeballed him and crossed her arms over her chest, clearly mimicking his action. "No."

"What?" He would never make the cat go outside in this weather, but damn—did she have to fight him on everything?

"Jesus, what's your problem, Jude?"

He lowered his hand and cradled his hard cock, raising an eyebrow mockingly.

She threw back her head and laughed out loud. Her

laugh moved him just as irrevocably as her orgasm had last night. A year without her. He'd been half dead when he saw her in Beirut a few weeks ago. Right now, in this moment, he needed to go to his knees and thank whoever was listening upstairs that she was alive and with him.

"Poor baby. You didn't handle that last night?" she asked coyly, lowering her hands and sauntering over to him.

He shook his head and waved his fingers. "Why go imitation when the real thing is naked and snuggled right there against you?"

She ran a finger down his arm, across his abs and then lower, stopping near his belt buckle, waiting for what Jude had no idea. "Jude, Jude, Jude, you poor, neglected man. Give me a truth, why don't you?"

She was going to play it that way, huh?

"I want my dick buried inside your pussy so bad I could probably hammer nails with it right now," he told her with a smile.

"I guess one truth deserves another, doesn't it?" she asked him, unbuckling his belt, and slowly, so slowly, unzipping his pants. The only thing between her hand and his cock was the cotton of his boxer briefs.

"It really does," he affirmed with a nod of his head. "Hurry up."

She laughed, the sound entirely too serious to be joyful, then leaned up on her tiptoes. This put her lips right at his ear. "When Dresden had me strung up in chains, the only thing that got me through was remembering your taste."

"Goddamn it, Ella. Don't do that. Don't bring him here," he begged her.

"He's always here now. I'll tell you everything, Jude. You just have to give me time, okay?"

His cock had softened with her words. There was no pleasure for him when her pain was right there bared between them. He moved to fold her into his arms, but she pulled back.

"Jude, that was only part of my truth," she said, eyes shining with tears.

He stilled. "Then give it to me, woman. I can handle anything you give me."

She held her head up, looking him straight in the eyes. "Ella, you don't have to—" he began.

"No," she stated emphatically. "You'll give me this, and I'll give you what truths I can."

He fisted his hands. "Not this way, baby."

"All my body had was pain, but my heart and my soul had...*you*. You were a phantom covering me, protecting me, always there with me. All I had were memories. Last night, you gave me all of you, taking nothing for yourself. Here's my truth, Jude. There's not been a step I've taken during the last year that wasn't for you. There's not been a thought I've had that you weren't immersed inside of. Not a breath I took that wasn't with the sole purpose of getting back to you, saving you."

He closed his eyes against the pain in hers. Then he opened them because not witnessing this was akin to denying her suffering, and while he had no idea what had been done to her, he was willing to let her take from him again and again and again if it eased her.

"You saved me, Jude. And all I can give you right now are the pieces of me that aren't bargained away to a monster. Will you take what I can give you?" she asked plaintively.

"No," he said. "But I'll start with that."

She took his hand and led him past the cat that now lounged on Jude's countertop, watching them cautiously. She led him up the stairs, her tiny hand in his, her body calling to him. She led him to his bedroom, where she slowly removed her clothes and took down her hair. Then she looked at him and smiled.

"I want you. That never changed and probably never will. I need you. Something else that will remain unchanged for millennia, I've no doubt." She brushed a hand over his chest and down to his hip. "I need your cock inside me, driving out the darkness and leaving room for nothing but you, Jude. That's the rest of my truth, right here, right now."

Jude felt the weight lift off his soul. He had no way of knowing if what they were about to do was being done in the correct order. There was so much unresolved between them. But his body recognized her need and demanded he meet that need with his own.

So whether it was right or not, it was absolutely what they both needed. He was going to let her take from him, and then he'd take from her in turn. In the taking they would both give and strengthen the bond that had stood unbroken the last year.

There would be no sun today, only gray skies that would pour forth their frozen wonder. The room was darker than he'd like, so he flipped on a switch and watched as the yellow glow flowed over her creamy skin. He noticed her flushed chest and peaked nipples, and the frantic pulse at the base of her neck.

The mountains outside his window would crumble before he stopped loving this woman. The sky would fall into the ocean before he stopped needing her.

He removed his T-shirt, sat down on the edge of the bed, and untied his boots before toeing them off, and then he removed his jeans and brief in one motion. "Turn around," he instructed her, grimacing at the gravelly sound of his voice.

Her eyes widened, fear darkening the depths before she tugged her lower lip into her mouth. He motioned with his hand for her to do as he bade.

Slowly, reluctantly, she turned around, facing the floor-to-ceiling windows that stared out into the freezing day. He approached her stealthily, like a cat about to pounce. He wanted her to feel his determination and strength, and he wanted her to be soothed by it, not scared.

Goose bumps broke out over her skin. He knew her nipples had furled tighter, wanted them in his mouth but bit back the lash of that particular want before he overwhelmed her.

With four strides he was at her back, nose in her hair, inhaling her fragrance and letting it calm him. He raised a hand and stroked it from her neck to her shoulder and then down her arm. "Your skin is so soft," he whispered gutturally. "I used to watch you get ready and wonder what the hell you were doing to make it so damn silky. Every night I've been able to sleep since you've been gone, I've woken up with the feel of you on my palms."

He kissed her shoulder and then placed both of his hands on her back. He moved them out to her sides, back up, and then down to the dip of her hips. The raised surfaces on her back told him a story of unimaginable pain and anguish. Her gorgeous flesh sliced open intentionally to hurt and maim. He lowered his mouth and kissed each scar, licking the length of every mark until he was on his knees behind her, his head bowed and resting at the curve of her back.

"I'll know what happened eventually, but Ella, you should know that every mark I've just kissed is a mark of courage. They taste of strength and resolve. They are as much a part of you as the skin I love to touch and the hair I love to feel on my chest when you sleep. They're reminders that you survived...that you held on to come back to me. I used to watch you enter a room and remember every second of every time I'd had you under my mouth. Nothing has changed for me. Every night I've been able to sleep since you've been gone, I've woken up with your taste sliding down my throat."

He turned her, coming to his feet as he felt the hot drops of her tears on his skin. He brushed them away from her cheeks before licking them from his fingers. He buried his hands in her hair and stared down at her.

"I dreamed of you when I was awake too, Ella. I dreamed of your eyes always finding me across a crowded room. I remembered your laugh when Micah or Chase teased you. I remembered your sighs when I slid so deep inside you there was no line marking where I began and you ended. I dreamed at night too. And every night I've been able to sleep since you've been gone, I've woken up with your name on my lips."

A broken sob escaped her as she reached for him, climbing up his body until she had her legs wrapped around his hips and her face against his throat. She shook so hard Jude thought she'd fly apart.

So he held her tighter. And when she kissed his collarbone, he knew she was ready for him, for them.

He placed her on the bed, the dark plaid of the duvet cover a benevolent canvas for Ella's perfection. She'd changed in subtle ways over the last year. She was thinner, though her breasts still overflowed his big hands. Her waist was tucked tighter, making her hips seem to flare even more. Her legs were long, thighs curving just right into slim calves. She was small-boned, and he was struck anew that she'd managed to survive as an operative.

She was so damn breakable.

She reached for him, and he followed her down, cataloging every breath and gasp, feeling her body give under his, welcoming.

"Love me, Jude," she whispered.

"There's nothing else for me to do, El," he responded.

She cupped his cheek, pulling him to her mouth. She arched up into his body, demanding he move faster, give her more. But it was the first time in a year that he'd had her under him. There was no rushing this.

"Slow, Ella. Let me love you slowly." Then he proceeded to do just that.

He stroked her flesh, tongued her hills and hollows, pressed against her skin until the heat between them made them one. He kissed her mouth, tugging on the curve of her lower lip until she hissed in a rough breath. He licked her neck, bit down on the spot he knew she loved, and felt her belly contract.

She tugged at his hair, stroked his chest, and sank her nails deep into the muscles there. She leaned up and licked his nipple. His balls drew up tight, and he had to hold himself still to stave off his orgasm.

"Do that again, and this will go much faster than either of us want," he growled down at her.

She smiled, a sweet curving of her lips, sexy and so blinding he wanted to howl. She arched up again, and he used his palm to push her back down. "No. I'm going to be inside you when I come, and I'll be feeling you contracting around my cock as I do it."

She reached between them and stroked him. He felt the heat of her pussy so close, so tempting. She wrapped her fist around him and squeezed. His eyes crossed. "Damn, woman!"

She laughed. "You're moving too slowly. I need you, Jude. Come inside me."

She bent her knees, held on to his shoulders, and pushed up with her hips, her velvet sheath seeking his steel.

She was a siren, and he couldn't deny her any longer. He allowed her to lead him to her precipice.

"I love you," she said, and her voice rang out in the silence of the room.

"Always," he responded as he sank deeply with one thrust.

He stilled and stayed that way for long moments, allowing her body to adjust to the intrusion of his. His muscles locked—the joy of being back inside her so absolute that his blood sang. His heart clicked into place, and his body began a slow dance with hers. Stroke, retreat, lick, kiss, repeat.

He lifted her leg and pushed it toward her chest, opening her so he could settle deeper in the cradle of her hips, hitting her clit as he entered her, sliding home.

Their breaths mingled, heat rose, their scents peppering the air with a fragrance that was all them.

She pleaded with him to never stop. He vowed he wouldn't. She pleaded for him to finish her. He promised he would.

Over and over, their bodies met, melting into each other before moving apart, his cock leaving her warm haven only to return home time and time again. The pressure at the base of his spine built. Her moans became jagged pleas, and still the wave of their desire rose. The headboard banged against the wall, sweat slicked their skin, and light coalesced behind his eyelids.

"Come with me," he demanded of her.

"I am," she mouthed, though no sound escaped her.

Pleasure reached its crescendo, peaking inside them and spreading out, offering bliss beyond anything Jude had ever known. Every sense he had heightened as he came. He watched her pupils dilate as the pleasure pulled her under. The draw of her pussy walls on his cock forced his release to go on and on until he felt wrung dry but born anew.

He had no idea how he found the strength to hold himself off her enough so she could breathe, but the thought of pulling out of her and moving off her body wasn't one he was comfortable with. So he stayed where he was, arms shaking as he gave her enough room to draw breath but not separate from her.

He rested his forehead on hers.

"That was…" Her words drifted off.

"Yeah, I'm pretty amazing," he said with a small laugh. "You ready?"

She opened her eyes and stared up at him. "For what?"

He slowly pulled out of her. They both groaned at the feel of his cock leaving her snug confines. It was an ecstasy all its own.

"For that," he answered, and even he heard the smugness of his tone.

He rolled over onto his back and she followed him, snuggling into his side as if she couldn't bear to be parted from him for any length of time.

"You're full of yourself," she said with a laugh.

"Yeah, but just a second ago you were full of me too."

She snickered. It had always been effortless between them.

"I forgot that humility was never your greatest attribute," she mumbled sleepily.

"Is it vain to know I please the hell out of my woman?" he asked, covering his eyes with his forearm. He would love a nap.

"Nah, but you could at least make an effort to be humble. Gloating is not your best look," she pointed out.

Her hands stroked his chest, running through the light mat of hair on his chest. They'd once had a discussion about hairy chests versus hairless and which she preferred. He'd been prepared to have every bit of hair on his chest waxed off if that's what she wanted. "I prefer you," she'd told him, and it had been the perfect answer.

"My best look is on top of my woman," he responded.

"Or your woman on top of you," she quipped. "Let's try that next."

He peeked out from under his forearm. "I'm ready when you are."

She opened a single eye, reached under the duvet

he'd brought over them, cupped his semihard cock, and then she smirked. "Sure."

He laughed and pulled her closer. "Keep your hand right there, baby, and it'll take no time."

She wrapped one of her legs over his, draped her arm around his chest, and rested her head on his shoulder. "A truth," she offered.

"I'm ready."

"You took him away. The feel of Savidge's hands on me, the feel of the blade he used, it's gone. That's my truth right now."

His heart stopped for a split second. "Good."

Within minutes, she was asleep.

He felt something bounce on the bed and raised his head. The stray cat she'd let into his house sat at their feet, staring at him. "Stop looking at me. She'll be awake soon, and she'll find you something to eat."

The cat continued to look at him.

"Seriously," Jude complained. "Go away."

Ella made a sound at being disturbed, and Jude held her tighter.

There was no telling where they'd be at emotionally when they both woke up, but right now, they were where they were supposed to be.

Chapter 16

THE WIND HOWLING WOKE ELLA. OR MAYBE IT WAS the demons chasing her in her sleep. Whatever it was, she woke before Jude. They faced each other, only inches separating them, their legs tangled beneath the covers. She relished the feel of his hairy legs against her smooth ones, the heat of him seeping inside her cold soul, warming her.

Nina had once said that Jude was like a burly bear of a man—not attractive by any stretch of the imagination but sexy as hell. Ella had laughed at the comparison but frowned at her friend's description of Jude as "not attractive." To Ella, he was the most beautiful man she'd ever seen. She knew his crooked nose and scars took away from any prettiness his face may have once promised, but his features were a gorgeous picture, giving insight into who Jude was before he ever said a word.

Of course Nina had also said Jude had the finest body she'd ever seen. Ella had been kinda pissed because that meant Nina had been *looking* at her man. Ella remembered Nina laughing at the expression on her face.

Ella hadn't even realized she was possessive until she'd opened herself to the man sleeping in front of her. She'd seen him, met his gaze, and everything inside her had gone silent, accepting that she had just met the man who would own every piece of her.

She wasn't fanciful. She'd grown up on the streets

of Chicago, moving from one foster home to another, somehow managing to do well enough in school to skip a couple of grades, graduate from high school early, and go to college on a scholarship.

She'd gone to Stanford University on a full-ride scholarship, graduating with honors and a double major—in foreign languages and in international finance. She'd dabbled in computer programming and knew just enough to be dangerous. It was while at Stanford that she'd drawn the notice of the CIA. Her story was much like any of the other analysts she'd talked to. The CIA recruited heavily at colleges, though they did it quietly and hardly ever drew notice.

Ella had always known she was a throwaway person. She had no discernible history, had a certain set of skills valuable to the agency, and nobody would miss her if she left or disappeared.

Her memories of her parents were vague at best—a feeling of love, a memory of gardenias and cigar smoke, but that was all she had of them. She'd formed no lasting relationships in any of her foster homes or at school.

When she saw Jude, everything in her world had clicked into place. He became her home so fast she hadn't even noticed the feeling of impending doom until the Piper approached her about a mission within a mission.

Ella had spent every day of the last year regretting that she hadn't told Jude as soon as the Piper had come to her. But she'd been so afraid that Jude was in danger, and she was the only one who could prevent Dresden from going after him. She wanted to hate Noah Caine for manipulating her by using her love for Jude. She should hate him. She'd taken the Piper's bait with barely any lure.

And she and Jude had both paid for it.

This man who'd taken her body yesterday—twice, and made her toes curl and her heart sing—was so precious to her.

And regardless of what Nina or anyone else thought, he was the most perfect-looking man in the history of men. She smiled at her musings.

When he slept, he was even more so. Something about sleep allowed his rough edges to smooth out. He looked younger than his thirty-two years and definitely not as burdened.

The shutters rattled against the wooden frame of the cabin, and Ella wondered how much longer she could burrow here, hiding from her responsibilities. Despite regretting that she'd taken this mission from the Piper, she had to finish it. The need to get Anna Beth Caine away from Dresden and safe was like a drumbeat in Ella's skull.

Dresden had to be taken down from the inside, and that plan could now be in great peril. By her estimation, she'd been out of contact with him for two entire days. She needed that computer. Hell, she needed a satellite phone again. She needed to make contact with the Piper as well.

Ella eased from the bed, watching for any sign Jude had woken. Once she pulled her clothes on, she tied her hair up in a knot because her ponytail holder was somewhere on the floor and she didn't have much time.

She made her way gingerly down the stairs, nearly falling when the cat came bounding down after her. Whose cat was it?

Ella had no idea, but the weather was too cold and snowy to let the animal back into the wild. She found a can of Vienna sausages in the pantry, opened it. She chopped the tiny sausages into bite-size portions for the cat and placed them on a saucer. The cat attacked the food as if it hadn't eaten in a year.

She poured some water into a bowl and placed it beside the cat.

The cat stopped eating, looked up at her, blinked slowly, and went back to eating. "Girl," Ella said. "With that much attitude, you've gotta be a tough chick. I think I'm gonna call you Chica."

The cat sniffed delicately, which Ella took as approval.

Now that the cat was cared for, Ella walked to the den and located the computer on the coffee table. She knew Jude had a communications room somewhere in this house, but she didn't have time to search for it. She needed information now.

She opened the computer, again surprised to find no password protection. It was outfitted with security and encryption though, probably thanks to Vivi.

She made a cursory search of the databases on the hard drive, searching for Vivi's signature spying software. Ella found none, so she proceeded to the Internet. She'd only had time to send Brody a limited amount of information last night before Jude had pulled at her attention. She'd uploaded the information she had on Dresden's mansion in Ukraine, and then she'd disconnected. It had been quick.

The computer pinged a few times, searching for a secure connection, and once she had it, she looked up the date first. She'd been with Jude for *three* days. Damn.

That didn't bode well for Anna Beth Caine. But Brody was on it now. The woman had hope.

Next, Ella pulled up everything she could find on Noah Caine, a.k.a. the Piper. She scanned several entries, committing them to memory for later recollection and dissection. She had a nearly photographic memory and a propensity for languages. That's what had drawn the CIA's eye.

After that, she looked up Anna Beth Caine and found absolutely nothing. No mention of either Cameron or Anna Beth.

She pulled up Google and logged into one of her many Gmail accounts. She searched quickly for a response from Brody about the thumb drive she'd sent him the other day—the one she'd retrieved from the train station at Cameron Markov's behest. There was nothing from her teammate.

That foreboding feeling she'd felt during the last year returned in full force. Brody was a crack at deciphering code, and if he couldn't get it, he'd turn it over to Vivi. Ella had known the risk of Endgame getting the information before she did, but she'd felt the benefit outweighed that risk.

"Damn it," she said around her thumbnail.

She penned a quick email to Vivi Granger and had just wrapped it up when she felt, more than heard, Jude enter the room.

"Just couldn't wait, could you?" His voice held no small amount of accusation.

She looked over at him and noticed his shirtless chest and hooded gaze. Her hands itched to touch him, and her mouth watered for a taste. "I just emailed Vivi. If

I'm hiding anything from you, I'm sure she'll tell you what it is."

Jude walked over to her, taking the computer from her hands and placing it on the coffee table. He sat in front of her on that same table, just watching her.

"Can we eat first?" she asked.

"I could eat," he responded, face blank, tone equally so.

She nodded and stood. He grabbed her hips and held her in front of him. She glanced down, intent on asking him to let her go, but his words stopped her.

"I don't ever want to wake up without you in my bed. Ever again, Ella. Do you understand what I'm saying?"

Her heart melted into a great big puddle at his feet. She brushed his hair off his forehead. "Oh, Jude, I can't promise that."

"Just give me the words, Ella. I'll help you hold to them," he promised her.

"What you've yet to realize is that I'm always with you, Jude. You hold my heart in your chest. You have from the moment I saw you. Corny, right?" She laughed mirthlessly. "I've loved you from the first time our eyes met. You were as much of a storm in my life as the one raging outside."

He nodded and kissed her palm. "You don't know what it was like…" His voice trailed off, breaking at the end as his pain at her desertion communicated loud and clear.

"I don't. I left. I didn't give you what I should have, which was my trust. I'm responsible for that. I have to live with that for the rest of my life. But, Jude, until I've finished this, I can't make you any promises other than that I'll love you until the breath leaves my body."

He stood then and ran a hand through his hair. "Don't say that! Don't you talk about dying!"

She fell back to sitting on the couch. He stalked away from her, and she sat there accepting what she'd done to the man she loved and resolving to somehow fix what she'd torn apart.

Pans banged in the kitchen, and she followed the sounds.

He moved with contained violence. It shimmered in the air around him, but Ella wasn't afraid of her man. He was mad *for* her. Not *at* her.

He stopped what he was doing, dropping a pan on the floor as he stalked to her. "What is going on? Tell me right now."

"Let's eat first, Jude. A truth?" she queried softly.

He nodded once, his eyes burning into hers.

"I really need you to put a shirt on. And I'll make this truth a twofer. I'll tell you everything after we eat."

She had to. She'd waited too long already. After what he'd given her in that bedroom, she needed to shed any preconceived notions about protecting Jude. She'd hindered him way more than she'd ever protected him, and in the process, she'd nearly destroyed them both.

He drew in a deep breath, and she felt the violence recede. He ran upstairs and came back wearing a gray T-shirt. Jude walked over to the pot he'd dropped moments ago and picked it up.

"You want a really late breakfast or lunch?" he asked her cautiously.

"Lunch."

He nodded and began gathering the makings for lunch. She watched him as he moved, soaking up his presence like a sponge. God, what he did to her by simply breathing. She moved to the counter and began working alongside him as he heated up what looked like…

"Is that Tia Rosa's hot pepper chili?"

He grunted, which Ella took as a yes.

"Damn. Do you have Coronas?"

Another grunt.

"Hot damn, Jude! I needed this today!" Her mouth was already watering. She pushed him out of the way because he was taking too long to get the chili thawed and heated. "Grab some bread or something—get it sliced and toasted," she ordered as she stirred and adjusted the temperature beneath the simmering pot.

Ella heard him behind her, doing as she'd asked. It took him about five minutes to slice the bread, warm it, and set the table. Once the chili was ready, she placed the pot on the table. "Is there any butter?"

He pointed, still clearly wallowing in his anger. She couldn't blame him, so she didn't give him hell about it. She just pulled the butter from the mammoth refrigerator he'd pointed at and placed it beside the bread on the table.

"Beer, Jude? We must have beer," she told him.

He rolled his eyes, but another small smile tugged his lips up as he stood and opened a smaller fridge set into the island counter. He pulled out two beers and placed them on the table.

"Let's eat," Ella said enthusiastically.

Jude grunted again. Three grunts. She'd take that after being caught with his laptop.

She took the first bite, felt the warmth of the chili tickle her throat. She closed her eyes, savoring, and then the burn hit, tearing her eyes behind her lids, making her

This was going to be so damn hard.

"Just start somewhere, Ella. It'll come as it comes," Jude said gruffly.

Always, he cared for her. Even when he knew what she had to say was going to hurt him.

"The Piper approached me about four months after I joined Endgame." Her opening foray fell like bullets into the silence of the room. A log fell in the fireplace and popped, sending sparks outside the grate. Jude didn't move. Ella didn't either.

Instead, she locked her eyes on his and drew strength from him.

"He had concerns and information about Horace Dresden and some underground society comprised of influential leaders who were looking to take over the world—real Illuminati-type stuff." Ella glanced at the fire. Hearing her own words, she would have laughed had she not seen proof that what the Piper had described was very much a truth. They weren't Illuminati; they were much, much worse. "He had Endgame hot on Dresden's heels, but there was something he knew that he hadn't shared with the team yet. Dresden was a lynchpin. He was the head of his own organization, but he was also a key into that mysterious group the Piper kept hearing about. So he determined that he needed someone inside Dresden's organization.

"The Piper approached me shortly after Dresden went after Vivi. He told me he had inside information that Dresden was coming for everyone in Endgame, and he was going to start with you. He said that the only way I could protect you was to insert myself into Dresden's organization and divert his attention."

"Goddamn him," Jude bit out. He wasn't lounging against the back of the couch anymore. He was sitting upright, muscles tight, hands fisted.

"I fell hook, line, and sinker. All I could see, all I could hear, was that Dresden was coming for you, and I had the opportunity to stop him. I jumped in with both feet," she admitted.

"Goddamn you too," Jude said harshly.

She held up a hand. "I can't do this if you're going to do that. I need you to listen to me, Jude. Reserve your judgment until the end, okay?"

He nodded, but she could tell it cost him a lot. Poor man. He'd already paid too much.

She swallowed and took a cleansing breath. "The Piper had no particular plan he'd made me aware of, had said only that I needed to be diligent, and that when the time was right, he'd call me up. I told you in Russia I had no idea that op in Beirut was meant to insert me into Dresden's operation. And putting together everything now, I don't think the Piper planned it that way. But once I was down, he didn't do anything to get me out. He saw it as his way of obtaining an objective with minimal effort."

"He couldn't have known Dresden wouldn't kill you. It was too much of a risk," Jude bit out.

"Gray Broemig didn't know that either, but one of his main intentions of inserting me into Endgame was to pursue Dresden. He and the Piper were making the same moves." Ella bit her thumbnail and glanced at Jude. "I wonder if they even knew."

She shrugged lightly. "I do think the Piper knows a lot more than he lets on and not enough about what he doesn't."

Jude breathed out roughly. "What he's doing is borderline criminal."

Ella didn't disagree. "I wondered for a long time if it wasn't the Piper who'd given Dresden the information about our mission, but it didn't make sense. He created Endgame. He had no reason to risk destroying you all just to insert me. Plus, I've looked him in the eye, and this team is *his*. He wouldn't destroy what he'd built and the men and women he'd built it on. He might sacrifice an operative to the greater good, but the whole team? I don't buy it.

"I've also since found out that Loretta Bernstein most likely leaked the information to Dresden about our incursion in Beirut that night. She'd mined Gray Broemig for information, using other contacts to put pieces together. I believe she gave Dresden the information. He fired the RPG that brought us down, and the rest was just shooting fish in a barrel."

She winced at her comparison. A fine man had lost his life that night. Micah Samson, Jude's best friend, had perished. Only Brody and Ella had been allowed to live.

"Savidge shot Micah, where I couldn't tell. I just knew he fell. He got Brody in the neck and winged me on the temple. I remember hearing you call my name in my earpiece. And I remember seeing Brody fall. But then my vision washed in red, and I was out. When I woke up, I was facedown on a dirt floor, naked and cold."

Jude stood and began to pace. She let him. It was hard to recount. It had to be hard to hear.

"Dresden wasted no time allowing Savidge to break me. 'Get them before their spine strengthens,' he said. Savidge laughed and then clapped the manacles around my wrists. He pulled on a long chain until I hung from a bolt in the ceiling. They'd leave me hanging for hours at a time in the dark, bleeding, hungry, and cold. Then Savidge would come in, hit a lever, and lower me to the ground where I'd lie for hours more.

"I started making marks in the ground to count the days. The sun would pierce a high window in my cell. It would travel the sky and go away. That would mark one day. By the time I had five days crossed off in the dirt, they'd begun bringing Brody into my cell."

She stared into the flames, feeling colder than she'd been in that cell. Memories hurt.

"The things they did to Brody made me scream. But eventually he screamed louder. I vowed in that dirty cell that I'd watch the life leave Horace Dresden's eyes." She glanced at Jude, noticing his jaw was bunched and his face wore a tortured expression. "He's mine, Jude. You may want to kill him, but it will be me who takes him."

Jude nodded at her demand.

"They finally took Brody away. He lost his voice for a long time. Probably lost more than that, but he's never said a word to me about what happened in that room, and I haven't either until just now." She wiped a tear away. "By the time they took him away, eight days had passed. When Savidge would hit that lever, and I would fall to the ground beside Brody, I'd talk to him. I lied, Jude. Every minute I was with him, I lied to him."

"Look at me, Ella," Jude demanded in a hard voice.

She did. But the words had started, and now she couldn't stop them.

"I told him we would be saved. That you were coming

for us, and King would be right behind you. I told him our team would get us out of that hell. But you never came," she ended with a whisper.

He picked her up, pulling her body to his before he sat down and arranging her in his lap. She laid her head on her chest and listened to his heartbeat.

"Listen to me, Ella," he ordered. He raised her head until her gaze met his. "We watched you all fall. We thought you were all lost. Then hell broke open, and we had to fight for our lives. By the time the secondary helicopter made it to us, Dresden, Savidge, and all of your bodies were gone, as if they'd never been there. We never left you. We didn't *know you were alive*."

"But when you found out? Why didn't you come then?" She hated that she sounded like a little child begging for an answer.

"We didn't know anything for sure until Loretta Bernstein showed King a video that Dresden had made of the entire thing. That was two months ago, Ella. I had heard rumors of a dark-haired woman with eyes of frost and a scar at her temple, but I thought I was chasing a ghost, baby. I had no idea you were really alive." His voice was terrible. His pain giving it a deep, rough, mournful quality.

"When I found out you were searching for information on me, I got scared. Brody did everything he could to throw you off the scent," Ella said with a teary smile. "God, I had forgotten what a pit bull you can be when you catch a scent."

"It ripped me to pieces when I saw that video. I saw with my own eyes that you'd left breathing, and I finally had verification that the rumors I'd been chasing were true. I hated you when I watched it. How could you have not come to me as soon as Dresden let you leave?" he asked.

She stood off his lap. It was her turn to pace. "I told you that Dresden used you as a tool, Jude. A tool to hone me. Keep me compliant. The Piper hit the nail on the head when he said Dresden was coming for you. He still is. He'll do whatever is necessary to keep me in line, and he thinks you're the only way to do that."

Jude shook his head. "Why does he want you so badly?"

She looked at him then. "Dresden is twisted that way. He wants me because he knows that using me hurts Endgame because it hurts you. His ultimate goal is to watch each of us fall by his hand or his machinations. He's driven, and he's motivated by a hatred so deep it can only be personal, Jude."

"And now it's personal for me," Jude replied. "That bastard is wily, and he has information he should never have. Someone in the White House is supplying him with information."

A chill skated down Ella's spine. "You know that he was on the team with Rook and Knight that went belly-up in the Hindu Kush four years ago. And at some point he's had dealings with King. I haven't been able to ferret that out yet."

Jude nodded.

"My gut tells me Dresden's hard-on for Endgame begins in the Kush. But he despises those three men with the passion of a thousand white-hot suns. His objective, as unattainable as it sounds, is world domination. But along the way, his driving force is to end Endgame Ops."

A ring sounded from another room.

"Hold on, Ella," Jude urged as he exited the den, returning a minute later with a sat phone to his ear. "Yeah. I get it." Then, "I'll ask her and call you back later."

He disconnected and glanced at Ella before placing the phone on the table between them.

"That was King," he told her. "Chase has radioed in. He's got a doctor who was working with Doctors Without Borders in his possession."

"Possession?" she asked carefully.

"Apparently, she was his objective per the Piper. Another mission within a mission, it would seem. Her name is Gabrielle Moeller. Name ring any bells?" Jude asked her, a note of betrayal in his tone.

"No. I have no idea who that is."

"You don't have any idea why the Piper wants her brought home?"

"None. Wait, what was Chase's original mission for the team?" she queried quickly.

"Recon on the warlord Abrafo Nadege."

"Oh damn. That's not good at all. Nadege is a killer, and he's in bed with Dresden."

Jude glanced at her. "We knew he was an associate of Dresden's. What is the relationship between the woman Chase is getting to safety and Nadege?"

Ella shook her head, her mind whirring. "Maybe the association isn't with Nadege, but with Dresden? Give me your laptop. Hurry, Jude!"

He left and returned with his laptop. She opened it and got busy. Twenty minutes later, she'd managed to amass only minimal information on Gabrielle Moeller. A plastic surgeon turned trauma physician, Moeller seemed a nonentity.

And then Ella saw a picture that added another piece to the puzzle.

"Look at this picture," she said to Jude.

"Just two women in graduation caps and gowns," he replied with a shrug.

"This," she said, pointing to Moeller, "is Gabrielle."

His brows lowered. "And?"

"The other woman… Read her name for me so I don't think I'm imagining it."

"Anna Beth Caine," he read from the old newspaper clipping.

"Damn," Ella whispered. "That's not good."

"What is it, Ella?"

"That woman? Anna Beth Caine? She's Horace Dresden's former fiancée."

"I hate to keep repeating myself here…and?"

"She's also related to a man named Noah Caine," Ella said softly.

"The Piper," Jude stated and hung his head.

"When your operative took me from Dresden's house, I left Anna Beth behind. Dresden has Anna Beth Caine, Jude. She's locked in the same cell I was locked in, and though she wasn't in as bad a shape as I was, her fortune could turn any minute…possibly already has."

Jude's face went hard and cold. "Dresden has the Piper's daughter."

Though he'd not asked a question, she still responded. "Yes."

"There's something else I need to tell you, Ella. Harrison Black tracked Anton Segorski to a flat in Russia. He's bugged down and not moving. No one has seen the prime minister in four days. We could very well be the last ones to have seen him alive."

"Dresden doesn't suffer fools well. Segorski is a small player, but his political machinations helped put Crimea's oil rights into Dresden's hands so the bastard could bargain with it. I can't believe Dresden would knock off the prime minister though. He wanted his money too badly. No, it just doesn't make sense, unless…"

"Tell me, Ella. Unless what?"

"Unless it was never about the money."

Jude hissed in a breath. "What are you saying?"

"I'm saying that if Dresden didn't need the money, he had another fish on the hook all along. That oil will net him enough money to do what he's always wanted—effectively rule the world. He'll be the single richest entity on the globe. Richer than any sovereign nation, richer than Croesus. And that much money would allow him to control everything, Jude. Everything."

"Who do you think the fish is?"

"I don't think it's a who. I think it's a group of whos."

It must have hit him then. "No way, Ella. You're talking treason. There's no way someone, or a group of someones, would sell out their own countries for money."

"Remember me telling you about that mysterious group the Piper was always talking about?"

Horror masked Jude's face. "No. I can't believe it."

"What if people in the White House are involved with this group? I don't have enough yet. Let me search. I need to talk to Vivi," she told him, but it came out a request. "I think at this point we need to start considering that the Piper is either onto this group and playing a dangerous game, or he's as thick with them as Dresden."

Jude nodded. "Give Brody a call while you're at it, okay? King said the man's champing at the bit to talk to you."

"That's good news. Give me a few minutes to talk to him, and I'll explain why," she informed him.

Ella glanced up and found Jude right in front of her. He'd always moved like a big jungle cat—stealthy and silent. He reached for her face, cupping her cheek in his big palm and thumbing the dent in her chin.

She'd always hated that dent. Jude had always loved it.

"A truth?" he asked.

She gazed up at him, her answer on her face.

"I don't think you betrayed your team."

Relief washed through her.

"But we still need to talk about what you did do, Ella. You should have come to me immediately and let me help you. You didn't trust me, trust us, enough to come to me, and that hurts, Ella. It hurts bad."

She sank her teeth into her lower lip. That small bite of pain centered her. "I messed up. I'm trying to correct it, Jude."

"I need you to promise me you won't leave, Ella. I need you to go all in with me, with your team." His voice stroked along her nerves. Jude was an excellent interrogator. He could cajole and get information and promises out of men even when they knew they were dead men walking.

Could she make that promise though? In her mind, the only solution was for her to go back to Dresden. He would make it hell for her, but that was the only way she was going to be able to get the information Endgame needed to take him down. And it wasn't as simple as a bullet to the temple—Dresden was only one head. The entire organization could have many, and all of their organizations had to be dismantled.

She needed to find out as much as she could about the mysterious group Dresden was a part of. And there was the matter of Anna Beth Caine.

Ella was her only hope, and she wouldn't leave the woman with Dresden to suffer. She needed to hit Brody up again and see where he was with that. She didn't believe Dresden would kill her—Anna Beth would lose her value then—but he could break her, much as he had Ella.

"Give me the words, Ella. I'll help you hold to them."

It was the same thing he'd said to her last night.

"I won't leave you, Jude."

"All in?" he asked.

She nodded, and he kissed her forehead, pulling her tight against his chest and just holding her there.

"Jude?" she asked after long moments.

"Yeah?"

"I need to make some calls," she answered with a smile in her voice.

"And I need to hold you," he responded.

She laughed, and he pulled away from her. "Make 'em then. You've got ten minutes," he told her gruffly.

Her mouth dropped opened.

Jude shrugged. "I don't know how much longer we'll be able to stay here. I'm starting to realize how badly Dresden wants you, and we need a head start if he's headed our way."

He handed her the sat phone and walked out of the den. "Hey," he called. "When you're finished, come to the door under the stairs."

"Code?"

"5572463."

"Give me a few," she said and sat down on the couch. She dialed Brody first.

"What do you want, Keeper?" Brody's broken voice called over the line.

"Madoc, it's Ella."

"Ella-Bella—you call, give me limited information, and bail. What the hell have you gotten me into?"

She chuckled. "How are you?"

"Still alive, same as last time we talked," he told her.

She'd take that from Brody. It meant he hadn't decided to eat a bullet yet, and damn but she'd struggled to pull him out of that hell for a year. She didn't want to lose him now. "I'm okay with that. You eating? What about the meds?"

"Did you become my mother over the last month or so?"

"Nah, but somebody's got to look after your mean ass. Now, eating? Meds?"

"Yeah. I'm doing all that shit. Look, I got your information, and I've got some for you. That drive you sent me? Damn, Ella, do you have any idea what that holds?" It was hard to gauge Brody's attitude or demeanor from his voice. He sounded like someone had shoved his vocal cords into rubbing alcohol after using a cheese grater on them. Most times it came across very gruff and very hollow. He'd once told Ella it hurt to talk.

She believed him.

"I do. I need confirmation," Ella said.

"I had to do a detailed decryption on it, and still it took almost forty-eight hours. The first file is a list of all of

Dresden's holdings. The second file is a list of associates. The third file, Ella, that's where shit gets real interesting."

Ella held her breath.

"It's got pictures."

"Let me guess—Noah Caine, Anna Beth Caine, and Cameron Markov?"

He grunted. "There's some other woman too. I'm running face recognition on her as we speak…no clue who she is. There are pictures and video. Whoever took the videos didn't do a great job. The audio is horrible. Vivi is working on cleaning it up right now. Most of the meetings are between, wait for it, the Piper and Horace Dresden."

It fell in line with what Ella was beginning to suspect was going on, but that wasn't good news. "What else? You're holding out on me," she said, warning in her voice.

"There's a file encrypted so tightly I couldn't break it. Vivi is trying to break it, but even she has doubts about how she's going to get it done. She says it looks like there was a fail-safe on it. We need to know who has the fail-safe. And Ella, the file is labeled 'Endgame.'"

"Anna Beth Caine," she whispered.

"The woman I'm busting my ass to get away from Dresden?" Brody asked.

"Yeah, that one. Anna Beth Caine either is or knows the fail-safe," she whispered. It's why Cameron had been so insistent that Ella get to the drive and tell her father to protect Anna Beth.

"How is she related to the Piper?"

"Daughter. Where do we stand on getting her out of there, Brody?"

"I'm working on it…tugging on every resource I have in that area, but you gotta know going in there is suicide without my team."

Ella did know. "Yeah…no heroics. My take is he's not going to kill her. Not until he's flaunted her for the Piper."

Brody went silent for long moments. "It's what he'll do to her in the mean-and-between-time. You know that, Ella."

She knew that too. "We'll get her. I don't know if she's innocent, but nobody deserves Dresden. We get her out. It's got to be a priority."

Brody grunted, and she took that as agreement.

"I'm sending you and Vivi everything I have on our secured link. Have Vivi look at it all and put together a board for me. I'll be in Port Royal as soon as I can. We'll put it all together then," she told Brody.

"Got it," Brody said. "Later."

"Later," she promised and disconnected.

She knocked the phone against her forehead. There was still something she was missing. She needed to meet minds with her people like they used to do, and then the picture would be clearer.

She dialed Vivi's number.

"Damn you, Jude. Where's Ella?" Vivi yelled into the phone.

Ella laughed. "Good to hear your voice, Viv."

"Ella? Damn that man for not putting you on the phone with me immediately! Are you okay? Tell me you're okay!" Vivi spoke so fast that Ella couldn't respond.

She laughed again. "I'm okay, Vivi. Done any riding lately?"

"Rook took the Hyabusa away from me. Said it was too heavy and I'd kill myself, which would kill him, therefore I couldn't drive it anymore. Pissed me right off." She paused long enough to draw a breath. "Enough about me. How's you? Been a long time. You couldn't hit a bitch up and chat?"

"Long time, my arse. You had tabs on me the whole time, and you know it," Ella said, frustration leaking into her tone.

She could imagine Vivi rubbing her nails on her chest before blowing on them. "I'm good, but it took me months to find you. I had to sneak into your profile chart at the Agency. I had to *research* you, Ella, before I could put together a viable code to find your ass. So as good as I am, you're not too bad your-damn-self."

High praise indeed coming from Vivi. "I'm chatting now."

"Your man went through hell," Vivi said, her voice now low and carrying just a tinge of anger.

"So did I," she responded.

"That over now? You all in?" Vivi queried.

"Jude left me no choice. My heart left me no choice," Ella responded honestly.

"Finally," Vivi said breathlessly. "Listen, I'm working on that drive Brody sent me. There are actually two files, not just one, that are encrypted so tight with a fail-safe that it will destroy them if I dig much deeper."

"I think I know who the fail-safe is, or at least who knows what the fail-safe is," Ella said. "I'm sending everything to Brody via our secure link. He'll get it to you."

"I'm kinda jealous you have a *secure link* with Brody but not me." Vivi's tone indicated her pout.

Ella snickered. "We'll correct that once I'm in Port Royal."

Vivi chuckled. "Fabulous. I'll see you when you get home."

"Oh, I'm already home," Ella said before she could stop herself.

"Where are you?" Vivi asked, confusion coming down the line.

"With Jude."

Vivi sighed. "I love that for you."

"Me too." Ella smiled. "Okay, I'm logging off. Brody will get you the information. I'll see you soon."

"Soon, Ella," Vivi said. "Oh! One more thing, I was about to hit Keeper up when you called. According to my sources, Dresden is in the States. I don't have a location. I'm trying to track him now."

Chills ran down Ella's spine. What had she said to Jude? Nowhere is completely safe. Was Dresden coming for her even now?

"Ella?"

"Got it, Viv. I'll tell Jude."

"I'm out," Vivi said and disconnected.

Ella got up from the couch, her heart pounding but lighter than it had been in months. How could she have forgotten what *team* meant?

She made her way to the door Jude had mentioned under the stairs. She punched the code in and entered. The door closed and locked behind her. She walked down a set of stairs into a cavernous room that had literally been carved out of the bedrock the house sat on. Or maybe it was a naturally occurring cave?

Jude sat at a large bank of computers, watching a monitor above him intently.

"Hey," she said softly.

He opened his arms and motioned her over. She went eagerly. He wrapped his arm around her, pulling her close. "Whatcha' lookin' at?" she asked.

He pointed at the monitor. "See that tree right there?"

"Yep." It was blowing in the tumultuous wind and looked as if it had snapped in half at some point.

"It wasn't like that last night," he said absently.

"The wind is blowing," she reminded him, fear creeping up on her like a wraith.

"Well, Miss I Put on Shoes, I did a perimeter check last night long before you got up and walked around in the snow half dressed to perform your own."

She arched a brow at him and made a hurry-it-up motion with her hand.

He snorted. "The tree wasn't snapped then. Hell it doesn't look like it snapped at all. It looks cut. I've got motion sensors a half mile out from the house in all directions. Animal, man, wind, they all trip the sensors."

She was missing it. "And?"

"No tripped sensors. That falling tree should have tripped the sensor in that quadrant."

"Malfunction?" she asked as she looked more intently at the tree.

He shrugged. "I guess anything is possible."

"Vivi said Dresden is in the States," Ella told him.

Jude went so still that she wondered if he'd stopped breathing. His face went blank, and his mouth thinned.

"Tell me, Jude. Do you think it's him?" Ella asked, unable to keep a quaver out of her voice. The thought of going back into Dresden's hell made a mockery of all her brave plans to get more information and save Anna Beth Caine.

"I'm not saying anything except that I'm about to make another perimeter check," he told her.

"I'll go with," she said as she started to turn around.

"No. You'll stay here," he told her.

Frustration gnawed at her. "I'm not helpless."

He held up his hands in front of him as if warding off a blow. "I didn't say you were. But that terrain is deadly, and I can't check the perimeter and watch out for you at the same time."

Her anger evaporated. She was going crazy. "Of course."

"You good?" he asked, caution in his tone.

"I'm good."

"I'll be back in a few. Then you'll tell me what you talked to Madoc about?"

She nodded. "Jude?"

He turned back to her. "Yeah, woman?"

"I love you."

He smiled, and it took her breath away. "Always."

Chapter 17

JUDE LOCKED THE HOUSE AND MADE HIS WAY NORTH OF the cabin. He was going to start in the quadrant where the tree had fallen and work back from there. It was about a half mile from the house, right at the edge of where he'd placed sensors. He'd just checked the alarms the night before last. His gut told him there was no way that alarm hadn't been tripped. And with the information that Dresden was in the States, well, it wasn't looking good.

If the alarm hadn't been tripped by nature, he was left with one answer: it had been deliberately tampered with. Losing that tree left a perfect line of sight to the cabin.

His skin prickled with more than the cold surrounding him. He had no way of knowing how anyone could have found them. But logic never played well with others. He'd have a look himself and determine any potential threats.

He stayed in the trees, the white of his outer clothing giving him perfect cover in the snow. Jude forced his mind away from thoughts of Ella. This was all about protecting her, but he couldn't carry her with him right now. He'd promised her she was completely safe, and he'd give his own life to ensure that.

The wind continued to blow ruthlessly, but the snow had stopped falling. The storm was passing, leaving a blanket more than five feet thick on the ground. To his left, a twig snapped. Jude stilled behind a massive cedar and waited.

His senses screamed at him. Someone was in the woods with him. How many?

He eased from behind the tree and made his way on his stomach to a slight depression about three hundred yards from the tree. Nothing moved except the canopy swaying in the wind.

A shrill blip sounded to his right. It cut off almost immediately, but it wasn't his alarm and it didn't belong in these woods.

He flipped his mic on. "Ella?"

"Here."

"There are two go bags under the bed. Grab them both and stay in the comm room. Hit the code on the panel by the door on the inside, and head to the back of the room. Wait for me there."

"Ten-four," she responded, a slight tremor in her voice.

"I'm not going anywhere, and neither are you. Safe, Ella," he whispered.

"Ten-four," she responded again, the tremor gone.

Good girl, he thought. He had to get to the trees again. His clothing had been made with a two-fold purpose—camouflage in the snow and to eliminate any heat signature he may give off. The light was low now, and thermal imaging couldn't spot him. The only thing that could give him away was his movement, so he had to proceed slowly and carefully.

It took him twenty minutes to move three hundred yards. There were no more sounds, and nothing disturbed the falling evening. But Jude's neck told the story. Someone was there.

An enemy.

He'd made it to the tree line and turned over to sit up when two shadows fell from the trees above. He got to his feet and turned, meeting the first fist with a quick deflection and a punch of his own to the man's ribs. The first man fell. The second one had a gun to Jude's head in less time than it took to blink.

"Put your hands behind your back," he ordered.

Jude had two options—fight or accept the restraints. His entire world was in the cabin below them. Fight it would be.

He was faster than either man who'd jumped him, and he attacked with a ferocity born of fear for Ella. He switched his mind down and let his instincts guide him. His KA-BAR knife was in his hand before he drew a breath, and he stroked it across the throat of the man holding the gun. That took two seconds. The man fell as the other one came up firing his weapon. Jude threw the knife, and it embedded in the other man's eye.

Jude pulled it out, wiped it on the man's clothing, and sank down beside them. Searching the woods around him, he didn't notice anything out of place. He grabbed the walkie-talkie one of the men had and listened.

"Do you have him?" a voice asked excitedly.

The men he'd just taken out were scouts. "Yes," Jude answered.

"Dresden is coming up the pass now. Hold him until the boss gets there," the man said.

Goddamn! Dresden had found him.

Jude got up, ran back toward the house, and hurried inside, the cat following him, meowing like the end of the world was upon them. Jude opened the door to the comm room, and the cat flew in behind him.

"Ella!" he called out.

"I'm here," she said, rushing to his side.

"Get dressed. The smaller bag is yours. I'm going back out. Dresden is coming up the pass, and I've got to prepare the traps. I need you to stay here. See that door right there?" He pointed behind her.

She turned, saw it, and nodded.

"I'll be coming through that when I come back. Nobody can get in here except you and me. I'm letting King know what's happening. They won't make it to us in time to help, but if I go down, you stay here until King calls you. Do you understand me, Ella?"

"No, Jude! I can help you out there," she pleaded.

He grabbed her face between his hands. "You can't. I'll be pulled in two different directions. You're a hell of an operative, Ella, but Endgame needs you alive. The world needs the information you have. And I need you safe."

"I need *you*, Jude," she responded.

"I'm right here. I'll always be right here," he promised, holding his hand over her heart. "I'm not planning on dying today, but you need to be prepared, Ella."

She nodded. She'd become a better soldier while she'd been away from him, but she was still soft.

He had about fifteen minutes before Dresden topped the pass and was at the house. He led Ella to the console in front of the computers. "See that button right there?"

She nodded.

"See that monitor?"

She nodded again.

"When you see me hold up my fist, press that button and then take cover. I had the cave surveyed. It should hold up, but I don't know what Dresden is packing, and I'll never take chances with you."

He sidestepped her and began walking to his armory.

"Uh, Jude?"

"Yeah?"

She didn't say anything, and he turned around. She was holding his Knight's Armament Mk11 SWS. Best sniper weapon in the game. SEALs always used the best. "Hooyah!" he said with a smile. "Loaded?"

She rolled her eyes and handed him three ammo packs. "You need more than that, you gotta hit me up. It's all I had time to load while you were gone."

"Load more. There's an H&K in there for you. Load up, and then settle down," he said as he slung his weapon over his back.

"Jude, come back to me," she demanded.

"No other place I'd rather be, baby," he said with a grin, then headed to the door. "Lock this after me." He had about twelve minutes now.

"Oh, one more thing," she called before he walked out. "There's another front rolling in bringing even more snow. It's on us now."

He nodded. That would be to his benefit. These were his mountains, and he knew them sun or snow. "Safe," he said, his voice deep and dark.

She held up six fingers, and he walked away, out of the comm room—listening for the snick of the electronic bolts that locked the door into the stone surrounding them—and then out of the house.

He made it up to the north quadrant and began loading

his traps. He'd built them in the first two months after Ella died. He'd never stayed in the house, but he'd come here and prepared for any war anyone wanted to bring to him.

War was now. If Dresden was coming, he wanted Ella alive. Jude was going to make sure he didn't make it to her at all.

He worked fast. Realizing he didn't have time to set the traps on the southern side of the property, he began stringing wire across the road that led to the cabin. He was only able to set two incendiary bombs along the road that he would remotely detonate before he heard the sound of vehicles heading up the pass.

He hightailed it back to the fallen tree and settled into the snow beside it, lying on his stomach and prepping his rifle. Once he had his sight trained on the road, he waited.

He hit the ear mic. "Ella?"

"Here."

"There are two vehicles coming up the pass. Both of them SUVs. I'm going to guess that between the two of them, there are six, maybe seven men including Dresden. More will be coming though. Once he has confirmation we're here, he'll call in a strike team. I've got to take them out. If he calls back to a strike team, we could be in trouble. You're going to hear the explosions, and I'll be out of contact. Stay in the room, baby."

"Ten-four."

She was a great partner—a great operative, he thought again. And she was going to let him do his thing, trusting he'd keep her safe. He pulled his satellite phone from his pocket and hit 1.

"Talk," King McNally said by way of greeting.

"I just sent you coordinates to my cabin in the Sangre de Cristo Mountains. I also forwarded satellite images of the cave system I built the house over. I'll be coming out on the north end of the property. There's an entrance to the caves hidden in the side of the mountain. I've got Ella, and Dresden is moving on us. She's in the comm room, if I don't make it. I don't think he can get her as long as she stays there. I need you, Your Highness."

"I'm coming, Keeper," King said and disconnected.

He'd done everything he could. There should have been no way Dresden could have found him. Unless...

"Ella?"

"Here."

"Go to the armory. There's a small handheld scanner in the second drawer of the tool cabinet. It detects the presence of embedded tracking devices. I need you to scan yourself."

"Oh no..."

"Do it, Ella."

"On it."

The SUVs made the last hill on the pass, moving at a rapid clip and getting harder to see amid the switchbacks up the mountain. The wind had died down a bit, which could be good and bad.

"A little closer," Jude whispered.

The first SUV topped the hill and started back down as Jude blew the first device. It exploded, toppling the vehicle and sending fire shooting into the sky. The other SUV sped around the first one.

"Come on, motherfuckers, I've got something for you too."

He peered through his scope and waited until they'd come close to his second device. He pushed the charge on the second device, but nothing happened. No boom. No explosion. The SUV continued to thunder up the pass. A couple of men made it out of the wreckage of the first vehicle and scattered.

Through his scope, Jude located the driver of the second SUV. He lined up his shot and took it. The driver's head exploded, and the SUV rolled to a stop about eight hundred yards from Jude's location. Three men in black poured out.

Jude fired relentlessly just to keep them guessing. He managed to line up another shot and once again pulled the trigger.

He dropped one man. The others dispersed, taking cover and waiting. Four men were trying to take a shot at Jude, but no sign of Dresden yet.

Wishes were for fools, but damn if he didn't take a second to regret that he hadn't had time to set more devices.

Bullets began to pepper his location, his own rifle fire having given him away. They were about to rain hellfire on his location. He had to move.

"Jude?" Ella called over the mic.

"Yeah?"

"There's a tracker in my hip," she told him. She was calm.

"Hold the scanner over the tracker, baby, and press the blue button on the top. It will disable the device."

"Ten-four."

One of Dresden's men stuck his head and shoulder out from behind a tree a little too long, and Jude took his shot. A scream rent the air. Not a kill shot though. The others were quick, moving like they'd been trained, and Jude wondered who the hell had signed on to work with that bastard. Hell, they moved like trained spec ops— SEALs, Rangers, Force Recon.

Taking out a fellow soldier would be a bitch, he thought.

Then again, if they'd signed on with Dresden, they were no longer his fellow soldiers. They were the enemy.

Dresden finally made an appearance, easing quickly out of the SUV before glancing toward where he had to know Jude was. Then he smiled, and the hate in Jude's heart for the man ramped up to unforeseen levels. Jude aimed but lost his shot because the bastard ducked back behind the door. Jude fired a shot anyway and then froze when he saw what Dresden pulled out behind him.

"Goddamn it," Jude bit out. "Ella, he's going to hit the cabin hard. Take cover."

"I'm settled, Jude. Now go to work and get that bastard," she demanded.

He smiled. "Ten-four."

He fired until his ammo packs were empty, and then he blew the last two incendiary devices. That didn't stop Dresden.

He lifted the enormous launcher, and as Jude watched, Horace Dresden fired the RPG, a white, foggy trail in the air highlighting its path directly into his home. The home his woman was holed up beneath.

The RPG struck, and the cabin shuddered as a hole ripped through Jude's bedroom. Glass exploded outward, and the subsequent explosion rocked Jude. Fire raced up and out of the hole. Jude wasn't worried about

Ella. There were three feet of steel and another five feet of rock between her and any threat. She had a separate ventilation system that wound into the caves below the room. Jude had strategically placed the cabin in this area because of those caves.

It was imperative always to have an escape plan. Ella was right. Nowhere was completely safe, but Jude had been determined to keep his family as close to that state as humanly possible.

Now his home was gone.

He lowered his eye to his scope and cataloged Dresden's face as the man watched what he'd wrought. His eyes were blank, but a smile played about his lips. Jude still didn't have a shot, but he fired a warning that skated close to Dresden. One of his men who'd taken position beside his boss fell, and Dresden dove back into the SUV.

Then they opened fired on Jude's location, spraying the area with automatic and semiautomatic rounds. One of the men loaded the launcher with another RPG.

From the communication unit he'd stolen from the first two dudes he'd taken out, Jude could hear Dresden calling in his strike team. They were at least an hour out. Soon Jude would be outnumbered and outgunned. He picked up his rifle and made haste down the tree line until he came to where the monitor he'd shown Ella was. He held up his fist and then fled the scene, heading toward the southern quadrant. An RPG landed and took out trees and earth, rocking Jude. Trees fell, and somewhere in the distance, a coyote howled. The silence left by an RPG explosion was eerie. Jude took off again, and it took little to no time for the ground behind him to explode. He rolled with the pitch of the earth and came up with a smile. They shouldn't have screwed with him. Sure, they had RPGs. Jude had C-4 and claymores.

He began his trek to the east side of the property and headed north again.

Along the way, he stopped and set as many traps as he could, but that wasn't many. He heard one of his claymores trip.

Bastards, he thought. *Come for my woman? Oh, hell no*.

He doubled back and had just begun heading north when a figure stepped in front of him from the darkness. Another scout—had to be. Jude didn't have time to reach for his weapon. He just dropped low and swung wide with his leg, taking the man off his feet. He followed the man down and delivered a punch to his throat that missed, grazing instead of hitting full force. The man coughed and rolled, shaking Jude off.

Jude reached behind him for his handgun as the man came up faster than Jude had expected delivering a blow that sank into Jude's side.

Knife.

Not very deep, but it stung. Jude channeled that pain and focused. He stepped to the side of the next blow, lifted his gun, and fired a single shot to the man's forehead. He fell. Jude started running.

He was bleeding, but the wound didn't seem that bad. In his periphery, he could see his cabin burning.

Anger simmered in his gut.

As he crested the rise that would lead him to where he needed to be, he had a decision to make. Fight Dresden here and now, or get to Ella. Choice made, he glanced in front of him. It was a long way down, and he'd have to scale the rock wall with nothing more than his hands.

"Dagan!"

Dresden.

Jude turned and saw Dresden with one other man coming up behind him. That man bled from the shoulder wound Jude had given him moments before. It was Jude smiling then.

Jude clicked his mic on so Ella could hear.

"Where is she?" Dresden called out.

Jude cocked his head. He only had his handgun. They'd cut him down before he fired a single shot. He had to get back to Ella. He took a step back, and a shot fired at his feet. "King always said you were a pussy and a bad shot," Jude said.

"But I'm the pussy with the upper hand, Dagan. Now where is Ella?"

"Somewhere you won't find her," Jude called out, and then he stepped off the rise.

Jude fell about ten feet before he was able to grab a small outcropping of boulders. It stopped him and nearly wrenched his shoulder out of its socket, but he held on, using his feet to draw himself up and over the boulders. He tucked himself into a nook against the rocks. "I'm good, Ella. Stay where you are." She didn't respond, but he hadn't expected her to. She was a good soldier. Soft in the heart, but a great warrior.

Bullets rained down on his location, but Dresden and his man couldn't see Jude, so he was safe for now.

"He's gone," Dresden bit out.

"Long way down," the other man said, and there was a smile on his voice.

"I'm going to find her, Dagan," Dresden called out anyway. "I never took the time to taste her when I had her last. I'll make sure to correct that this go-round. I'm sure I'll enjoy it. I doubt she will."

Jude bit his tongue and kept his mouth closed.

"Enjoy the weather, Dagan. I hope you freeze to death."

Jude waited for two hours, sure that someone had been left to watch for him. He shed his white outerwear and threw it off the side of the rise. At some point, he'd lost the radio that gave him insight into Dresden's next moves. Probably dropped it in the fall. No shots came his way, but he could hear Dresden and the other man scouring the remains of his cabin.

Steel and stone, that's what remained between Dresden and Ella.

Jude's muscles tightened with the need to move. He'd waited as long as he could. He shimmied down the rise to a small hollow, thanking his Creator that the moon was hiding behind the clouds. He pulled a packet of QuikClot out of one of his pockets and coated the rip in his side with it. It wasn't bad. The knife hadn't gone deep before he'd wrenched the other man's arm so hard his elbow had popped. Jude drew in a deep breath and eyed the night around him. A creek ran the length of his northern property, and he followed it up, farther into the mountains. He walked for an hour before he found the entrance to the cave system.

Pulling out his flashlight, he peered into the opening. It was winter, and there were bears in these mountains.

He hit his ear mic. "Ella?"

"Talk to me, Jude."

"I'm here. I'm coming to you. You okay?"

"I can hear the earth shifting above me. I heard the cabin go. I also heard gunfire. You okay?"

"Nothing I can't handle. It'll take me about an hour to get to you. Hold on, baby."

"I'm here," she said.

He entered the caves cautiously but swiftly. He needed to see her. Touch her. Just be with her.

He didn't encounter any bears, thank God, but it took a little longer than an hour to make it to the comm room. There'd been a rockslide inside the natural tunnels, and he'd had to clear it enough so he could get through.

He made it to the room, hit the code on the pad on his side, and sighed in relief as it opened.

She was on him right then.

"God, Jude! You're bleeding," she cried.

"Just a surface wound. Come here," he ordered as he closed the door and hit the code again. They were as safe as he could make them until the cavalry arrived. He dropped his weapons and held out his arms.

Ella jumped into them, and all he knew was her.

He took her mouth, probably too roughly, but he had to have her. Right. Now. And she responded so beautifully.

Jude pulled her shirt up, going for her skin even as she went for the buttons on his pants and he went for the buttons on hers. Then his cock was out and she was bared to him and he lifted her, sliding into her heat and feeling her body take him deep, so deep.

"Love you," he said as he sank until he couldn't sink anymore.

She moved her hips, clasping him tight with her inner muscles.

"It never stops," she whispered as her tongue licked up his neck and into his mouth. "Love me, Jude. I need it."

He took them both to the floor, not caring that it was cold, only knowing that he needed to be inside her, moving, making her cry out for him—pleasuring her, loving her.

He pulled out and sank back inside her heat. She lifted to him, pulling him flush on top of her so that no part of them was separated. He thrust up into her and stilled, fighting off the call of orgasm, wanting it to last and last.

"Need *you*," he bit out.

"I know," she said softly.

Their breaths mingled, and his skin prickled where her breasts pressed against his chest. His heart thudded, and he thought hers did too. He moved faster inside her. In and out, over and over, ecstasy building in waves that promised to drown them. Heat and wetness coating them both, sweat melding their bodies together, and still they moved as one, reaching for the finale.

His spine tingled, and her pussy clamped down on him. He was done, exploding inside her, feeling her internal muscles pull everything from him. He rolled over and pulled her on top of him. Better he had the cold floor than her.

"The floor's cold," she mumbled against his neck.

He chuckled. "I think you killed me, and all you can talk about is how cold the floor is?"

"If I'd known you were going to jump me as soon as you walked in, I'd have set up a pallet," she argued.

"There's a bed over there." He pointed somewhere behind him.

Her head came up at that. "Seriously?"

He nodded as a smile split his face. "Would I lie about a bed?"

She bit his pec through his shirt. He laughed.

Then he cradled her head and forced her to look at him. "A truth?"

"I'm game."

"I'm going to keep you safe."

She stared at him, her big, gray eyes warm and accepting his promise. "Is that right?"

He nodded.

"I'm going to keep you safe too."

His cock stirred again, but an alarm began to sound and Ella moved off him. "I've got to clean this and get it bandaged."

He started to open his mouth, and she shot him a glare. "Do your worst."

It took her about five minutes to clean the shallow cut and Steri-Strip it. Then she put gauze and tape over it and lowered his shirt.

He kissed the top of her head. She burrowed into his neck. They stood that way for a few precious seconds. The need to move pressed on him then, and he obeyed it.

Jude moved to the monitors and cursed. The cameras in the trees surrounding the cabin showed Dresden's current plan of action clearly. "Ella, put on the outer-wear in your go bag. Right now."

She did as he bade. Dresden was about to use explosives to get in. Jude knew the man had a larger contingent of men winging their way toward the cabin's location. They had to move. There was no way Dresden could penetrate the steel, but maybe he was hoping he could tunnel under. What Dresden didn't know was that there wasn't soil underneath the comm room. There was a massive cavern. In theory, he could hit the structure hard enough to force the cavern beneath to crumble. As with the rockslide Jude had encountered earlier, it *could* happen here.

Jude didn't think it *would* happen. After all, the room had been built to survive a nuclear holocaust. A little overboard, but Jude knew what the world was running toward, and he'd wanted a way to protect his family. But he wasn't God to know if the cave system would hold up to that much of an explosion.

So they'd have to run.

"What about the cat?" Ella asked as Jude changed his clothing into warmer wear. He shoved new outerwear into his go bag and moved to the armory.

"What about it?" he asked absently.

"Chica goes with us," she said firmly.

He stopped loading ammo into another knapsack long enough to check the monitor and throw Ella a look of disbelief. "You named it?"

The cat meowed.

"I named her, and she goes."

His woman was worried about a stray cat? When Dresden was about to try to blow them sky high? Damn.

"Shove her in your go bag, zip it up, and she can go," Jude told her, grabbing the last bit of ammo he could stuff into his knapsack before he zipped it shut.

"Chica?" Ella called, and damn if the cat didn't immediately go to her.

Jude watched in bemusement as she put the cat gently into the sack, talking to it like it was a child and could actually understand.

"Do we have a couple of cans of Vienna sausages down here?" she asked him, her gray eyes pleading.

He thought his eyes were going to bug out of his head. But he threw a thumb over his shoulder and said only, "Check under the sink over there."

She did and made a triumphant sound as she shoved two cans into the sack with the cat.

Jude gave one last look to his comm room.

"You can rebuild," she offered.

He nodded in affirmation. Maybe he would, but only with her.

Jude reached for her hand and tugged her to the door. "Got your weapon?" he asked.

"Yeah. Holster at my back," she answered. "And I've got one in my boot. Oh, and I stole a KA-BAR from your armory."

"I approve." He held out a rifle to her. "Put your go bag on first, then strap that over your back."

She did as he told her. No questions. Not even the cat complained.

"We've got about an hour hike out of these caves. It'll still be dark when we exit. I go first, and if there's any sign of danger, you tuck in and wait for my orders. We clear, Ella? I need your cooperation here."

"I'm clear," she said in exasperation. "How the hell did I manage to survive a whole year without you?"

Oh, her sarcasm. He'd missed the hell out of that. He rolled his eyes. "I don't know. I'm sure it was touch and go."

She threw back her head and laughed. Loud. It was beautiful. "And that's a truth you can take right to the bank. Cash that shit out and run for Mexico."

He grinned at her, checked the monitor again, and punched in the code. "I'm first. Always."

"Yes, sir," she replied smartly.

"Smart-ass."

She turned her head and tried to look over her shoulder at her butt. "You think?"

He shook his head as the door swished open. He stepped into the tunnel and checked for any disturbance. "We're clear. We've got to move fast. I don't know how the cave will hold up when those explosives he's almost finished setting go."

"Let's move then," she said. "I've got you, Chica. Hold on for the ride."

His lips curved again, and he swore he hadn't smiled so much in a year. "Let's do it."

They moved quickly. They'd made it about a quarter of a mile through the tunnels when the first explosion rocked the system. The way the walls and ceiling of the cave's tunnels shook didn't bode well for them.

"Run," Jude said, turning around to get behind her. "Run fast," he urged as he took off his headlamp and put it on her head.

The concussion of another blast nearly took them off their feet. He refused the fear that climbed up his throat. He wouldn't lose her here. The earth rumbled as it absorbed the impact and sought to hold. Wind rushed by him, the wind of the approaching dust headed their way.

"Run, Ella!" he yelled, and she did just that.

He tore after her, but they weren't fast enough. "Duck down, and cover your face," he called as the dust caught up to them.

Jude covered her body with his as yet another rumble

rocked the walls around them. The fear knocked on his mind again, and he again refused it entry. Instead, he held her close, making sure she kept the cloth in place over her mouth and nose. He shoved her face into his chest and bowed low over her, breathing through her hair and letting the silk of her tresses filter his air.

Another boom, and her body shook. His world was about to collapse around him. Horror choked his throat, and his hands clenched tighter around his woman.

He was scared he'd found her only to lose her again. And in the midst of one of the greatest terrors of his life, Jude was smiling because all he could hear was Ella talking softly to the damn cat.

Chapter 18

GODDAMN DRESDEN! HE WAS GOING TO BLOW UP THE whole mountain! Ella's entire body trembled, and she wondered if she'd just come back to Jude to lose him to Dresden anyway.

"We've got to move, Jude," she said against his chest. She pushed against his side to get him to move, and he hissed in a breath.

He laughed, and it was rueful in the sudden awful silence.

"Let me look," she ordered, pushing his hands away as she moved to her knees in front of him.

"No time," he muttered. "We'll patch it again when we're safe."

Ella gazed at him, either to judge his words for truth or to see if he was simply placating her.

She nodded at what she saw in his eyes. They would run, and she'd care for him later.

He stood and helped her to her feet.

"I've got you, Chica," she said softly to the cat zipped inside her go bag. The cat meowed back. "You're getting a gold bowl when we get home."

"We're keeping it?" Jude asked, dismay hugging his tone.

A laugh escaped her. "Her. We're keeping *her*."

Jude grunted.

As she began following him once more through the

caves, it struck Ella that over the last forty-eight hours she'd fallen back into team mode. The past year she'd been solo, with the exception of Brody. She'd conditioned herself to the reality that she was the only one she could count on 24-7.

Jude had erased that line of thinking in two days. That was indicative of how tired Ella was, but more than that, it was a clear sign that she trusted him. Their connection hadn't disappeared. It had *grown* in strength.

She still didn't know if she'd survive Dresden, and she knew she had to go back in, but she'd cross that bridge when she came to it. Dresden wouldn't stop coming for her. She didn't know everything about his operation, but she still knew too much. And he didn't like being beaten. He wouldn't take losing Ella to Endgame lying down, as evidenced by the continued explosions that rocked the caves.

She watched Jude's back, kept her gaze trained on him. One foot in front of the other, she followed him without question.

He stopped once and sank down behind a cave wall. She lowered immediately. He held up his hand and waved her forward. "That wall wasn't there when I came this way. It's caved in, and I'm going to have to move some rocks so we can squeeze through."

He took off his go bag, his weapons, and the light he'd taken back from her. "Train that light on the wall so I can see."

She did, and he began moving rocks. And then he moved more rocks. And finally more rocks. The wall didn't seem to be shrinking, and there didn't seem to be any holes opening up.

"That's not good, huh?" she asked.

He hung his head, glanced at her, and smiled. "Nope."

She blew a strand of hair out of her face. "Do you have reception on the sat phone?"

He rubbed his forehead as he pulled out the phone. "No."

"We're stuck?" she asked, unable to keep the quaver from her voice.

"No," he said, assurance in his voice. Then he started moving rocks again.

The cat meowed, and Ella opened the bag. The cat ventured out, looked around, and stepped right back into the bag. "Huh. She likes the bag," Ella mused.

Jude grunted.

"Can I help?" Ella asked.

"No."

She cleared her throat. "I really can't help?"

"No."

"Do you know any other word at the moment?"

"No," he said, but there was a laugh in his voice. "You feel that?" He held his hand up above his head.

"No," she responded with a smile. "Feel what?"

"Fresh air," he told her and began to move faster.

He moved three more fairly large rocks, and a gust of fresh air rushed into the cave. He grinned. "We're almost there."

He climbed up the rocks a little and moved more. "Need you to move, Ella. Some are going to fall."

She picked up their stuff and moved back, watching as he opened up a hole big enough for them to climb through.

"Let's get out of here," he called down.

Ella handed their gear, the headlight, and his weapons up to him. He pushed their things through and then slithered through the hole. Ella was left alone. The gaping maw of the cave rose behind her, and she shuddered. She hated the dark.

Jude was back through the hole in a minute at most, holding out his hand to her. "Climb up, baby," he ordered.

She climbed after giving him her go bag. She slid through the small opening and reached back for the bag. He handed it to her, and then Ella wasn't alone in the dark anymore.

They made good time to the mouth of the cave system. Again, Jude went ahead to do recon and came back telling her they were going to bed down there.

"It's snowing hard," Jude told her. "The opening is hidden, and I doubt anyone will move tonight."

"Do you think Dresden breached the comm room?" she asked him.

Jude met her gaze. "No. But I think he destroyed it, and until he can verify you're either dead or gone, he'll be busy trying to dig through tons of rock to get in."

"He's smart, Jude. Don't underestimate him," she warned. "He's a master strategist and will think of every move I could have made, including escaping. Don't doubt he's looking for that opening right there."

"He's the devil, Ella. I never underestimate evil like Dresden."

She nodded and moved to set up a place to bed down. "Can I let Chica go? Do you think she'll come back?"

"Let her out. She's not going anywhere. You're feeding her. You talk to her. She's yours now, whether you like it or not," he said.

Another ray of hope speared her chest. "I've never had a pet."

"And now you do," he affirmed with another patented Jude grin.

Ella rubbed the area over her heart. She was afraid to trust how much her world had changed in just a few days. She'd gone from wanting to shove a wineglass stem through Dresden's eye socket to teasing parlays with Jude.

But it felt good. It felt right. So she'd take it and keep moving until she had to change directions.

Jude hunkered down in front of her as she unzipped her go bag. He reached for her hand, pulled it to his mouth, and gently kissed her palm. "He's never getting to you, Ella."

"You can't promise me that, Jude. And the fact remains that I may have to return."

His gaze darkened, and he lowered her hand as he stood again. "Over my dead body."

"That's what I've always been afraid of," she whispered.

"We're going to talk about this habit you have of trying to protect me. But right now you're going to sleep. I'll take first watch. You rest," he ordered.

Fatigue pulled at her. She watched as Chica remained in the bag, refusing to leave. The gorgeous cat curled into an indistinguishable ball of brown, white, and black fur, then went to sleep. Ella lay down beside the bag, petting the cat. "Wake me when it's my turn," she told Jude around a yawn.

"Will do," he promised.

⌁

He was going to allow them an hour at the most before he woke her and they left this cave. Dresden was a former

Navy SEAL. He'd have gone over every possibility before blowing up the ground Jude's house had sat on. That meant he was definitely searching for Ella's path of escape.

Dresden knew damn well that Jude wouldn't have left her safety to chance. Nothing was one hundred percent. Not even safe comm rooms built into rock.

Jude took a few moments to watch her sleep. He loved her with every molecule of his being. She was never going back to Dresden if Jude had anything to say about it.

Her hand rested on the cat's back. Jude shook his head and let a smile curve his lips. Only Ella with her soft heart. She was still the most beautiful woman he'd ever seen. His gaze traveled over her face—over the scar at her temple, across the slope of her cheeks, down past her lips to the small dent in her chin.

She was everything to him. He could admit it here in the darkness of the cave that sheltered them. Hell, he'd admit it to the world. He just had to convince her that he could keep them both safe before she left again.

There were so many angles to this thing with Dresden. The Piper, his daughters, Anton Segorski, people in Jude's own government, and on top of that, there was now some nameless organization attempting world domination?

"What the hell have we gotten into, El?" he asked softly.

She turned her face to his, a frown creasing her brow as if she'd answer him, but her eyes never opened. She was tired. God knows she'd been through hell during the last year. He needed the entire story, but right now he needed to get them safe.

Jude stood, pulled a thermal blanket out of his go bag and placed it on top of Ella. He headed toward the mouth of the cave and sank down behind a big boulder, watching and listening. Dawn was about an hour away, and the moon was hidden behind the clouds that still dropped snow on the earth. There had to be at least six feet on the ground now. It was so thick that it'd already covered his tracks from earlier. It would definitely slow down anyone who tried to move in it.

The night was quiet; nothing moved in the cold and precipitation. Jude didn't even see signs of forest animals moving in this weather. A twig snapped just outside the cave entrance. Jude raised his rifle and peered through the scope. Nothing but darkness. He got down on his belly and crawled to the entrance, settling behind a snowbank. He slowly created a hole in the snow and put his rifle through. He listened. He waited.

Nothing moved.

A shadow separated from behind a cedar. Big and stealthy, it headed toward Jude's location. Everything narrowed to that shadow, though Jude's other senses flared out, seeking more threats. Nothing else moved. No sounds of weapons hitting cloth or feet moving over snow hit Jude's ears.

Just that shadow.

He'd never seen anyone but Jonah Knight move that silently. But this man was shorter than Knight—hell, shorter than any of Jude's Endgame teammates.

The shadow drew closer. Jude pulled out his KA-BAR, palmed it, and lowered his rifle. He'd take the man as quietly as he could. He didn't want anything to draw other scouts to this location.

The man reached the mouth of the cave, which put him right beside Jude. Jude flowed to his feet, rising above the man and stroking the knife across his neck. Jude's movements were too fast for the man to be prepared, so he went down fast and easy. Jude ripped the man's balaclava off and exhaled in relief when he didn't recognize him.

Jude dragged the man farther into the cave, checking for a radio and finding none before he hid the body behind a boulder so Ella might miss it when they left. He had to do recon, and that meant leaving the cave. He checked on Ella, made sure she still slept, then moved back to the cave's entrance.

He was wearing another set of white camo outerwear, and it remained pitch-black outside. He blended into the snow effortlessly. Jude used every last ounce of his training as he slithered out of the cave and into the tree line beyond the caves. Jude glanced back, checking the cave to make sure he'd hidden his path, and saw it still looked pristine.

The cave's entry was hidden by low, overhanging trees that grew out of the sides of the rock. The mountain was a formidable foe, but life grew in the most bizarre places. The man he'd just taken out had to have known it was there, and that wasn't good. It meant Dresden knew, or had guessed, about the caves.

Jude worked quickly, finding no one else hiding in the immediate perimeter. He hustled back to Ella. "Baby, get up. We gotta move," he urged.

She was up in a second, asleep one moment, completely alert the next. His hands fisted. She'd been conditioned to do that by Dresden, no doubt. Yes, she had training, but nothing that would have prepared her for that instantaneous alertness. That only came from combat situations, and Jude was finally realizing that's what her entire year alone with Dresden had been. Combat.

Ella zipped the cat in, folded the thermal blanket, and handed it back to him. He shoved it in his go bag and helped her load her bag and her weapon onto her shoulders. She was dressed exactly like him. He was about to test her endurance as they trekked up the mountain, hopefully reaching the pass that would take them down the other side.

"We're heading up the mountain. We have to move quickly and silently. You loaded?" he asked as he strapped his bag to his back and checked his weapons.

"Yes," she whispered, her voice husky from sleep.

"Dresden knows about the caves. You stay right on me, Ella. Step where I step, and do what I say when I say do it," he commanded.

She didn't bristle, and that more than anything told Jude she understood the precariousness of their situation.

"He's not getting you," Jude bit out.

She threw back her head. Ella had her game face on as she pushed her comm device into her ear.

Jude took a moment to trace the curve of her brows before he leaned down and kissed her lips. "Let's handle business."

They made their way out of the cave cautiously. Jude's neck wasn't prickling, but that didn't mean Dresden wasn't close. They hit the trees, and Jude forced a hard pace as they scaled the mountain. The path was rocky, and the forest began to thin out, their cover disappearing too rapidly. Jude motioned her to take cover behind a big cedar, and then he sank to the snow and pulled out his ocular scope.

He scanned the vista below him. In the distance, he could make out tendrils of smoke from his still-burning house. He didn't hear any signs of big earthmovers, although he'd expected Dresden to be searching the crater he'd created when he blew the explosives.

But the mountain was silent.

"He's here," Ella's voice whispered across the ear mic.

Jude nodded. Dresden's strike team had arrived. The air quivered with their presence. "Stay where you are. I'm going hunting."

"I've got your six."

"Safe, El."

Jude belly-crawled through the trees. He'd pinpointed two areas where Dresden could funnel men through the trees. He pulled two claymores from his go bag and set them in those places. He could hear a low drone now, the sound of snowmobiles echoing up the mountain.

Dresden was coming. Those claymores would slow them, but he and Ella had no choice but to run now.

"Get up, Ella," he called out. "Run southwest. Hit the tree line."

She was up and running, Jude on her heels, when the first claymore exploded behind them.

BOOM!

BOOM!

The second one followed the first. Screams of the men who'd been taken out by the explosives echoed in the mountains. Dresden was hitting them from both points.

Ella sprinted to the trees, feet sure in the snow. She hit the edge of the forest before Jude.

A bullet gouged out a slice of snow to his right. Jude turned, went to a knee, lifted his rifle, aimed in the direction the shot had come from, and fired.

A shout rose as the shooter fell. Jude eyeballed the scope and got off two more shots, two more kills, before he slung his weapon over his back and took off after Ella.

More shots peppered his path.

"Run, Ella. Keep running," he called out.

Then he heard a sound that froze his heart. Ella cried out, the sound cut off as fast as it had split the air.

Jude pumped his legs, chasing that cry. Behind him, Dresden and his men fired at will on Jude's location. In front of him loomed a small drop-off that Jude feared Ella had gone over.

He slid to the edge and peered down. Ella had landed on a tree trunk about three feet below him. She was sprawled over the trunk, her weapon and bag falling off her back. Her eyes were closed, and she was squeezing the trunk with her arms and legs.

"Let the bag and weapon go, Ella," he said.

"I don't want to drop Chica," Ella called back.

"Ella, do you trust me?" he asked.

Behind him, hell was being unleashed. Dresden had indeed come prepared for a war.

"Yes," she replied instantly.

"Drop the damn bag. Do it now."

She dropped the bag with a soft cry.

"Now slither off that trunk and get on the ground, woman," Jude demanded.

She did as he asked and looked up at him in confusion. She'd only fallen about a foot to the ground.

"Run, Ella," he told her. "Run and don't stop until King gets here."

"Where are you going?" she asked, fear a tremor in her voice as she grabbed her pack and gun. No way was his woman going to leave that damn cat.

"Talk later, baby," he said as he ducked the shots coming through the trees. "Run!"

He didn't look to see if she'd done as he asked. He rose, turned, and began firing, reloading, and firing again.

"Don't die," she pleaded over the ear mic.

He couldn't respond. He ducked behind a rock and prayed that King got there soon.

Just then, the night exploded, the sounds of men crying out in pain echoing in the air around Jude. Another explosion, and the trees in front of Jude toppled, fire ripping through the night.

Jude didn't question it. He just slithered down the small rise and followed Ella's path. He ran until he reached Ella and then they both ran, down the mountain, through the creek, and through the trees.

In the distance the *whump-whump-whump* of helicopter blades broke the silence of the lightening sky. Jude pushed Ella down behind some boulders and pulled out his satellite phone.

It was ringing.

"Goddamn it, Keeper. Where the hell are you?" King demanded.

"Heading south, down the mountain. I'm heading toward a shed that's about five miles from my current location. Head southwest of the coordinates I gave you, and you'll find the shed. Is that you in the chopper?"

"No, that's Black. I just blew Dresden's men to

kingdom come. No sign of Dresden yet. There's no sign of any more men, Jude."

"We'll be at the shed," Jude said and disconnected.

"Let's go, Ella," he called. "Follow me, baby. The cavalry's arrived."

"Thank you, God," she breathed out as she stood.

It took them about an hour to reach the shed. Ella didn't falter, and Jude was so proud of her resilience. The shed rose out of the foggy morning, a silent emissary offering safety. He urged her to the back of the shed and put a finger to his mouth, shaking his head.

She nodded. She wouldn't move.

Then he stepped around the side of the shed and whistled.

An answering whistle rent the air. King stepped out of the trees. Jude almost went to his knees.

Instead, he reached deep, adrenaline close to failing him, and went back to Ella.

He pressed her body against the shed. "You're safe, baby."

She gazed up at him, the low light of a snowbanked morning kissing her features. "I never doubted it, Jude."

"King's here. He's going to get you home," Jude whispered at her ear.

She grabbed his shoulders. "Where are you going?"

"Hunting."

He looked to his left and saw King approaching. He didn't look at Ella again, afraid he'd go with her. He knew now, more than ever, that he had to eliminate Dresden. Ella wouldn't be safe until that bastard was ashes in the wind.

"Don't leave me." She whispered the plea.

Jude didn't respond, just pulled away and stepped to King, who reached out. Jude clasped the man's forearm.

"Don't be brave," King commanded.

"Be accurate," Jude responded immediately.

"Hooyah." King stepped around Jude and walked to Ella.

"Damn it, Jude!" Ella cried out behind him.

"Let him go, Ella," King said softly.

Jude began walking, shedding her pleas, shedding most of his humanity. He was about to hunt down a man and do his best to kill him. That required a level of animal Jude couldn't affect if he didn't drown out Ella's voice.

"Dresden is mine," she demanded on a shout. And then, "Come back to me."

Jude walked away into the trees, blending seamlessly. He'd track Dresden, but he had a feeling the man was running even now. Jude didn't care how far he had to travel or how long. Ella would be safe with King.

And contrary to what Ella thought, Dresden was all Jude's.

Chapter 19

"It's good to see you again, Ella."

Ella glanced at the hand held out in front of her face and reached for it. She was encased in ice, but she could do this—look at the woman she'd helped Dresden and Savidge go after. She could do it and act like she wasn't ashamed to have confirmed the other woman's identity to a monster. An act of desperation, it still left a bitter taste in Ella's mouth.

The danger she'd put this innocent woman in! Even though she'd done it to keep Jude safe.

"How you doing, Allie?" Ella was proud her voice didn't break.

The petite woman with white-blond hair shrugged and leaned back into her man. King McNally wrapped a hard arm around his woman's midsection and pressed a kiss to that sunlit hair. They fit. Like pieces of a puzzle. Ella had seen the hint of it in Spain. It was even more apparent now.

Deep inside Ella, anger burned. She wanted her puzzle piece, but Jude had been gone for a day and a half with zero contact. Ella had begged Vivi to help her find him. Vivi had refused, and Ella knew why.

Her team didn't trust her.

Ella didn't give a shit. Her man was out there hunting a madman, and he was doing it *alone*. Dresden was dangerous. When he was cornered, hunted, he was insanely crafty. Ella didn't doubt Jude's ability, but Dresden was a monster. If he caught Jude before Jude caught him... Well, he'd make Jude suffer. And that would destroy Ella. Everybody had a reason—for living, breathing, putting one foot in front of the other. Jude was Ella's.

She had to get to Dresden before Jude. That was proving impossible because her teammates, including Brody, were with her every single minute. Nobody called it *guard duty*, but that's exactly what it was.

"I'm good," Allie Redding said with a grin, pulling Ella back to the conversation.

Ella decided she had to take a new tack if she wanted to evade her team and get to Ukraine. She'd gone over every scenario she thought Dresden would engage in. He'd suffered losses in New Mexico. But men were a dime a dozen for Dresden. He seemed to have an unlimited supply. He'd hole up in Ukraine because he had oil to sell.

Allie cleared her throat. "Don't know that I ever thanked you for the help in Spain."

Ella snorted. "Considering I helped put you in the hot seat, it's the least I could do."

"You talked to Vivi yet?" King asked.

Ella narrowed her gaze on him. "Why?"

"Well, I think it's time you gave us a debriefing, right? I mean, it's been a year, Ella." His voice communicated a vein of distrust, but Ella knew he wouldn't let Allie anywhere near her if he thought she was a danger to the team.

She nodded, but her words belied the action. "Maybe."

"Maybe, hell," Rook said from the doorway. "Time is now."

"Still pissed about Russia, Granger?" Ella asked, keeping her voice low.

Rook grinned. "Damn straight, Ella-Bella. Ain't no chick gonna take me down and not suffer for it."

Speaking of chicks, her cat, Chica, strolled into the room, jumping into Ella's lap and nudging her nose against Ella's chin. "Hey, baby," she whispered, burying her hands in the cat's soft fur.

The cat had taken to Endgame Ops like a cat to, well, milk. The team complained. Sometimes King fake sneezed, but for the most part, they'd accepted Ella's surprise animal like they did everything else involved with the team—easily. Besides, Vivi had a cat too. Knight liked to feed him Twizzlers.

"It's time, Ella," Vivi said from the door, alarm in her voice.

Ella's head snapped up, her gaze pinning Vivi.

"It's not good," Vivi responded. "I've got everything set up in the war room."

Ella was up that quickly, following Vivi to the house's former ballroom. It had been converted into a large communications room, similar in feel to Jude's in New Mexico. His old one anyway. The entire house had been fortified with steel, the windows bulletproofed. It was a mini Fort Knox, each member having donated their specific skill set to ensuring it was as safe as any building could possibly be.

Ella had spent the last thirty-six hours searching for clues to where Jude had gone. She'd also searched for clues that Dresden was back in Ukraine. She'd researched Noah Caine and his daughters, along with Gabrielle Moeller, to the nth degree. And she'd begged Vivi for help. Ella wasn't eating, was barely sleeping—because how could she sleep without Jude surrounding her? She was close to breaking.

King must have realized it and demanded they do this right now.

Ella walked into the room, noticing nothing had changed since she'd been here last. It would have felt like home if Jude had been there with her.

But he wasn't, and it was time to go to work.

King, Allie, and Brody sat on the left side of the war table. Rook and Ella sat on the right side. Vivi stood at the head.

"Where are Black and Knight?" Ella asked no one in particular.

"Looking for Chase and Dr. Gabrielle Moeller in Burundi. Apparently, Abrafo Nadege took a liking to the lovely Dr. Moeller, and Chase has had a bitch of a time keeping her safe," Brody informed her.

Gabrielle Moeller is just another pawn on the chessboard, Ella thought. She wondered what the woman's role would be in the game. Her gaze sought the big, white boards behind Vivi. On one board were pictures of Moeller, Anna Beth, and Cameron Markov, and of course, their father, Noah Caine, the Piper. On a second board were pics of Dresden, the prime minister of Russia, and Anton Segorski. A map of Crimea was highlighted in yellow between Dresden and the prime minister, and a line went from one board to another, delineating the connection between Dresden and Anna Beth Caine. On the third board was a picture of the White House, several lines coming off it with a picture of Noah Caine, the chairman of the Joint Chiefs, in the middle. Ella wondered who the other lines were for.

Vivi cleared her throat, and it was so quintessentially Vivi that Ella felt a smile almost curve her lips. Then Endgame's chief analyst started talking, and the potential for a smile lessened significantly.

"Let's start with Africa, shall we? Burundi is a hotbed of unrest, along with most of Africa. Dresden has cemented his foot right in the middle of it, and from everything I have been able to dredge up, he's aligned himself with Abrafo Nadege in an attempt to secure weapons and, get this, diamonds." Vivi tapped her lips with her marker as she moved to the second board and pasted a grainy photo of Abrafo Nadege on the board beneath Dresden.

She consulted some notes on her iPad and said, "Nadege was born in Rwanda forty-three years ago, but his parents escaped the political and social unrest, fleeing to London where Nadege was raised among the elite of London society. Schooled at King's College of London, he graduated cum laude with a PhD in political science. He's traveled extensively his entire adult life — moving back and forth between Africa, London, and the United States. He began as a professor and somehow insinuated himself into London politics for a time. Long enough to forge political ties in his home of Rwanda anyway. He falls off the face of the earth about seven years ago, leaving a wife and three small children in London, not showing up on my radar until Ella gave Brody his name a month or so ago."

Ella speared Brody with a look. He raised an eyebrow and shrugged. He cleared his throat, and Ella knew the action hurt him. "You were in trouble. Shit was speeding up. I needed Vivi. Hell, *you* needed Vivi."

She couldn't be mad at him. "Thank you."

He nodded and turned his gaze back on Vivi.

Vivi and the rest of the team looked at Ella.

"Nadege came on the scene with Dresden shortly after I entered his tender, loving care. Nadege is well spoken, attractive, a big man with big aspirations. He has no conscience, which Dresden adores in his subjects. He's also a master strategist, and he's formed solid bonds with tribal leaders all over Africa. When you speak with him, he comes across as sane. When you see him deal with his people, he's a despot. He controls his people with fear and rage. He's made a fortune in his own right through diamond mining and running guns for Dresden.

"Diamonds are the trade in Africa. Diamonds and people. Money doesn't mean much, but diamonds mean power. And to reach the upper echelon of that power scale, you must go through Dresden. Nadege is intelligent enough to realize that he'll get further with Dresden than without him, and he's effected a change in the scenery of terrorism in Africa. He owns a lot of land as well. Possession is everything. His hands are on it; it's his. Rumors are that terrorists are setting up shop to train all over Africa."

Ella drew in a rough breath. She remembered a time when she'd made a pickup for Dresden in Burundi from Nadege. His courier had been missing four fingers from his left hand and his right ear. He'd handed Ella the bag full of diamonds and fallen to his knees pleading for mercy. Nadege had laughed and laughed and laughed. "Tell your Boko Haram leader I let you live because I'm gracious, but if he interrupts my supply line by invading any more villages, I'll kill you all. Tell him, and I'll continue to let you live." She shuddered.

"Nadege controls all terrorism in Africa, and if Al-Qaeda, Boko Haram, or anyone else thinks to step on what he considers his, he destroys them. They don't move unless they've approved it through Nadege. That's the kind of control we're speaking of. Yes, they're training all over the continent. Because he allows it. There are rumors of other activities going on in Africa as well. Always there are rumors."

"You're telling me he's stronger than Al-Qaeda?" King asked in disbelief.

Ella glanced at King. "He's not as diversified or as zealot-driven, but yes, he's stronger—in Africa at least—than Al-Qaeda. Might is right in that area of the world. And right now, Nadege, with Dresden's backing, has the might.

"Nadege brings us to Dr. Gabrielle Moeller. Twenty-eight years old, graduate of Johns Hopkins University School of Medicine. Said to show great promise, she was slated to perform her residency at Walter Reed Medical Center in Bethesda, Maryland, but never followed through. She's the daughter of Harold and Caroline Moeller, deceased some twelve years ago. Her father was at one time the ambassador to China, and he was a two-time senator from Maryland. Gabrielle Moeller went to an all-girl private Catholic high school, and here's where things really get interesting—she met Anna Beth Caine at Saint Pius, and they became inseparable until two years ago when they both disappeared off the face of the earth."

"Lots of people falling off the face of the earth,

Vivi," Rook said, an edge to his voice that displayed his concern.

"Yeah, Granger. They disappear, but they don't realize I'm the one looking for them," Vivi said with a grin.

Rook grunted.

Vivi huffed. "I really hate when you do that."

Ella just wanted her to hurry the hell up. She needed to get to Jude. It was a driving mantra in her head. Every second her teammates traded loving quips or secret grins was another second she was without him.

"Okay, what's the connection between Moeller, Anna Beth Caine, and Dresden?" Allie Redding tossed out.

"I'm not sure where Moeller falls in other than her connection to Anna Beth. And let's talk Anna Beth Caine," Vivi said, taking a deep breath and once again consulting her iPad. "Born twenty-six years ago, second daughter of Noah Caine," Vivi said, pulling her glasses down as she looked each person in the eye. "Our Piper."

Everyone nodded. By the pall in the air, everyone understood the weight of his picture on the board.

"Anna Beth is Caine's second daughter. Cameron, married name Markov, was born two years previous. The Piper's wife died in childbirth with Anna Beth. Caine took the loss hard and moved his daughters to the Maryland countryside, buying a property that butted up against… Anybody?" No one answered, and King made a motion with his hand to hurry Vivi up. She huffed again but continued. "He bought the property beside Harold and Caroline Moeller."

"Is there a reason for that information?" Ella asked, a queasy feeling in her gut.

"I'm not sure. Maybe we can figure that out. But

allow me to continue," Vivi answered. "Caine was just beginning his stint on the Joint Chiefs of Staff. Harold Moeller was the ambassador to China. I'm digging, but I'm thinking we'll find out these two families were close, and no, I don't know what role that plays in things.

"Anna Beth and Cameron were schooled at Saint Pius, and there are hints that when the Moellers died in a car crash, Piper took on the raising of Gabrielle Moeller. Gabrielle and Anna Beth both dual-enrolled at Johns Hopkins University their senior year in high school and entered medical school the summer after they graduated from college. Gabrielle's focus was plastic surgery. Anna Beth's was psychiatry. But again, though they graduated, they never completed residency. Where was Cameron through all this though? I searched and searched and couldn't find Cameron, and then I turned to your dad's files, Allie, the ones you sent me last night?"

Allie nodded, disquiet marking her features.

"Dresden wants Gabrielle Moeller because of her specialty," Ella said aloud, the possibility too great to ignore.

"He wants to disappear under another face?" Brody asked in horror.

Ella nodded. "It's the only thing that makes sense."

Silence reigned for a few moments as everyone absorbed that tidbit.

"Big risk to take…letting someone who never even completed their residency carve on your face." King pondered the thought.

"Back to the files." Vivi spoke up again. "Cameron is mentioned once and never again. She entered a CIA training camp at age seventeen at the behest of her father."

"My dad took a seventeen-year-old on to train?" Allie asked in surprise.

"Guess who trained her," Vivi urged.

Allie swallowed hard, but it was Ella who answered. "Loretta Bernstein."

Vivi slow-clapped. "Bitch shows up everywhere. But I don't know where Cameron went after training. There's no mention of her again, and there's not enough information for me to build a code to search for her aliases or operative code name."

"She married Yevgeny Markov, now deceased. And Cameron, known as Svetlana, is dead now. I think Dresden is responsible for the sniper that took her out in Moscow. She took a bullet to the chest and head, but not before she gave up the thumb drive's location and asked me to tell her dad to protect her sister," Ella bit out. God, it played out like a bad movie behind her closed lids. Svetlana Markov, a.k.a. Cameron Caine, had married the devil to get further into Dresden's organization. Had her father groomed her for that duty? And if he had, that meant he'd known Dresden was about to go rogue. How would he have known that ten years ago? And why in the hell would he use his *daughter* to keep track of the bastard? Maybe Dresden hadn't been his initial objective.

Ella's head hurt trying to figure it all out.

"Jesus Christ," Brody muttered. "Who are we working for?"

King held up his hand. "There's more, Vivi. I can see it in your face."

She nodded. "While Cameron Caine was becoming Svetlana Markov, her sister, Anna Beth, was hitching her flag to our good old buddy, pal Horace Dresden. They became engaged shortly after Dresden graduated from BUD/S training. There are no society pictures, only a small announcement in the *Washington Journal*, but it's there."

"Something happened though," Ella began. "Because they most definitely are no longer engaged, and that was six years ago. Move forward two years from their engagement, and Dresden is betraying his teammates in the Hindu Kush and moving on to world domination. Four years later, Anna Beth Caine is a prisoner in Dresden's cells."

Vivi mumbled something around her pen tip before she sighed. "I'm trying to account for their whereabouts the last two years. It makes no sense that they simply disappeared, leaving their lives incomplete and hanging, and now they're both back on the scene. Moeller in Burundi, right in the heart of Abrafo Nadege's backyard. And we all know where Anna Beth Caine is."

King turned to Ella. "Tell me how you found out about Anna Beth."

"After I left you, Rook, and Jude in Russia, I returned to Ukraine. Dresden was going to want answers about what happened in Moscow, how his grand deal had gone to shit. When I arrived, he said he had something to show me. It was Anna Beth Caine—living in the same cell I'd resided in after Beirut."

"You okay, Ella?" Brody asked. He'd know what thinking about that time in the cells would do to her.

She gave him a small smile. "We've got to get her out, Brody." Ella tapped her finger on the table and swallowed hard. "Dresden told me about Svetlana

Markov being Cameron Caine and how Anna Beth was his former fiancée and Cameron's sister. The connection to the Piper was right there, and Dresden taunted me with it."

"The link was there the whole time, but we had no idea to look for it. The Piper has a connection with Dresden—and it's so goddamn personal he created an entire team to take the bastard down?" King asked in exasperation. "It doesn't play out to me. There's information we're missing."

Ella both agreed and disagreed. "It's more than personal, but don't any of you fool yourself, it's also *very* personal. So Rook, you guys want to share what happened in the Hindu Kush?"

Rook closed his eyes before he drew in a deep breath and opened them again. Ella swore she could see the memories in them, violent and ruthless.

Vivi covered her man's hand and looked over at King. "Let me handle this?"

King and Rook nodded at her.

"When I first met Rook, he was at Leavenworth Correctional Facility. Rook had saved my brother long enough for me to say goodbye. That alone merited my help. But when I started looking into the reason behind his incarceration, I discovered he'd been tried and imprisoned on faulty information." She took a deep breath. "I busted Rook out of prison." She glanced at her man and smiled. "You were a right ass when I first met you."

"But sexy," he responded with a grin. "Don't forget sexy."

"Too much for my own good," she answered with a

grin of her own. Her expression hardened. "And don't think for two seconds I'm not pissed as hell about you not letting me have access to that file. I can crack it, Rook. I know I can!"

Ella cleared her throat. Loudly. "Can we keep it moving?"

Allie laughed. King grunted. Vivi smiled.

"During the course of trying to clear Rook, we also found Jonah Knight. He wasn't dead at all, but that's a story for a different day."

"I'll finish this, Viv," Rook said. He glanced at Ella. "Knight and I were on that failed Hindu Kush op. It was a joint team operation. Dresden and another man were the SEALs of the group. Me and Knight were the Rangers. There were two CIA agents with us as well as four Force Recon marines. We were to meet with a tribal chief, Abu Bakr-Kabal, for information on Al-Qaeda and another shadowy group that was making waves on the terrorist map. We couldn't get a bead on them or the organization, but it smelled bad so we needed the intel. We had about two million on us. Bakr-Kabal wasn't giving up information for free.

"Once we arrived at his village, sugar went to shit. We were targeted and viciously attacked. Knight, the other SEAL, and the four Force Recon soldiers didn't make it out. Dresden disappeared, and for a while we thought he was dead. Only the two CIA agents and I walked out. I headed home and continued with life. I never heard anything else about the failed operation or Dresden until Endgame started being bandied around with Vivi. Endgame was the name on the disk Vivi knew of. It was the name of the Piper's privatized black ops outfit, but it was also the name of the operation we ran in the Kush."

Something Rook had said stuck with Ella. "What were the names of the marines?"

Vivi shot her a look and put her glasses back on. "Gimme a second," she said. Two minutes later, she said, "David Small, Warren Gent, Henry Grant, and…oh shit!"

Vivi's eyes went round, and she leveled them on Ella. "Drake Cain. No *e* on the end."

Ella nodded. It made sense. "In your research of Caine, you never ran into a son?"

"There's nothing. He's buried so deep that not even I turned him up."

"Probably the *e*," Ella mused.

"So the Piper, the chairman of the Joint Chiefs of Staff, had a son on our op?" Rook asked, his gaze on King.

King ran a hand over his forehead. "Makes sense why he was buried so deep now, doesn't it?"

"Dresden betrayed us, made off with the money, is responsible for the Piper's son's death, so he sets up an entire team to take the bastard down? Risked his daughters?" Rook asked in disbelief.

"I still think the big picture is unfolding. You forget, he's lost two children to Dresden, and his last one is in Dresden's hold. There's something bigger the Piper is after," Ella warned.

"Ask him," Allie said as if it were the most logical thing in the world. "Just ask him. It's obvious this is much bigger than any of you realize. If people in the White House are doing everything they can to silence and come after you, it's apparent that Noah Caine is an island under attack. I don't think the Piper is the enemy."

Ella agreed. But… "Doesn't excuse his methods. He's playing with our lives."

"Agreed," Allie Redding admitted. "But outing him at this point doesn't serve any purpose. And we have no way of knowing who's friend or foe at the moment. My dad was betrayed by his second-in-command. Best course of action is to just pin the Piper down and ask him."

"You'll have to find him," Brody interjected. "He's on a tour for the president that's taking him all over the Middle East and, oh yeah, Russia."

"How has he evaded Dresden?" Vivi asked absently.

Ella knew this one beyond a doubt. "It's a game to Dresden. He's keeping Caine on the line to hurt him. It's deep between those two. Also, Dresden is part of a group that I can't get a bead on. It sounds mysteriously like the group Rook was just telling us about."

"Man, this is a cluster," King said around a sigh. "I haven't heard from the Piper in a week. Strange. Worrisome. But we aren't shut down. We still have access to our accounts. It's almost as if he's telling me something without telling me."

"Maybe he figured you'd discover the truth. Especially now that I'm back with the team," Ella added with a shrug. "Vivi, I need Jude."

Every gaze slammed into Ella.

She stood. "If Dresden gets him first, I'll lose him. And if I lose him, I'll set the world on fire, team leader."

"Vivi, do you know where Keeper is?"

Vivi glanced uneasily at Rook.

"I'm right here, Vivi," King said in a hard voice. "I'm your team leader."

"Don't talk to her that way, King," Rook warned.

"This is my team, Granger." He shot Rook a hard look. "Tell me, Vivi," King demanded in a softer tone.

God, these men, Ella thought. Alpha. Badass. But so soft on the inside it defied expectation. She wanted hers back. Now.

"He's in Ukraine. According to my sources, he met up with Georgia Banks, FBI agent on loan to the CIA for covert ops. She's known Jude for a while," Vivi said, her eyes on Ella.

"She's the one who knocked me out and brought me to Jude the other day." Ella grimaced. She would not get pissed off that he'd met up with another woman when he'd refused to let Ella go with him. "What's their location in Ukraine?"

"Sevastopol in Crimea," Vivi answered.

"Vivi," Rook warned. "No more."

"I told him where she was. Right is right." Viv was emphatic.

Rook shook his head. King laughed. Allie looked uncomfortable.

Brody stood up. "We headed out, Ella-Bella? Sounds like we got two folks to corral now."

She looked at Brody in shock. "No way, Madoc. You're here. I'll not—"

"What you'll not do is tell me how to live. I get it, Ella. I do. But I won't hide from that motherfucker. Now when do we leave? If Keeper is setting up to give that bastard some, I'm going to be in on it," Brody stated patiently.

She gave up. She couldn't protect everyone. She loved Brody like a brother, but she wasn't his keeper. *Keeper... Damn you, Jude,* she thought. "Do you still have that contact in Sevastopol?"

"Yeah," Brody replied with a grin breaking across his face. "She's probably missing me." He rubbed a hand down his stubbled jaw. Brody was a huge dude and attractive. The scruff covered the scars on his lower face. Savidge had ravaged her friend's face like he'd ravaged Ella's back.

"Tap her and set up a puddle jumper. We'll head out tonight. Adam Babic owes me another favor. I'll tag him for transpo…get him to set us up on board his next flight to Odessa. From there, we'll hit the puddle jumper to Sevastopol," Ella said, giving details as she rose and planned in her mind.

Brody nodded.

"There's one more thing, team," Vivi called out.

"There's more?" Rook asked in disbelief.

"I got a kickback on one of our burner cards two weeks ago. I had put a trace on it because it wasn't in Nina's things when we picked them up from the hospital after she…" Vivi trailed off. There was no reason to say it.

Ella rubbed her chest. Nina and Micah. She missed them.

"And?" King prompted when Vivi didn't continue.

"It was used in Utah to purchase a plane ticket to Anchorage, Alaska."

Nothing niggled at Ella about Alaska. "Were you able to get any footage of who purchased it?" she asked Vivi.

"Yeah." Vivi turned around and pulled up the email, clicking on a link to the requested footage. "I just got the email response as we talked."

As they watched, grainy CCTV footage at the Provo, Utah, airport showed a woman walk up to the Alaskan

Airlines desk and purchase a ticket. She turned back toward the camera, and the shock nearly took Ella to her knees.

"No way," she said breathlessly.

"Let's enhance this," Vivi mumbled, doing her mojo. In seconds, a clearer picture of the woman's face showed on the screen.

"Nina?" Ella whispered.

"What the hell is this?" King roared. "She's dead. We buried her outside DC!"

Vivi took the image down. "The plane landed in Anchorage on time yesterday morning. I'm looking for anything I can find after the plane landed. It may take me awhile with everything else going on. But, yeah, that looks like Nina Lassiter."

"I want to know where that woman is when we return, Vivi," King demanded, pointing at the screen.

Ella looked at her team leader. "You're going?"

"You don't seriously think I'm going to let my team go without me?" he asked in a hard tone.

She shrugged. "You left us in Beirut." It came out before she could stop it.

"We didn't know," King said in her face, his voice tortured. "You are my team. You're part of me," he claimed, slamming a fist to his chest.

Ella felt a single tear trek down her face.

King grabbed her shoulders and pulled her to him, hugging her tight. "I would never have left you in Beirut if I thought you were alive, Ella. You, Brody, Nina, Micah...you're as much a part of me as my arms, my lungs. Hell, you're not just team, you're family."

"I know," she mumbled against his chest.

King stepped back and lifted her chin. "We're going to get Jude. I need you all in, Ella. Get in the game. Can you handle this?"

She notched her chin higher, tears drying. "That's my man walking into danger. I've spent the last year trying to keep him safe. Nothing will stop me now."

He nodded. "Get ready. We leave as soon as you talk to your transport. Rook, get ready. Call Knight and Black and make them aware as you get an update on Chase's situation. Tell them we'll upload Vivi's notes as soon as they have a clear connection. They need to know what we're dealing with. Oh, and tell them to make sure Dr. Moeller gets back here in one piece. I think she and Anna Beth Caine have a lot of intel we need."

"On it," Rook said as he walked to Vivi and pulled out his satellite phone.

"Let's move, Endgame. We've got a player on the board. Let's get his six," King called out as he left the room.

Ella glanced at Brody and smiled. "Let's do this."

Brody nodded. "I'm point, Ella. Keeper already wants a piece of my ass for the last year. If you aren't behind me in this, he'll lose his mind."

Ella's back snapped straight. Then her anger deflated.

"Poor Ella. If it helps, I'm not a badass CIA operative either," Vivi called out with a laugh. Rook pulled her close to him with a laugh of his own.

"Screw you, Granger. I'm as badass as they come," Ella said in a tone as mean as she could affect.

"Straight up," Vivi agreed.

"I hear you, Brody, but remember, I've trained, and I'm not as weak as you men seem to think. I can handle myself. How about this? I'll stay behind until I have to move in front," Ella said hopefully.

"I'll take it," Brody agreed. "Now move."

She did, heading up to her room and grabbing her go bag that she'd repacked the moment she'd reached Port Royal. Chica meowed from the door. "Come here, baby girl," Ella crooned.

She grabbed her cat and hugged her close, and the cat allowed it. Ella took comfort in the feel of the cat's fur and purrs beneath her palms. Jude was in trouble, and he'd allowed someone else to have his six. Ella wanted to be pissed, but she understood him. Hell, she had spent the last year doing the same thing.

The cat hopped off her lap and headed for the pillow at the head of the bed. She walked in a circle twice and lowered herself gracefully to the soft, downy pillow, closing her eyes, still purring.

Nina might be alive. Jude was heading for Dresden. Anna Beth Caine needed saving.

And it was all okay, because Ella had her team at her back.

It was time to kick some ass.

Chapter 20

JUDE WAS COLD. SEVASTOPOL IN THE CRIMEA REGION of Ukraine wasn't a pleasant place in the midst of winter, and as he watched Georgia head his way with a bottle of whiskey, his current state of mind made the location even less so.

"Have one," Georgia said with a grin as she tossed back a shot of amber-colored liquor.

"I'll pass," Jude told her. "And maybe you should lay off a bit?"

Georgia had proven to be a valuable asset when he'd needed to get Ella out of Dresden's house. On this go-round, she was proving to be a pain in the ass that he was struggling to keep sober. The woman could drink Jonah Knight under the table, and that was saying something. Jude had once watched Knight down an entire bottle of Scotch, then start in on a fifth of gin on the same night.

"You my daddy all of a sudden, Dagan?" Georgia asked, quirking a brow at him.

"Nope. You do you, G," Jude replied with a shrug. His neck prickled. "What do you see?" he asked, leaning in as she gestured him to come closer.

"Looks like we've got company," she whispered in his ear. "Fedir and his men just walked in."

Jude glanced up as the man walked up and sat down, grabbing the whiskey Georgia had been drinking and pouring himself a snifter. "You the one needs ride to

Simferopol?" His English was bad and so accented it was hard to follow.

"Yeah, I need transpo," Jude said, "and Georgia told me you've got architectural plans for that mansion," he added with a smile.

"I've got them. Cost you big," Fedir said. "And I want know why you want."

Jude shook his head. "Not your concern. I'll pay whatever you're asking."

"I want go with," Fedir said suddenly. "The devil in that house has my sister."

"I don't do rescues," Jude said impatiently. What had Georgia gotten him into? He just wanted a fucking reliable vehicle and the plans to the bastard's house.

"I go or no plans," Fedir stated implacably.

He threw Georgia a look full of retribution.

"Come on, baby, let's help him out," Georgia wheedled. Something in her tone told Jude this was important to her too. He wished he knew why.

"You go, you handle your own business. I want the plans," Jude bit out.

The man handed over a rolled set of plans and tossed back another whiskey. It seemed that was all people did here…drink.

"I always take care myself," the man said darkly.

Jude grabbed the plans, stood, and tossed some money on the table. "We leave in the morning. Six."

He walked out of the bar and headed toward the ship docked in one of the berths along the shore. He'd tracked Dresden out of his mountains and all the way to Ukraine. He had one mission—blowing Dresden's head off.

Ella would be free. Jude would be free. Hell, the world would be free. That's all that mattered to Jude right now. He didn't give a shit about any shadowy group on the fringes of society looking for world order or power. He didn't give a shit that the Piper was invested in all of this for personal reasons. He cared about two things: Ella and his team.

"Wait up," Georgia called. "Jesus, Keeper, what's your issue?"

He turned on her as they came to the ship. "Why are you here? What's your op?"

She couldn't meet his eyes, gazing instead over his left shoulder. "I'm only here helping you."

"I'm calling bullshit."

"Then call it," she huffed, turning around and walking away.

"What do you owe the Piper?" he called out.

She stopped on a dime, spine stiffening, and Jude knew. She was in the Piper's pocket. "You don't want to know," she whispered.

But Jude heard.

"I'm going to suggest you head back stateside. I've got it from here," Jude replied.

"I can't," she said miserably.

"Tell me why," he demanded.

"Because I'm not here for you, or Endgame. I'm here for Loretta Bernstein. She's my objective."

"She'll eat you alive," Jude told her. "I don't know why the Piper involved you in this, but you'd do better heading home and taking refuge at Quantico. You aren't cut out for CIA work, Georgia. They have no soul and will suck yours from your body to compensate."

"I know, I know!" She paused. "But I owe him. He helped a friend of mine a few years ago when he was in a sticky situation in Afghanistan."

"And that put your ass on the line? Must be a helluva friend. Because let me assure you, Loretta Bernstein will knock you down and keep moving," Jude assured her. "The woman is a stone-cold killer. And how do you know she's here anyway?"

"Got intel right before you called me wanting help here. I was coming and decided to let you hitch your wagon to mine."

"Bullshit. The Piper told you I was headed this way and thought I'd help *you* out. I'm getting pretty sick of him manipulating me," Jude growled.

She shrugged. "Okay, maybe."

"Just like Fedir, you're on your own. I've got one mission...eliminate Dresden. Other than that, nothing else matters to me. We clear? In, out, home."

She nodded.

Jude's satellite phone rang. He ignored it. In fact, he turned it off. He was solo now.

"You realize Endgame is headed this way?" she asked him suddenly.

"It doesn't matter. I have a head start, and hopefully, I can put a bullet in Dresden's brain before they get here." His words were a vow.

"I'm heading back into town. There's more information to be gained," she told him.

He snorted. "Stop drinking, G."

She snapped her fingers. "Shucks, you figured me out. Look, my only other outlet is sex. You game?"

He shook his head. "I'm off the market."

"Ella locked you up tight, eh?" she asked with a grin.

"Never any doubt," he answered, and the absoluteness of it rang in the air between them.

She nodded. "Good for you. At least one of us has their shit locked up tight." Then she walked away.

Jude headed inside to look over the plans Fedir had given him. He needed this over so he could go home to his Ella. That was all he wanted.

———

"He's not going to be happy about this," Georgia said to King.

Ella looked the woman over, dismissing her as a threat. She may once have had a relationship with Jude, but Jude was Ella's now. Her conviction was bone deep.

"Which slip?" King asked.

"Three," she answered before she turned to Ella. "He's all yours."

Ella smiled, hoping it was more than just a baring of her teeth. "I know."

Georgia laughed.

Ella walked over to the bar. "She's the Piper's, according to Vivi," Rook said from the corner of his mouth.

"She told me Jude has the plans to Dresden's mansion," King told them as they sat down around the small table by a window.

Ella sniffed lightly. "We don't need them. They're probably out of date. Dresden remodeled shortly after taking it from the previous owner."

"You going in first, Ella?" Brody asked with a quirked eyebrow.

"Yeah. Right after a shot of vodka to fortify myself,"

she said around a laugh. Brody motioned for the woman behind the bar to bring them a round.

"I think we all need one," he said in agreement.

They each took a shot, slamming their glasses upside down on the scarred wooden surface.

"We'll bunk on the ship tonight. According to Georgia, Jude is set to leave at oh six hundred. Be ready," King warned.

They each stood and made their way down the docks. When Ella came to the third slip, she breathed in deeply. He was going to be pissed.

She didn't give two shits.

She stepped onto the boat, steps nearly silent, wind tossing her hair to and fro. She entered the main cabin and froze as a gun was leveled at her temple.

"Goddamn it, Ella!" Jude pushed out between clenched teeth. "What the hell are you doing here?"

"Get the gun off me, Jude," she demanded.

"Then take yours out of my gut," he said ruefully as he lowered his weapon.

Ella did the same. Then they were face-to-face. Darkness had fallen hours ago. It had been a hard ride to Sevastopol from Odessa. Puddle jumpers never failed to wig her out. The moon shone bright over the water and highlighted the cabin.

"I'll accept your apology once we're home," she whispered, and they both knew she was referring to his leaving.

"I can't do this if you're here," he said, once again through clenched teeth. "You'll pull my concentration."

Ella cocked her head. Frustration gnawing at her. "Well, you won't be doing it without me here, so looks like you've got a choice to make."

The others stepped in behind her.

"Take her home, Your Highness," Jude said softly, his gaze never leaving Ella.

"No." King was implacable.

Finally, Jude moved the weight of his gaze from Ella to their team leader.

"You'll do it with your team, or we'll do it without you," King said firmly.

Jude ran a hand over his head. She felt his tension, wanted to ease him.

"He tried to kill her. Blew my cabin apart to find her. Had his men fire shots at her. I can't let her go back into that."

"We go together. I understand why you left, Keeper, but there's shit you need to know, and Ella was coming after you whether we came or not," King informed him.

"Then you should have locked her ass up," Jude bit out.

"That shit don't work, man." Brody spoke up. "Even Dresden figured out real quick that Ella doesn't do real well locked up."

Jude dropped into a chair by the captain's table. He hung his head and took deep, even breaths. He was struggling with it. With having her here.

"I spent the last year tortured every day with thoughts of Dresden possibly killing you. I have done things I won't ever receive forgiveness for. The least you could do is look at me when you talk about me," Ella demanded.

His gaze rose to hers.

"When he shot me in Beirut, I thought it was over. When I woke up, I knew I was going to suffer and then die. You were there with me every step. And now, when you need me the most, you're shutting me out. I want to know why."

"I would die if I lost you again," he said simply.

Every word was a bomb dropped right on her heart.

But she raised her head and nodded. "And I would do the same. It's why I suffered the last year—doing the Piper's dirty work, dealing with Dresden, doing every last thing I've done to help that monster. Don't shut me out because you think I'm weak and can't handle it. If you don't understand what I gave up when I stayed gone, letting you think I was dead, then we have nothing between us."

He stood at that and rushed her, taking her arm and moving her to the back of the forty-foot boat, as far away from the others as he could get. He slammed a door behind him, and they were enclosed in a small space. Too small to contain the aggression pouring off them both.

Ella opened her mouth, and he was on her. Mouth closing over hers, tongue demanding entry. "Take it all off," he whispered savagely.

"You first," she returned stubbornly.

He had to realize that while she wasn't as strong as he was physically, she was an equal in this. Dresden was hers. For everything that bastard had done. He was hers.

Jude ripped her shirt in half. Okay, she really wasn't as strong. She pushed her hands under his tee and pushed up. "Get it off," she pleaded.

His lips left hers long enough for him to tug his T-shirt off. Then he was back on her. He unbuttoned her pants and pushed them down her legs. She stepped out. Her panties followed. She reached for his fly, unbuttoned and unzipped him, then reached in and freed his shaft.

"So hard, Jude. I need it," she said, desire coating her words, making them thick in her throat.

"I'm going to give it all to you," he replied, following her down as he laid her on the small bed.

He was inside her as soon as she parted her legs, sliding home with a groan.

"God," she prayed reverently. "I love you, Jude."

His response was to push deeper, forcing her body up the bed with the sensual ferocity of his thrusts.

She wrapped her legs around his hips, sank her fingers into his shoulders, and held on for the ride. Over and over, he dove and retreated, his cock filling her up and then emptying her. She spiraled up, felt the heat of his skin melt into hers, and then saw the sun behind her eyelids as he took her to the peak.

"Give it all to me, Ella. Every last bit of you," he begged harshly.

"It's yours," she promised as she exploded around him.

He rode her through the orgasm, slowing for a time, never leaving her body, using his pelvis to build the fire between them again. He rotated his hips, and she lifted hers.

"Don't let me go," she whispered in his ear.

He cursed and withdrew from the clasp of her body, turning her over to her stomach and using his legs to spread her. "On your knees, Ella."

She complied, her body begging for what he was about to give her.

"Relax, baby. I've got you."

His voice in his ear was a low growl of need. His

cock parted her folds and slid so deep that he was the center of her world. He sank inside, pulled out all the way, and dove back in.

Every hard stroke was a loving declaration, a promise of ecstasy, a vow fulfilled between two people who only knew that their hearts resided in the other's chest.

When release came, it slammed into her, a supernova of pleasure as his body curved over her back, his voice in her ear praising her body, her desire, and the way she gave both to him without reservation.

His release followed hers, and he groaned her name, soft, seductive. She was reborn in the sound of it.

Ella fell to her stomach, her body limp and sated. He fell on top of her but rolled to the side, his hands tracing her spine as their breathing calmed.

Ella opened her eyes and found him watching her in the darkness.

"You shouldn't have come, but I get it."

The pressure in her chest released. "You shouldn't have left, but I get it."

He snorted, then pulled a blanket over her body. "Stay here," he said, getting off the bed and dressing. "I need to talk to the team. Rest, Ella. It's a big day tomorrow."

She didn't argue with him. But she didn't sleep either. She wouldn't do that until he came back and slid in beside her.

Chapter 21

"WE'VE GOT TO HIT HIM FAST," BRODY SAID, AND FOR the first time since the man had returned to his team, Jude noticed the sandpaper roughness of his voice.

It wasn't so much that he hadn't noticed before, but that he'd ignored it. After losing and then finding himself inside Ella's body and heart, he couldn't help but hear the pain in the man's voice—the echoes of the torture he'd suffered in that room with Ella.

"We've got the layout now," King said. "Rook, you've got point. Brody, you've got Keeper. Ella's with me."

Jude nodded. It was best that Ella stay with King. She messed with Jude's mind, and he absolutely couldn't have his thoughts divided when he got a bead on Dresden. "I'm good," he said easily.

King inclined his head, accepting that. "It will take about two hours to reach Simferopol. Dresden's place is on the northern outskirts of the city. It's walled, but we're heading in with the cleaning crew."

"Fedir, the guy who gave me the plans, is driving the truck," Jude pointed out. He shrugged his shoulders when Rook threw him a look. "I had no choice. He provided those worthless plans. Says his sister was hired by Dresden and can't leave. He's got a scheme to get her out."

"And he's using our attack as cover? Great. Who else are we dragging along?" Brody asked, his tone grumpy.

"Nobody. Georgia is out. She's in the Piper's pocket. Said she was heading in for Loretta Bernstein. The Piper wants Loretta in a bad way apparently." Jude sighed and ran a hand down his face. His mind was on the planning. His heart was back in that tiny bed with his woman.

"We don't need Loretta, but if we get her, it's a bonus," King said. "Vivi?" he called out.

"Your Highness?" she answered via the satellite phone.

"I need coordinates sent to my GPS by oh six hundred. Will you have satellite coverage for this op?" King asked.

"You'll have two hours to get there, but my satellite access should not be in danger on this op. In spite of that, you need to get in and out. Dresden doesn't have a huge contingent of men on his property, but he does have access to more men, if he needs them. Operational details have been sent to your personal comm units. Full disclosure, guys—my reach in Ukraine is limited. You'll be pretty much on your own, should the local police or, God forbid, the Ukrainian military get called in." She hummed a bit to herself, which wasn't unusual. Vivi was always all over the place. "Oh, one more thing. I received video of the occupants of the plane disembarking in Anchorage. It's much clearer than the Provo video."

Silence held sway as Jude looked at King, confusion swimming through him. King held up his hand.

"Baby, come on, what'd you find?" Rook prompted.

"Facial recognition confirms it's Nina Lassiter," she told them, her voice hushed.

"You have got to be kidding me!" Jude exclaimed. "She's alive?"

"According to my software, it's a positive match. I'm running further analysis as we speak. I've also asked a friend still with the Agency for help in locating the woman," Vivi announced.

"No," King said emphatically. "Call them off. I don't want Broemig having this information."

"Future father-in-law is a real gem, isn't he?" Brody teased.

King threw him a sardonic grin. "Vivi, call your friend off."

"Done," she stated. "I'll do the legwork."

"Wait until we get back stateside, Vivi. You and Allie lock up tight. Black is headed your way. Fill him in on things, and keep an eye out for Chase and Knight to be headed your way too."

"Ten-four, Your Highness." She cleared her throat, and then uttered a tentative "Rook?"

"Yeah, woman?" Rook was staring out one of the cabin windows. Jude followed his line of sight and noticed the Black Sea, an endless, velvety blackness beyond the glass.

"Come home to me," she whispered.

"Done."

"Good night, Vivi," King singsonged and then disconnected.

Jude rubbed his chest. Vivi wasn't cut out for wet work. She sucked in the field. But without her, Rook was only half a man. Much like Jude without Ella. It was the first time he didn't envy Rook and Vivi. He had Ella here with him, and even though she was soft, she'd proven she more than had the chops for fieldwork. She was a damn fine soldier.

He'd have to tell her.

"I'm going to bed down," he told his teammates. "I'll

take last watch." He glanced at his tactical watch. "I'll be up at oh three hundred."

He made his way back to Ella. She was quiet, but he could feel her attention. He wondered if she'd eaten over the last couple of days and decided she probably hadn't. The woman was too thin. When they got home, he was going to keep her fed. And sexed up. Definitely sexed up.

She curved her body into his as he settled back down on the bed with her. "Hey," she murmured sleepily.

"Shh, go to sleep. I've got you, El," he whispered against her hair.

His hands calmed her back down into sleep, and Jude just held her there against him, feeling waves rock the boat.

He fell asleep with her scent in his nostrils and her heat against his skin.

Chapter 22

ELLA BREATHED IN THE SALTY WIND AND PULLED HER hair into a tight bun. She was dressed in black, her combat boots chafing because they were so new. Over her black field suit, she wore blue, faded overalls. Cleaning crew, indeed.

Jude had been up at oh three hundred for watch. She'd taken it with him. They hadn't talked—that's not what watch was for. But she'd been eased anyway because they were together.

She watched him strap on his guns. Keeper. He was every bit his call sign. He wore a double shoulder holster with a 9mm handgun in each pocket. He had cleaned them earlier and loaded ammunition. Rook, King, and Brody had sat at the table with him doing the same.

Ella had cleaned her guns prior to leaving Port Royal. She'd spent the gut-churning ride in the puddle jumper loading her ammo. As Jude strapped on multiple knives, Ella admired the play of muscle over solid bone. Those arms had held her all night.

She was going to make sure they continued to do so.

She pulled on her own holster, loaded herself down with her weaponry, pulled up the coveralls, zipped them, and cleared her throat.

The men all stopped in the process of pulling on their overalls and glanced at her, questions in their gaze.

"Anna Beth Caine," she said by way of explaining her interruption.

"The Piper's daughter?" Jude asked. "What about her?"

"She's there. Whatever happens today, we don't leave without her," Ella explained.

Everyone nodded.

Brody ran a hand over his beard. "You mentioned something about her being a fail-safe?"

Ella nodded. "Yeah, we never talked about that the other day in the war room. Vivi can't open those last two files on the thumb drive Cameron Caine gave me. I think Anna Beth knows how to crack that code."

"Do you think that's why Dresden has her?" King asked.

She shrugged. "Maybe. Maybe not. Either way, we need her. Oh, and again, she's a person in the hands of an evil bastard," she finished sarcastically.

"What if she doesn't want to come?" Brody asked.

Ella huffed. "Jesus, Brody. Did he break your brain in that cell?"

"You'd know better than me," Brody said with a wink.

"Psshh, you're an ass." She glanced at Jude and found him watching her intently.

"We'll get her," Jude said as if it were a foregone conclusion.

But Ella knew those were few and far between. They hadn't even begun this op, and he was giving her assurances.

King's satellite phone pinged, and he hit a button.

"Good morning, Endgame. Your op starts now," Vivi chanted. "Ride's outside waiting on you."

"You got eyes on us?" Rook asked, strapping his rifle to his back and pulling a skullcap over his head.

"I do. Now get moving. You've got limited time to reach Simferopol. Word on the street is that Dresden has a plane being fueled, and he's pulled maybe fifteen or twenty men in to his property."

"How do you always know everything?" Jude asked.

"It's my job," Vivi said matter-of-factly.

"Touché," Jude responded.

"He knows we're coming," King said on a sigh. "He always knows we're coming. I'm getting sick of this."

"He may know you're coming, but he doesn't know how. You've got the heads-up. You aren't walking in blind," Vivi reminded them.

Jude pulled on his skullcap, covering his hair and donning his soldier persona. This was business now. So Ella pushed everything she felt for him to the back of her mind as she shielded her heart.

"Safe, Ella," he said as he put his rifle over his back.

She held up six fingers.

He smiled. Her stomach settled.

King gave a short whistle and they all fell out, hitting the deck and making their way to the waiting truck.

"Good see you, American," the man named Fedir said with a grin.

Jude grunted.

Ella nodded and loaded up. King sat beside her in the back. Rook, Brody, and Jude sat across from them. Georgia was in the front seat with Fedir.

Jude's jaw hardened when he saw the woman. "Told you to head home, G."

"Told you I have a mission, Jude. Looks like I'm going with," the woman said, her gaze roving over Jude and then moving to meet Ella's.

Ella raised a brow and then purposefully looked away. The woman was no threat to her, regardless of what she was trying to intimate. Brody chuckled. "Fish in a goddamn barrel, Keeper. How do you get such pretty women to fall for that ugly mug?"

Jude looked at Ella and only Ella. "I just got it like that, Madoc." He slid his gaze to Brody. "You need lessons?"

"From your mama maybe," Brody snapped back.

Jude winced. "Leave my mama out of it."

Brody made a kissing sound, and for a second Ella was thrown back to the morning she'd been called up for the Beirut op. By the end of that day, she'd been shot and Micah Samson and Nina Lassiter had both been dead.

But maybe not Nina. Maybe, somehow, improbably, Nina was still alive.

Ella remembered the feeling of doom she'd had setting out on that Beirut op. She shivered and glanced at Jude, seeing concern drawing his face into harsh lines. She shook her head and gave him a small smile.

She refused to let that doom back in. She would make sure this op went exactly the way they wanted. Ella rested her head against the wall of the truck and went over the op again.

It took them every last minute of the two hours Vivi had given them for arrival in Simferopol. It took them another thirty minutes to skirt the city and hit the road to Dresden's house.

"Target is still on-site, Endgame," Vivi said into their earpieces. "You'll be there in five minutes. Go to the second gate and let Fedir do the talking. King? I just got word from Knight that he's on the ground in Simferopol."

"What the hell?" Jude exclaimed. "I thought he was with Chase and that Moeller chick heading back stateside."

"They've sent Dr. Moeller my way. She should arrive in the States in about nine hours. They are heading your way," Vivi explained. "It's an Endgame party, guys. Get ready."

"Fedir?" King called out.

The man turned. "Yes?"

"Stop the truck," King ordered.

Fedir put on the brake and turned around.

"We'll wait for them," King told his analyst. "We'll need all hands on deck for this not to go completely FUBAR."

"Ten-four." Thirty seconds later, Vivi was back. "They're two minutes from you. Can you hold?"

King raised an eyebrow at Fedir. "Get out, and act like you're working on the truck."

A few cars passed them, but Dresden had eyes everywhere and the repairs needed to look genuine. Knight and Chase arrived, jumping out of their Volvo and into the back of the truck. Chase looked like hell—like he'd been up for days without rest and he was barely holding on. Knight didn't look much better.

"Let's move, Fedir," King demanded as he tossed each new man a pair of coveralls. To Chase and Knight, he simply said, "Sit rep."

Chase ran a hand down his face. "We were able to catch Black before he left. We got him and Dr. Moeller on a plane, and they're headed to DC, then Port Royal. Nadege was relentless, Dr. Moeller is a pain in the ass, and I'm ready to kill Dresden."

"Hooyah," Jude replied with a grunt.

"Nadege just let her go?" King asked in disbelief.

"Not quite," Knight said with a grimace. "He lost a

lot of people, and finally the bastard ran. It gave us time to get her out and on a plane."

"She won't give us any information. She'll be a tough nut to crack." Chase's voice was hard. He finally noticed Ella, and his jaw dropped. "Ella-Bella?"

She hadn't seen Chase in over a year. He might have known she was alive, but he hadn't seen her so it was probably shocking.

"Chase Reynolds, as I live and breathe," she said in a very fake southern accent. Chase would appreciate her effort, being the Alabama boy he was. Ella wanted something to replace that look of frustration on his face.

He laughed, but it was forced. "Damn, girl, I'm happy to see you."

"No offense, but you don't look all that happy."

"Well, I've had a rough week," he said, and it seemed a huge understatement.

Knight snorted. "Good to see you, Ella," he said with a nod. He punched Jude in the arm, probably bro code for *You got her back*, Ella thought.

"Chase, Knight, I've loaded the op onto your comm units. You've got five minutes to read through it," Vivi stated calmly.

They got busy. Jude and Rook shared a weapon each and some ammo with Chase and Knight.

"Knight, you're with Rook. Search the house for any intel we can take with us. Keeper, Brody, you'll hit Dresden. Chase, you're with me and Ella. We'll hit the cellar," King stated.

"No—" Jude began.

Ella silenced him with a look. She knew he wanted to protect her from her memories—from what had happened to her there—but she knew that cellar like the back of her hand. She needed to be the one who went. Her look quelled his instant, protective response.

Then he nodded, as did the rest of the men. Rook and Knight had worked together for so long that they moved as one sometimes. Jude was badass no matter who he was grouped with.

"We're here, Americans," Fedir called out, pulling into the gate.

"Chase, Knight, get behind us," King ordered. They did, and when the guards opened the back door to check them, they saw nothing but men and women dressed for cleaning.

Ella breathed out heavily and thanked God. That could have started everything off poorly.

"Dresden's pilot has arrived at the airfield. If you're going to move, do it now, Endgame. You will have a welcoming committee once they realize you're on-site." Vivi told them, no urgency in her voice. She was always the calm in their storms. Ella gave thanks for Vivi too.

Then again, they did this for a living. They lived and breathed FUBAR situations. Dresden getting ready to leave could definitely throw a kink in the works.

"He wants her for something big," Chase said, staring hard at the side of the truck.

"Who?" Jude asked.

"Gabby," Chase informed them. "Dresden's been after her for a few years now."

"Let's chat later, ladies," King said quickly. "It's time to move."

The truck stopped and they all got out, including

Georgia and Fedir. They spread out, grouped loosely but very coordinated. There were no guards posted, which set Ella on alert.

It made no sense. Normally, Dresden was surrounded by guards, and Vivi had told them he'd amassed a lot of men. If he suspected they were coming, had even a hint, she would have guessed he'd meet them with guns blazing. Something was up. Something bigger than they'd guessed. She glanced across the courtyard to Brody, and he nodded as their gazes met, his mind obviously traveling where hers had.

They entered the house and split up. She got one last look at Jude.

"Safe," he mouthed.

"Six," she mouthed back, and then he was gone around a corner, out of her sight.

"Let's move, Banning, Work to do," King urged. "Where are the men, Vivi?"

"I'm searching my feed. Satellite is getting grainy," Vivi answered.

King glanced at Ella. "Where are the cells?"

"Follow me," Ella said, taking the lead. King and Chase followed her.

The house was eerily silent. They met no staff and still no guards.

"Vivi, any intel on guard locations?" Chase questioned the analyst.

"Negative," Vivi responded. "House appears to be empty."

"We need to find Anna Beth Caine. She could be in the cellars. Keeper, Brody, we're headed that way now. You might want to hit the western wing of the house.

He's got rooms there. Dresden also has an exit from the lower level in that wing," Ella said calmly.

"Ten-four," Jude responded, his voice very dark and very deep. Soldier.

A shot rang out as Ella peered around a corner of the hallway that led to the stairs to the cell. She dropped to a knee, put the barrel of her rifle around the corner, and fired. The sound of a short scream indicated she'd made a hit. "One down," she reported.

She quickly glanced around the corner, didn't receive fire, and felt King move around her, taking point. "Down the hall, last door on the right," she said over the ear mic.

With King in front and Chase behind her facing the opposite direction, they moved toward the cells.

"Tango," Chase murmured. The suppressed sound of his rifle thudded behind her, and she kept moving. "Two down," Chase reported.

King stopped in the hallway, raising his rifle to his shoulder and shooting once. "Three down."

They moved to the door, not encountering any more fire. King took the stairs, followed by Ella and Chase. She noticed the pall first, normal for the cells, and yet…not.

Then the smell.

Someone had died very badly and very recently. The smell of death permeated the air, and Ella's skin chilled. *Please, not Anna Beth Caine.*

She waited for King to give the all clear signal, and then she moved to the first cell. She threw it open and was both relieved and horrified by what met her eyes.

She heard King in her ear, heard Jude and Brody both calling her name, but she was suddenly, irrevocably in the midst of her memories and pain. Everything seemed to fade around her except for the tableau before her.

The chains.

The dirt floor.

The darkness.

Anton Segorski hung suspended from the same bolt in the ceiling Ella once had. He'd been tortured and ultimately disemboweled. Stuffed into the enormous cut in his stomach was money—hundred-dollar bills, a lot of them.

"Ella?" Jude called over the comm unit.

"I'm good," she whispered and swallowed hard. It took another few seconds, but she got it together.

"Goddamn, who does something like that?" Chase said around a gag.

"Dresden," Ella said succinctly. "He knew I was coming. This is for me."

She turned and checked the other cells quickly. Nothing. "He's got something planned," she said and ran toward the step.

"Banning!" King called out. "Stop."

She didn't. Segorski had been a resource for Dresden. A way to get the Russian prime minister in Dresden's pocket. Then Segorski had turned on Dresden and paid the price. His presence in that cell was meant as a warning for Ella.

She had to get to Jude. "Jude, what's your location?"

King grabbed her arm, and Ella turned on him. "We have to find Jude," she demanded.

"All we're going to find is a bullet if you don't slow down," King told her furiously. "Get your shit together, Banning."

"Jude, what's your location?"

Static met her ears.

"Brody, what's your location?" she tried.

Nothing.

"He's got them," Ella said, fear climbing up her throat.

"Team leader? Brody and Keeper found Anna Beth Caine. They handed her off to Rook and Knight and are headed across the property to head Dresden off. Knight and Rook are en route to your location. Brody says Dresden is moving and has men surrounding him," Vivi informed their team leader.

"Goddamn it," Chase bit out. "We cannot let him get away."

"Why don't we have comm?" King asked.

"Don't know, could be interference. If you don't hurry, we'll lose everything and I'll be blind," Vivi reported. "Head to the back of the property. The airfield is about a mile from the house. You need to move now."

Ella took off after King and Chase. She ran as the cold seeped under her overalls, past her vest, and deep under her skin. Terror shook her core as she searched the large expanse of lawn for Jude. He was her every thought. She couldn't lose him.

She could see Rook and Knight settled into a depression about three hundred yards from the tree line. The trees formed a natural barrier around the edge of the property and were about a half-mile thick from the road to the lawn. A small plane was parked another four hundred yards or so past them, obviously ready for takeoff.

Men ran toward them from the woods, surrounding the plane. So that's where his men had been—pulled back, waiting for this moment. As one, they went to their knees and began firing.

Ella dodged, zigzagging her steps and knowing sheer luck prevented a bullet from finding her body. She kept her eyes on her target, that depression where her teammates were, and noticed a woman in between them cowering, her body shivering. Ella reached the depression and went to her knees beside the woman, unzipping her blue coveralls, pulling the material down, and unstrapping her bulletproof vest.

"Is she hurt?" she asked Rook.

"No," he answered and settled down to reload his weapon. Both he and Knight were firing, but Ella couldn't tell if they were even making a dent in the wall of men surrounding the plane. Chase dove into the slight depression and asked for a sitrep.

"FUBAR," Knight replied.

Chase nodded, wedged into position, and began firing.

"Here," Ella told Anna Beth Caine.

The woman glanced at her, eyes blank, as if there was absolutely nothing going on upstairs. "Anna Beth," Ella said firmly. "Look at me. I told you I'd come for you, right? Here I am. Put this on."

Her tone must have gotten through to the woman, because her gaze cleared and she reached for the vest. Ella strapped her in it. "Stay down," she ordered.

Ella wiggled out of the cumbersome coveralls while searching for Jude. From the opposite side of the airfield, a car pulled up and Abrafo Nadege exited. Gunfire continued to pepper the air around them.

"Son of a bitch," Chase whispered. "I kinda feel like we brought a knife to a gunfight."

"Been in worse places," Knight warned. "Remember Syria last year?"

"Been trying to forget," Chase replied with a grin.

"Where's Dresden?" Rook questioned.

"Vivi, I need eyes," King demanded.

"I'm searching," Vivi responded in their ears.

Ella lifted her rifle, hunting for Jude and Brody but not finding them.

In the distance, the sound of helicopter blades splitting the winter air bounced off the low-hanging clouds.

"Who is that?" King demanded. "Vivi, who's in the chopper?"

"On it, Your Highness," she replied, her voice more harried than Ella had ever heard it.

The helicopter swung down from the clouds, flying low over the trees and raining hellfire on Dresden's line of men. Nadege ducked behind the car and dropped to the ground. Ella pushed Anna Beth down and began firing.

"No clue who's in the chopper, Your Highness, but they're cutting Dresden's men down," Vivi reported.

"Let's move," King ordered.

As one, they stood and—still firing—began moving forward in the same zigzag pattern Ella had used. Knight grabbed Anna Beth Caine and put her hand on his waist. "Run with me," he commanded her. The woman nodded and immediately did as he'd ordered. She was holding her own, considering moments ago she'd been Dresden's prisoner.

He hadn't broken her, which gave Ella hope for the woman.

Ella fired, and when her rifle ran out of bullets, she pulled her handguns from their holsters and used them. From the air, the helicopter continued to fire, and still there was no Jude or Brody.

King, Rook, and Chase were now engaging men hand to hand. A couple of Dresden's men were running for the woods, while others fell under the barrage of machine-gun fire from the helicopter. They simply didn't have a place to hide from the chopper.

The wind whipped Ella's hair as she ducked and spun under a roundhouse punch from one of Dresden's goons. She pulled her KA-BAR from its sheath at her boot and came up punching the blade into the man's chest. He fell, a look of stunned disbelief his final act.

She turned and took a fist to the shoulder before she could duck. She stumbled and shook out her arm before she grabbed her final knife from its scabbard, flipped it, and tossed it directly into the man's throat.

"Ella, move!"

Jude's voice. She turned and started to run, but an arm snuck around her throat and hauled her back against a hard body.

"Did you really think I'd let you go, Banning?"

Dresden.

Her heart stopped, then kicked into overdrive. She went deadweight, hoping to catch him off guard, but he laughed and clamped down on her throat harder.

"Take the shot," she heard King call over the comm units.

"No!" Jude protested.

"Take the shot, Brody," King ordered.

Dresden lowered his head, tucking his chin between her neck and shoulder and pressing down until he knew no one had a shot without going through Ella's head first. "Tell them to stand down," he whispered in her ear.

All around her, action ceased. The helicopter hovered and turned right, disappearing back over the trees.

Ella couldn't breathe, spots swimming in front of her eyes. But in between the spots was Jude, walking toward them, rifle held at the ready, face promising death.

"Stop, Keeper," Dresden called out when Jude was about fifteen feet away. The pressure on her throat eased, but a gun pressed into her temple now. "I don't *want* to kill her, you know?"

"Let her go, Dresden," Jude said, his voice low and cajoling. He wouldn't meet her gaze. He knew. He knew damn well this was it for Ella.

"I don't want to kill her, Keeper," Dresden said as he began moving backward, pulling Ella with him. "But I will."

The plane was only yards away. If he got her on it, she was dead.

"Take the shot, Brody," Ella said softly.

"Shut your mouth, Banning," Dresden demanded, and though his words were spoken softly, they were loud in Ella's ears.

"Don't," Jude pleaded. His voice was still low, but it was filled with fear now.

One of them wasn't making it home today. Ella accepted that and determined it would be her. She'd known this was her probable outcome, and she'd signed on anyway because keeping Jude alive was everything to her.

"Take the goddamn shot, Brody," she said easily, almost conversationally.

"There is no shot. Stand down, Brody," King ordered.

Behind Jude, her teammates stood, weapons raised, all aimed at Horace Dresden. She saw Chase, Rook,

Knight, and Anna Beth Caine. They wouldn't leave here
without her this time. She knew it. She'd be dead, but
they'd take her with them this time.

Dresden continued to move toward the plane. Jude
moved as Dresden and Ella did, slow and steady, his
gaze never leaving Dresden, his black eyes cataloging
the man's every move.

"I love you, Keeper," Ella whispered.

Finally, his gaze met hers, and the pain in his eyes
skewered her.

Jude threw his weapon down and opened his arms.
"It's me you want, Dresden," he growled. "Take me."

Ella felt Dresden's chest rise and fall. The bastard
was laughing. "Oh, I will, Keeper. No doubt, I'll definitely be ending you, and I won't harm a hair on your
head to do it."

They were almost to the car that was parked beside
the plane.

"Nadege, get on the plane, will you?" Dresden queried sharply.

"Don't you fuckin' move, Nadege," Chase called out,
his rifle aimed on the man.

"You think I can't find Dr. Moeller, Chase? You
think you can hide her from me?" Dresden asked conversationally. "None of you can hide from the truth of
this. I own you all."

"Let her go, Horace," a small voice said from behind
King.

Dresden's spine snapped taut, and his grip around
Ella's throat hardened. Once again, Ella's airway was
constricted, but she didn't struggle. He still had the gun
at her temple.

"Anna Beth, you were never any good at staying where I put you," Dresden said. "Warren? Take the shot."

A shot rang out, and Anna Beth cried out, her body bowing at the waist before she fell to the ground.

"She thought I wouldn't do it," Dresden said at Ella's ear. He eased the pressure on her throat. Ella knew her time was limited. "She thought I wouldn't find her, thought I wouldn't hurt her, just like your Keeper thinks I won't cut you down. But neither of them realizes that I tend to get rid of the things that no longer have use to me."

"Who is it, Dresden?" she pushed from her aching throat.

"You want a name, Ella? You think you deserve a name? You think you deserve something for all the hard work you've put in?" Dresden asked with a laugh. "Maybe you do. After all you've killed and maimed, and now you'll die for it."

"Give me a name. Who pulls your strings?" she asked. "No way you're the top."

His grip tightened, and Ella's vision winked. "I will be," he said.

"Name," she forced out.

He shrugged. As if it was nothing to give her this information. "Okay. I'll give you a name. You can take it to the grave with you...Ricker. William Ricker. You don't know him, and he can't be found. And in a few moments you'll be too dead to do anything about it."

Ella had no idea who that was. None at all. But it was a place to start. She'd worked within Dresden's clutches for a year for this single name. Relief and something else flowed through her. She'd call it disappointment. All of this for a single name.

But maybe her team could use that name to dismantle Dresden and whoever he worked for.

"Let her go, Dresden," Jude called out again, taking another step forward.

"He's going to kill you, Horace," Ella whispered.

"And just like you, he'll fail," Dresden said with a laugh.

She was watching Jude's face and saw his eyes widen the split second before Dresden pushed her away. She tried to catch her balance, but the suddenness of his action had her going to her knees facing him. In slow motion, she watched him raise his weapon and fire a single shot. She fell forward, her hands bracing her fall.

"Two birds, one stone," Dresden said.

His words brought her head up. There was a smile on his face.

It was gone a split second later as a hole formed in the center of his forehead.

He crumpled to the ground. Dead.

Just like that, Horace Dresden was dead.

Jude called her name, his tone agonized, and all Ella wanted to do was comfort him. He was safe. Dresden was dead, and Jude was alive.

She brought her hand to her side and pulled it away as Jude went to his knees beside her. In her ear, she heard rapid-fire commands from King, and she heard that damn helicopter making a return trip.

Who was in that damn thing?

"Ella!" Jude demanded.

"Jude?" she said, a cough rumbling up from her core, pain spreading through her body like fire. There was blood on her hands. A lot of it. Jude pulled her into his lap, and the pain of his movements stole her breath.

She recognized this for what it was. Her ending. "I love you. Be safe."

"Hold on, Ella. You hold on for me!" Jude demanded.

She couldn't hold on. Everything faded but the pain. She needed to breathe—God! Why was it so hard to breathe?

"Love you," she pushed out again. *Drowning must feel like this,* she thought.

"Don't, baby," Jude said, and he was there, holding her now. How could she not feel him? She was so cold and needed his warmth. "Don't leave me."

She tried to reach for him but couldn't make her arms work. So she smiled, and Jude threw back his head and screamed at the sky.

He was alive. That's all that mattered. One more thing though.

"Wi...Ricker..."

"What?" Jude asked, wiping her face, his own tortured.

She swallowed around her tongue. "Tell the Piper... William Ricker."

She dropped her arms and stared at the sky. It was done. Ella was done.

A last look at Jude, and then her world winked black.

Chapter 23

JUDE PICKED HER UP AND RAN. HIS TEAMMATES FORMED a barrier, but Nadege was on the plane and Dresden's men—the ones who hadn't fallen to Endgame—were fleeing. The plane's engines screamed and it took off, fleeing the destruction Dresden had wrought.

The military helicopter that had peppered Dresden and his men with artillery shots made another appearance, but it was too late.

"Piper sent the cavalry," Vivi said over their earpieces. "She's going to land it, Endgame. Get Ella and your asses on board."

"Is that Loretta Bernstein?" Rook asked in disbelief.

Jude heard him but didn't give a shit if it was the pope. He had to get Ella somewhere safe.

"Put her down, Keeper," Brody demanded. "We've got to look at her. She's losing a lot of blood."

Jude could feel it running down his arms. But put her down? He wouldn't do it.

"Keeper!" King yelled. "Put Ella down, now. That's an order, soldier."

Fuck his orders. Jude glanced down and saw her pale face lolling against his chest.

"She needs help, man. Put her down!" Brody yelled this time. It was his voice, so broken and grating, that finally got through to Jude.

He lowered Ella to the ground and stood. "Help her," he demanded of the woman, Anna Beth Caine.

Her gaze was glassy, she was only half-dressed, her clothing having been torn either during her captivity or the run from Dresden's house, and she wore Ella's vest. The vest that could have saved Ella's life. The vest that had indeed saved Anna Beth's.

The woman shook her head. "I-I-I can't," she cried out, and it seemed to be a plea.

Jude leaned down in her face. "Help. Her. Now."

"Keeper, goddamn it, stop this shit," Brody demanded, his broken voice no longer moving Jude.

Suddenly, the woman shuddered and seemed to come back to herself. She lowered beside Ella and began checking the gaping wound in Ella's lower chest. Knight handed her a first-aid kit, and she took it cautiously as if it were a snake about to bite her.

"Hurry up," he said, his voice cold and brooking no argument.

Jude glanced behind Brody and saw the helicopter landing. Wind whipped all around him as he stood over his woman, protecting her from the goddamn air because he hadn't been able to protect her from Dresden's bullet.

Anna Beth Caine worked over her, shoving something inside her chest. A gasping cough, and then Ella was breathing again.

"Bullet collapsed the lung," Anna Beth said, her voice trembling. "I can't do much more."

"Just keep her alive," Jude demanded, uncaring that he was probably making an impossible request. "She dies, you've got a problem." He would never hurt a woman, but he was gone, and though he recognized it, he couldn't stop it.

He'd watched Ella fall. Dresden had shot her and laughed, and because he'd been using Jude's woman as a shield, Jude hadn't shot him first. Hadn't killed him. Brody had taken the kill shot.

"You guys screw it up for her again?" Lo-Lo Bernstein's voice sounded from behind them.

"Shut up, Lo-Lo," Rook hissed.

"Yeah," came a woman's voice behind Jude. "Shut up, Loretta."

Georgia had made an appearance.

Loretta smiled, and it was ugly. "Send a child to do a woman's job? Poor Gray Broemig. He's desperate now, eh?"

"I'm not here for your boss," Georgia said, her voice arctic.

Loretta cocked her head. "Who?"

"The Piper," Georgia said. "He's not real happy about you cavorting with Baron in Moscow. Got a lot to answer for, Lo-Lo. Shall we?" she urged, holding out a hand and gesturing for Loretta to follow her.

"She's tight in the turns, Your Highness. Make sure Knight knows that," Loretta said softly. And then unbelievably, the former CIA operative followed Georgia, and both women disappeared into the trees.

"Load her," King said.

Jude picked up his heart and placed her in the chopper. Blood seeped from Ella's lower chest, though more sluggishly now.

"She's going to live," he said.

"She is," Brody said. "She's not going to give up."

"Knight, there's a Ukrainian air base about thirty minutes away. The on-base physician will look Ella over, make sure she's as stable as we can get her. From there, you'll load onto a transport plane and head to Odessa. That's an hour and a half from your location. I'll have medical staff meet you at the airfield. I'm downloading coordinates to the copter's autopilot," Vivi said over the comm units.

Ella didn't open her eyes, but she was breathing. It was labored, but she was breathing. Breathing was good at this point.

"Don't let her bleed out," Jude demanded.

"She's not going to bleed out," Anna Beth snapped. "But you should know, I'm a psychiatrist by training, not a trauma doctor."

Jude clenched his teeth against his rage. The woman once again on her knees tending Ella wasn't responsible, but Jude wasn't logical at the moment.

He'd watched her fall.

His heart had stopped.

And if hers didn't continue to beat, he might damn well follow her.

"Get her as stable as you can," Brody told the woman.

Anna Beth nodded and went about cleaning the wound. "I need to pack this wound," she said.

Jude pulled off his outer shirt and vest, then tugged off his undershirt and handed it to her. "Use this."

"Can you hold her?" she asked softly.

Jude went to his knees and lifted Ella. She didn't make a sound. The puddle of blood beneath her scared the hell out of him. He held her though, refusing to stop.

He held her until medical staff boarded the plane in

Odessa and pried her from his grasp. Then he followed her as far as he could—until Brody stepped in front of him and Jude had to watch them wheel her away for surgery.

"Live for me," he whispered.

"That's all she's been doing, Jude. That's all she knows," Brody said passionately, clapping a hand on Jude's shoulder.

Then Jude sank into a chair near the OR and waited.

Chapter 24

THEY WORKED ON ELLA FOR TWO HOURS. THE BULLET had done damage by bouncing off a rib before deflating her lung. They'd transfused a pint of blood. Each member of Endgame had offered up their own for her. She was AB positive, the universal recipient. That was something in their favor when so much had gone wrong today. When the doctor who worked on her came out, he looked haggard, but there was a small smile on his face.

"You guys got lucky," the man said in perfect English.

"How's that?" King questioned.

"My specialty is trauma, specifically the lungs, and I just arrived yesterday on loan to this hospital from Johns Hopkins. My military residency requires me to practice here for six months. I got the Chairman of the Joint Chiefs' call as I landed, was able to bypass customs, and voilà, I'm here," he told them.

Jude heard it all from a distance. His blood pounded in his ears.

"Ms. Banning suffered some blood loss and a collapsed lung. Her lung has been repaired, and we've reinflated it so she's breathing easier. She'll be sore for a few weeks due to the gunshot, but she's in excellent health, so barring anything unforeseen, she should make a full recovery rather quickly. I'd like to keep her a couple of days." He checked his chart and shook his head. "No way. You can't take her back tomorrow.

She'll not be ready to fly for another week or so, maybe longer."

"She goes tomorrow," Jude said firmly and stepped around the doctor.

"Where are you going?" the young physician asked worriedly.

"To see my woman," he growled, and he pushed open the doors to the recovery room.

She was the only patient. So tiny against the bed, her skin leached of color. But the monitors she was hooked to showed a steady heart rhythm, and her chest rose and fell evenly.

God, he thought he'd lost her.

Again.

"She's going to make it," Brody said from behind him.

Jude nodded but said nothing.

"Anna Beth Caine is heading back with us," King said as he walked into the room.

"Where's Chase?" Rook asked as he and Knight entered the room.

"He headed back to get Dr. Moeller settled in a safe house outside DC," King answered. "We head back tomorrow. Vivi will make sure Ella has what she needs the second we land."

Jude sat on the metal chair beside Ella's bed and grabbed her hand. She hadn't woken from surgery yet, but Jude would be here when she did.

"Knight, you'll head back to meet up with Chase. Get Dr. Moeller settled, and then come back to Port Royal," King said as he took the seat on the opposite side of the bed. He stared at Jude. "Dresden knew we were coming."

Jude didn't respond. The hows and whys didn't

matter here and now. The only thing that mattered was the elimination of Horace Dresden. He looked at each of his teammates. "Bastard is dead now."

Brody sighed but stepped forward. "He is, but this shit has gotten deeper."

King shook his head, and the gesture made him seem weary. "We've got to plan. There are still way too many unknowns in this. We will all go home tomorrow. We'll plan. And then we'll destroy whatever Dresden was working to build and whoever was pulling his strings."

Jude stared at his team leader, knowing it was the right tack to take, but his blood pounded through his veins. He didn't want to *wait*. He wanted the people responsible for Dresden in his hands. *Now*.

"He's right," Brody said, his broken voice loud in the eerie quietness of the recovery room. "Dresden has been plotting and planning for years. We've had to play catch-up. He's gone now, but this is something we have to figure out before we make another move. Let's go home, Keeper. We'll fill you in on everything you missed in the last war room. We'll plan. And we'll kill all of them. Dead."

Jude hung his head, took a deep breath, and pushed the rage down. It seemed his last year had been spent doing that—battling his rage. It all came back to him in a second: watching Ella fall in Beirut, the year spent mourning and searching, and finally finding her. He'd experienced the lowest low when he lost her. Then the highest high when he'd seen her again, very much alive in Beirut.

He'd buried himself in her again. Found every piece that had been missing since she was taken from him, and then he'd almost lost her one more time.

Never again.

He looked at the woman lying so still on the bed in front of him, glanced at her monitors, and felt the rage click into place inside a space that wouldn't touch Ella.

She had a long road to recovery ahead of her. He had to be right there for her.

"We'll plan," he said with a nod. "Then we'll hunt."

"Hooah!" each member said softly, but the cheer resounded in the room.

With Endgame behind him, he could do this.

They called him Keeper.

So that's what he'd concentrate on—keeping Ella safe.

Chapter 25

ELLA HEARD HIS VOICE IN HER SLEEP. JUDE. HER love. Her life.

"Come on, baby, wake up," he urged softly. His deep voice filtered inside her, warming everything left cold.

She hurt—felt as if an elephant had copped a squat on her chest—but she pushed through the fog and fought to open her eyes. She'd been hurt, that much was obvious. But how? When?

"Come on, baby," he demanded. "I need you to open your eyes."

"Trying," she mumbled. Damn, even her throat hurt.

"God," he whispered harshly. "Thank you."

She pried her eyes open and found him above her, black eyes intent and…wet? "Why are you crying?" she asked, wincing as every word felt like a blade on her tender throat.

"I'm the Keeper, baby. I don't cry," he said with a smile. His face was haggard, stubble covering his chin, and the look in his eyes was nothing short of desperate. She couldn't remember the last time, if ever, she'd seen Jude with that look on his face.

She concentrated on raising her hand. It took every effort she could muster, but she placed her hand on his cheek and rubbed the black stubble. "Me likey," she whispered.

"It itches," he complained. "But I'll keep a permanent five-o'clock shadow if you'll stay awake." One big hand stroked the hair away from her face, while the other grabbed her hand on his face and brought it to his lips. "Hey, baby."

She smiled, or thought she did. "Hey, Jude."

She was missing something. How had she ended up horizontal and in more pain than she'd ever felt, even at the hands of Vasily Savidge? "How?"

"Let me get the doctor in here to check you over. You've been in and out for a couple of days," Jude said as he lowered her hand and moved away from her.

She glanced around, though lifting her head was nearly impossible. Soon a woman in bright-green scrubs hovered over her, poking and prodding around her chest, checking her pupils, and then writing on a chart for a minute or so. She was in a hospital.

But why?

"She's awake," the doctor said.

Jude snorted. Ella smiled. He was holding on to his sarcasm, and she wanted to praise him for it.

"Vitals look good. She's healing well. I'll need to get some labs and an MRI to check how that lung looks, but if she's coming along as it appears she is, she should be able to go home today," the doctor said and left.

"She's awake," she heard Jude say. He was on his satellite phone. "Yeah, today."

She slowly took inventory, moving her hands, her feet, performing a systems check of sorts. Her side hurt like someone had stabbed her with a hot poker, but other than not remembering how that had happened, and some pretty serious weakness, she seemed okay.

"I'll be bringing her home, but yeah, send Brody," Jude said. "Got it, Your Highness."

Then he was in front of her again. A nurse came in and asked Ella how she felt.

"Like I've been shot," Ella replied.

"Sounds about right," the nurse said and then asked if Ella wanted anything to drink.

She did, but the nurse only gave her ice chips. She wanted answers, but Jude stood there watching the nurse fuss over her, arms crossed over that delicious chest, staring at her like she was his entire world and he'd die if he couldn't see her face.

She decided she really liked it when he looked at her like that.

"I've got to take her down for some tests," the nurse told Jude.

"I'll go with you," he said implacably.

She started to argue, he shot her a look, and she sighed. Then the nurse was wheeling Ella's bed out of the room and down the hall. After the MRI, the nurse wheeled Ella back to her room and asked if she wanted the head of her bed raised.

Ella nodded, but as the bed lifted, she winced when her wound pulled.

"Stop," Jude said harshly.

The nurse stopped.

"Leave it there," Ella encouraged the nurse. She was nowhere near vertical, but it was an improvement over being flat. The nurse left, and Ella gazed at Jude.

"Baby," he whispered reverently.

"He shot me," Ella said as images from the last time she'd seen Dresden flashed through her mind.

Jude nodded as he sat on the bed beside her, raising her hand to his lips again and kissing her fingers slowly, one at a time.

"How bad?"

"Bullet hit a rib and punctured your lung," Jude told her, his voice tortured as if the memory was too bad to be borne.

"I heard you," Ella whispered, breathing through the pain and her own memories. "I saw him smile, and then he fired and I heard you calling me."

Long moments of silence passed between them.

"I thought I'd lost you," she said, squeezing his hand and bringing it to her lips. "I thought I'd lost us."

"You fought, lady. Like a beast, you fought to stay with me," Jude responded.

Her heart thumped in her chest. "I love you, Jude Dagan. I don't ever want to leave you again."

He closed his eyes and swallowed. "You won't."

"Did you get Dresden?" she asked tentatively.

He nodded.

A tear fell down her cheek. It broke his heart.

"Look, he has no place here, even dead. I need you to rest so I can take you back to Port Royal and get you completely healed. We've got a rough couple of days coming up. There's so much to bring you up to speed on."

"Nina?"

He nodded. "She's alive."

"She's scared," Ella said firmly. "She wouldn't run and hide if she wasn't scared."

"We've got to find her. If she's scared, she knows something, and for her sake, we need to find her," Jude stated. "But first, we get you out of here."

Twelve hours later, her MRI showed no concerns and that she was healing nicely. Jude had brought her up to speed on her injury and how she'd come to be at Walter Reed. He'd told her everything, leaving nothing out, and by the time he had finished, Ella had been crying but so had Jude.

Once her tests returned clear, she was ready for discharge. Jude listened intently to the doctor and took notes on her upcoming care. She was scheduled to follow up with a doctor in two weeks. She could be cleared as early as then.

It was a two-hour drive to Port Royal, and they made it in the middle of the night. Brody brought the vehicle to the hospital door, and Jude carried her down to the SUV, placed her in the backseat, and moved in beside her while Brody drove.

She slept most of the ride, having no energy to do much but lie on Jude. He seemed fine with that, his hands never far from her, his voice in her ear telling her what she meant to him, how he was never going to let her go.

Brody said two words, "Goddamn, Ella-Bella," but he smiled to alleviate the reprimand. He'd always said she got into more trouble than she was worth, yet he'd always been there with her in the midst of it. Now was no different. She guessed they'd kinda saved each other in that cell of Dresden's.

She didn't remember falling asleep or being carried up to her room. She remembered waking up cold and needing to pee, so she tried to get up on her own.

Jude was there that fast. "Ella, let me know you need to get up, okay?" he admonished.

She threw him a nasty look and then let him lift her.

"I really can walk, Jude," she informed him, tempering the frustration in her tone.

"Just let me do this for a little while longer," he said, holding her against his chest and then setting her on her feet.

She used the bathroom, brushed her teeth, and washed her face. He stood right there, just in case she was too weak to handle the mundane tasks, but she felt remarkably well considering two, almost three days ago she'd been shot in the side at nearly point-blank range.

"I don't want to lie down," she warned him.

He held up his hands in surrender but stayed close as she walked to an enormous chair that looked brand new. It was butter-soft cream leather, and she sank into it gratefully, leaning back. "This getting shot shit sucks," she told him softly.

"Yeah," he said, a grin curving his lips. "You hungry?"

"I'd kill for some chili," she whispered.

He raised his eyebrow and smiled. "You can't handle my chili right now, lady."

"I can try?"

He crossed his arms over his chest, and she licked her lips. He laughed. "We talking chili or fucking?"

"Yes," she said with a laugh.

"None of that for a while, baby. Heal, then we'll burrow like rabbits to make up for lost time."

She pouted, and he kissed her lips, very slowly and very thoroughly. "I need a little more of that," she urged.

"You think?"

She nodded and smiled. It felt good.

"Francisco is going to stop by periodically to check

on you. And you'll have to go back to the doctor for clearance, but we'll get you better, El."

"I know. I never doubted. It'll be good to see Francisco again," she murmured.

Ella glanced out the big window he'd placed the chair beside and noticed the river winding below them. "I need to tell you some things." It was past time, and better she do it now, so that as she got back on her feet, they had nothing between them, none of her secrets or lies.

Worry passed like a cloud over his face, but he pulled up an ottoman and sat in front of her. "I'm here."

Just like that. He had always been a rock for her.

"You didn't get rid of the beach house, did you?" she asked suddenly.

"I rented it out, but the lease expires in a month," he said. "Why?"

Ella took a deep breath, locked down her pain, and opened her box of secrets. "When I woke up in Dresden's cell, I smelled the sea, and for just a moment, I heard your voice in my ear. I'd like to visit the beach house soon."

"What was I saying?" he asked cautiously.

Ella met his gaze. "'Move heaven and earth to get back to me, El.'" She swallowed thickly, and Jude handed her a bottled water. She took a healthy swig and stared at him. "That morning, before we left the beach house you said you'd move heaven and earth to get back to me. Those words gave me strength because, Jude, he made me suffer in that cell."

"Give it to me, Ella. Let me help you carry it," Jude demanded softly.

She nodded. She could do this. "I told you about the

first few days with Dresden and Savidge. And you know Savidge was responsible for the scars on my back. But it's what they did to Brody that nearly broke me.

"Brody saved me in that hellhole. As they'd work him over, he'd stare into my eyes, and I tried to take as much as I could." She sobbed and caught herself before more came out. "I tried to give him as much of my strength as I could. I hurt so bad, and I remember the feel of dried blood because they never had anyone treat the bullet wound on my temple. Sometimes, it would split back open and the blood would flow into my eyes. But I always gave Brody my eyes because he needed that. He needed someone to witness his pain, because he refused to give them what they wanted by screaming and begging. They did things to him, Jude, I can never tell another soul because it would betray Brody and he deserves so much more than that. But they hurt him until I gave Dresden what he wanted—confirmation that Allie Redding was Gray Broemig's daughter." Ella hung her head, still unable to believe she'd given over an innocent, yet convinced she'd do it again to prevent Brody from being hurt.

"He put up with so much pain in that cell with me." She took a deep breath and reached for the calm. "But Brody didn't break until I did. I couldn't stop screaming the last night Savidge cut me. He'd brought acid that night, and he dribbled it on my cuts, never letting it drip down my back, just making sure it stayed in the cuts. I screamed and screamed, and they made Brody watch. I couldn't give him my eyes, and eventually he screamed too. He pleaded for them to stop, to give him any punishment they felt I deserved. He screamed because he hoped that's what they wanted, for him to break in my pain. I screamed in pain and despair, and I screamed because I wasn't strong enough to hold my silence for him, like he'd done for me."

She broke apart then, tears flowing down her cheeks, and through it all, Jude sat there, holding her hands, saying nothing, just giving her his gaze as she struggled to put her pain in place.

"Brody screamed because of my pain. And he yelled until he bled from his mouth, his vocal cords shredded, and he was choking on blood. Then they laughed, hit the lever, and let me fall to the floor beside him. We lay there the whole night, broken." She drew in a shuddering breath. "They took him from me the next morning, and I didn't hear his voice until about nine months later...in fact, right before I saved King's ass in Spain."

She glanced out the window, watching the river flow. "When I first agreed to work with Piper, I was all God and country. I knew Dresden wanted Endgame—you, Rook, and King specifically—but my purpose wasn't solely selfish." She went quiet and looked back at her man. He continued to gaze at her with acceptance, love, and strength that she could draw on. Her rock. "God help me, Jude, but neither God nor my country meant a damn to me when I found out you were searching for me. All I knew was terror that Dresden would find out and cut you down before I could take him out.

"I lost my mission. It became personal for me. When I saw you in Beirut, all I wanted was to run to you, but I knew, I *knew*, Dresden would find out and come for you."

"Dresden was a master manipulator. Much like the Piper. We have all been tools in this game they're playing. But Ella, make no mistake…I never stopped loving you. I don't care what you've done, where you've been, or how you came back to me. I love you. You're the air I breathe, the food I eat. I'm so proud of you, lady, because you came back to me. You survived, and you're here." He picked her up and settled her in his lap, taking her place in the big chair. "I'm not going to let you go. Ever. If I have to follow you into death, by God, I'll do it, because there is no life for me without you. I know. I've tried it and wasn't very successful."

She lifted a hand and traced his lips. "All I've known the last year is fear and longing. I didn't think you'd want me once you realized what I'd done, no matter my reasons for doing it."

"I won't lie to you and say it doesn't bother me that you didn't trust me enough to come to me in the beginning when the Piper approached you," Jude told her. "But I can't equivocate over that. He's good at what he does, and he'll answer to me for that. But maybe part of the fault for that lack of trust is mine. I know I'm an asshole sometimes, taking more than I give."

She shook her head. "This isn't on you. I do trust you. I didn't trust myself. And that's what it comes down to. I haven't made many bad choices in who I surround myself with. I'm a pretty good judge of character, but I didn't trust myself enough to trust anyone else."

He nodded. "I've been there."

"You came for me, refused to let me go. I believe you when you say you love me. Can you forgive me?" she asked, unable to stop the tremor in her voice.

Her heart stuttered as she waited. Without his forgiveness, they couldn't move forward no matter how much love was between them.

"There's nothing to forgive. You're the other half of me," he murmured at her lips.

Ella sank her hands into his hair and held on. He parted her lips with his and drank her in. It wasn't a kiss of need; it was a kiss of absolution. He soothed her soul and put balm on her heart.

He healed her.

"I need to talk to Brody," Jude said when he released her lips.

"Be careful with him, Jude," she warned.

"I owe him. He kept you alive and killed Dresden. You need to warn him to be careful with me," Jude said with a laugh.

A knock sounded on the door, and Harrison Black stuck his head in.

"Nobody said to come in, Brit," Jude grumbled.

"Whatever, Keeper. You want privacy, lock the door. Meeting in the war room in an hour," he said before tipping his head and waggling his eyebrows at Ella. "Rook said there was a bet in Russia over you two. Since nobody won, there's a new one."

"Yeah?" Ella laughed around her reply. "What's the bet?"

"Everybody's giving it two weeks before they hear the headboard knocking against the wall," Black told them, then snickered. "I put five on it."

"Five hundred dollars?" Ella asked in disbelief.

"*Ten* dollars, Ella-Bella," he said with a frown. "We Brits leave nothing to chance, including our money. I personally only give it a week. It wasn't such a nasty hit you took, but you are a woman, so…"

Ella flipped him off, but she couldn't stop the laugh that bubbled up. Harrison Black truly didn't understand that women were universally the stronger sex.

Jude snorted, but she felt his chest rumbling with his own laughter.

"See you both in an hour," Black called and then shut the door on his chuckle.

"Want to change?" Jude asked her.

"Nah, I think my pajamas are about all I can handle at the moment," she said as she snuggled deeper into his hold. "In fact, I'm going to take a short nap while we wait."

"Go ahead, woman. I've got you."

Ella knew he absolutely did, so she closed her eyes. Surrounded by her man and all the love they shared.

Chapter 26

JUDE PLACED ELLA IN A CHAIR AND TOOK THE SEAT beside her. Rook and Vivi were already in their seats. Black and Brody were across the war table from him and Ella. He'd asked Brody a few minutes ago for a moment after the meeting. He had some words to say to the man who'd saved Ella in that cell.

Because Jude had no doubt that had Brody not screamed, Savidge would have devastated Ella and she might have died that night. He owed Brody his life. Without Ella, Jude didn't have one.

Vivi stood as King walked in and began to set up her boards. Allie Redding followed King, and behind her came Anna Beth Caine. Jude had only seen her once they'd returned to the States. She stayed holed up in her room and didn't say much to anyone. Jude had no idea why Anna Beth was there. Normally, war room meetings were reserved for the team.

King, Rook, Knight, Chase, Black, and Madoc settled in their normal places. Jude reached for Ella's hand and felt the sun shine in his soul. She was still so pale, but her gray eyes were clearing of the clouds she'd carried with her, and she was alive. It was more than he'd dared hope for. She had news she needed to impart at this meeting, and he worried about the single name she'd given him earlier.

"We ready?" King asked, pulling Jude from his thoughts. Vivi nodded. "Let's do this." Rook's wife cleared her throat and pushed her glasses up her nose. "Nina Lassiter is very much alive, according to my facial recognition software."

"Lots of people we thought were dead are showing up alive," Rook mused, tossing Ella a look.

"There are a lot of threads here, Rook. It's why we're meeting. We need to work up an angle, figure it all out, and determine what our next move is," King reminded him, motioning for Vivi to continue.

Chase tapped the table. "Not to overstate the obvious or repeat what Rook said, but we've got Ella and Madoc, both of whom we suspected were dead. And now we've got Nina?"

"Best way to hide is to die," Knight said from his point at the end of the table. He'd know, Jude mused, because he'd hidden his presence after the failed mission in the Hindu Kush with Dresden and Rook.

"Truth," Harrison Black chimed in. "It's why MI6 demands irrefutable proof through a body and matching DNA before they'll accept the death of one of their agents."

There's a story there, Jude knew. Black had left MI6 amid scandal. He had fit right into Endgame.

"I can only speculate as to her reasoning. I've done everything I can to determine how she's hidden from us and what happened when she disappeared, supposedly dying of poisoning. I'm working on it, but I'm only one person. Allie is doing what she can, tapping some of her resources, but it's hard because King has put an information blackout on Endgame. He doesn't want anyone knowing what we have and where we're heading." Vivi pulled up a video feed on the screen that hung from the ceiling. "Here's Nina buying the ticket in Provo, and here she is disembarking in Anchorage. I have no idea where she went from there. Surveillance video shows her leaving the airport on foot, and I've lost her trail."

"Why Alaska?" Jude asked suddenly, something scraping at his memory.

"She's changed," Ella said softly. "Thinner, leaner, and her hair is longer. Nina hated long hair."

"Wig?" Vivi asked.

"No, I think it's hers," Ella answered, running her index finger along her lower lip.

Jude noticed that the bruises from Dresden's blows were gone. Ella glanced over at him, seeming to read his mind because she licked her lower lip. Jude's heart turned over in his chest.

This woman. She'd changed him.

King cleared his throat and gave Jude a look. Jude smiled and engaged in the conversation again. "I gotta ask again, why Alaska?"

"Nina had no family. She was like me when she joined the Agency...from the foster system. I think she was originally from Vermont. She graduated from MIT, went to school with you, right, Vivi?" Ella asked.

Vivi nodded. "She was a year behind me."

"She never mentioned Alaska to me, and when we talked about her past, it was pretty cut and dried. She had no one," Ella told the team.

"Did she have a man?" King asked.

Jude felt something click in his mind.

"She was a loner. If she had dates, I never knew about them. When we weren't on ops, she was at the condo we shared in DC. You know what though? The last few weeks before Beirut, Nina had been dressing up, using makeup and such. I just remembered that. I was going to ask her if she'd met someone but, well…Beirut," Ella finished in a near-whisper.

Jude reached for her hand again and squeezed. He remembered Nina as a behind-the-scenes analyst who backed up her team from base. She was almost as good as Vivi and Ella with information analysis and computer programming. The difference between Vivi, Ella, and Nina was that Nina had trained with Rangers at Fort Benning in Georgia. She'd gone through Ranger training and graduated top of her class. She'd been a soldier through and through. Jude didn't remember ever thinking of Nina as anything other than one of them. He'd never seen her as a woman.

"She's either in Alaska, or she used that as a jumping point. Thing is, she used the card, and that just smells to me," King murmured. "Why would she use a card that she had to know would ping with us?"

"Maybe she thought we would have shut that card down?" Rook offered.

Vivi shook her head. "No, she knows how we operate. She knows we never close cards unless we have proof they're compromised. It's how I was trained to keep track of rogues for the Agency. Someone gets burned, they go to ground, but they are trained to have three cards memorized. The Agency refuses to leave one of their agents, even a burned one, without resources to survive. They always hope they can retract the agent and determine what happened. Anyway, once an agent goes rogue or gets burned, those cards are put into a special system that monitors activity so that when they ping, we can track the agent. Nina knew this."

"That means she did it on purpose," Allie said, confirming what Jude had been thinking.

King nodded. "Why? She didn't look hurried or scared on those videos."

"Desperate people don't always *look* desperate," Ella reminded them. "And Nina was really good at hiding what she was feeling. We were friends—I think out of necessity and convenience rather than because we were so much alike—but I didn't know much about her. Hell, I'm just now realizing I hardly knew her at all. Just basics."

"She was good," Vivi said. "And now she's in play. I've heard talk about a rogue agent with information for sale."

"No way," Ella said, slapping her hand on the wooden table in front of them. "She's not a traitor."

Jude winced. He'd once called Ella that. Hell, they all had when they thought she'd been the one to betray their spec ops for that Beirut mission. "There's something we're missing."

Black snorted. "Lately, that's the name of the game."

Brody nodded.

"Alaska though…" Jude trailed off. Something about that niggled at him and wouldn't leave him alone.

Then it hit him. Micah had set up property in Alaska. Between the western edge of the Denali National Park and Preserve and a tiny village called Nikolai.

Jude had thought Micah had met someone. Micah had mentioned it before that Beirut mission, had said Jude wouldn't believe who it was when he told him.

"I think I know where she went." Jude breathed out.

King narrowed his gaze on him.

"Micah and I both purchased property about three years ago under shell corporations Micah set up for us. We wanted off-grid homes where we could bury ourselves so deep nobody could find us," Jude began. "I purchased in New Mexico. Micah bought property in Alaska."

"I'll start a search there. Can you give me coordinates like those you gave King for your property?" Vivi asked, making notes on her iPad.

"I don't have them, only a general location," Jude explained. "Look, Micah was my best friend, but when it comes to someone's personal safety, or that of any family they planned on having, they don't trust anyone with that information. It can be pulled out of even the strongest ally by the right person, by the right torture."

King grimaced. "True. Can you give us the approximate location and let Vivi begin searching?"

"I'll give it to her, but it's a long shot. There are hundreds of thousands of acres out in that wilderness. I'm just throwing it out there, hoping it sticks. Micah had started dating someone, said I wouldn't believe who it was, but we never got to talk before Beirut. He was always busy, and I was too," Jude said, glancing at Ella.

She smiled, and her lips curved in that secret way she had. She'd told him earlier that she remembered every time they'd ever been together, and he thought she was thinking of one now.

"But he was preoccupied before Beirut."

"None of that matters," Brody tossed out. "Micah died in Beirut. I have no idea why, but they buried him in one of the only Christian cemeteries in Lebanon.

He's dead. Why would Nina head to his property? How would she even know about it?"

Ella shrugged. "Maybe they were closer than we can imagine."

Brody's gaze went dark. "I don't buy it."

"Me either," Chase said. "Micah loved women. I seriously doubt he'd ever settle down, much less with a mouse like Nina."

"Damn, Chase," Knight grumbled. "Did you ever really look at Nina?"

Chase shrugged.

Black smiled. "She was actually beautiful underneath that faded-brown, dyed-from-a-bottle hair."

"I never really looked, I guess," Chase said, his tone clearly indicating his angst at the oversight.

"Let me run a search, and we'll revisit this. I just wanted you all to know she's alive, from what I can tell, and she's in play again," Vivi murmured. "Next thing up for discussion...Anna Beth Caine."

The woman in question kept her gaze on the table, her hands twisting in front of her. Jude felt sorry for her. He wasn't thrilled with her parental unit, but he felt bad for the daughter. He wanted a few moments alone with the Piper. Just a few.

"Anna Beth has been helping me crack the code for the thumb drive Ella retrieved in Russia. She tells me her sister had secrets upon secrets, and that she doesn't know what those were because she was locked up in an institution the last four years," Vivi recited softly.

"There's a story there," Brody murmured. "You'll tell us eventually."

No question. Brody punctuated his statement with a quick tap of his fist on the table.

Anna Beth Caine jumped and then glared at the big soldier. *Well, that's interesting,* Jude thought.

"Anna Beth," King began. "We need all the information you can give us about your sister, your father, and your brother."

The woman's head snapped up at that. "I—"

Ella glanced at Jude, brows raised, a question in her gaze.

"Don't lie to me," King said, his voice low with just a hint of a growl. "We know about Drake."

"How?" she asked.

"Doesn't matter. We figured it out. And I want everything you have on your brother. I know he's dead. I want to know how he plays into this, and you're going to give us that information." King's tone left no other alternative.

Brody glared at King.

Jude rolled his eyes. So much drama. "Brody, chill out. King, there's no reason to threaten her."

King speared Jude with a glare of his own. "It's not a threat. We are all in play because we've been used as the chess pieces in her father's personal vendetta." He turned the full force of his gaze on Anna Beth. "I want everything you have, and you'll give it to me, or I will make the creator of this team suffer. I want to know your relationship to Horace Dresden. I want your sister, I want your brother, and I want you. Soon. I'm giving you another twenty-four hours before we meet again, and, Ms. Caine, if I have to pull it out of you, I will."

Anna Beth hissed in a breath. "You threaten me and

talk crap about my father. But here's a truth for you. He's saved all of your asses. None of you would be here without him."

"You'll have to expand on that for any believability," Knight muttered. "Because right now, the picture doesn't match the sound."

King glanced at Ella. "Don't," he warned her. "Anna Beth, I'm not threatening you. Stand down, Brody."

Ella went red in the face. Brody's fists were clenching and unclenching.

Jude thought shit was about to go nuclear, and then Anna Beth Caine defused the situation.

"He's right, Ella. I know the truth, but you guys don't. I'll give it all to you, but I need to get it together in my head. I've been…" She trailed off and then seemed to snap back. "Look, just give me another day or two, and I'll give it to you," she said clearly.

King nodded. Ella blew out a breath. Brody sat back.

Vivi cleared her throat. She did this for the sole purpose of drawing their notice. It was one of her patented moves. Like Rook grunting, Vivi cleared her throat.

"Tomorrow then," she said and made a note on her tablet. "Dresden is dead. Gabrielle Moeller is in a safe house outside DC, and now we've got Nina on deck."

"Has there been any significant troop movement along the Russian-Crimean border?" Ella asked.

Vivi gave a negative shake of her head. "Not yet, but there are murmurs."

"But you can bet your sweet ass Russia will begin making military moves to protect that oil. Dresden never got his money, but someone wants it. Which brings me to some information I need to share," Ella stated.

She took a deep breath. Jude rubbed her leg under the table. Any comfort he could give her, he would. "I was with Dresden for a year, trying to gather information on the group he worked for or with. I still don't know the specifics. I did things I can't take back. Saw things that will haunt me for eternity. But it wasn't until right before he shot me that I got a name I'd been seeking for a year."

"You don't want to do that," Anna Beth Caine interrupted Ella, fear a tattoo on her face. "Not yet. That name is too dangerous."

Ella looked at Anna Beth, clearly not surprised the other woman knew the name she was about impart. "It's okay, AB. We're team. We'll protect you."

Silence reigned as everyone waited.

"William Ricker," Ella said in the quiet.

Anna Beth shook her head. King hung his. The other men and women around the table frowned.

"Okay, this seems a little melodramatic, but who's William Ricker?" Black asked.

"I don't know," Ella said.

"I don't either," Vivi stated. "But I will soon." She gave Anna Beth a pointed look.

"How do you know Dresden wasn't lying?" Knight asked.

"Because he gloated. He knew he was going to shoot me. The dead don't tell tales," Ella reminded him.

"Unless they're not dead," Chase said. When everyone looked at him, he threw up his hands. "Look, I'm just saying." He pointed at Knight, Ella, Madoc, and the board that held Nina's picture. "Dead, then not dead. Seems to me Dresden made a horrible miscalculation."

"True that," Jude bit out. "And I'll thank God every day for it."

Ella grabbed his hand, interlocking their fingers and holding on.

"The Alliance," Anna Beth whispered. "William Ricker has ties to the Alliance. Ricker owns a global conglomerate that contains everything from the largest pharmaceutical company in the world to an automaker. And I can't tell you more, because I don't have it. I can help you crack the fail-safe, but I don't have any more than that. Please don't ask."

"Vivi, get on it," King ordered.

"That's the group," Ella said aloud, reaching for Jude's leg and squeezing, her worry and fear communicated clearly in the gesture. "The Alliance. That's the group the Piper is hunting. It feels right."

"Or he's running from it," Black threw in. "I've heard of them before, a splinter group, real Illuminati-type stuff, that's been talked about for years now. Just hints and rumors, nothing concrete. Let me tap some of my resources in London. I'll get back to Vivi with what I find."

King nodded. "Okay, so everybody knows the balls we're juggling—Nina Lassiter, the Piper's location and story, and now William Ricker and his Alliance. We all need to be ready to move. Black, I need you on Dr. Moeller. Can you bring her to base so we can pick her brain as well? I think Anna Beth would like to see her friend too."

Black nodded but not before glancing at Chase, a question in his gaze, almost as if he was asking permission. Chase just shook his head; his face hard, his eyes even harder. Anna Beth didn't say anything, and Jude thought that unusual. Jesus, there were too many secrets. They'd spend eternity digging out from under them.

"I say a couple of us head to Alaska, see if we can't find Nina Lassiter. Who's in?" King asked.

"Me," Jude offered immediately.

"I'm in," Black said right after Jude. "I'll grab Dr. Moeller and be back tomorrow."

"Get on it. Brody, you and Rook are here. Chase, I need you and Knight back on Nadege. Take him out. It's what you do; handle it. No capture. Straight kill order."

Chase and Knight nodded. Brody looked pissed. Rook looked bored.

"We good?" King asked.

Everyone affirmed.

"Don't be brave," King said into the sudden silence.

"Be accurate," the team responded automatically.

Jude helped Ella up the stairs and to their room. He helped her shower, making sure her wound was covered so she could get in the water. He stood behind her, washing her body slowly and thoroughly. He was as clinical as he could be, considering she was his woman and he loved her body.

She quirked a lip at his hard cock, and he shrugged, completely unrepentant. Ella laughed, and Jude smiled at the sound. He dried them off, dried her hair, and got them both dressed.

He settled her in their bed and climbed in behind her, her body curving into his as effortlessly as always. Her cat, Chica, jumped lightly on the bed, walking in a circle before she curled into a ball at Ella's feet. Jude shook his head. Only Ella could find a goddamn cat in the middle of a snowstorm.

"Will we rebuild in New Mexico?" she asked softly, twining her fingers with his.

"Maybe," he murmured at her neck.

"Have you talked to Tia Rosa?"

"She's fine. She knows the house is gone, and she knows you're alive. Says she can't wait to see you again," Jude told his lady.

"She wasn't shocked?" Ella asked, worry in her tone.

"Nah. She's the one who taught me that not everything is as it seems," Jude said into her hair.

"Hmmm," Ella mumbled as she turned over in his arms and rested her head on his chest.

Long moments of silence passed, while Jude soaked up the fact that she was with him, alive. He listened to her breathe and drank in her scent, running his fingers through the silken strands of her hair, basking in her presence.

"You'll be careful." She wasn't asking; she was telling him. He, King, and Black were heading out late tomorrow to Alaska. Nina Lassiter had to be brought in.

"Only way I can be when I know I have you to come home to," he assured her.

Ella yawned as she settled into his body.

"My heart never gave up on you, El," he whispered.

She kissed him right over the organ that had never let her go. "I know," she replied sleepily.

He felt her breathing even out and her body settle into the pattern of sleep. But he had one more promise to make before sleep took him.

"Safe, baby," he said so softly it was barely a breath. She was already out, and he didn't want to wake her.

But Ella smiled, her lips curving against his skin, and he realized she wasn't as asleep as he'd thought. She raised her hands from under the covers and rested six fingers on his chest. "I've got your six, Jude."

Joy lit the last dark corner of his heart. She'd come back to him. Or maybe he'd chased her down. Either way, she was his, heart and body—and Jude would never take that for granted again.

"Always," he said.

Epilogue

NINA WAS TIRED. IT FELT AS IF GRAINS OF SAND HAD embedded themselves in her eyeballs and no amount of rubbing helped ease the discomfort. She'd been up for two days straight. Fear and adrenaline continuously punched through any attempt at rest, not allowing her a respite. She'd gone through Ranger training and not had this much difficulty staying on top of things.

And now the car she'd purloined in Anchorage, the Honda she'd thought would run for miles and miles and miles due to its Japanese engineering, had met its match—Alaska.

She groaned as she shoved the car door open and stepped out. Steam rose from the front of her vehicle, the ghostly tendrils of gray mist startling against the backdrop of a brilliant pink-orange sunset. The sight held her attention for a long moment. It really was pretty in a this-sucks-ass kind of way.

Somewhere, a tree limb cracked and fell to the snow-shrouded ground, disturbing the sudden silence. At least, she hoped that's what the noise had been. She didn't know if she could protect herself from anything other than a stick right now.

The car must have become motivated by the sound of the limb falling because it chose that moment to creak ominously, the engine coughing and hissing before the whole body shifted, sinking into an impressive gangster lean.

Then, right before her eyes, one of the wheels fell off and rolled down the road. "Well…damn," she whispered.

She had driven the wheels off the car. Literally. Apparently not finished with its sighing and groaning, the Honda shuddered violently and gave up the ghost. The steam billowing out from under the hood stopped, and she was left once more with silence.

Losing the tire must have broken its heart.

She had no idea where the first laugh came from. It startled her, made her question her sanity. Because sure as hell, none of this was *funny*. Her gaze caught on the animal moving over the snow ahead of her. The cause of her current trouble trotted up a steep hillside as if it hadn't a care in the world.

Stupid elk. The animal didn't look any the worse for wear after meeting her borrowed Honda ass to fender. The Honda?

Yeah…it was hurt. It was hurt real bad.

With the rapidly falling snow and not a soul in sight she knew, *real bad* was a death sentence for the car. Probably for her too. She was so close to her destination. Even though she felt like she'd traveled to the end of the earth, she had to be close.

The frigid breeze reached under her knit top and sank fangs into her skin. She blew roughly on her hands as her toes curled inside her fur-lined hiking boots. She had to get moving. Too long out in this weather, and she'd die. She hadn't survived hell to die frozen in Alaska. Contemplation made her angry, so she shoveled that energy into pulling on whatever she could find from the backseat of her car. Layers for warmth because it was damn cold here, and it appeared she had a long walk in her near future.

"You just couldn't pick Tahiti, could you? Had to pick Alaska," she grumbled aloud. "Who picks Alaska to set up their retirement home? You had to be crazy before Ricker got hold of you. That's got to be it."

She rubbed her chest because the pain that settled in her heart when she thought about Micah had the ability to take her to her knees. She breathed through it. He was gone. She was going to have to make peace with that eventually. But not before she destroyed the man who'd taken him from her.

After putting on every last bit of the clothing in her go bag, she decided she resembled a vagrant marshmallow woman. She shrugged. It was irrelevant. She gathered together as much of her stuff as she could, cramming her laptop, satellite phone, and a small notebook into her go bag before she punched the key fob lock. She shook her head, sighing loudly as the car alarm snort-wheezed and then let out a last mournful wail. Why she was attempting to lock it was a mystery.

The car she'd appropriated—okay, fine, the car she'd stolen in Anchorage—was over fifteen years old. The beating it endured during her cross-Alaska flight, followed by being smacked upside the head by that damned elk's behind, had relegated it to toast status. It wasn't salvageable and would probably be consumed by the forest surrounding her. The car mimicked her sigh and then deflated, the other front tire going flat with a pop and hiss.

If cars had a soul, this one's had just crossed over. She stared at the gray hunk of metal, and tears pricked her eyes. If she could make it to Micah's hideaway, she'd buy herself some time to research and plan. She'd waited for a year to make this move. Making it to his place would allow her safety and access to the high-tech systems she knew he had hidden in his war room.

She'd never been here. But he'd promised that one day he would bring her.

Wiping away a tear, she wanted to scream at the agony racing through her. He should be here with her.

Goddamn Dresden! Goddamn Ricker! Goddamn the Piper!

She glanced up at the sky again and forced air through her lungs. She could do this. She'd baited the hook for Endgame. She'd used burner credit cards and shown her face on closed-circuit television. They'd come looking for her as she wanted, but they'd struggle to find her so she'd bought herself some time. Micah had given no one the location of his house. Not even Jude, his best friend. Eventually, they'd find her, but she estimated she had at least a month or two before that happened. And that was plenty of time to plan.

She gazed around at the majestic beauty of the scene before her. No doubt, Alaska was gorgeous, but she could not, for the life of her, figure out why a man born and bred surfing in the waves of the Pacific off the Southern California coast had wanted to live in the vast, cold wilderness that was Alaska.

Then again, once upon a time she'd wanted to hide as far away from civilization as she could get. Become lost in a tourist town and not come up for air. Instead, she'd entered the CIA and found herself smack-dab in the middle of international espionage and intrigue.

She hitched her go bag over her shoulder. The last sign she'd passed had said the big city of Nikolai, Alaska, population ninety-four, was approximately ten miles ahead.

Somewhere on the periphery of Nikolai was where she was headed. It was as remote as anyone could get, and right now her target location seemed farther than the moon.

She had a hell of a walk in front of her. She recalled the coordinates on the handheld GPS she'd purchased in Anchorage and cursed when the battery went dead.

"Keeps getting better and better," she groused.

She raised her sleeve, hit a button on her watch, and waited as the tiny electronic marvel calculated her location and gave her directions to the coordinates Micah had loaded into it fourteen months ago.

He alone had known her secrets and done everything he could to protect her from her mistakes. He'd done it selflessly, not realizing the price he'd have to pay. She angrily swiped at another tear.

She needed to get her shit together.

A hawk's cry pierced the air, and she glanced skyward. Soft, bitterly cold flakes fell on her cheeks. She'd be in heaven if she were twenty years younger. She'd make snow angels and snowballs. She'd make slushies and snowmen, really live it up like she had back in Vermont. But she wasn't six, and right now this looked like a frozen version of hell.

She patted the dented hood of the Honda. "You were a good car. I appreciate all you've done."

With one last glance at the car, she blew out a rough breath and turned away from the road, heading just into the edge of the forest. One minute she was walking on snow-covered dirt; the next she was slipping on snow-covered pine needles. Uphill she trod, passing boulders as she put one foot in front of the other.

Her feet were like ice blocks. She wiggled her toes

experimentally, wishing she'd thought to purchase warming packets. Her breath sawed in and out of her lungs. It was a loud sound in an otherwise silent forest. She laid a hand on her chest, pressing as if she could make her heart settle just by that action. It pounded so hard she had to stop, sit down, and catch her breath. She'd not been the same since the poisoning.

The snow fell heavier, coasting to the ground with a whisper that spoke of all things not related to warmth. She rubbed her eyes, wincing when the roughness of her driving gloves scraped her cheek.

Night was upon her, and as she sat there trying to determine if she should just make camp, a strange knowing slid down her spine. Someone, or something, was watching her.

The knowledge she'd become prey settled in her mind even as it danced on her skin. She allowed her gaze to go unfocused, searching her periphery for signs of any movement. If it was a wild animal, she could only hope she had time to shoot. She lowered her hand, reaching for her sidearm. A branch snapped, and the shushing of falling snow reverberated like a bomb in the sudden silence.

Nina couldn't shake the sudden feeling that branch snapping had been intentional.

She stood and turned in a complete circle as she withdrew her gun. She backed up, her back hitting a tree, and she went still, waiting.

The feeling persisted, but nothing jumped out or made a sound. If it were a bear, she'd hear its grunting and chuffing. A wolf would be too silent to anticipate. Maybe she was just paranoid?

Surely it wasn't a person. This place was entirely too isolated to have people running around in a threatening blizzard.

She picked up her go bag and secured the strap onto her shoulder. She turned, keeping her gun out, and then she walked again.

Periodically, she'd stop and listen, but upon hearing nothing, she kept on. One foot in front of the other. Then the canopy emptied of birds. A screech, a caw, and they were airborne, lifting as one into a darkening sky. It startled her so much that she instinctively picked up speed—her walk nearly a run now.

She was tired though, and as a small hill gave way in front of her, she miscalculated her steps and slipped on a rock. Then she was down, rolling and tumbling along a snowbank before she landed heavily against a boulder.

"Oomph!" Her breath left her, her back slapping against the rock and sending pain down her spine.

From somewhere behind her, another twig snapped. She was being hunted. And still the damn snow fell. She rolled to her side and pushed to her knees, tiny frozen crystals pelting her from a darkening sky. She was so cold. And now her back hurt.

One more twig snapped, and with it, her tentative hold on anger. She searched for her gun and located it about ten feet to her left. She hadn't survived poisoning to die in this forsaken wilderness.

Snow crunched beneath heavy steps, and Nina knew that whoever, or whatever, was chasing her was too close for her to make it to her weapon.

She threw back her head to scream at the sky, to curse the enormity of this task she'd set for herself, and stopped when the barrel of a gun pressed against her temple.

Her eyes shifted sideways as she prayed. She needed retribution. Micah deserved redemption, and by God, she was going to get it for them both. It would damn well not end this way.

Then the smell of the ocean permeated her senses. The ocean was hundreds of miles away. Micah's smell had always reminded her of the ocean—salt, sand, and sweet air. It was as if she'd conjured him.

But it wasn't possible. She must've hit her head in the fall, because surely she'd lost her mind. He was buried in the only Christian cemetery in Beirut.

The gun didn't move, the air didn't shift, and the damn snow sure didn't stop falling. Tingles shot up her spine now, replacing the pain with a bittersweet ache. She closed her eyes and swallowed hard.

But in that second, as the steel of the gun pressed into her temple, Nina swore everything in her calmed. The peace she'd not had in fourteen months stole over her as she looked up and up and up into eyes so blue that they were the color of a cloudless sky at midday.

The refrain repeated: it just wasn't possible.

And then he spoke.

"Who the hell are you, and what are you doing on my property?"

About the Author

Lea Griffith has been reading romance novels since a young age. She cut her teeth on the greats: Judith McNaught, Kathleen Woodiwiss, and Julie Garwood. She still consumes every romance book she can put her hands on, and now she writes her own compelling romantic suspense. Lea lives with her husband and three teenage daughters in rural Georgia.

EVERY DEEP DESIRE

First in a sultry, swampy romantic suspense series
from author Sharon Wray

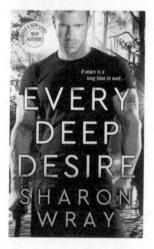

Rafe Montfort was a decorated Green Beret, the best of the best, until a disastrous mission and an unforgivable betrayal destroyed his life. Now, this deadly soldier has returned to the sultry Georgia swamps to reunite with his Beret brothers—as well as the love he left behind—and take back all he lost. But Juliet must never know the truth behind what he's done...or the dangerous secret that threatens to take him from her forever.

For more Sharon Wray, visit:

sourcebooks.com

I AM JUSTICE

First in an action-packed, band of sisters romantic
suspense series from award-winning debut author
Diana Muñoz Stewart

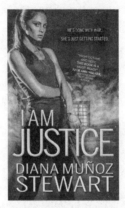

Justice Parish takes down bad guys. Rescued from a brutal
childhood and adopted into the wealthy Parish family,
Justice wants payback. As a trained assassin, she's targeted
a sex-trafficking ring in the Middle East. She just needs a
cover so she can get close enough to take them down…

Sandesh Ross left Special Forces to found a humanitarian
group, but saving the world isn't cheap. Enter Parish
Industries and limitless funding, with one catch—their hot,
prickly "PR specialist," Justice.

If they don't kill each other, they'll end up making a great team.

"High-octane and sexy, this book is a must-read!"

**—Julie Ann Walker, *New York Times* and *USA Today*
bestselling author of the Black Knights Inc. series**

For more Diana Muñoz Stewart, visit:
sourcebooks.com

BLACK KNIGHTS INC.

These elite ex-military operatives are as unique and tough as their custom-made Harleys

**By Julie Ann Walker, *New York Times*
and *USA Today* bestselling author**

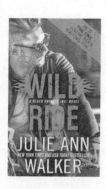

Wild Ride

Former Navy SEAL Ethan "Ozzie" Sykes is the hero everyone's been waiting for. When he's stuck distracting reporter Samantha Tate, he quickly loses his desire to keep her at bay…

Fuel for Fire

Spitfire CIA agent Chelsea Duvall has always had a thing for bossy, brooding covert operative Dagan Zoelner. It's just as well that he's never given her a second look, since she carries a combustible secret about his past that threatens to torch their lives…

Hot Pursuit

Former SAS officer and BKI operator Christian Watson has fought for his life before. Doing it with the beautiful, bossy former CIA operative Emily Scott in tow is another matter entirely.

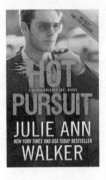

Built to Last

Jamin "Angel" Agassi is a spec-ops virtuoso whose cover can't be broken. That is, until he encounters Interpol agent Sonya Butler—the one woman who knows everything about him.

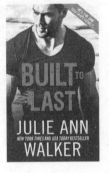

SURVIVE THE NIGHT

Third in the thrilling Rocky Mountain K9 Unit series

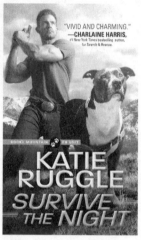

K9 Officer Otto Gunnersen has always had a soft spot for anyone in need—but for all his big heart, he's never been in love. Until he meets Sarah Clifton

All Sarah wants is to escape, but there's no outrunning her past. Her power-mad brother would hunt her to the ends of the earth…but he'd never expect her to fight back. With Otto by her side, Sarah's finally ready to face whatever comes her way.

"Vivid and charming."

—Charlaine Harris, #1 *New York Times* bestselling author

For more Katie Ruggle, visit:
sourcebooks.com